THE GIRL ON THE TRAM

S D MARSON

First published in Great Britain in 2024.

SECOND EDITION

Stephen Marson has asserted his right under the Copyright, Designs and Patents Act 1988 to be identified as the author of this work.

This book is a work of fiction and any resemblance to actual persons, living or dead, is purely coincidental.

This book is sold subject to the condition that it shall not, by way of trade or otherwise, be resold, hired out, or otherwise circulated without the author's prior consent in any form of binding or cover other than that in which it is published and without a similar condition, including this condition, being imposed on the subsequent purchase.

Dedicated to my partner Tracey and our black lab, Riley. Thanks also to my editors, Rebecca Klassen and Rebecca Weber, without whom this book wouldn't have been as good as it is. Thank you to my early readers, Joanna and my mum. Your comments, enthusiasm and feedback have made a real difference.

And thank you, Carrie, a distant, relative from the past who inspired this story.

I'd always wanted to write a story, and I had this idea in my head that wouldn't go away. When I finally had a chance to start writing, two things happened. Firstly, I came across a newspaper report from the 1900s, about a tram that crashed in my home town, killing a passenger.

The other thing that happened was when I was researching my family history; upon opening an old metal chest I found a pile of cards sent between family members back in 1900 or so. One of my relatives wrote about her first time on an omnibus; an unusual sight in those days. Her name was Carrie and a story started to form itself in my head.

THE GIRL ON THE TRAM was born, and the heroine had to be Carrie of course...

1

A tram, a bridge and a woman in blue

The ringing in my ears is excruciating. My mouth tastes disgusting, and I'm lying on my front, the side of my face on the dirty, cobbled road. I slowly open my eyes. Nothing but dust.

Grimacing, I gingerly lift my head and look around as the dust settles. I'm on the bridge, the early morning river mist swirling like ghosts, gradually clearing as the sun does it's best to break through. People run in all directions. Carriage horses struggle against their harnesses, their owners desperately trying to get them under control.

Though still muffled, my hearing is gradually returning. People are shouting as I struggle to my feet, my skirt covered in dirt and grit. My new employer will be furious if he sees me like this. I've only been working at the solicitor's office for a month, and I need to prove to Mr Edwards (and my father) that I'm worthy of the position usually reserved for men, even now in 1910, despite the suffragette movement. I can't be late again; it would be the third time in as many weeks.

'What happened?' I call out to a man sitting on the ground, blood running from a nasty gash on his head.

He looks up, dazed. 'The tram. It ran down the hill and crashed into the railings. The horses have bolted.' He points behind me with a bloodied hand. 'Nobody could have survived that, miss.'

Feeling dizzy, every bone and muscle in my body aching, I turn. One of the town's trams is on its side, the yellow stencilled number 19 on the front, the horses nowhere to be seen, their harnesses lying tangled in the road. Several men clamber onto the smashed tram, trying to climb into one of the broken windows, shouting, 'Get help. Summon a doctor!'

It all comes back to me in a rush. A sudden memory of a tram racing down the hill. People running to get out of its way, women screaming, children crying, men yelling. The terrifying noise of wood splintering, glass smashing; the tram sliding down the road on its side, crashing into carriages and carts until it races past me and into the bridge railings. I have a hazy recollection of being struck by something. Instinctively, I raise a dirty hand to my forehead and feel a large bump but, thankfully, no blood.

I grab my leather bag, scratched and covered in grit, and stumble towards the carnage. My head hurts, and the muddy smell of the river below fills my nostrils. On the side of the road, next to the broken and twisted tram is a young woman in an extraordinarily bright blue dress. So bright that it makes the rest of the scene appear black and white in contrast.

She is lying on her back, not moving. No one else seems to have noticed her as I run over. A voice in my head. Holmes. Quickly, Carrie. She needs your help.

The woman is badly injured. Her dress is covered in blood, and her leg is bent underneath her body. Her eyes are closed, and she is perfectly still, except for a gentle rise of her chest, the faint sound of a breath exhaled. I kneel in the dirt and cradle her head. 'Stay calm. Help is on its way. Can you hear me?' I say, taking off my shawl and pressing it firmly to her stomach where most of the blood seems to be.

I look at her face - she is so pale. A loose strand of blonde hair curls over her face. I brush it neatly over her ear. Her eyes open, and she looks at me, puzzled. She doesn't seem to be in pain. She grabs my arm, but there's no strength in her grip.

'It wasn't an accident, miss,' she whispers, blood dribbling from the corner of her mouth. 'It wasn't the

8

Over the doctor's shoulder, I notice a big man with dark hair and a pale face. He is fiddling with a tall, wooden tripod, a camera apparatus sitting on top. He ducks under a black sheet out of view. Surely he isn't taking photographs of this terrible scene? How distasteful.

The doctor breaks me from my thoughts. 'Come on, we can't help her now.' He stands and picks up his case. 'You seem a sensible young lady. I need your help with the gentleman over there. I think he's the driver.' I look across, and sure enough, Mr Hoskins, the tram driver, is sitting against the bridge railings, his head in his hands, sobbing. A police officer stands beside him, making notes in a notebook. He bends down and says something to Mr Hoskins before walking off and talking to another bystander.

I follow the doctor as he strides across the road and crouches next to Mr Hoskins. The doctor gently places his hand on the driver's arm. 'Where does it hurt, sir?'

Mr Hoskins looks at the doctor and blinks in confusion as he notices me standing at the doctor's side. 'Carrie, my dear, what are you doing here?'

'Hello, Mr Hoskins, don't you worry about me. Let the doctor focus on you.' Mr Hoskins drives his tram by our house, his route running through our street, heading for the town. He often waves to me if he sees me by the roadside. We are acquainted as I went to the same school as his daughter.

He turns back to the doctor. 'My head hurts, but it's not too bad,' he says with a confused expression. 'I didn't see you onboard today, Carrie.'

'I decided to walk, Mr Hoskins. Don't worry about me. The doctor here will help you.'

The doctor repeats his examination procedure as he did with Rose, starting at Mr Hoskins' head, working down his neck to his shoulders and finally his torso.

driver's fault. The tram was broken.' She takes a breath and winces in pain.

I touch her shoulder to calm her. Blood trickling down her face from a cut on her forehead makes me feel weak.

'Don't worry about that now. Let me help you. My name's Carrie. What's your name?'

'Rose. My name is Rose James,' she says as her eyes flutter closed.

'Excuse me, miss, let me through,' says a voice behind me. A young man with a doctor's case approaches. I move slightly to the side, leaning across, still pressing down on my shawl covering her wound.

The doctor kneels next to me and examines Rose. He places his hands on the top of her head and feels down her face and neck. He is gentle and thorough with his examination. He gently lifts the shawl I still have pressed against her stomach, but releasing the pressure suddenly brings a gush of red. The wound is messy. He quickly presses my hands back on the shawl. 'You did the right thing with your shawl, miss. Keep the pressure on her stomach. The wound looks quite bad. Let me have a look at her leg.'

I try to comfort Rose by holding her hand and squeezing it gently. She opens her eyes and looks at me with a frown, grimacing as she struggles to reach into her pocket. She hands me a crumpled card. 'Speak to this man and to my husband. They know the truth.' She stares at me. I nod, take the card and put it in my pocket.

Before I can ask her about her husband, the doctor moves the woman's leg, and she lets out a soft moan. Her eyes look beyond me as if she can't see me at all.

I feel useless as the young doctor puts his ear to her mouth. 'She's dead, miss. There's nothing we can do for her now.' The doctor softly takes my bloodied shawl and covers Rose's face.

I place Rose's hand on her stomach and smooth her hair, straighten the shawl. She looks so peaceful. So beautiful.

'Everything looks fine, sir. You have a nasty gash on your head, but nothing a few stitches can't fix. Do you feel pain anywhere else?'

'I am aching all over, but that could be my age,' Mr Hoskins says, winking at me and attempting a smile that turns into a grimace. I help the doctor wrap a bandage around Mr Hoskins' head, holding it in place as the doctor ties it carefully. He puts a comforting hand on the driver's shoulder.

'This bandage is only temporary. You need to go to the hospital for further treatment. I don't think you'll be driving any trams for the time being!'

'Thank you, doctor, and thank you, Carrie. I'm so glad you weren't on board today. It was the most frightening experience I've ever endured in all my days.'

'What happened, Mr Hoskins?' I ask.

A frown creases his forehead. 'The damnedest thing, Carrie my dear. We were stopped at the top junction when the brake lever stuck in the holding slot. I've never had trouble with the braking lever before. I tried with all my strength to release the damn thing, and when it finally let go, it went with a bang.' He pauses, rubbing his chin before continuing, 'The noise it made must surely have been heard over the river.'

With a helping hand from the doctor, Mr Hoskins slowly gets to his feet and is led away by a nurse to a waiting hospital carriage. Several other people are already on board, some with bandaged heads, others with arms in slings.

The doors slam shut, and the carriage slowly makes its way through the crowd who are still gawping at the scene. Once clear, the carriage speeds up and heads for the hospital.

I don't know what to do, so I sit on the kerb, my head swimming. An elderly woman in a red shawl touches my shoulder and gently pulls me to my feet.

'Are you all right, dear?' she asks with a concerned face, looking me up and down. I gently touch her arm.

'I'm fine, thank you.'

I sling my bag over my shoulder and push through the expanding crowd, and notice the man with the camera ahead of me, carrying his bulky equipment over his shoulder, a heavy case in his hand.

I trudge up the hill, some paces behind the photographer, the excitement of my day ahead now gone and replaced with a miserable feeling that seems to press down on me. I think of Rose, and my heart hurts. She was so young. I've never seen someone die before.

The streets are busy with people heading to work. Shopkeepers are opening up for the day, cleaning the steps outside their shops, and putting out their wares to entice customers.

I don't notice that the photographer has stopped outside a shop until I nearly bump into him as he struggles to open the shop door, his case on the pavement beside him. His camera contraption is leaning against the window, still attached atop the wooden tripod, threatening to slide and fall at any second. The photographer pushes the door open, grabs the camera and his case, and steps inside.

As I pass the shop, I glance in the window, noticing a carefully arranged collection of framed photographs featuring smiling families, their eyes eerily following me as I walk past. The sign on the door says Studio Family Portraits. Why would a Studio Photographer feel the need to capture pictures of vehicles in the street? And crashed ones at that.

I continue walking up the hill, parts of the crashed tram littering the road. People rush to get to the crash site. News travels fast in this town and there's nothing like a gruesome scene to delightfully tell friends later. A young couple with a child stare at me as they pass, shocked at the state of my clothes and my face. The blood on my blouse. I ignore them and they carry on, racing to get a good view of the carnage.

As I reach Samuels, the jeweller, I look up. The big clock, famous for keeping accurate time, shows half-past eight, so I might just have time to pop into the newsagents to pick up today's edition of The Strand for my father. Since starting my job, I had promised him I'd collect his newspaper every day on the way to the office. Tuesday's edition is special, as it features a chapter from a Sherlock Holmes adventure. Being an avid fan, even a tram crash won't deter me from picking up a copy. Sherlock's stories are all I read. No wonder I keep hearing his voice in my head.

I emerge from the newsagents, newly purchased newspaper folded in my bag. My pace quickens as I realise I might be on time if I hurry. Even though the sun is out now, the early morning mist burnt away to reveal a perfect October day, it feels suddenly colder, so I push my hands deep into my pockets. In my left pocket, I feel the crumpled card Rose handed me. Taking it out and looking at it closely for the first time, I see it's a calling card, dirty and blood-stained. The front is barely legible. Turning it over, there is a scrawl on the back in pencil:

Mr Shute, Estuary View, Church Hill - £100. Monday Night. Tram 19

Who is Mr Shute? Tram 19 was the one that crashed this morning. One hundred pounds for what? That's more than I could hope to earn in a year! Rose told me it was no accident, she seemed so sure. Someone must have caused the crash, but to what end? I intend to find out. It's the least I can do for poor Rose.

2

The night before the crash - a card game and a fight

It was unusual for Detective Sergeant Jeffries to be in a public house with his colleagues from the station, but they had insisted, and his wife had told him to have a night off now he was back home from his course in London. So here he was, enjoying a pint of beer with his fellow officers. This particular public house wasn't one of his favourites for an evening out. Too noisy and boisterous for his liking, and the beer too strong for his taste. But his colleagues were in high spirits, keen to congratulate him on the successful completion of his detection course and eager to hear more about his new skills.

Jeffries had felt the eyes of the other officers on him since he'd arrived at the bar. They might be celebrating with me, but they're probably jealous. They'll have to work harder to cover my old beat, he thought. They all knew the new detective rank was common in London, but here in the southwest, the position was seen as an expensive and unnecessary addition to the regular ranks.

Jeffries was a big man. Not fat, but broader and taller than most of his colleagues. It was well known he ate more than his fair share, often seen with a pasty or a sandwich in his hand. 'Where do you put it all, Robert?' his mother always used to ask. He wore a moustache as was fashionable with older men, younger men seeming to prefer a clean-shaved face. Jeffries often covered his moustache with one finger, considering the effect in his shaving mirror, always changing his mind at the last minute.

The detective sergeant contemplated his future as he sipped his warm beer. He was now responsible for all cases with results that remained elusive to the uniformed police employing regular methods. He had a lot to prove to his superiors and colleagues.

As was a habit of his, Jeffries cast his eyes around the smoky room, noticing the coarse, rowdy women as they tried to get the attention of the young, naive men. Waitresses scurried about with plates of food and pints of beer. A group of men huddled over a small table by the bar. No doubt planning some illegal activity, Jeffries thought cynically, deciding to ignore the men this evening. It was his night off, after all, although, from the way his colleagues kept talking about work, you wouldn't have thought so.

Beer in hand, he took in the room, his eyes resting on a poker game in progress in the far corner. Tired of his colleagues' incessant talk about work; long shifts, the poor pay, he wandered over to take a closer look. He was curious to watch from the side-lines. Games out in the open like this were usually low-stakes affairs that were perfectly legal. The hidden games in backrooms were where the serious money changed hands, and where the fights usually ensued. Fists flying over a lost hand of cards. Accusations of cheating.

Four players were at the table, all men. Half a dozen customers watched as a fresh hand was dealt. Jeffries noticed that except for one bored-looking woman, all the observers were men.

Jeffries' eyes were drawn to one player in particular. A smartly dressed man with a narrow, clean-shaven face. He was of an age that was difficult to pinpoint, perhaps in his mid-twenties. On the table to his left was his hat, and on his right, a bottle of whisky and a half-full glass of amber liquid. The man was clearly on a winning streak as the pile of coins next to him testified. With a subtle shift of his head, the young man glanced at each of the other players in turn, studying them casually.

One by one, the other players threw down their cards and shook their heads in despair. They all looked at the young man with the pile of money, who grinned and fanned out his cards face up. To Jeffries' eyes - and he was no poker player - the young man's cards didn't look exceptional. Not a picture card or an ace amongst them. He at least expected a Royal card or two, given the young man's expression. These cards held no obvious pattern at all, save for a pair of twos.

One of the other men abruptly stood, his chair falling over with a crash, the glass in his hand spilling beer across the table. 'You only held a bloody pair of twos! I could have beaten that with my pair of Jacks.'

The young man shrugged. 'But you folded, Arthur, and I had the best hand left in play. That's how poker works.'

'But it's a crap hand. How can you win with a pair of bloody twos?'

The young man smiled. 'Come on, Arthur, it's only a few shillings. You should have stayed in the game if you thought you had a winning hand.'

Jeffries watched as Arthur slammed his drink on the table and reached into his jacket pocket to withdraw a folding knife. Flicking it open and waving it from side to side, the short blade flashed, catching the light from the single gas lamp hanging above the table. 'Perhaps you and I need to go outside and talk about the rules of poker.'

The young man held out his hands, palms facing out. Smiling, he kept a wary eye on the knife. 'Come on, Arthur, get a grip, man. It's just a friendly game of poker.'

'Friendly?' The man said. 'You think it's friendly to swindle a fellow player out of his hard-earned money? I don't know how you do it, but I lose every time you play, so what's your game?'

Arthur strode around the table. The young man quickly stood and stepped back, his chair clattering to the floor, his bottle of whisky toppling over, spilling the contents, swamping the playing cards. As the two men looked each other in the eye, Jeffries put his glass on a nearby table and positioned himself behind the man with the knife. The young man noticed but didn't take his eyes off his

16

opponent. Jeffries sighed. What a night off this turned out to be, he thought.

With one swift movement, Jeffries stepped to the side of Arthur, reached across to his knife hand and grabbed his wrist. With a twist, he turned the man's hand in on itself, forcing it open and releasing the knife.

The knifeman snarled, but before he could recover from his position, Jeffries turned the man's arm behind his back and forced him to the ground, holding his arm in place. Jeffries leaned in close and said quietly, 'Now, sir.' He paused, smiled and nodded towards the front door. 'I suggest you get up calmly and go home to sober up before I decide to break your arm.'

Jeffries released his grip and the knifeman crumpled to the floor. Jeffries bent and picked up the knife before expertly closing the blade and slipping it into his pocket. He stood to his full height as the knifeman got to his feet, rubbed his shoulder, glaring at Jeffries before stumbling to the front door, turning back to face the room, pointing to Jeffries. 'Mark my words, men who interfere with another man's fight get what's coming to them.'

The landlord, who had now moved from behind the bar with his cloth slung over his shoulder, nudged open the front door with his shoulder and nodded in the direction of the street. 'Get off home, Arthur. I don't want trouble in my public house. Come back tomorrow when you've cooled down.' As Arthur walked through the open doorway, the landlord added, 'And you're barred from playing poker in my pub for the rest of the month.' The landlord slammed the door shut, strode back to the bar, shook his head, and grabbed a glass for the next customer.

The other poker players left the winning man to his haul, picked up their beer glasses and headed to the bar for refills, laughing and joking as they each settled on a barstool for the rest of the evening. The small group of onlookers wandered off, searching for something else to entertain them.

Several officers had congregated at the bar, where Jeffries now found himself, empty beer glass in his hand. He tried to get the attention of the woman behind the bar but as he did so, his glass was taken from him, replaced with a full one.

'Beers are on us, Jeffries!' Said one of his colleagues, his name forgotten at that moment. Several men patted Jeffries on the back. A job well done.

'Didn't think you still had it in you, Sir.' said one officer, grinning. The others laughed. The atmosphere had switched from one saturated with tension and fear to one of celebration and, in the case of Jeffries, relief.

As a rule, Jeffries didn't like violence, but sometimes something more than gentle persuasion and a quiet word was needed to prevent things from getting out of hand. He could have arrested the man and thrown him in jail to cool off, but it was his night off, and he wanted to forget about work for at least one evening.

Sipping his drink, the froth settling on his moustache, Jeffries looked around the room once more. His eyes settled on the young poker player, gathering his winnings, downing his drink. The poker player looked up, smiling broadly. His eyes met Jeffries' who walked across. 'Thank you, sir, that could have become nasty. Care for a game?'

Jeffries laughed. 'Not against you, that's for sure!' He never could play poker; he didn't have the patience for it. 'I'd be keen to learn how you do that, though.'

'Do what?' The man said, tilting his head to one side.

'Work out what cards the others are holding,' said Jeffries.

'Buy me a drink, and I'll tell you if you like.' The young man downed the last of his whisky and scooped his winnings into his hat.

Both men walked to the bar, and Jeffries signalled to the barman. The young man turned to Jeffries and held out his hand. 'My name's Francis, by the way. Francis Smith. My

friends call me Frank. Welcome to my local public house, the best place for a friendly poker game.'

Jeffries shook his hand. 'Robert Jeffries. Most people just call me Jeffries. Pleased to meet you.' He pointed to Frank's empty whisky glass. 'Now, would you like another whisky or join me with a beer?'

'I think I'll have a beer, thank you.'

The two men sat at a table in the corner, beers in front of them. Frank dropped his winnings into his pocket, took a long swallow of his drink, placed the glass back on the table and wiped his mouth with his sleeve, a habit Jeffries detested.

'So,' said Jeffries, taking a sip of his drink. 'How do you work out if you have a winning hand, and how do you stay focused with so much whisky inside you? You don't even look tipsy.'

Frank tipped his head back and laughed. 'To begin with, I stay sharp because I don't get drunk. It's ginger beer in the bottle, not whisky.' He looked around the room, lowered his voice. 'I have a little arrangement with the barman. I don't usually tell anyone, but you look like you'll keep my little secret. And the other player's cards? That's easy. I watch them like a hawk, looking for their own little tell.'

Jeffries frowned. 'I don't understand. What's a tell?'

'Everyone has a tell. Next time you speak to someone you think might not be telling the truth, watch them closely. They'll give it away with the tiniest of twitches. That's what we call a tell. It might be a scratch on the nose or a wrinkle on the forehead. It might be a shift in their gaze. I'm working on a theory that everyone does it. Most people normally do one thing when telling the truth, and quite another when they're lying.'

'But how does that help you work out what cards they have in their hand?'

'I don't know the cards they have, but I do know if they have a good or bad hand and if they're bluffing. Take

Arthur as an example. He's a classic. If he picks up a card that's of no use to him, he'll wrinkle his nose ever so slightly. But, if he picks up a card that he thinks will win the game, he'll rub his chin. If he has a bad hand and he's hoping to bluff his way to a win, he'll be even more nervous, so he'll rub his chin some more. He doesn't even know he's doing it. It's actually quite funny.'

The two men spent the rest of the evening talking and laughing. Jeffries liked Frank. Although younger than Jeffries by a good few years, he felt they could chat for hours. He was glad he'd spent the evening in the public house for a change. The two men talked about all manner of things, but neither of them discussed work, which was a refreshing change. Sometimes work was best left out of an evening's entertainment.

The barman rang the brass bell behind the bar, bellowing, 'Last orders, gentlemen!' Jeffries drank the last of his beer and Frank stood to pull his coat on. The two men walked across the sticky floor to the front door. The barman, busy collecting dirty glasses, raised his free arm. 'Goodnight, gentlemen.' Jeffries and Smith returned the gesture.

Most of the other patrons had already left, Jeffries' colleagues no doubt disappearing off to some other, less desirable tavern. Jeffries didn't mind. He was ready for a good night's sleep. Leave the young ones to it. Frank held the door open for his new friend.

'We must do this again. I enjoyed our conversation this evening,' said Frank. Jeffries stepped onto the pavement outside, the wind bitingly cold. 'By the way, you didn't tell me what you do for a living, Jeffries.'

Jeffries didn't want to spoil the evening as it usually did when he told people he was a policeman, so he simply smiled. 'Oh, nothing very interesting. I'll tell you next time.'

3

A new suit and a stiff collar

Stepping into the police station the morning after his night out, Jeffries was surprised to see that workmen were still painting the walls and ceilings in the entrance hall. The redecoration work had started before Jeffries had gone on his training course weeks ago, and showed little sign of being completed any time soon.

Jeffries rubbed his head. His slight but persistent headache from the night before was gradually wearing off, and the hearty breakfast prepared for him earlier by his wife, Edith, was speeding up his recovery.

Avoiding a stepladder and stepping over pots of white paint, Jeffries managed to navigate the cluttered entrance without getting anything on his new suit. He walked through the door into the main office and noticed that the workmen were preparing the walls, repairing holes and sanding smooth the surfaces, the ceiling already complete. Jeffries looked around the office, now much brighter, despite the dreary day outside. The white finish certainly made a difference.

The office buzzed with the clattering of typewriter keys and a constant hum of chatter as officers typed up reports. Others stood in groups, discussing cases. Or last night's excitement at the poker game, more likely, thought Jeffries as he slumped into his chair. His desk before him was piled high with files. Certainly more files than when he left for the course. He sighed, reached into the top drawer and rummaged about until he found what he was looking for.

The photograph of his young son was faded somewhat and a little dusty. Sighing, Jeffries wiped the glass, put the picture back in the drawer, aware of the paint splatters that might damage the frame. It had been nearly two years since the initial diagnosis, and he missed his boy as much now as he did that first awful day. He straightened his collection of pens and pushed the pile of paperwork to one side. I'll start on those later, he thought, adjusting his collar and loosening his tie. The jacket sleeves were a touch too long, and the collar of his newly starched shirt stiff. Wearing civilian clothing instead of the regulation uniform might be one of the benefits of being a detective, but he felt like a fish out of water among the uniformed officers in the station. Jeffries smiled as he recalled the course, the completion of which culminated in his new promotion to Detective Sergeant. The title had a nice ring to it.

He wasn't keen at the start of the course. A fat lot of good this new qualification will do in sleepy Devon, he had thought. He'd changed his mind after only a few days, the tutor surprising him with some insightful ideas Jeffries now wanted to bring into play. He had initially agreed to attend the course only when the inspector had promised that with the new position, he could avoid long days patrolling the streets, dealing with low-life criminals and violent racketeers. Now in his mid-fifties, he hoped the promotion would present interesting and varied cases that called for more intellect. Exercise his old brain a bit more.

Jeffries knew that most officers retired through stress or injury by the time they reached their late fifties, but at fifty-six, Jeffries felt he had a few years left in him, despite his wife pressing him to hang up his boots and take early retirement. That wasn't for him, though. He disliked some of his life on the force, despised the politics and was increasingly surprised at the depravity some criminals would reach. Mostly though, he enjoyed the camaraderie amongst his fellow officers and found the work challenging and satisfying, especially when they cracked a case. That sweet point in time when the penny dropped and the realisation that the elusive clue was right before their eyes. Those moments were to be cherished.

Jeffries' attention was drawn to the desk beside his, an aroma of bacon making his nostrils twitch and his stomach rumble, despite the piled-high breakfast from earlier.

Constable Macintosh was hungrily biting into a greasy bacon sandwich, a cup of steaming tea next to him. Jeffries liked a bacon sandwich himself, but not in the office. It seemed unprofessional.

Jeffries shook his head, wafting the air as he looked around the room. Nothing much had changed in the two weeks he'd been away, apart from the freshly painted ceilings and some new lights. Looking over at the inspector's office, he noticed that the door was closed, a light showing through the frosted glass panel. Voices and laughter could be heard coming from the room. Jeffries looked back at Macintosh, his bacon sandwich already demolished. 'Who's with the old man, Mac?'

Macintosh wiped his mouth with a grubby handkerchief. 'Ah, that's the new recruit.'

Jeffries raised his eyes at this news. 'New recruit? Good. It's about time we had more men on the force. We can barely keep up with the cases we have already.' He considered the pile of crime reports in front of him, threatening to collapse at the slightest nudge. 'This lot will take me months to work through.'

Macintosh grinned. 'Well, we thought that with your new training, you'll be able to crack those in no time.'

'Funny,' said Jeffries, unsmiling. 'So what do you know about the new recruit? You're the one with his ear to the ground; nothing gets past you.'

Macintosh took a slurp of his tea and joined Jeffries, sitting on the side of his desk and leaning in close, the aroma of greasy bacon on his breath. 'I hear he's to be your new accomplice.'

Jeffries moved back in his seat. 'Really? What on earth do I need an accomplice for?'

Ignoring the question, Macintosh glanced over to the inspector's office and continued, 'I heard he's none other than the chief inspector's son. Bit of a clever one, I hear. I've been a Constable for five years. I put in all the hours, can never get promotion though. Seems you need to be

23

well-connected in this game.' He folded his arms and looked back at Jeffries. 'That's probably why you were sent on the course, to pass on your skills to your new partner. Sounds like the men upstairs are taking this detective thing seriously after all.' Macintosh laughed, returned to his desk and picked up his empty cup. 'Want a brew, Detective Jeffries?'

'Very funny,' muttered Jeffries, holding out his own cup. 'No sugar, Constable.'

Later, draining his tea and sorting through the pile of documents, the door to the back office swung open and the inspector appeared. Jeffries' superior was a short, dumpy man with bloodshot eyes and a red nose. His fashionable moustache was wider than his round face, and it drooped at the ends, a sign it needed waxing. He looked across at Jeffries.

'Ah, Jeffries, just the man. Welcome back. I have someone for you to meet. A new recruit. The first of many, hopefully. Come and meet your new partner.'

Sighing, Jeffries rearranged the files into three piles, more to prevent them from falling over than any thoughts of being organised. He stood, straightened his tie, and went to join the inspector in his office.

Entering the room, warm from the little fire in the corner, Jeffries looked around, taking in the newly painted walls and smart furniture. The redecorating in the inspector's domain had been completed well ahead of the main office. No expense spared here, he thought. Two chairs faced the inspector's huge mahogany desk. One chair held a pile of documents and files; the other was occupied by a young man, the new recruit, his back to the door. He held a crystal glass in his hand, half filled with an amber liquid. Very cosy, thought Jeffries.

The inspector closed the door. 'Meet your new colleague, Jeffries. Allow me to introduce our new recruit, Constable Smith.'

The young man set his glass on the desk and turned as he stood.

Jeffries almost gasped out loud. The man standing before him was none other than Frank Smith, the winning man from the pub last night, only now he was wearing a smartly pressed uniform, the smartest Jeffries had ever seen on an officer in thirty years on the force.

'Well, I never.'

Constable Smith smiled broadly as he held out his hand in greeting, and the two men shook hands as they nodded to each other.

'Hello again, Detective Sergeant. I had a feeling that I'd see you in the station somewhere. Didn't quite expect that it would be in the same office.'

Jeffries smiled. At least this recruit is a decent man. Intelligent too, he thought.

Still smiling, Jeffries turned to the inspector who was looking on, a frown creasing his brow, clearly surprised that the two men had already met. 'We met yesterday at a, er, drinks event,' explained Jeffries.

Smith grinned. 'Yes, a very pleasant evening it was too.'

Jeffries turned back to Smith. 'So why did you expect to see me here? I didn't tell you I was a police officer.'

'Let's just say that you gave it away on several occasions,' said Smith, tapping the side of his nose.

The inspector coughed. 'Well, gentlemen. Perhaps you can continue this cosy conversation in your own time.' He picked up his notebook, squinting as he consulted his notes. 'In the meantime, we have a new case, Jeffries. There's been a serious tram crash on the bridge at the bottom of Fore Street. A woman has died.'

He nodded towards Smith. 'Constable Smith was at the scene earlier. Young Smith here noticed a crowd of people heading to the river and, using his initiative, decided to follow them and see what the fuss was about.' The inspector pointed to the main room. 'A pity the other officers are not as conscientious.' He turned back to

Jeffries. 'Anyway, Smith tells me a very important lady was on board. Thankfully, Mrs Brody wasn't hurt too badly, just a few scratches, I hear. She's good friends with the chief inspector, so we need to tread carefully on this one, Jeffries. She'll no doubt report back, and we'll be in the firing line if the chief thinks we're not doing a thorough job.'

Jeffries groaned inwardly. Just my luck to be lumbered with a case that has connections with one of those upstairs. His superiors. That means the inspector will be on my back, he thought.

Jeffries listened to the inspector drone on about the chief and possible promotion prospects. Or damage to those prospects. Typical of the inspector to only be thinking about the important lady. He didn't seem concerned about the young woman who'd died or any other passengers who may have been hurt.

The inspector put his notebook back on his desk. 'Driver error is the most likely cause of the accident, of course, but I need you, Detective Sergeant Jeffries, to investigate if foul play caused the crash. Our new recruit here already has a list of witnesses for you to interview. Let's see if this course of yours was worth the money! Take Smith with you and do some of your detecting, would you? And Jeffries? We need a quick result on this one. A week should be enough time for a man with experience and your new skills. That's all.'

'Yes, Sir. Come on, Constable Smith, no time to waste,' said Jeffries. Reaching for the door handle, he paused and faced the inspector, now sitting at his desk. 'Just one thing, sir.'

The inspector looked up. 'Yes, Jeffries?'

'If Constable Smith here is to help me with my enquiries, he'll stand out like a sore thumb. His neatly pressed uniform may look commendable, but I learned on my course that a successful detective needs to blend in. An

officer in uniform just won't work. He needs to be in civvies. Sir.'

The inspector twirled his moustache. 'Very unusual. Not really the done thing. Policemen should be seen to rise through the ranks. But you may have a point there, Jeffries.' Turning to Smith, he said, 'Smith, I believe you live nearby? Best you get back home and change into your suit. To blend in, as the detective says.'

Smith turned to the inspector and said, 'I live just a five-minute walk away. I can be changed in no time.'

Nodding to the inspector, Jeffries opened the door. The other officers had stopped typing and talking. No doubt trying to listen in to the conversation, thought Jeffries.

Later, Smith and Jeffries stood outside Smith's house in Longbrook Street, Smith having changed into his suit, adding a black Derby hat that suited him well. Jeffries straightened his own hat, a grey Fedora, looking rather worn with daily use. His wife had often mentioned he needed to buy a new one, but Jeffries liked this one just fine. He considered the man in front of him. The suit accentuated Smith's muscular arms and solid shoulders. Jeffries thought he might be a keen swimmer.

On the street, Jeffries said to his new accomplice, 'How many witnesses do you have on your list, Constable?'

Smith consulted his shiny new notebook, most of its pages still crisp and unused. The first page was full of neat handwriting. 'I spoke to the lady the inspector referred to, Mrs Brody, and the driver, both of whom left for the hospital soon after I arrived at the scene. The driver, Mr Hoskins, looked in a bad way. The doctor said he'd taken a nasty knock to the head but should recover and be back on his feet in a few days. Mrs Brody looked in better shape, and insisted on accompanying the driver to the hospital.' Smith turned a page in his book. 'The driver was talking nonsense when I tried to speak to him, no doubt due to his injury to his head, and Mrs Brody didn't have much to add to what I'd already seen with my own eyes. One other witness I tried to speak to was a Mr Westlake. An interesting fellow. He's a photographer who owns a small shop on Fore Street. He was supposedly taking photographs of nearby buildings at the time of the crash but when I tried to ask him questions, he seemed in a hurry to get away from the scene. He was packing away his camera apparatus when I approached him. Another bystander had distracted me, and the cameraman wandered off before I could talk to him properly.'

'Do we know the name of the woman who died?'

Smith turned the page. 'She was called Rose. Mrs Rose James. Not long married, apparently. The driver knew her. It seems he knows all his passengers, as they are mostly regulars. Quite a jovial chap, according to his passengers. Not when I spoke to him, of course. He was very distressed, as you can imagine.'

Jeffries thought for a moment. 'Yes, I'm sure he was. Poor man, just going about his business, a normal day that ends in tragedy. Right, let's go and see this photographer fellow, Mr Westlake, first. Then we'll inspect the wreckage tomorrow, assuming it's been taken to the tram workshop on the quay.'

Smith closed his book, returning it back to his coat pocket. Jeffries considered his colleague, 'Come on Smith, what's on your mind?'

Smith smiled, realising Jeffries had noticed him in deep thought, 'Just a feeling, sir. The photographer was at the scene before the crash, with his camera set up already. It just seems, I don't know; convenient?'

'We'll make a policeman of you yet, Smith. I was thinking the same thing. If we time this right, we can have a chat with our photographer friend and be finished in time for coffee. I'll be ready for some grub by then too, I shouldn't wonder.'

Smith laughed. 'I have heard about you and your eating habits. Apparently, you eat all day, but you never put on weight. How do you avoid getting fat?'

'I burn it off with hard work, Smith. Come on, where is the photographer's shop? Is it near a café?' Jeffries said with a smile. Normally content with working alone, he was warming to the idea of having an accomplice. Even a poker-playing one.

4

A cup of tea and a tin of biscuits.

What seems like hours after the crash, but what is, of course, just a few minutes, I wearily climb the steps to the office, hoping Mr Edwards doesn't see me arrive in my dishevelled state. Out of breath as I reach the top step, the front door swings open, and William Edwards Jr is there, gaping at me. His fair hair glints in the morning sunlight, the handsome dimples in his cheeks drawing my attention. He never fails to make my face turn an embarrassing red. My stomach flips.

'What the hell happened to you?' William says, looking me up and down. 'You look terrible. You're lucky my father is out, or he'd probably fire you on the spot, looking like that!'

My skirt is ripped, and my blouse is filthy. My hair is full of dirt. I'm a mess. I sweep my hair back, adjusting the hairpin. 'A tram crashed on the bridge. A young woman died. It was awful,' I bluster, stepping inside. William follows me as I walk to the little front office where we both work. There's barely room for our two desks, our chairs almost touching the wall. A tall cupboard with shelves and drawers occupies the rest of the available space. I pace up and down, absent-mindedly inspecting the spines of the legal books lining the shelves.

William looks at me with concern, his eyebrows drawing together. 'You're shaking like a leaf. Sit down, and you can tell me all about it over a cup of tea. I was just popping out for milk, but we have enough for now. I'll put the kettle on.'

William hurries to the kitchen behind the office, and I hear him rattling the tea caddy and rummaging in the cupboard for cups. The office is warm. William has already lit the little fire in the corner of the room. The coals crackle and spit. I sit at my desk, lean back in my chair and stare blankly at the wall. I'm starting to shake more now. I'm cold; I left my shawl on the bridge. My stomach turns and I feel sick.

'There, one cup of sweet tea,' William says as he places a chipped cup on my desk and flops into the chair opposite. He gently blows on his own tea and takes a sip. 'Tell me everything about this awful crash and leave nothing out!'

I take a noisy sip from my cup and grimace. I like sugar in hot drinks, but William has overdone it. Thankfully, the sugary taste makes me feel better almost immediately, and I begin to tell William the account of my morning.

'I was on time for a change this morning, so I decided to walk as it was such a lovely day, and the tram is not always quicker anyway. I remember taking my usual route down my road, saying hello to my neighbour. She was busy cleaning her front step. It was all very normal. Just like any other day. The sun was shining, and it didn't feel particularly cold for October.' I lean forward, crossing my arms on the desk, thinking back.

'I started to cross the bridge at the bottom of Fore Street. The water smelt awful, as usual. You probably don't know that, as I expect you don't venture south of the river.' I smile ruefully. People tend to stick to their own side of the river, suspicious of the other side. Taking another sip of my tea, I continue. 'Before I started up the hill, I noticed one of the town trams was stationary at the top. I don't really know what made me stop and stare. All I remember is the horses seemed to be having trouble pulling away from the junction. They were making an awful racket.'

'This is the South Street junction?' asks William.

I nod, 'Yes, that's right. Whenever I take the tram to town, I usually jump off there as it's a short walk to the high street. Anyway, as I watched, the horses broke free and bolted. The tram started to roll backwards, gathering speed, rocking from side to side. I suspect the driver was trying to stop it from careering down the hill. It was awful, William. It just got faster and faster, smashing into a horse and cart, throwing the cart driver into the road.' I wrap my hands around my cup, thinking back. 'The tram fell onto its side, smashing its windows and breaking up as it scraped along the ground. As it slid past me, something must have flown off it and hit my head because the next thing I remember, I was lying in the road, covered in dirt.'

'Are you hurt? You have a nasty bump on your forehead.'

I reach to feel the bump. 'My head hurts, but not too much. My back was aching, but it's feeling better after my walk to the office.' I look down at my clothes. 'I need to get cleaned up before your father gets back. Where is he anyway?'

William waves his hand, shoves paperwork to one side, and puts his cup on the desk. 'He won't be in for ages. What happened next?'

'Well, I came to my senses and stumbled across the road to the wreckage, and this is the really awful part.'

William leans forward but says nothing.

'There was a woman. A girl, really, lying in the road. I tried to help her, and a doctor arrived to care for her, but it was too late. She died in front of us.'

'That's terrible, Carrie! No wonder you look a state,' says William, sitting back, clearly shocked at what I have just told him.

'But the oddest thing,' I say. 'She was alive when I reached her, and as I held her hand, she said that it wasn't an accident and to talk to her husband. Apparently he knows the truth. Isn't that an odd thing to say while lying injured on the road?'

'Well, I …'

I raise my hand to interrupt William and reach into my pocket. 'That's not all. She handed me this card before she died. Here, what do you make of it?'

William takes the card from me and examines it closely, squinting as he does so. 'I can see it says Exeter, but the rest is smudged and difficult to read, and it's torn right through the middle of what looks like a company name.' He turns the card over. 'Who is Mr Shute? And what does the mention of the hundred pounds mean? That's a lot of money.' He hands the card back, and I push it into my pocket. 'Are you going to speak to her husband? How will you find him?'

'First, I need to clean myself up before Mr Edwards arrives. And as far as Rose's husband is concerned, I was hoping that you'd know how to find out where she lived. Do you have any ideas?'

William smiles as he arranges some documents into a pile and lines up his pens. 'I thought you'd ask that. I have a friend who might be able to help. Leave that with me. Do you need any other help? Checking through these boring wills is sending me to sleep.'

I smile back and sip my tea, reaching for a biscuit from the tin William keeps on his desk. I feel much better now, and I really want to find out what happened and why Rose thought it was not an accident. I can't imagine it was the driver's fault, as Mr Hoskins is so experienced, having driven the trams for years. William and I could work together. How exciting! 'It will be extremely helpful if you can find out where Rose lived. Thank you.' I think for a moment. 'Shouldn't we tell your father?'

William shakes his head. 'Let's keep this to ourselves for now.' He drums his fingers on the desk, thinking. 'The accident happened on the bridge, but you said the tram was at the top of the hill when it started reversing. It's fairly steep at that point, and I've seen how the drivers need to firmly hold the brake at that junction. There's quite a technique to it. Perhaps part of the mechanism simply broke.'

'I agree, but Rose was determined to tell me it wasn't an accident. I'm sure she knew something, but she died before she could reveal more.'

'Well, there is one way we could find out,' says William, finishing his tea in one gulp and reaching for the last biscuit. 'I'm meeting a good friend of mine for lunch. As luck would have it, he's an engineer in the workshop where they maintain and repair the trams. You could join us and chat with him to see if he has any ideas.'

'If you're sure he won't mind. It sounds like a good idea,' I say.

William stands and picks up a bundle of papers. He straightens them and puts them into his worn briefcase, handed down from his father. 'Don't worry, John won't mind. We've been friends since school. And he owes me a favour or two.' He snaps his case shut, grabs his overcoat from a hook on the wall, and checks his timepiece. 'I'd better get a move on. I need to deliver these documents to the court this morning. Let's meet outside Deller's Café at midday. Do you know Deller's?'

'Yes, I know the place. I'll quickly tidy myself up before Mr Edwards arrives.' I stand and brush biscuit crumbs from my skirt. William leaves the office, which suddenly feels very quiet. I go to the little washroom behind the office, locking the door. I inspect my face in the little mirror above the sink. The bump on my forehead is a fierce purple, and blood is smeared across one of my cheeks. When I notice the dried blood on my hands, I realise it's not my own. My stomach turns. I think of poor Rose, lying in the street, covered by my bloodied shawl. Across my chin is a streak of mud and grit. I look dreadfully tired. I feel like I've been made up for a play, but at the same time, I can't imagine laughing or smiling right now. *Come on, Carrie. Focus, says a voice in my head. The game is afoot.* Yes, Sherlock, it most certainly is.

Pulling out my hairpin, I vigorously brush my hair and tie it up back into a bun. I hate to wear my hair like this as I prefer it loose, but at least it now looks reasonably tidy. I wipe my face with a towel and I begin to look presentable. The worst of the dirt and blood on my blouse won't easily wipe off, but it's covered by my jacket. Hopefully, it won't look odd if I keep the jacket on, even if it is warm in the office. My skirt is a different matter entirely, but I will be sitting at my desk when Mr Edwards comes back, so he won't notice the dirt.

I return to the office, sit at my desk and reach for this morning's post just as the front door opens, and Mr Edwards strides in. A slim man in his fifties with hair greying at the sides, William's father is dressed in his usual dark suit and carries his rolled-up umbrella like a cane. He gives me a cursory glance and mutters, 'Good morning, Miss Grey.'

'Good morning, Mr Edwards.' At the door to his office, he turns to look at me, then shakes his head slightly and enters his office, leaving the door open. He's clearly still not keen on having a woman working here. It's only because he knows my father that I have the job. I think back to my father's words this morning at breakfast. "Don't forget that Mr Edwards is a stickler for time. He is a good friend of mine; don't let me down!"

My mind still firmly on the accident throughout the morning, I absentmindedly arrange the letters by type; general enquiries for William to deal with, and signed papers and bills for Mr Edwards Senior. There are more bills than enquiries.

The ticking of the clock punctuates the silence in the office. The only other sound comes from Mr Edwards' room as he huffs and puffs, reading documents that obviously don't please him. Eventually, the clock hands move to midday, and it's time to meet William and his friend at Deller's.

I stand and go to pull my shawl over my shoulders before remembering I'd left it at the scene of the accident earlier. It's probably in the morgue now with that poor girl. Tapping on Mr Edwards' door, I lean into his office, careful not to reveal my dirty skirt. 'I'm going out for some lunch, Mr Edwards.'

'Yes, of course. Please don't be late back.' He pulls out his pocket watch, the light momentarily catching the polished brass. 'I shall be watching the time, Miss Grey.' He snaps his timepiece shut and drops it back into his pocket.

I step out of the front door and take a shortcut, passing the Ship Inn - Sir Francis Drake drank here once, according to the little sign by the door - and emerge into the cobbled street next to Deller's, the cream stone of the Cathedral opposite glowing in the sunshine. William is already here, looking out for me, hands deep in his pockets. I enjoy working with William. He's kind and compassionate, and despite only meeting him a month ago, I feel as if I've known him for years. I walk up to him and smile as he holds the door open for me. Time to meet his friend, who will hopefully help us get to the bottom of this mystery.

5

A camera, a darkroom and a wife

Harry Westlake was in his processing room behind the shop, thoughtfully boxing up the photography plates he had exposed in his camera earlier that morning on the bridge, the resulting pictures already developed and displayed in his shop. The room was dark, save for a red-tinted light that cast an eerie glow on the walls, long shadows running from the floor to the ceiling. A knock at the door pulled him from his thoughts.

'Just one minute,' Harry called out, shaking his head, annoyed. Why his wife couldn't answer customer queries this morning without troubling him was beyond him. It was her job to manage the shop, after all.

'There are two police officers here, Harry,' his wife called through the door. 'They said they need to speak to you urgently.'

Harry sighed, carefully set the box on the shelf above the bench, and strode across the room. He opened the door to find two officers, their hats in their hands, looking at the photographs displayed on the walls. They turned to face Harry as he appeared in the doorway. Harry recognised the younger man from earlier as Constable Smith, who had asked him questions about the crash. He was wearing a uniform then, but now wore a well-fitting suit under his overcoat. The other man appeared older, hair greying at the sides and rather unkempt as if it needed a comb. Like the constable, he also wore a suit under his unbuttoned overcoat and, from his demeanour, was obviously the one in charge. Harry wondered why the constable had changed out of his police uniform.

'Can I help you?' asked Harry. A nervous tic made his eye twitch.

Jeffries took a step forward and, with a friendly smile that he hoped would disarm the man, said, 'Mr Westlake?'

'Yes, that's me. Please call me Harry. Is this about the tram accident?' Harry tilted his head at Constable Smith. 'I've already given my account of what I saw to your colleague.'

'Allow me to introduce myself, Harry. I am Detective Sergeant Jeffries, and I have heard the brief account you gave to my colleague, but I have some more questions.' Jeffries liked the photographer's look of concern at the mention of the word 'detective.' The addition to his rank was starting to give Jeffries a good feeling.

The photographer absentmindedly picked up a camera lens from the counter. 'I don't know what else I can add.'

Jeffries sensed a note of defensiveness in Harry Westlake's tone. 'Perhaps you can tell us again how you came to be at the scene of the accident.'

Harry fiddled with the lens, turning it over and wiping imaginary dust from the glass. 'Well, as I said earlier, I was photographing the historic houses on West Street for a book I am working on. Portrait work alone doesn't pay the rent. I need to sell books and postcards to earn more money.'

Detective Sergeant Jeffries took out his notebook, flipped it open and scribbled a note with his stub of a pencil. 'I see, so you were in a good position to see the crash. What exactly did you witness?'

Harry glanced at his wife standing next to him, pretty in a smart red dress, her hair tied in a bun. Her brown eyes were clear and alert, looking at each officer in turn as she played with a loose strand of hair. Jeffries caught the briefest look of resentment the wife gave her husband. Harry didn't seem to notice and looked back at the police officers. 'My camera was set up and ready to use when I heard a commotion at the top of Fore Street. When I looked up, I noticed a tram at the top of the hill having some kind of problem at the junction.'

Jeffries stopped writing and looked at Harry, indicating to Smith with his pencil, who was paying more attention to a little desk pushed up against the wall next to the door. Smith was making a mental note of the contents sitting next to the blotter. A set of matching pens, a pencil, a pad of cream notepaper. And an open tin. Leaning ever so slightly, Smith peered inside, and raised his eyebrows. His attention was snapped back to the room as Jeffries continued. 'When you spoke to my colleague, you said you saw the tram racing down the street to the bridge. You didn't mention that you noticed it having problems at the top of the hill. I was under the impression that you didn't see anything until the tram ran down the hill.'

'Well, I remember now,' said the photographer, annoyed. His eye twitched again. 'I could see that the tram was struggling to move forward. At first, the horses slid back, then they broke loose and bolted. The tram started accelerating backwards down the hill, crashing into other carriages and getting faster and faster.' Harry paused at the memory. 'It was so strange. Everything seemed to freeze in place. Time seemed to slow down. I remember looking around at people as they watched the scene unfold. Everyone looked terrified as the tram raced down the hill. It hit a horse and carriage, crashed onto its side and slid to a halt on the bridge, jammed against the railings.'

Sergeant Jeffries glanced at Mrs Westlake, curious as to why she hadn't said anything, and then turned his attention back to Harry. 'And what did you do, Mr Westlake? Did you try to help?'

'Er, no. My camera was ready, so I took some photographs of the scene.'

'So while people were probably trapped inside, likely badly injured, you simply took photographs?' Jeffries said, raising his eyebrows. No wonder Westlake's wife looks embarrassed, thought Smith.

Harry carefully put the lens back on the counter. 'Well, it's my job. I felt I should record the event. For posterity.'

Constable Smith stepped away from the little desk. 'May we see the photographs? It might help us to understand what caused the crash.'

Harry turned to a stand by the counter and selected a handful of pictures. He passed them to the constable, who looked at each in turn, flicking through them like cards in a poker hand.

The detective sergeant looked at the remaining photographs on the stand and scratched his jaw. 'These photographs have prices on them. You are selling photographs of a fatal accident, sir? That is scandalous! What kind of man records such an incident and then sells the images?' Smith handed the photographs to the detective sergeant for him to inspect.

Harry's wife looked down at the floor as her husband explained, 'It's business, officer. I've sold dozens already. People like to buy them to show to their friends and family.'

Jeffries looked at his colleague. 'Can you believe this, Smith? Do people like to gloat? A young woman died in this accident!' He slipped the photographs into his inside pocket. 'You'll be hearing from us again, Mr Westlake.'

The officers turned to leave. 'Wait, the photographs are threepence each,' Harry spluttered.

'No, Mr Westlake, these are evidence. Good day to you, sir.'

6

Pie and gravy with new acquaintances

'I was starting to think you weren't coming, Carrie,' says William.

I smile. 'Very funny. You know I couldn't leave until twelve on the dot. I'm only two minutes late!'

William bows theatrically as I pass him and step through the open door into the cosy café. I laugh; he is a true gentleman. The room's aroma hits me as soon as I walk through the door, a delicious fragrance of roasting coffee beans and something that reminds me of gravy. Meat pie, perhaps.

Being lunchtime, it's busy. The place is warm and welcoming, with watercolour scenes on the wood-panelled walls. People sit at tables set with cream cloths, menus and shiny cutlery.

William looks across to the back of the room and raises his hand. At a table by the window, a dark-haired man notices us and smiles. His white shirt is grimy, the sleeves rolled back, exposing strong arms; it's obvious he's an engineer. He stands and waves us over.

'That's John,' William says, gently taking hold of my elbow and leading me past tables to his waiting friend.

I take in the scene as we walk across the crowded room, squeezing past tables and chairs. Three men at one table wear smart suits, looking at some documents with serious expressions. At another table, a man and woman are deep in conversation, their heads almost touching. Across the room, a small group of young women laugh as they enjoy each other's company. In the corner, an old man reads a newspaper, pipe in one hand, a steaming mug of something hot in the other. Concentration etched on his craggy face.

The two men shake hands, and John slaps William on the shoulder. 'Are you going to introduce me to your delightful friend?' he says, his smile warm and friendly. Is

41

this why women go weak at the knees? I think. What nonsense!

Blushing slightly, William sits opposite his friend. 'This is Carrie, my colleague from the office. She has only been with us for a few weeks.'

'So nice to meet you, Carrie,' John says, beckoning me to the seat next to him. He looks at William. 'I've already ordered our usual.' Turning to me, he says, 'I'll order another dish and a drink for you if you're staying for lunch?'

I realise I'm starving. 'That would be lovely, thank you.'

John must be a regular here, as he easily catches the eye of a waitress. Seemingly having a hidden signal between them, she simply smiles, nods and returns to the kitchen, presumably to arrange an extra dish for me and whatever they are drinking. I do hope it's not beer. Not at lunchtime, at any rate.

He's obviously good friends with William. While they chat, they share knowing looks and laugh at the same things. It's almost as if they reach into each other's minds. I smile, hoping they'll accept me as a friend. I suspect we'd make a great trio.

Despite his unkempt appearance, or perhaps because of it, John is a handsome man with a ready smile. He beams at every opportunity, revealing white teeth, bright against his grubby face. He saves his best smile for the waitresses, who always smile back. He's obviously a ladies' man, the way he captivates them with a simple grin. He reaches for his glass, his hands oily from a hard morning's work. His nails are grubby. Considering his job, I suppose it's inevitable.

John seems to read my mind. 'I've ordered the same food we're having and lemonade for you, Carrie. I hope that's ok?'

'Lemonade is perfect. Thank you.'

'So, what's been happening to you two today?' John looks at my blouse and skirt. 'Have you two been fighting? Looks like you came off worse, Carrie!'

I look at William, silently checking that we can trust John with my story. He nods and turns to John. 'Carrie had an awful experience this morning, and we need your help with something.'

John's face is suddenly serious as he realises his joking is inappropriate right now. 'Sorry, Carrie. How can I help?'

I sit up straight as I describe my morning, pausing only when the waitress serves our food: three steaming plates of pie and gravy. The savoury aroma makes my stomach grumble, and, thanking John for lunch, we all tuck in.

Between mouthfuls, I continue my account of the morning, John nodding and frowning as I tell him the part about Rose dying in the road while I held her hand. 'How awful,' he says as he reaches for his beer, taking a long drink before placing the glass back on the table and wiping his mouth with a napkin.

I leave out the part about Rose handing me the card. William must notice because he gives me a pointed look when I omit that piece of the story, and I shake my head a little. Some things might be better if they stay between us for the time being.

John says, 'As William probably told you, I work at the engineering shop where the trams are maintained and repaired. The tram you saw this morning has already been brought into our workshop. It's in a terrible state, as you know. We begin repairs tomorrow. If it can be salvaged, of course. From what you've told me and from what I've seen, it's probably only good for scrap. A shame, as we'd only just finished carrying out maintenance on it the day before.'

William looks up from his lunch. 'What sort of maintenance work, John? Could the work have been faulty?'

John shakes his head. 'Just a routine job on the harness. Nothing very involved, certainly nothing that would have caused the tram to crash.'

I think about this. 'Surely the police will want to look at the wreckage before you touch it, won't they? They won't want you tampering with any evidence.'

William smiles and says to John, 'Carrie's a bit of a detective buff. She reads those yarns about Sherlock Holmes. I think she sees herself as a bit of a Watson, isn't that right, Carrie?'

'Or perhaps Sherlock himself,' says John, his eyes crinkling as he smiles.

I feel myself blush. 'Guilty as charged. I do like the Holmes and Watson stories. I just think that the police will want to find out what happened, and there might be evidence in the wreckage.' I don't tell either of them that I often hear Sherlock's voice in my head.

'The police probably think it was the driver's fault,' says William.

'Impossible!' I answer a little too loudly. A couple at the next table look across before returning to their conversation. Or talking about us, more likely.

'Mr Hoskins is a careful and experienced driver, and the woman who died...' I abruptly shut my mouth.

'The woman spoke to you? What did she say?' asks John, suddenly serious again.

I realise that to ask for John's help, I'll have to tell him the missing part of my story. After relaying my conversation with Rose, I show him the card. 'She was convinced it wasn't an accident, and certainly not caused by the driver. She gave me this card, telling me to speak to her husband and the person whose name is written on the back, a Mr Shute.'

John takes the card from me and reads it carefully. When he turns it over, he frowns, holding the card up to the window to get a clearer look. 'Interesting.'

'What is it? We could read some of the words, but it's not very clear,' I say.

'It's smudged, but when I hold it to the light, I can just about make out the wording. It says Shute Lighting Company. I know them. They have offices and workshops near us on the quay. They are one of the biggest employers in the town. They make electric lighting components for businesses, I believe.'

William shakes his head. 'Not just businesses. Some wealthier homes now have these new electric lights as well. Ordinary people can't afford to change from gas and oil.'

I look around and see the café still has the old gas lamps on the walls, the wallpaper behind them blackened by the smoke. 'Not always wealthy people,' I say. 'Some of our neighbours have recently replaced some of their gas lights with the new electric ones.' I nudge William in the arm. 'Perhaps you can speak to your father about it and convince him to change to electricity in the office. I hear that the light is so much brighter.'

William sighs as he puts his knife and fork down, pushing his plate away and wiping his mouth with his napkin. 'I have already suggested making the change, but I think it will be a while before my father puts his hand in his pocket!'

Turning to John, he says, 'Do you think we can have a look at the wreckage in your workshop? Carrie wants to find out what really happened, and the idea of investigating the cause of the accident sounds interesting. Certainly more exciting than working on legal documents!'

John thinks while leaning back in his chair, his plate scraped clean. 'I can't let you in during the day as visitors are not allowed, but we can have a look tonight if you would like? I have a key to the workshop.'

I don't hesitate. 'That would be perfect. Shall we, William?'

William grins. 'Sounds like an adventure. Count me in!'

45

With a rough plan in place, we finish our drinks and arrange to meet up outside John's workshop at seven o'clock tonight.

7

Coffee, a steam car and a photograph

The two policemen stepped out of the photography shop into the bright autumn sunshine and strode purposefully up the hill. The street was busy and bustling with activity; coalmen, dustmen, tinkers, carpenters, street sellers and messenger boys all going about their business.

Deep in thought as they walked to the top of South Street, Smith was about to say something when Jeffries suddenly stopped in the middle of the pavement. A woman walking behind them nearly bumped into Jeffries. 'Look out, mister!'

Jeffries turned around and touched the brim of his hat. 'Sorry, Madam.' Smiling at Smith, he said, 'Why don't we find a quiet café and have some coffee and a bacon sandwich? We need to have a proper look at these photographs, and I'm starving.'

'Only if you're paying,' said Smith, smiling and shaking his head, bemused by his new colleague's obsession with food. Wondering where he put all this food.

Jeffries led the way, turning the corner and quickly walking past other pedestrians. He patted his belly and decided he'd have to cut back on pastries and bacon sandwiches in future. The excellent, if over-indulgent, food on the training course had added a pound or two to his already substantial frame. Perhaps he'd start tomorrow, but today, he needed food to think.

As they waited to cross the street, a noisy vehicle painted shiny black with bright yellow wheels raced past within inches of the two men. A steam cloud belched from a tube at the back.

'Watch out, Smith!' Jeffries grabbed hold of his colleague's arm and pulled him away from the edge of the road.

The horse-less carriage thundered past and off up the road. People jumped from its path as it sped up the hill, making a noise like a little steam train, leaving a white cloud in its midst.

'What the dickens was that, sir?'

Jeffries smiled at his younger colleague. 'That, my friend, is a steam carriage. A Stanley, I believe. They are popular in London, but that's the first one I've seen in Exeter. Apparently, they are the future of transport, quieter than the new petrol engines and destined to replace the horse and carriage. They say they will soon be cheap enough for every family to own one!'

'Well, let's hope they find a way to slow them down before the damn things start killing people,' muttered Smith as he nervously stepped into the road. 'Who was the driver? I have a mind to report him.'

'That was none other than Mr Downe, the shipping magnate. He lives in a fine house overlooking the town. He collects cars in his spare time, and that looks like his most recent addition to his collection. Come on, my coffee is calling me.'

They reached a café that didn't look too busy. Jeffries preferred Deller's, but this one would have to do. It was closer.

'After you, old chap,' Jeffries said, beckoning for his companion to lead the way. 'Find a table in the window. I like to watch the world go by while I enjoy my coffee.'

Smith walked to a vacant table overlooking the street. They took off their heavy coats, removed their hats and sat opposite one another with a satisfied sigh. They'd been on their feet all morning, and the prospect of a strong coffee and a mouth-watering bacon sandwich was just the ticket.

Both men took in their surroundings. It was quiet, with just a few of the other tables occupied. Steam rose from the kettles behind the counter, and a waitress was busy filling a display with tasty-looking cakes and biscuits. A waiter fiddled with a steaming contraption, its brass and steel tubes gleaming as the steam hissed into a shiny jug. Seemingly satisfied, he carefully poured hot milk into a tilted cup.

Jeffries watched the waiter perform this long process. Wrinkling his nose, he said to Smith, 'What is that contraption, Smith? They seem to crop up everywhere. Deller's has one too.'

Smith smiled. 'It's a coffee-making machine. It makes a frothy, milky coffee. An Italian import, I believe. The idea is to create a foam on the top of the coffee, by carefully pouring the milk over the top.'

Jeffries didn't look impressed. 'Not for me, thank you. I enjoy a simple coffee; black with plenty of sugar. Nothing fancier than a kettle is required to satisfy my needs.'

As they waited for a waitress to come over and take their order, Smith said, 'How much do you think Mr Westlake makes from his portrait business?'

'Not a lot. His customers are probably ordinary people who don't have much money to spend on such luxuries. Why do you ask?'

Smith smiled and said, 'That's what I thought. Then why does he have a pile of five-pound notes in his shop?'

'How on earth did you know that, Smith?'

'I glanced at his desk by the door while you talked with him. I noticed a tin on the desk and risked a quick peek. The lid was open anyway.'

'Go on.'

Smith paused for effect. He was enjoying himself. 'There was a bundle of five-pound notes inside. I couldn't count them, of course, but it looked like a substantial amount of cash to me.'

'Well done, Smith. I wonder why he has so much money in the shop. Cash like that should be kept in the safe. Interesting.'

Smith frowned. 'Something's going on with those two. Did you notice how nervous they both were? Curious fellow, our Mr Westlake. And Mrs Westlake was very quiet. She knows something, I reckon.'

Jeffries shrugged, 'I don't know, Smith. I think she was embarrassed that her husband had taken photographs of the crash and then started selling them to the public. In any case, we need to have another chat with them both, and ask about the cash in the tin. Let's have a look at those pictures of the crash.'

Jeffries twisted round and withdrew the photographs from his coat pocket. He carefully spread them out on the table. They looked at each one with interest.

Each photograph showed the same view with slight differences. The first showed the crashed tram on its side, debris scattered across the road. A crowd of bystanders were gathered around, held back by three policemen. Constable Smith could be seen at the edge of the photograph. The bridge railings were on the right of the picture.

The second photograph was similar but without so many people standing around.

Jeffries frowned as he inspected this image. 'This one clearly shows the accident immediately after it happened. See how there are hardly any people at the scene. He pointed to the next photograph in front of them. 'In this one, the passengers are climbing from the vehicle as if it has just crashed. Our photographer was lucky to be at the scene with his camera equipment just as it happened.'

'Certainly convenient,' Smith said, looking up as a waitress appeared, her notepad and pencil poised.

'Mm, yes, it was convenient, wasn't it?' Jeffries said, stroking his chin. He looked up at the waitress. 'A coffee, strong and black for me, please.' Jeffries nodded to Smith. 'One of those fancy frothy coffees for my colleague and bacon sandwiches for both of us. Thank you, miss.'

The waitress nodded, scribbled, and walked back to the kitchen.

A few minutes later, as the two men continued inspecting the photographs, the waitress returned with a tray.

'Your coffees and sandwiches, gentlemen.' She expertly lowered the tray and placed the food and drinks on the table. A heady aroma from the greasy bacon sandwiches and mugs of steaming coffee filled the air.

'Thank you, miss,' said Jeffries, taking a sip of his coffee. 'Mm, that's better. Just what the old brain needed!'

Smith took a big bite from his sandwich, the grease running down his chin. He deftly wiped his mouth with his sleeve and slurped noisily from his cup, leaving a line of frothy milk on his top lip.

Jeffries frowned, Smith lacked proper manners, despite being the chief inspector's son. He turned his attention to the photograph with the most people around the debris. Pulling a magnifying glass from his suit pocket, he peered closely at the image. He could see several people in the picture, some watching from the pavement and others sitting on the road. Just the driver's cab was visible; the rest of the tram was out of view. Jeffries concluded that the photographer must have altered his position slightly to frame this picture.

'Not much here to help us,' said Jeffries, slipping his magnifying glass back into his pocket. 'The photographs show the result, not the cause of the crash.' He leaned across to gather up the photographs.

'Wait,' Smith said, reaching out and putting a greasy finger on the last image. 'That girl sitting on the ground looking directly at the camera - I know her. That's Mr Grey's daughter, Carrie.'

'How do you know her, Smith?'

'I don't know Carrie Grey directly, but I know Mr Grey from the social club. He told me that he had managed to find his daughter a job with one of the solicitors in the town. Edwards and Son in Castle Street, I'm sure of it.'

Detective Sergeant Jeffries looked again at the photograph, quietly pleased to be paired up with Smith, who was proving to be quite astute despite his inexperience. 'Miss Grey is sitting next to someone who is being attended to by the doctor. That's definitely Doctor Swithens there. I'd wager from the looks of things that the person lying on the ground is the woman who died in the crash.'

Jeffries drained the rest of his coffee. 'Come on, Smith. Let's get back to the station. While I write up our report for the day, I need you to arrange our visit to the workshop early tomorrow morning. Get a message to the foreman to make sure the tram has arrived in his workshop, and tell him not to touch anything until we've inspected the damage. When we've had a look, we'll go and have a chat with this Carrie girl. There's no point in seeing the driver today. He's probably still in shock from the crash, and we won't get anything useful out of him yet. Tomorrow is going to be a busy day. I suggest we meet at Deller's for breakfast to avoid getting delayed at the station.' Jeffries lowered his voice. 'The coffee is better at Deller's, and don't worry, they have one of those fancy coffee machines, so you'll be happy.'

Smith smiled. 'Any excuse for coffee and food, eh, Detective Sergeant?'

8

A contraption and a theory

At Deller's, John had handed me a crude map, scribbled on a napkin to show the location of the workshop. It's a short walk from my house, and William should be on his way to meet me there. I hope he hasn't lost his nerve.

As I walk, I can see my breath in the light of the street lamps. My hands barely keep warm in my thick woollen gloves, and I have my favourite hat pulled down over my ears. I hurry down the cobbled street towards the quay, my route taking me past the bonded stores where tea and coffee from overseas are stored after being unloaded from the quayside. The enormous stone-built warehouses are closed and quiet now but will be full of activity early tomorrow morning. I walk faster as I pass. The buildings look ominous in the dark, a tingle runs down my back.

I reach the little bridge over the stream that joins the main river. A chill rises from the murky water, and a thin mist swirls about my feet.

As I cross the rickety bridge, the worn wooden boards creaking with each step, I hear footsteps behind me. Quickening my pace, my heart racing, I chance a look over my shoulder. A man with a cane and a long coat is approaching. I start to run, almost slipping on the wet boards. The workshop is in darkness ahead of me now, an amber light glowing in the windows above the big double doors.

'Carrie!' a voice shouts from behind me. With a sigh of relief, I realise it's William. I turn and put my hands on my hips. 'You gave me a fright. I thought I was being followed by some stranger!'

'I'm sorry, I should have called out earlier. I didn't mean to frighten you.'

'I like your hat and cane. Very posh,' I mock.

'The hat keeps me warm, and like most gentlemen, I don't need a cane but it improves my posture.' William raises the fine walking stick above his head, 'And it comes in handy if I'm approached by any villains. You never know who's about on a dark night, especially in this area.'

'Well I certainly feel safer with you and your cane. I don't mind admitting I was a little nervous back there. Come on, let's see if John is here yet.' William walks alongside me, his cane clicking on the cobbles in time with his pace.

We reach the workshop. The sign over the door swings gently in the breeze, the hinges squeaking. 'John should get those greased. It's not a good advert for a maintenance company, is it?' William whispers.

'Why are you whispering?'

'I don't know.' Just then, the door swings open, and John appears from inside, an oil lamp in his hand throwing a weak light onto his face. He has a big, mischievous grin, clearly enjoying the adventure.

'Quick, come inside,' he says, looking left and right as he ushers us into the workshop.

The interior is dimly lit by oil lamps placed strategically on workshop benches, the light flickering on the walls. There is a cocktail of smells that I can't identify. 'What is that smell?' I ask, screwing up my face.

John joins us after slamming the doors shut with a bang and throwing the bolt across, making William jump. Satisfied, he turns to us. 'It's the grease and engine oil. I'm used to it. Welcome to my workshop.'

It's not actually his workshop, as he just works here, but I smile as I realise John likes the idea of it being his domain. He clearly loves his job, despite the grime and manual labour.

William and I follow John across the workshop, careful to avoid tripping over wheels, lengths of wood, bits of metal, and all sorts of mechanical parts littering the floor.

As we reach the far end of the workshop, the area opens up into a much larger section. The ceiling is higher here, and workbenches line most of the back wall. Tools and contraptions of all sorts hang on hooks, occupying every available space.

In the middle of the floor are the broken remains of the tram. The main body is upright, with pieces scattered in piles around the wreckage, organised for the police inspection.

'If we want to find out why the tram crashed, where on earth do we start?' says William, brow furrowed. I think he was expecting this to be easier. I am still excited and eager to find the answer. I've only been working at the solicitor's for a matter of weeks, and already I'm in the middle of an exciting mystery, in a place I shouldn't be, in the dark with my new sidekicks in tow. Though I'm no longer cold, my hands shake a little, and I remind myself to concentrate on the task ahead. Sherlock would be proud!

John touches the peak of his cap and smiles. 'Allow me to demonstrate the cause of the crash.'

'Wait, you've already worked it out?' I say.

'Of course. I'm an engineer, aren't I? Come and see. I've set up something on the bench that will help explain it to you amateur engineers.'

John beckons us to one of the benches and places his lamp next to a wooden contraption. The dim light barely illuminates the structure. John lights another lamp so we can see more clearly. I lean in for a closer look. There is a small wheel fixed to a frame with a wooden bar raised at an angle. The lower end of the bar touches the side of the wheel.

William peers at the contraption, a deep frown on his face. Mechanics is clearly not something he is interested in, and I don't expect his hands have ever been dirty like John's. Except from ink from his inkwell, perhaps.

Pointing at the wheel, John explains. 'Imagine, if you will, that this is the wheel on the tram. Each one is identical, of course, and much smaller than the one on the tram. Now Carrie, turn the wheel, and you'll see it runs freely.'

I take hold of the wooden wheel and turn it as he instructs. It turns easily, and I can spin it at speed.

John looks at William and points to the wooden bar. 'This is the brake lever, and by pulling the top part backwards, you'll see that the lower end presses this wooden block onto the rim, thereby slowing the wheel. The more you pull, the harder it presses and the slower the wheel turns, eventually stopping it completely. This is a simplification of the actual braking system, but you can see the basic mechanics. Go ahead, William. Gently pull the lever while Carrie turns the wheel.'

Sure enough, as William pulls the lever, it's more difficult to turn the wheel, and when the lever is pulled as far as the contraption allows, I can no longer move it in either direction.

'Now think back to the few minutes immediately before the crash. What was happening?' John asks me.

I shrug. 'The tram was stationary at the top junction, so I assume the brake must have been applied to stop it from moving.'

William is still holding the brake lever. 'But imagine holding the real lever against the weight of the tram on a steep hill. My arm is tiring just using this model. How do the drivers manage with a tram? Are you suggesting the driver simply couldn't hold the lever any longer and let it go?'

I shake my head. 'I really don't think Mr Hoskins could rely on holding the lever like this to keep the tram stationary.'

John smiles and points to the top of the lever. 'Ah, well done. I'll make engineers of you both yet! If you look at the bottom of the lever, you'll see a small slot. Move the lever to your left into the slot, and you'll see how the top is prevented from moving, so the driver no longer has to hold the lever in the brake position.'

William does as instructed and lets go of the lever. The block stays in place, and I still cannot move the wheel.

I'm confused now. 'So what caused the crash? Was the brake faulty in some way?'

'Patience, Carrie! I'm getting to that part. If William moves the lever out of the slot and releases the brake, you'll see that the wheel can now be turned again.'

William releases the lever, and I can move the wheel easily. John retrieves a small, wedge-shaped block of wood from his pocket and places it into the space next to the lever, the narrow end pointing downwards. 'Try the brake again, William.'

William pulls the lever as before, and it goes as far as the slot, but pulling as hard as he can, the lever can't be moved into the parked position. As he tires of pulling, he releases the pressure on the wooden lever, and I can again turn the wheel.

'Are you suggesting that something broke and jammed against the lever?' I ask. 'Because if that's the case, it was a problem with the tram mechanism. That doesn't bode well for the maintenance team, which reflects badly on you, John.' I look at William and see the stiffness in his shoulders. He's realised the same issue. 'You don't seem worried. In fact, you look rather smug, if you don't mind me saying,' I add.

'I'm dismayed you both doubt our skills in this little workshop,' says John, shaking his head in mock disappointment. 'I inspected the brake section when the tram wreck was brought in, and I couldn't find any issues with the braking system or the condition of the mechanics. Let me show you.'

John picks up his oil lamp and leads us to the tram in the middle of the workshop. He points to the section beneath the driver's position. I can just make out a boxed section with screw holes where a cover has been removed.

'That's the mechanism where the end of the lever is attached to the brakes. I checked earlier, and there was no sign of anything broken.'

'I don't understand. If the mechanism isn't broken, what could have jammed the brakes?' William asks, looking perplexed.

'Carrie, you have small hands. Why don't you reach in and tell me what you find.' John stands aside, holding the lamp overhead.

I crouch beside the box section and push up my sleeve. I reach into the dark space, feeling around until my fingers touch something slimy. 'Yuk!' I say, quickly pulling out my hand. 'That's disgusting!'

'It's just grease. Put these on.' John passes me a pair of workman's gloves. They are too big for my hands, but I pull them on and try not to think of the grubby hands that last occupied them.

'Reach in lower, Carrie, and you'll uncover what I found earlier. I want you to discover it for yourself.'

I shift my position to reach as deep as I can beyond the grease. My fingertips touch something solid. I feel around, it's about four inches long, an inch square. It moves as I touch it. I get my fingers around it and carefully pull it out of the box.

I look at the object in the dim light of John's lamp. 'Bring it over to the bench,' John says.

William and I follow John, and I place the object on the bench. It's a wedge, just like the one in John's demonstration, but larger. Smooth and wooden, it narrows to a flat edge at one end. It has a hexagonal-shaped mark on the side.

John points to the indentation in the wood. 'You can see where the bolt that holds the brake in place has made a dent just here.'

'I've seen these wedge things before. It's a doorstop,' says William. 'This wedge would block the braking lever perfectly. Well done, Carrie, and you, John. This is quite a find. It proves the tram was tampered with.'

I lift the doorstop to the light, turning it over to see if there are any clues as to where it came from. 'We need to show this to the police. This proves that Mr Hoskins is innocent of negligence and that your colleagues are not guilty of poor maintenance.'

William leans in for a better look. 'There's usually a maker's mark on these doorstops, but this one is plain. Perhaps it was taken from a batch that hadn't been engraved yet.'

Pulling on a pair of gloves, John takes the wedge from me. 'We can't give it to the police. If we do that, they will think we put it there in the first place. I'll have to put this back where we found it and wait for it to be re-discovered by the police tomorrow.'

I nod. 'I agree. It's only legitimate evidence if there are official witnesses when it's found.'

'Elementary, Holmes,' says William with a grin.

John walks over to the tram, leans under the driver's seat and drops the wedge back into the box, where it lands with a thunk. He reaches for his toolbag. 'I'll put the panel back onto the brake section, and we'll see what happens when we show the wreckage to the police tomorrow morning. I'll tell them my theory and then discover the wedge again.'

I turn to William. 'It's getting late, and I need to get home. My father will wonder where I am if I don't hurry back. We can meet again tomorrow in Deller's at lunchtime, and John can tell us about the police inspection.'

In the dim lamplight, John smiles. I smile back. 'Lunch is on me tomorrow,' I say as we walk to the front door.

***

Later, while walking home, William says, 'There are still some questions we haven't considered yet.'

'I know what you're going to say. We know how the tram was tampered with, but we don't know who did it, and we also don't know why.' I say.

'That's exactly what I was thinking. And the person who did this must have extensive mechanical knowledge, access to the tram, and the right tools. I was also thinking that the brake section is quite well hidden. You'd have to know exactly where to look.'

'You don't think John had anything to do with the sabotage, do you? Perhaps someone paid him to tamper with the brakes when the tram was in the workshop. John did say his team had worked on the tram the other day.'

William turns to me, 'John? No, he'd never do anything of the sort. He's a good man, I'd vouch for him any time.'

'What about one of his colleagues? Any one of them could have had access to the tram when it was in for maintenance.'

William shakes his head, 'He said he'd worked on it himself as it was such an important job.'

'Well, someone interfered with the tram. The evidence was clear enough.'

We walk along the road to my house, deep in thought. 'Let's wait and see what happens tomorrow. See you bright and early in the office, William.'

William pulls his collar tighter around his neck, his breath steaming in the frigid air, 'I enjoyed tonight. Quite the adventure. I can see that working with you is never going to be boring! See you tomorrow. Goodnight, Carrie.' William turns down a side street towards his home, cane swinging as he walks.

I push open the gate, walk up the garden path and quietly open the front door, hoping it won't squeak. 'Is that you, Carrie? Where on earth have you been at this hour?' my father calls out.

I hang my coat on the hook by the front door, take a deep breath, and walk into the front room. Father is in his usual chair by the fire, drinking a whisky, his pipe on the tall ashtray by his side. Dark circles under his eyes. Time for me to make a stand. I'm twenty now, no longer a child, and I need more independence.

'I've been with William and his friend John. We've had a lovely evening enjoying a hot chocolate at Deller's and putting the world to rights, just like you do at the club.' I say, which is partly true.

'Well, I hope young William walked you home. It's not safe for you to walk about in the dark alone,' Father says with concern etched on his face.

'No need to worry. William was the perfect gentleman.' I sit in the chair opposite him and warm my hands by the fire. He looks at me in surprise and points to my forehead. 'What on earth happened to your head? You have an ugly bruise there.'

I sit back in the chair. 'It's a long story, Father.'

9

A cab ride and an engineering lesson

Jeffries paid the waitress for their coffee and food, and shrugged into his coat. As arranged the day before, Jeffries and Smith had enjoyed a plentiful breakfast, successfully avoiding going to the station, saving time and evading the inspector's attention, at least for the morning. Both men were eager to continue with the case and visit Carrie, their new witness. Smith slipped his coat on as he followed Jeffries to the door. 'Damn, it's raining,' said Smith as he peered outside.

Jeffries smiled. 'We are on expenses, Smith. We shall hail a cab!' He stepped out into the rain and raised his hand. In an instant, a cab clattered to a halt outside the coffee shop, the driver pulling on the reins to steady the horse.

'Castle Street if you please, driver,' said Jeffries as he opened the door for Smith. They settled in for the ride, thankful to be out of the rain, as the cab set off at speed.

The men looked out at the miserable day as they sped along, the cab bouncing alarmingly as it raced through the muddy streets. The two men peered through the murky windows, watching as people dashed to find shelter, some braving the weather under flimsy umbrellas or with their coats pulled over their heads. Despite the downpour, the streets were coming to life as tradesmen and shopkeepers set up for the day.

The cab passed the dilapidated houses that were a blight on the town, their occupants unkempt and weary as they stood in front of their homes, deciding whether to brave the weather or wait for it to pass. Two men in scruffy, ill-fitting suits stood against one house, sheltering in a doorway, smoking and talking. A woman with a young child by her side, a group of older children huddled under a doorway, all trying to keep dry in the deluge.

Jeffries and Smith turned away, feeling fortunate to have secure jobs. Homes in pleasant neighbourhoods.

Smith turned to Jeffries. 'By the way, the inspector thought I'd make a good detective, and I wondered if you could share some of your experience, sir? The inspector said I should learn a lot from you. I think he respects you, despite his abrupt manner.'

Jeffries smiled. 'Mm, I'm not so sure about that. You want my advice? Just remember this, Smith. People lie all the time. Don't believe a word anyone tells you. That's my advice. Oh, and trust your feelings.'

Smith frowned. 'Feelings, sir?'

'It's an instinct. A gut feeling if you will. You'll know when you get a feeling for something.' Jeffries held up a finger. 'You'll see.'

Smith pondered Jeffries' words as the cab raced over the bridge where only yesterday, the tram had lain wrecked. The two men gazed out of the window, deep in thought. Smith broke the silence. 'Those passengers were lucky the tram didn't crash right through the railings. The river flows pretty quickly here. They would have been swept to their deaths.'

Jeffries nodded. 'Indeed, Smith. Our investigation would be quite different.'

The cab continued through the town streets. The rain was easing, and the sun emerged as they reached Edwards and Son on Castle Street. The cab came to a halt, and Detective Sergeant Jeffries jumped out, pausing to dust off his coat as he called back to Smith. 'Pay the driver, Smith. Don't forget to tip him!'

The driver held his hand out. 'Three shillings, mister.' Smith stepped down to the pavement and reached into his pocket. He took out three shillings and added some copper coins before handing the money over.

'Thank you, sir,' the driver said, cracking his whip and setting off.

Smith joined his colleague at the top of the office steps just as the front door opened. A young man appeared with a cup of tea in his hand. He considered them both before saying, 'How can I help, gentlemen?'

Jeffries appraised the man. He was in his twenties and wore a smart suit. It looked new to Jeffries, creases in all the right places with wider lapels than his own. The corner of a red handkerchief stood to attention in the breast pocket. Jeffries subconsciously reached for his own pocket and tugged at the crumpled handkerchief within. He glanced down and decided it was probably best left hiding where it was.

The two officers presented their police badges. 'We're here on police business to speak to Miss Carrie Grey. May I ask who you are, sir?' said Jeffries, returning his badge to his pocket.

The man looked from one officer to the other. 'I am William Edwards; my father owns the firm. Miss Grey is my colleague.' He smoothed his tie, despite it being neat already. 'I'm afraid you've had a wasted journey. Carrie isn't here. She's on an errand and won't be back until later this afternoon. Can I help?'

Detective Sergeant Jeffries took a calling card from his coat pocket and handed it to William. 'We need to speak to Miss Grey as she witnessed the tram crash yesterday. Please ask her to contact us at the station as soon as she can. Good day, sir.'

The two policemen turned to go when William called out, 'Have you inspected the damaged tram yet? Carrie knows the driver and is convinced it wasn't his fault. Perhaps you should examine the wreckage instead of wasting your time with Carrie.'

Detective Sergeant Jeffries turned back to William. 'We are aware the tram needs inspecting, and that is our next appointment. Thank you for your concern, but perhaps you should concentrate on wills and probate, and we'll focus on police work.'

As the two men crossed the road, Smith smiled. 'That put him in his place, sir.'

'Cheeky bugger,' Jeffries muttered. 'Let's go and see the wreckage. It's the other end of town, but at least the sun's out now.'

After what Smith considered a route march, Jeffries striding ahead, the two men arrived at the quayside. The cobbled road was slippery with rainwater and fish oils as they made their way carefully along the quay to the workshop.

The area was bustling with activity. Men shouted orders as ships were being loaded with huge wooden crates hoisted by overhead cranes mounted on the quay wall. Two women in scruffy shawls leant against a wall. One called over to the two officers. 'Hello, gentlemen. Care to spend some time with me and my friend here, my lovelies?'

Jeffries blushed and Smith smiled as they walked briskly past the two women to the tram workshop, its huge doors held open by great steel posts. The sign above swung and squeaked in the breeze, proclaiming 'Repairs and Maintenance Workshop'.

The two officers walked through the giant front doors, to be greeted by a crescendo of noise. Several men in oily overalls and flat caps were hard at work, some on machines, others working with hammers and saws or carrying tools and materials from the work area to the benches along the walls. The workshop was lit by the daylight streaming in through the open doors. On the far wall, a giant furnace, its heavy iron door wide open, cast a bright orange light across the walls and faces of the workmen. There was a distinct aroma of oil and burning coal.

One worker, a young lad in his early twenties, approached to greet them. 'Hello, gentlemen. I'm John Sparkes. Are you the officers who asked to inspect the wrecked tram?'

'Hello, Mr Sparkes. Yes, that's right. I'm Detective Sergeant Jeffries, and this is Constable Smith.'

'We've been expecting you. I'm in charge today while the boss is out.'

Jeffries and Smith each held out a hand. The engineer waved them away. 'I wouldn't; my hands are filthy! Follow me. Be careful where you step; it can be a little cluttered here when we're busy.'

They followed John to the far end of the workshop to a bench covered with tools and engineering parts of all descriptions. John moved the tools to one side and pointed to a wooden contraption. 'I have set up a model of the braking system to make it easier to explain why I think the tram lost control.'

Smith and Jeffries exchanged a look. Smith took the lead and said to John, 'You mean to say you already know what happened? I'm impressed, Mr Sparkes.'

John smiled. 'I'm an engineer, and I live and breathe mechanics. You probably think about crime and criminals all day. With me, it's all nuts and bolts. Gears and levers and such. Let me show you what I think happened.'

After showing the officers the same demonstration he presented to Carrie and William the night before, he led them to the tram, sitting forlornly in the middle of the workshop floor.

He reached into his toolbelt, took out a screwdriver and removed the screws that held the brake cover in place. Jeffries looked on in interest. 'I assume this is the brake box you mentioned. Where you expect to find a blockage of some kind?'

John looked up. 'That's correct. I haven't had a chance to inspect the box yet,' he lied. 'It's just a theory, but I'm confident this is what happened.'

As John had removed the bolts the previous evening, he didn't need to try too hard to unscrew them, but he made it look as if they were tight by breathing heavily as he

66

worked. Straining with the spanner as if loosening a stubborn bolt.

Once they were removed, he lifted off the cover and invited the officers to reach in and find whatever had blocked the braking mechanism. Smith didn't hesitate. He stepped towards the box section, pulled up his sleeve and reached into the dark recess of the brake box.

10

Bad news comes in pairs

Father looks up as I walk into the kitchen the following morning. It's Wednesday; halfway through the week already. I give him a quick kiss on the cheek, grab the remaining sausage from his plate and take a bite.

'Excuse me, I haven't finished my breakfast, young lady!' Father says, removing his glasses and looking over his newspaper at me.

'You are drinking your coffee and reading the financial section, which you do only when you've finished your breakfast. I, therefore, deduce that the remaining sausage is surplus to requirements.' I smile, finishing off the sausage.

'And I deduce, Carrie, that you've been reading too many of those Sherlock Holmes stories in my newspaper recently.'

Father folded his paper, laid it on the table and pointed to the photograph of the crashed tram occupying most of the front page. 'There's a big story about the crash today. Front page, no less. The police will probably appeal for witnesses. They may want a word with you, especially after what you told me last night. Do you remember anything else about the crash?'

I shake my head. 'I haven't remembered anything else. Do you really think the police will want to speak to me? I'm not sure how I can help.' I look up at the kitchen clock. I omitted to tell Father last night that I was hiding behind the office door when the policemen called. It was William's idea. He said I was in no state to speak to them so soon after the crash. 'I need to hurry, or I'll be late for work.'

As I enter the hallway, Father calls out, 'Be careful today. Probably best not to ride the tram this morning. People are saying that they aren't safe.'

I slip on my coat. 'Don't worry, Father. I'll be careful, and I enjoy the walk anyway. See you at dinner later.'

I open the front door to a beautiful day, the sky a perfect blue with just the odd wispy cloud. I hurry down the garden path to the street. Today is going to be an exciting one. I can feel it in the air.

I reach the bridge and hesitate. Workmen are repairing the damaged railings and sweeping the road as I cross to the other side. The familiar smell of the river brings back memories of yesterday. Rose's face. The loose strand of hair. I start my familiar walk up the steep hill, which is bustling with men in suits or overalls heading to their offices and workshops. Women hurry to the shops with their baskets to buy provisions for dinner.

I smile as I watch messenger boys run up and down the hill with their heavy shoulder bags. The regular postal service takes a day or more, but a messenger can deliver and collect a message within the hour. Despite the slightly higher cost, businesses and busy households rely on the regular and fast messaging service.

I can't help shielding my eyes from the sun and studying the junction at the top of the hill. I'm thankful there are no speeding trams racing down the hill this morning.

Halfway up the hill, I look up at the big clock above the jeweller's shop and check my watch. It's a new routine for me, and surprisingly, I'm actually early for work. I even have time to look in some shop windows this morning, but my mind remains elsewhere. Before I realise it, I've arrived at the office. William is already there, opening up.

'Good morning, William,' I say, startling him so that he drops his keys. 'Sorry, I didn't mean to startle you.'

'Ah, good morning Carrie. Did you sleep well last night?'

'I did, actually. I thought I'd be too excited to sleep.'

'I lay awake thinking about what John showed us.'

'We're meeting him today, aren't we? I can't wait to hear what the police thought about his theory.'

I spend the morning busying myself with filing and tidying up the office. Anything to encourage those slow clock hands to move quicker towards our midday meet-up.

Eventually, the time shows noon. I had previously agreed with William that we would leave separately to prevent his father from asking awkward questions. I grab my coat and call out, 'I'm going out for lunch, Mr Edwards. I'll be back before one.'

I don't wait for a response. He always seems so miserable! Always frowning, muttering to himself. I don't think I recall him smiling at all. William looks up, smiles and goes back to his work. I close the front door behind me and hurry down the steps to the road, eager to get to the café and find out news of the tram inspection. Two men walk past me, carrying stepladders and tins of paint. Women walk briskly to the shops, pushing perambulators and dragging older, reluctant children along the pavement.

I reach Deller's, slightly out of breath, and wait while a man opens the door for me, frowning as he does so, probably thinking all women of a certain age should be with a chaperone. So old-fashioned.

A delicious aroma of coffee and food fills the air. I look around for John and spot him at the same table as yesterday. He stands as I approach, not sporting his usual wide grin. 'I've already ordered coffee and sandwiches. I assume you haven't eaten?' He sits, and I take the seat opposite him, folding my coat over the back of the chair.

'Thank you, I'm starving! Well, what happened this morning?' I say conspiratorially, leaning across the table, almost knocking over the condiments. 'Did everything go as expected?'

'Should we wait for William to arrive? Ah, he's here,' he says, standing and waving.

I see William making his way past the other tables, now all occupied with people talking and eating, drinking coffee and browsing menus.

John pulls a chair out for William and shakes his hand before they both sit. The waitress arrives with our drinks, and we sit silently while she wipes the table and places the cups in front of us. 'I'll just get your sandwiches,' she says. John looks up at her, smiles and looks back at William and me, his smile vanishing.

'It's not good news, I'm afraid.' John pauses when the waitress returns with our plates. Sandwiches for William and me, and a hot toasted sandwich for John, which steams as a cheesy aroma wafts over us.

'Well, go on,' I say, taking a gulp of my coffee, scalding my tongue.

John takes a bite from his hot sandwich and, mid-chew, says, 'The police arrived as expected. There were just the two of them. I don't think they knew what to look for, so I offered my theory about what had happened. I explained the idea just as I did with you last night. I even showed them my contraption. They were quite taken by it.' John takes a sip of his coffee, savouring the flavour.

'And you showed them the doorstop we found last night, I assume?' William says, concern on his face.

'Well, that's the thing. They both felt around in the brake box and found nothing. I even dismantled the whole box. The wedge had disappeared.'

I blink at John, then look across at William, who sits frozen, sandwich mid-journey to his mouth, a slice of tomato dropping onto his plate. 'That's ridiculous,' I finally say. 'I saw you drop the wedge into the box. I even heard it hit the bottom. Someone must have removed it after we left. You were the last one in the workshop after we all went home, John.'

'Well, I can assure you, I didn't remove it,' John says, shrugging. 'Why would I? And why would I explain everything to the police and show them the box section? I felt a fool, having persuaded them of the theory only to find the evidence missing.'

I think back to the workshop. Was there someone else there, watching us? I didn't think so. 'The same person who tampered with the tram must have broken in again after we left last night. Or this morning before you arrived, and removed the evidence.' I say.

John shrugs. 'I wondered that, too. I checked, but there was no sign of any damage, and none of the doors or windows had been forced open.'

'Who else has a key to the workshop?' Says William.

'I'm the only one with a key. Apart from the boss, of course. There's a duplicate in the office cupboard, but that's kept locked. I also have the cupboard key. I opened up, as usual, this morning. I was in early, and the other men arrived a little later.'

'It doesn't make sense.'

John thought for a moment. 'Well, however they got in, they were very clever about it, and they must have used the same way both times; once when they originally tampered with the tram and again when they retrieved the wedge, removing the evidence at the same time.'

We eat in silence, each of us considering theories of our own. John finishes his toastie, wipes his mouth on his sleeve and looks at us. 'That's not the only news.'

We both look up and push our plates to one side.

'There's been another crash.'

11

A messenger boy and pots of paint

Jeffries and Smith sipped their cups of weak tea, Jeffries grumbling that the tea and coffee in the police station were not as good as the offerings in the local cafés. 'I just don't understand how they can make such awful tea and coffee in this place. It can't be that difficult, surely.'

Smith smiled across the desk. He didn't really mind. Tea and coffee were welcome at any time, no matter the quality, as long as the drink was hot and sugar was involved in the brew. He had to admit, though, the frothy coffee served in the café was his favourite.

Both men were despondent. Their trip to the tram workshop had given them no additional clues.

'That John fellow had a good theory about something getting jammed in the brake section. I was quite excited. Nothing but grease in there, though. My wife is going to have a job cleaning that off my shirt sleeve.'

Jeffries dumped his notebook on top of his pile of paperwork, leaning forward, steepling his hands in front of him. 'Yes, well, theories are one thing, Smith. Solid evidence is something else entirely.'

Smith fiddled with his pen, twirling it in his fingers. Jeffries looked at him. 'Come on, Smith. What's on your mind? Something's obviously bothering you; let's have it.'

Smith put his pen to one side, looking at his colleague. His boss. 'I was just thinking that it's strange the inspector sent you on that course. I mean, why send you and not a younger officer? Surely it would make more sense as you're not far off retiring, and the course must have been expensive.' Smith looked awkwardly away, adding, 'He should've sent me.'

Jeffries smiled at his colleague. 'Oh, what little you understand, Smith. The reason they sent me and not one of you young men has nothing to do with cost, nor is it to do

73

with age.' Jeffries leaned back in his chair, the springs complaining. 'You see, Smith, the inspector sent me because,' Jeffries looked around and lowered his voice. 'They want me to train you.'

Smith's raised his eyebrows but before he could comment, the door to the office crashed open, and a messenger boy ran in, breathless. As Jeffries and Smith were the only officers in the room, the boy ran straight to them, and stood in front of Jeffries' desk, leaning over, his hands on his hips, catching his breath.

'Well, boy.' Jeffries said, standing and looking down at the lad. 'What's all the hurry about?'

The boy regained his composure, reached into his bag and handed a sheet of paper to Jeffries. 'There's been another of them trams crashed, sir. Top of North Street. Damaged a shop and wrecked a lamp post. No one killed, though. A constable sent me to give you the message, but I already knows what it says. Obvious, really.' The boy held out his hand. 'The constable said you'd pay, sir, as he didn't have any money on him.'

Jeffries took the message paper, shook his head and waved the boy away. 'Nonsense. You know as well as I do that all constables carry coins for sending messages, and I also know you wouldn't have risked delivering this without being sure of getting paid. I may be old, young man, but I'm not stupid.' The boy stood his ground, pouting as he looked the sergeant in the eye. 'Ran all the way, I did. Knew it was important, being the police and all.'

Jeffries sighed, reached into his pocket, pulled out a small coin, and handed it across. 'Here's a farthing for being cheeky. Now be off with you.' The boy grabbed the coin and ran to the door, looking over his shoulder. 'Thank you, sir.'

'Cheeky monkey.' Jeffries handed the note to Smith. 'Come on, Smith, grab your coat. We need to get to North Street before the crowds arrive. Anything else in the note we should know about?'

Smith scanned it. 'No, it's all as the boy said. Tram crash at the top of North Street. Shop damaged. Two casualties. Request assistance. It's signed by Constable Kelly. That's it.'

Jeffries was already at the front door, struggling to push his arm into his coat sleeve as he shouldered the door open. Smith buttoned his own coat as he followed his colleague.

The two men walked briskly down the hill, taking a shortcut to the top of North Street and the crash site. A noisy, chaotic scene awaited them, with people pushing and shoving to get a better view of the damaged tram, no longer on its rails but on the pavement. Jeffries led Smith towards the tram. They squeezed through a narrow gap between a carriage and a delivery wagon, paint tins stacked haphazardly in the rear section of the open-back wagon, some tins on their side, leaking paint all over the wooden floor. Jeffries noticed the wagon was one of the new petrol-driven vehicles, the front grill smashed in. Steam hissed as it rose in a white cloud from the bonnet. Oil dripped onto the road, forming a black puddle. The engine clicked as it cooled.

Constable Kelly had already called on two of his colleagues, the three of them now desperately trying to hold the inquisitive mob back. Through a gap in the crowd, Jeffries noticed a doctor and a nurse attending to a young man as he lay on the ground, twisting and turning as he cried out in pain. The doctor did his best to wrap a bandage around the patient's head while the nurse held the man still.

Scanning the gathering crowd, Jeffries noticed a mother and her young daughter sitting on a nearby bench, the girl playing with her teddy bear. The mother stared at the tram, tilted at an awkward angle, the rear end shoved into a fruit merchant's shop. The front was raised above the ground, the wheels still slowly turning. Smashed wooden crates of fresh fruit lay scattered along the pavement. A young boy was scrabbling on his knees, grabbing as many apples as he could stuff into his pockets. Astonishingly, the horses were both still harnessed to the tram, seemingly not at all disturbed by the incident as the breath from their nostrils steamed in the cold air, their hooves patiently scuffing the ground.

The uniformed tram driver stood nearby, taking rapid puffs from a cigarette, inhaling deeply then tipping his head back, blowing the smoke into the air. He had a bloody bandage on his arm, and his uniform was ripped in several places, the left sleeve hanging down.

Jeffries turned to Smith. 'Have a wander around, see if anyone witnessed the crash, and I'll have a word with the driver.'

Smith pushed through the crowd, holding up his identification as he gently nudged people away. He received some angry looks as he made his way to the front. He then faced the crowd. 'Ladies and Gentlemen, quiet please! I am Constable Smith from Exeter Police Station. Did anyone actually see the tram crash?'

A well-dressed man in a suit, his hat tilted at a jaunty angle, stepped forward, his hand held up to grab Smith's attention. In his late-fifties, Smith estimated. He carried a narrow, brown case and an umbrella. His tie was slightly askew. He strode across to Smith as the crowd grew quiet, all of them eager to eavesdrop any grisly details.

Smith guided the man through the crowd, pointing the way to a nearby shop doorway, away from the curious onlookers. He took out his notebook and pencil, flipped it open to a fresh page and noted a few details as the witness recounted the incident.

Mr Tyler, a bank manager, explained to Smith that he had been walking to an appointment with a client when he witnessed the whole thing. He leant on his umbrella, his case now by his feet, recounting what he'd seen.

Smith listened, scribbling in his book, as the man described how he'd been about to cross the road, the tram having already passed by, when he heard a motor wagon speeding up as it swung around the corner, the engine revving loudly. Mr Tyler remembered calling out in horror as he realised the wagon — a delivery wagon with tins of paint in the back, he recalled — could not possibly avoid a collision. He'd watched from the pavement as the wagon smashed into the tram with an almighty crash, forcing it off the rails and into the shop window.

Smith wrote furiously, noting everything in his notebook. Then he paused and looked up. 'The wagon must have been speeding at quite a rate to force the tram off the rails. What happened next?' He looked around. 'And what happened to the wagon driver? Is he still here?'

Mr Tyler didn't need to look at the crowd. 'He's long gone, Constable. He jumped out of the cab and hobbled up the hill. Went in the direction of the high street and disappeared around the corner.'

Smith looked up. 'Hobbled?'

Mr Tyler picked up his case. 'Well, he had a bit of a limp. I assume he must have injured himself in the crash.' He touched his hat, straightened his tie and nodded. 'I must be off, Constable. I have an important meeting to attend.'

Smith considered Mr Tyler's last remark about the wagon driver as he watched the man stroll away. He looked around for Jeffries and spotted him talking to the tram driver. Pocketing his notebook and pencil, he walked through the crowd to join his colleague.

Smith watched as the tram driver wandered off. Jeffries had evidently finished interviewing him. They both considered the damaged wagon, still steaming and dripping oil. The smell of petrol polluted the air. 'Any luck, Smith? And what do you make of the wagon?'

Smith recounted his interview with the bank manager and that the wagon driver had run away. Hobbled away, in fact. The two men walked around the wagon, inspecting the damage and noticing the company's name in a fancy typeface embellished on the side panels. Several paint tins had been thrown from the back section and had lost their lids, the contents mixing with the black oil on the road, creating a swirl of colour, reds and yellows mixing with the shiny oil.

Jeffries contemplated the company's name on the side. 'Have you heard of Warren's Paint, Smith?' Smith shook his head. 'No, not heard of them. I'll get back to the station, look up these Warren people, and pay them a visit.'

'Good man. I'll see if there are any other witnesses and meet you back at the station. I've sent a messenger boy to the tram workshop to get the engineers to tow it to the quay for repair.'

'Do you think the crashes are connected?'

'I'm not sure yet. Two crashes in as many days? I don't believe in coincidences, Smith. I spoke to the tram driver. He said he was happily driving along and the next thing he knew there was an almighty crash and the tram was on its side.'

**

Jeffries and Smith met later that afternoon back at the station to compare notes. 'How'd you get on with the paint company, Smith? Any luck there?'

Smith consulted his notebook, took a slurp of his tea, winced at the unsweetened brew, and reached into his drawer for a sugar cube from a packet he kept there, amongst old pens and pencils. An empty biscuit tin, left there by the previous occupant. 'It was easy to find the company. They were in this week's classifieds. They supply paint to shops and local tradesmen.'

Jeffries folded his arms and raised one eyebrow. 'Don't keep me in suspense, Smith. Do they know who was driving the wagon?'

Smith mirrored his superior by crossing his arms and leaning back in his chair. 'They know who drives that wagon, but that doesn't help us. Apparently, it was stolen early this morning before the men arrived for work. I spoke to the boss and his foreman at Warren's, and both said the wagon was loaded up the night before but had disappeared when they opened up this morning. The lock to their yard had been forced, but nothing else was taken. They weren't too happy to find it had been wrecked and was now part of a police investigation.'

Jeffries leant forward, his elbows on the desk, deep in thought. He looked at Smith. 'If the two crashes are connected, why does someone want to damage these trams? What's the point?'

Smith stood, walked to the window, and looked out onto the street. People were passing by, a day like any other, although Smith thought the pavements looked busier today. A tram trundled past on its way to the top of the town. The driver was the only occupant. Smith faced Jeffries, leant against the wall and crossed his arms. 'One thing's for sure, sir, the trams aren't full like they usually are. Now I come to think of it, each one that passed me on the way to work was nearly empty. So if someone is trying to damage the company itself, they're doing a good job. They can't be making a profit at the moment, with everyone avoiding the trams.'

Jeffries stood and joined his colleague at the window, peering at the street. 'That must be it, Smith. Whoever is responsible is trying to drive the tram company into the ground. They won't last long without paying passengers.'

Smith nodded. 'It seems a risky thing to do, nobble the trams, risk someone getting hurt, even killed. Just for some business advantage.'

'People do illegal things for all sorts of reasons, Smith. It always comes down to money in the end.' Jeffries nudged his colleague. 'Come on. We've done all we can here for today. I want to catch Miss Grey at her home this evening. We might as well go and pay her a visit on our way home.'

12

A bruise, a camera and a memory

The cold evening had kept most people indoors. The flickering gas lamps, not long set by the gas lighters, cast shadows ahead of the two officers. It had been a long day, starting with the inspection of the damaged tram, and then the news of the second tram crash. Deep in thought, hands in thick gloves, they trudged through the town's deserted streets. Smith used to feel out of place without his regulation uniform but was beginning to prefer his suit.

Jeffries broke the silence. 'How did you know where this young lady Carrie lives?'

'I have been to her father's home for drinks before heading to his club on a few occasions,' said Smith.

'Club, Smith? Surely you don't mean a gentlemen's club?'

'I only go for the beer.' Smith blushed. 'Most of the members are there to make new acquaintances and further their business interests,' he quickly added.

Jeffries smiled. 'It can't do any harm to further your own career, though, can it?'

'It never occurred to me,' Smith said, grinning. 'Here we are, number 81.'

Smith opened the gate, and they walked up the path through the small, well-kept garden to the shiny black front door. Jeffries rapped the brass knocker and stepped back, looking up at the little window above the door, the welcome glow of a gas lamp shining through the glass.

The door opened, and a young woman with black hair appeared. The two men immediately recognised Carrie as the same woman from the photographs of the first tram crash. Jeffries wasn't good at discerning ages, especially that of young women, but he put her age at about twenty. She wore a purple skirt and dark grey cardigan, the fashion for young women these days. A yellow bruise sat on her forehead above her left eye. Her brown eyes shone with intelligence. Jeffries noticed the way she fidgeted with her skirt, almost jumpy. He had the distinct idea that she wanted to burst forth with words that she could barely keep to herself. She returned Jeffries' look and, glancing at the other man, noticing their suits and overcoats, realised they were the same men William had said visited the office earlier. She smiled, recalling William greeting the officers while she stood, quiet as a church mouse, in the hallway while William lied, telling the officers that she was out of the office. She hadn't wanted to get involved before. Didn't want to relive the thought of Rose dying. It was silly, she realised now, and knew she should talk to the police. Perhaps even help them, now the initial shock had worn off. She nodded to the younger of the two as she now remembered where she'd seen him before. He had occasionally accompanied her father to the gentlemen's club. A rare event recently, but one that she knew her father enjoyed immensely. 'Can I help you?' she asked, directing her question at Smith.

'Hello, Carrie,' said Smith. 'I'm afraid we're here on a police matter this evening. This is my colleague, Detective Sergeant Jeffries. May we come in? We understand you witnessed the fatal tram accident, and we'd like to ask you some questions.'

Carrie paused. 'Yes, I thought I recognised you. Hello, Frank.' She smiled. 'My colleague said you'd visited the office. I haven't had the chance to call into the station as you'd asked. I did see the crash, but I don't really remember what happened. Please come in, and I'll help if I can.' She stepped back, and the two officers walked into the hallway, removing their hats as they took in their surroundings. Family portraits on the wall. An assortment of little china ornaments upon a mahogany cabinet.

Carrie closed the door when a voice called from the drawing room, 'Who is it, Carrie?'

'It's the police. They want to ask me some questions about the incident on the bridge.'

Her father appeared at the drawing-room door, wearing a colourful smoking jacket, holding a glass of whisky in one hand and a folded newspaper in the other. 'I should be with you while you are questioned. Hello, Frank. Good to see you again.'

Smith nodded. 'Mr Grey. I haven't seen you at the club recently. How are you?'

'I am well, thank you. I've been busy and haven't had time to go to the club lately. Shall we go into the kitchen to talk?'

Jeffries noticed that Mr Grey didn't ask how Smith was.

Mr Grey led his daughter and the two policemen into the kitchen, dropping his newspaper onto the cabinet as he passed. Jeffries noticed that it was the business section. He preferred the sports pages and had little time for the stock market and other financial affairs.

The kitchen was warm, and the delicious aroma of dinner recently enjoyed filled the room. Something meaty, a stew perhaps, thought Jeffries. His stomach grumbled. A cast iron wood burner sat in the corner, burning fiercely, and a pair of gas lights on the wall illuminated the room with a flickering light.

Carrie placed a kettle on the stove. 'Would you like a cup of tea, gentlemen?' Without waiting for a reply, she opened a cupboard and pulled out cups and saucers.

Jeffries sat at the head of the table, opened his notebook and placed it before him, the pencil in line with the edge of the book. 'Yes, that would be most welcome, Miss Grey. Thank you.'

Smith stood by the stove, warming his hands. Mr Grey sat opposite Jeffries, took a sip of his whisky, set the heavy glass on the table, and leant back in his chair.

While the two men waited for their tea, Carrie's father said, 'Do you have any indication as to what caused the tram to crash? I would have thought there were safety measures in place to prevent such an accident.'

Jeffries cleared his throat. 'We have a number of theories. Top of our list is the driver lost control at the top junction, and he was unable to stop the tram as it sped down the hill.'

Carrie turned from the stove, looked at Jeffries, and then at her father. 'Mr Hoskins is an experienced driver. I cannot believe he is responsible for the accident.' She turned back to the kettle, her hands shaking as she poured the boiling water into the teapot, nearly spilling it as she did so. 'Have you considered it might be that the tram was faulty in some way? Poorly maintained, perhaps? Or sabotage. Is it possible someone tampered with the mechanics?'

Carrie's father shook his head. 'Nonsense, Carrie! Really, where do you get these ridiculous ideas?' He looked across at Jeffries and smiled. 'Carrie likes to read the Sherlock Holmes chronicles. They are published weekly, and I find that part of my paper goes missing every Tuesday.'

Carrie placed the cups and saucers on the table and poured the tea. Smith moved to the chair nearest the fire and sat down, unable to shake the chill from their walk.

Carrie pulled out the remaining chair. She sat and took a tentative sip from her cup, remembering the last time she'd had tea. On that occasion, it had been too sweet when William had made it on the morning of the crash. Now, she'd have to tell her account again. 'What would you like to know, officers?'

Detective Sergeant Jeffries pulled his notebook towards him and turned a few pages before finding the one he needed. Taking out his pencil, the end of which he resisted licking, he looked at Carrie. 'Just start from the beginning, Miss Grey. What's the first thing you remember about the crash?'

Carrie paused, deciding where to start. 'I had just crossed the bridge and was walking up the hill when I happened to look up the road and noticed a town tram had stopped. The horses seemed to be having trouble pulling it away from the junction. I remember they made an awful racket. I think that's what made me stop and look up the hill.' She paused and took another sip of her tea. 'The next thing I remember is the tram racing down the hill, rocking from side to side, gaining speed. I was struck in the head by something.' Carrie distractedly touched the bruise on her forehead. 'I was out cold before waking up with an awful ringing in my ears. When I came to my senses, I went to assist people injured in the crash. Despite a doctor quickly arriving on the scene, the young woman I tried to help sadly died in front of me. I shan't forget that for a long time.' Her eyes started to well up.

Jeffries stopped scribbling and looked up. 'That must have been terrible for you to see. I'm sure there was nothing you could have done to help her.'

Carrie reached into her pocket, withdrew a card and slid it across the table. 'The woman, her name was Rose, she gave me this card while she lay in the road. I'm not sure if it means anything to you?'

Jeffries reached for the card, turned it over and read both sides. He passed it to Smith for him to examine. Jeffries made a note in his book. The name of the company printed on the card. The scribbled writing, or what little he could make of it. Noted for later. 'I've not heard of the Shute Lighting Company before. What about you, Smith?'

Smith shook his head. 'Doesn't mean anything to me. I assume this woman, Rose, had some dealings with this Mr Shute. It doesn't seem to connect to the crash in any way.'

Jeffries took the card back and placed it by his cup. 'I'm interested to hear what you make of it, Carrie?'

Carrie thought for a moment, and smoothed a strand of hair over her ear, an action noticed by Smith. 'I don't know. Rose handed me the card and she said the crash wasn't an accident. I thought it might mean something. Now I'm not so sure.'

Jeffries looked down and wrote something in his notebook. Smith said, 'Who else did you see at the crash site, Carrie?'

Carrie thought back, taking care of her next words. 'All I remember is the tram lying on its side in the road. I recall seeing a crowd forming, held back by police constables. It was very chaotic. People were crowding around, trying to see what was happening. There were a number of people injured and being helped into the hospital wagon. I spoke to Mr Hoskins, the driver. He was hurt but not too badly, according to the doctor. I don't know what else to say.' Carrie shrugged and tilted her head. 'There was one thing I do remember.'

'Oh?' said Jeffries.

'Mr Hoskins said something about the brake system jamming. He struggled to stop the tram and said there was an awfully loud cracking sound when something snapped inside the mechanism. That's all I remember.'

'That's really useful, thank you.'

Constable Smith prompted, 'Did you notice a man with a camera contraption? He was wearing a brown suit and had a black cloth he might have placed over his head. Photographers do this to be able to see the image they are capturing.'

Carrie rolled her eyes, smiled and said, 'I do know what a photographer is, and yes, I did see someone with a camera. He was packing away his equipment as I walked away from the accident. Is he relevant to your investigation?'

Carrie noticed the two constables exchange a glance.

'Possibly,' said Constable Smith.

'I'm curious. How did you know I had witnessed the crash?'

Jeffries slipped his notebook and pencil into his pocket. 'We talked to the photographer. He had some photographs of the scene and one showed you attending to the lady who died in the crash.' He nodded to Smith. 'My colleague recognised you from the photograph, and here we are.'

Carrie smiled at Smith. 'I see. Interesting.'

Detective Sergeant Jeffries finished his tea. 'Well, I think we have everything we need. Thank you for your account of the accident. And thank you for the tea; just what we needed on a cold evening.'

Carrie pushed her own tea away and looked at Jeffries. 'What about the other tram? Are the circumstances the same as the first crash?'

Jeffries looked at Smith, then back to Carrie. 'News travels fast. Thankfully, no one was killed, and the damage was minimal.'

Carrie folded her arms. 'It seems rather odd that two crashes occurred within a day of each other, wouldn't you say?'

Jeffries was about to reply when Mr Grey stood, cheeks reddening at his daughter's inquisitiveness. 'Well, Carrie, perhaps you should leave the police to investigate as they see fit. Will that be all, gentlemen?'

Jeffries and Smith rose from their chairs. Smith gulped back the last of his tea.

Jeffries extended his hand to Mr Grey and nodded to Carrie. 'Thank you for your time, Mr Grey' He turned to Carrie, 'and thank you, Carrie, for your version of events.'

Carrie looked at the two policemen. 'I hope you find the cause of the crash soon, officers. If you need to ask me anything else, I will be here in the evenings. I'd prefer it if you avoided visiting me at my place of work. Mr Edwards doesn't care for private business to be conducted in the office.'

'Of course, Miss Grey. Good evening to you.'

As Carrie's father led the two officers to the front door, Carrie cleared the tea cups and sugar pot when she noticed that Jeffries had left the card on the table. She picked it up and slipped it into her pocket, an idea forming in her mind.

As Jeffries and Smith left Carrie's house and headed for home, Smith was deep in thought. Jeffries broke the silence. 'I don't think Miss Grey has told us anything new about the crash. She just happened to be there and tried to help. More than that photographer did, that's for sure.'

'I'm not convinced, sir. I think she knows more than she's letting on. I don't know why; it's just a feeling.'

Jeffries laughed. 'That's a copper's nose you have there, Smith! I told you you'll get those strange feelings. Take notice of those sensations because they are usually trying to tell you something important. I'll make a detective of you yet, my friend.'

The two men reached the junction where Smith would turn right and head home, and Jeffries would turn left towards his own house.

'We're still no closer to working out what happened to the tram, and the inspector will want results soon. We're going to need more time,' said Jeffries as he and Smith stood under a gaslight. 'We need to speak to the photographer again. I'm not happy with his statement. He's definitely hiding something, and I noticed his wife fiddling with her hair - a sure sign of nervousness according to your theory, Smith. Who else do we need to speak to?'

Constable Smith covered a yawn with his gloved hand. 'She was definitely nervous about something, sir. We need to speak to the driver of the first tram, Mr Hoskins. The doctors say he should be well enough to see us in a day or two. He should be able to tell us what happened on the tram that day. Then there's Mrs Brody, of course. Why was she on the tram? As she's a friend of the Chief Inspector, I would think that she would have her own private carriage. I think we should have a chat with her.'

'I agree. Let's pay our photographer a visit first. Perhaps we can catch him in his shop if we call in early. Then we'll call in to speak to Mrs Brody.'

Jeffries smiled, pleased that the two of them got on so well despite his worries on their first day working together.

Jeffries was still smiling when they parted ways, each man heading to their respective homes.

13

A suspicious friend and a nervous wife

Glancing up at the clock, I'm disappointed to see it's only eleven thirty. The morning is dragging, and I'm quietly filing papers and thinking about the missing wedge and the second tram crash when Mr Edwards calls me from his office. 'Carrie? A moment of your time, please.'

'Yes, Mr Edwards?' I say, entering his warm office, the little coal fire crackling and flickering in the corner of the room. Mr Edwards is at his desk, signing papers. He looks up, reaches over his desk and hands me a bulky envelope. On the front is a handwritten address declaring 33 Fore Street. The back is stamped with our office seal.

'I need you to take these documents to the address on the front. Ask for Mr Goodchild and ensure he signs both copies in your presence. You're to bring one copy back to the office; Mr Goodchild will keep the other copy. Hurry now, he is expecting you this morning.'

'I'll deliver it right away, Mr Edwards.' I leave his office, walk over to my desk and collect my coat and umbrella. The package fits easily into my bag. I cross the strap over my head to protect it from bag snatchers who have been more active in the town lately.

'Enjoy your errand, Carrie,' William whispers as I walk to the front door. 'Lucky devil! I wish I had an errand to take me away from the office for an hour. I know that probate is Father's bread and butter, but it's not particularly interesting.' He dips his pen in the inkwell and continues carefully writing a client's will, his cursive script neat and precise.

I open the front door and look up at the darkening skies. 'You might prefer to stay in the warm and dry, William. It looks like it might rain.'

I shut the door behind me and hurry down the steps to the street. It might be threatening to rain, but there are still plenty of people in the town, going about their business. An empty tram trundles by, no one on board save for the driver.

I reach Fore Street within a few minutes, and while I look for number 33, I find myself outside the photographer's shop where the man with the camera went yesterday. Outside the shop is a display rack full of photographs. As I look closer, I realise with horror that the photographs are all of the crash scene. People are looking at the images, gossiping amongst themselves, eager to buy a photograph of the incident. I brush past these ghouls, realising that Mr Goodchild's house must be on the other side of the street. I check for traffic and, seeing it is clear, quickly step across. I knock on the dull brass knocker belonging to number 33, and after a moment, a woman opens the door. I smile, 'Mrs Goodchild? I have a document for Mr Goodchild to sign. I'm from Edwards, the solicitors. I believe that he's expecting me?' I remove the envelope from my bag.

'Yes, that's right. Come in, my dear. I'll fetch my husband for you.'

Later, having witnessed Mr Goodchild's signature (he took an age, checking the details and muttering to himself the whole time, not even offering me a cup of tea) I step out onto the street and notice the door of the photographer's shop open. A man emerges onto the street and slams the door behind him. Lingering for a second or two, he looks left and right, pushes his collar up and walks down the hill, his head bowed and hands deep in his pockets.

It's John. And he's furious for some reason.

I go to raise my hand to attract his attention but stop myself. I can't remember mentioning the photographer being at the crash yesterday. And now John is angry. What is he up to? I cross the road and approach the shop.

A bell chimes as I open the door and step inside. The shop is smaller than I expected, and the natural light is mostly blocked by an exhibition of portraits in the window. A pair of gas lights mounted on the wall add their share of light to the little shop, but it's still gloomy. A display cabinet runs along the back wall, and a selection of complicated-looking cameras sit behind the glass. To the left of the cabinet is a red door, slightly ajar with a hand-written sign hanging at a slight angle. Private, say the words in thick black letters. To my right is an open doorway, half-covered by a curtain, revealing stairs leading to the floor above.

A woman appears from the doorway, in response to the bell. She is slim and pretty, her hair loose about her shoulders. She has striking blue eyes. 'Did you forget something, John?' she asks. 'Oh, sorry, miss. I thought you were someone else. Can I help you?' She blushes, clearly a little embarrassed. My eyes drop to her blouse. The third button down is undone. She notices my gaze as her hands move to her blouse, and she fastens the button.

I look back at her face and reply, thinking on my feet. 'A friend recommended you for family portraits, and I'd like one of my father and me. How much would that cost?' I look around at the photographs lining the walls.

'My husband is the photographer but he's not here; he's at our studio, down at the quay. I have a list of our prices here.' The woman reaches for a leaflet from a pile on the counter. 'Oh, these are the old ones. My husband should have thrown these out. I'll fetch the new ones from upstairs if you'll wait, miss?'

'Thank you. I'll happily wait.' I hope it doesn't take too long. Mr Edwards will wonder where I am. The woman goes back through the curtained doorway, footsteps echoing up the stairs.

As I wait, I look around the shop and wonder why John was here earlier. The woman clearly knows him well enough to use his first name. He looked angry when he left the shop, obviously not happy.

My eyes are drawn to the red door. I can hear the woman rummaging around upstairs, and as I can't help but be curious, I walk behind the counter, absentmindedly running my fingers along the countertop. I stand in front of the door, glance back to the stairs before returning my gaze to the red door, the lock one of the new types that only needs a key on one side, the other operated by a lever.

The private sign is at an odd angle, which is strange, as all the framed photographs are level and inline. I reach up to adjust the sign, but in doing so, I knock it, and it clatters to the floor. I bend down to pick it up and notice it is wet. There's water pooling under the door. The moisture holds a slightly chemical aroma. The sign now forgotten, I push the door open and peek inside. The room is almost completely dark, save for a dull red illumination casting an eerie glow. I step over the pool of water and into the room. There's that smell again, quite unpleasant, stronger now. I wave a hand in front of my face, attempting to disperse the smell and pull the door closed. I need to hurry. The wife will be back in the shop any minute. My eyes grow accustomed to the dim light. This must be a photographic darkroom. I recall Sherlock and Watson apprehending a thief in such a place on one of their adventures.

I make out a bench along one wall and a table in the middle. I almost walk into a string stretched across from a wall to the one opposite. Photographs are pegged to it, and as I step closer to inspect them, my foot strikes something on the floor.

I look down and see a man's boot. As I round the table, I gasp. A man is lying on the floor. I drop my umbrella on the table and edge forward for a closer look. Behind me in the shop, the little doorbell rings again as someone enters from the street. I stoop to look closely at the man's face. In the dim light, I recognise him: the photographer from the crash. His eyes are open, looking right through me. I crouch next to him and reach out my trembling hand. His chest isn't moving. He's definitely dead. A deep, narrow wound runs around his neck, and there's a nasty gash on the side of his head. A small pool of blood glistens next to him. Not again. Another body; that's two in as many days. My heartbeat pounds in my ears.

I stand and steady myself against the table. My fingers brush against a small bottle, knocking it off the edge of the table, smashing into a hundred pieces as it strikes the floor. My pulse quickens. Water splashes my skirt. There's that odd smell again, which I realise now isn't water but some kind of chemical. I hear raised voices coming from the shop. There's no time to think. If I'm caught, I'll have to tell them about John leaving the shop. It will implicate him, and surely, he had nothing to do with this. And I'll need to explain myself, sneaking in here like a thief. Or a murderer.

I quickly look around the dim room. Spotting the service door on the back wall, I step over the body and stride across the room. Reaching the door in a couple of steps, I twist the handle and push the door, but it holds. I frantically turn the key in the lock. It's rusty and stiff, but with a forced twist, it turns with a loud click. I try the handle again and push the door - it swings open. Shouting comes from the shop. 'Mr Westlake. Harry. Are you in there?' A pause, then, 'It's the police; we're coming in.' I snatch the key from the lock, step into the alleyway beyond and pull the door shut just as the interior door swings open with a crash. In the alleyway, I shake as I push the key into the lock and turn it. Leaving the key in the lock, I run to the end of the alley into the bustle of the street.

'Look out, miss!' shouts a coalman, his face as black as the fuel he carries in a sack on his shoulder.

I run past him into the street and through a gap in the traffic to the other side. There's a queue of people gathered in front of the bakers, queuing for bread. A woman tuts and mutters something under her breath as I gently nudge my way through the crowd and look in the shop window, slowing my breathing. Why are the police there already?

Did they know the photographer had been killed? He must've been murdered. It certainly didn't look like an accident.

In the reflection of the glass, I watch the photography shop across the road. A man appears at the front door, looking up and down the street. The Detective Sergeant from last night. Jeffries. He looks across the street, quickly scanning faces. His gaze seems to rest on my back before he raises his arm, whistles and beckons. My heart is in my throat. Has he seen me? A messenger boy races past, spots a gap in the traffic, and runs across to the detective. Jeffries talks to the messenger boy, and points in the direction of the river. The boy takes a coin from the detective and runs off while Jeffries heads back into the shop.

I'm worried the photographer's wife will be able to describe me. I need to speak to John. What was he doing there, and why had the photographer been killed? And more importantly, did John kill him?

Trudging up the hill once more, dark clouds forming with a threat of rain in the air, my old friend curiosity creeps upon me. I just can't help it. I duck into a doorway, withdraw Mr Goodchild's letter from my bag and unfold it, quickly scanning the pages. It's an urgent reminder that the rent for 30 Fore Street is overdue, with a threat of court action if it's not settled in seven days. With a jolt, I remember that number 30 is the photography shop. Mr Goodchild must be the photographer's landlord. Just a coincidence, I think, as the first few raindrops hit the pavement. I reach for my umbrella and realise I've left it in the darkroom. Father will be mad, it was a rather splendid umbrella, he had it specially engraved with my initials.

14

A locked door and a dead body

Smith and Jeffries arrived at the photographer's shop as planned the night before. The little bell above the door tinkled as they entered. The photographer's wife appeared at the bottom of the set of stairs. With several leaflets in her hand, she looked around the shop, her forehead creasing. 'You two again. If you're looking for Harry, he should be back from the studio soon.'

'I see. We were hoping to have another word with him, Mrs Westlake,' said Jeffries, sighing. 'Where is his studio? Perhaps we can catch him there.'

'It's on the quay. We rent the floor above the tram workshops.'

Jeffries and Smith exchanged a glance. 'Perhaps we'll walk down to the quay and have a chat with your husband there.'

Mrs Westlake jumped at the sound of glass smashing, the noise seemingly coming from a room behind the counter, interrupting their conversation.

'What the hell was that?' said Smith. 'I thought you said your husband wasn't here.'

Mrs Westlake gasped, looking across at the red door. 'He definitely isn't here. It must be an intruder; Harry has a lot of expensive equipment in there.' She turned back to the two men. 'Do something! My husband will be furious if his camera equipment is stolen!'

Jeffries strode across to the door and twisted the handle. It was locked. 'Where's the key, Mrs Westlake?'

'Harry has the only key. He keeps his darkroom locked in case someone tries to walk in while he is processing photographs.'

Jeffries looked down and noticed a wet sign in the puddle of water at his feet. He pounded on the door and called out, 'Mr Westlake. Harry. Are you in there?' There was no reply. 'It's the police; we're coming in.'

Jeffries turned just in time to see Smith leaning into his shoulder, clearly preparing to launch himself at the door. Jeffries put out a hand to stop him. 'What do you think you're doing, Smith? Don't they teach you new boys anything? You'll break your shoulder doing it that way. Let me.' With that, he took a step back, raised his foot and launched his hob-nailed boot directly at the lock. The wood splintered, but the door remained firmly shut. Mrs Westlake looked on in horror as Jeffries kicked the same spot again, and the frame split. The door swung open and smashed against the wall with an almighty crash.

Constable Smith followed Jeffries as he rushed into the room, their eyes adjusting to the dim light from the red lamp, the only light source. From the far end of the room, daylight streamed in through an open door to the alley beyond, the silhouette of someone caught for an instant before the door slammed shut.

Once again in the red gloom, Jeffries strode across to the back door, the harsh scent of developer fluid assaulting his nostrils. There was another aroma he was only too familiar with. A metallic smell. The stench of blood. He reached the back door in two strides but found it locked. 'Damn,' he said under his breath. He turned and, in the dim light, saw a man lying on his back by the table, a dark pool of blood by his head. The man's eyes were open, reflecting the red light.

Jeffries crouched beside the man and felt for a pulse. The deep laceration around his neck confirming his suspicions as he searched for any sign of life. 'Damn,' he said again as Smith joined him, the photographer's wife following close behind.

Jeffries put his arm out. 'Don't let her see this, Smith.'

The light from the shop streaked across the floor to where the body lay. Smith turned to hold the photographer's wife back, trying to prevent her from seeing the body. 'Let's go back into the shop, madam.'

It was too late. She brought her hand to her mouth with a sharp intake of breath. 'Oh, dear god. Harry! What on earth's happened to my Harry? He can't be dead. He just can't be. I was next door. I would have heard something. Tell me he'll wake up. Harry?'

Smith gently guided her back to the shop and helped her into an armchair by the counter. She flopped into the seat, her hand on her forehead, tears pouring down her face.

Jeffries followed, closing the darkroom door behind him. He strode across to the front door, the little bell pinging as he pulled it open. Jeffries looked up and down the busy street for any suspicious movements, trying to see where the culprit had gone, vanishing into the hustle and bustle. Looking across to the shops opposite, he spotted a couple of messenger boys, one smoking a cigarette. He put his fingers in his lips and whistled, waving to get the boys' attention. The boy with the cigarette looked up, spotted the raised arm, pinched his cigarette end to snuff it out and stuffed it in his pocket for later. He ran to Jeffries' side. 'Want to send a message, mister? Only halfpenny to anywhere in the town, guaranteed service, delivery within the half-hour, mister.'

Jeffries pulled his notebook and pencil from his pocket, scribbled a quick message, folded it and handed it to the boy, pointing up the road. 'Take this to the Coroner's Office in Southernhay. Quick as you can. This is police business.' He found a coin in his pocket and handed it to the boy. 'Here's a penny for your service if you can be quick about it. Double the going rate. Do you know the Coroner's Office?'

The messenger boy put the folded note into his satchel, the coin disappeared into his pocket. 'Of course, sir. That's where all the dead bodies go. Proper creepy.'

'That's the place. With haste, young man.' The boy set off. Jeffries went back into the shop, shut the door, and hung the 'closed' sign in the window. Mrs Westlake was still in the armchair, sobbing quietly while Smith stood beside her, arms behind his back. He wasn't sure if he should console the poor woman or simply stand there. Hopefully, Jeffries would know what to do.

Jeffries gently placed his hand on the widow's shoulder. 'Madam, is there anyone who can sit with you? A friend or a relative, perhaps?'

Mrs Westlake sniffed, scrunched up her handkerchief and looked up, her eyes red with crying. 'My sister lives across the road.'

'What's your sister's name, Mrs Westlake?'

'Susan. Susan Goodchild. She lives at number 33.' Mrs Westlake pointed in the direction of the road. 'It's right opposite. Yellow front door.'

Jeffries took Smith to one side and said quietly, 'The coroner should be here soon, Smith. You have a few minutes before he arrives, so call across the road at number 33 and bring Mrs Westlake's sister here to the upstairs living quarters. Then wait for the coroner and show him the body. While you're waiting, get some light in that darkroom and have a look around before he arrives. Make a note of anything unusual, anything that strikes you as odd, no matter how insignificant it may seem. And Smith, don't touch anything.'

'Yes, sir. What are you going to do?'

Jeffries looked across to Mrs Westlake. 'I'm going to take Mrs Westlake upstairs, make her a cup of tea. Hopefully, she can answer some questions and will remember something that helps us find who did this.'

Constable Smith left the shop, leaving Jeffries alone with Mrs Westlake. 'I know this is difficult, but I need to ask you some questions so we can catch the scoundrel who did this terrible thing. Perhaps we can talk upstairs and have a cup of tea?'

Mrs Westlake nodded, rose unsteadily from her chair, and led the way to the stairs. Jeffries followed, looking around the narrow stairway as they made their way up to the first floor. The walls were tastefully adorned with photographs, most featuring portraits of people, some alone but mostly of family groups. Jeffries wondered if they were examples of the photographer's work or of his own family.

As they passed a bedroom on the landing, Jeffries noticed the bed was unmade. Clothes scattered on the floor. A book lay on the bed, open and face down.

In the little kitchen at the end of a narrow corridor was a table for two. Unwashed cups, saucers and plates were piled on the drainer. A saucepan with remnants of congealed porridge sat on the counter. Mrs Westlake pulled out one of the chairs and sat down, her head in her hands.

Jeffries filled the kettle and set it on the stove, hot from the logs burning in the grate. He added another log for good measure and reached up to the shelf for two clean cups. He emptied the teapot, rinsed it quickly and added tea leaves from a little caddy sitting on the counter.

Sitting at the little table, they sipped their tea. Jeffries put his cup down and pulled out his notebook and a pencil stub. Clearing his throat, and turning to a blank page, he started with a simple question. 'Can you tell me what happened this morning, Mrs Westlake? Tell me everything you can remember, no matter how insignificant. Any small detail might help.'

Mrs Westlake wiped her eyes and blew her nose with her handkerchief before stuffing it up her sleeve. She wrapped her hands around her cup and stared into her tea, thinking back. She brushed an errant strand of hair over her ear. 'We had breakfast together at about eight o'clock, as usual. Harry was up first; he always makes our porridge and boils the kettle for our tea.' At the memory, she paused to take a sip from her cup. Jeffries' mind drifted to his own wife, thinking how he was always telling her to lock doors and check windows. He would remind her again tonight. Mrs Westlake put her cup back on the table, gathering herself before continuing. 'We talked about our plans for the day. Harry had a meeting arranged for half past nine down at the studio, and I was going to spend the morning cleaning our rooms. We don't open the shop until midday on a Thursday, so I use that time to clean.'

Jeffries glanced at the plates on the drainer, remembering the unmade bed and scattered clothes. 'Go on,' he prompted.

Mrs Westlake pushed her cup to one side and looked about the kitchen. 'We finished our breakfast, and Harry kissed me goodbye. He pulled on his coat and went down to the shop. I think he was going to collect some things from the darkroom before heading to the studio.' Her eyes brimmed with tears, and she bit her lip. 'That's the last time I saw him.'

'Did you hear the bell ring when the front door opened?'

'Well, yes, I did. I do remember hearing the bell a few minutes later.' She looked up, her eyes wide. 'I'd assumed it was Harry leaving for the studio. Do you think that was whoever killed him? Harry must have let them in.'

Jeffries considered this. 'It would seem that way, Mrs Westlake. Do you know who Harry was meant to be meeting at the studio?'

'It was a new client who wanted him to take photographs of the cast of an upcoming play at the theatre. The client, I can't remember his name now, wanted to meet Harry at the studio to have a look around. See if it was appropriate for the job. We have one of the few studios in the town suitable for big groups of people, and the light is perfect, with the big windows facing the river.'

Jeffries considered his next question carefully. 'And you're sure that you can't recall the name of the new client? I would like to speak to him. Try to remember, Mrs Westlake.'

'I'm sorry, I'm not sure. A Mr Dobbs or Dodds, something like that. You'll find the information in Harry's notebook. He records everything in that book. Names of possible customers. Appointments. That kind of thing. He even keeps notes of camera settings to improve his photography. Always trying out new ideas, he is.' Mrs Westlake smiled. 'It's our private joke. You're not considered important enough unless you're in Harry's little black book.'

Jeffries added a note to search Mr Westlake's body for the notebook later. 'What happened after Harry left for his meeting?'

Jeffries watched her closely, noticing that Mrs Westlake fiddled with a lock of her hair as she recalled the rest of the morning. Jeffries thought back to Smith's revelation that everyone has a way of giving away they are not telling the truth. A 'tell' he called it. Is this Mrs Westlake's tell? He remembered how she'd fiddled with her hair the first time he'd met her. He'd ask Smith later. Mrs Westlake continued. 'I opened the shop at midday and served a young woman who was interested in our prices for a portrait session. It was odd. She said she'd wait while I looked for our price list, but when I came back downstairs, she had already left. That's when you and your colleague came into the shop. I was only upstairs for a couple of minutes. I suppose she must have been in a hurry and didn't want to wait after all.'

The hairs on the back of his neck pricked up. 'Can you describe this woman? What was she wearing, for example?'

Mrs Westlake rubbed her chin, recalling the woman. 'She was young. About twenty, I should think. She wore a dark skirt, I think it was purple, a white blouse and a black jacket. Quite ordinary really, except....'

'Except?' Jeffries prompted.

'She had a nasty bruise on her forehead. Just above her left eye.' Mrs Westlake said, pointing to her own forehead.

101

Jeffries scribbled 'Carrie Grey' in his notebook and underlined it twice. Now we're getting somewhere. The back of his neck itched. Something bothered him. A photographer just happened to be in the right place just as the tram crashed. A tin full of cash had been spotted in the shop. The photographer was now dead, and this Carrie woman seemed to pop up everywhere. Could be a coincidence.

Jeffries shook himself from his thoughts. 'Can you remember anything else about this morning? Anything at all? Did you hear anything unusual while you were cleaning?'

Mrs Westlake's eyes flicked to one side as she thought back. Jeffries noticed her fiddling with her hair again. 'No, I didn't hear anything. The windows were open while I aired the rooms, and there is always quite a noise from the street, so I wouldn't have heard anything from the shop. Apart from the bell, of course. In fact, Harry always complained I didn't hear him calling up the stairs for a cup of tea.' Mrs Westlake's eyes started watering. Their little quarrels didn't seem important anymore.

As Jeffries considered everything she'd told him, there was a quiet knock, and a woman's face appeared around the door. She looked just like Mrs Westlake but shorter and with darker hair.

'Oh, Sarah. How awful,' the woman said as she rushed in and hugged her sister. Mrs Westlake started sobbing. Jeffries decided this was the right time to leave them alone. He rose quietly, pocketed his notebook and pencil, and headed for the door. Turning back, he said, 'Thank you, Mrs Westlake. We'll find out who was responsible for your husband's death.'

Jeffries made his way down the stairs, trailing his finger along the dusty bannister. He wondered what Mrs Westlake had really been doing this morning, as it clearly wasn't cleaning.

15

Supper and police business

Another wet and windy evening. Jeffries led his wife along the garden path to Smith's front porch, the rain driving under Jeffries' brolly and soaking his overcoat. He struggled with the umbrella as a gust threatened to turn the fabric inside out. The light from the house flickered warm and welcoming. Just what the pair needed after a brisk walk from their own home, only two streets away.

He reached up for the shiny brass knocker, briskly knocked twice and closed his umbrella, shaking it vigorously before propping it in the corner of the little porch. He smiled at Edith, as she fiddled with her collar. She was always nervous when meeting new people. Smith had mentioned his new colleague to Ann, his wife, and she had then sent a message to Edith, introducing herself and asking them both to supper to get better acquainted. Jeffries thought it was a little early, having dinner and drinks so soon after meeting just this week.

In Jeffries' opinion, working and socialising didn't go hand in hand. Edith had disagreed, saying the two men's professional relationship would only improve if they got to know each other better, cementing their trust in one another and helping them learn what the other is thinking, which would prove helpful in their cases.

Jeffries and Edith could hear voices on the other side of the door before it opened, and the welcome light of the hallway flooded into the porch. Jeffries smiled. 'Hello, Smith, awful weather out here.'

Constable Smith smiled back. 'Please, call me Frank. We're not on official business this evening! Do come in out of this wretched rain.'

***

Later, having sampled Frank's fine wine and Ann's wonderful pork and potato dinner, followed by treacle tart and custard, the four of them sat around the dining table, enjoying the company of their new friends. Ann and Edith had recalled how they'd met their husbands, and realised they had common interests. 'We must arrange to meet for tea and have a proper chat,' Edith had said. Ann had readily agreed. 'That would be lovely.' Ann had replied. The conversation had naturally led to the two men and why they'd decided to join the force.

Smith held the others in captive silence with his childhood story. 'Two men broke in late one night and set upon my grandfather, demanding that he open the safe in the shop below. He refused, of course, stubborn man that he was, thinking he was brave and could outwit the thugs.'

Smith described how the intruders kept the rest of the family imprisoned in the bedroom all night while beating his grandfather until he'd finally revealed the combination to the safe. 'It was too late for my grandfather. The damage was done, and he died from his injuries a few days later. That's when I decided I would join the force when I was old enough. Become a police officer. The idea of a police force was quite new back then, of course.' Smith took a long drink of his wine, looked across at Jeffries and raised his glass. 'I didn't think I'd be working with a detective on my first day, though! Why did you join the police force, Jeffries?'

Jeffries turned his glass, examining the red liquid before looking up. 'It was so long ago since I joined. I can't recall why I had done so.' His wife had laughed and nudged him. 'Oh, come on, Robert. You know very well why you joined the police.' She turned to the others as Jeffries sipped his wine, looking a little sheepish, his cheeks a decidedly brighter red than before. 'Robert decided to join the police because he wanted to impress me! A few months before I met him, my parents had hoped I'd marry their friends' son, an army officer.' Edith looked around at the others before continuing, 'Robert knew that he had to impress my parents. He'd seen an advertisement in the newspaper, announcing a new police force that was to be set up. He had previously applied to the army, but he was turned down on medical grounds.'

Jeffries held his hand out. 'It was nothing serious, just a little deaf in one ear.'

Edith winked at Ann. 'Which suits him fine when I ask him to do something around the house.' She rested her hand on her husband's arm. 'And now he's a detective sergeant, the first outside of London. I'm so proud of him.'

Jeffries blushed as he reached for the wine bottle. 'Any more wine, anyone?' Smith pushed his chair back and walked into the kitchen, returning with a fresh bottle.

***

Later, the dinner plates piled up in the sink, the wine replaced with brandy for the men and sherry for the women. Jeffries and Smith retired to the drawing room, unable to resist discussing the crashes and the murdered photographer. Edith and Ann soon joined them.

'I can guess what you two are talking about,' said Ann.

Both men stood while their wives made themselves comfortable, settling into the velvet-covered sofa that had seen better days. Smith refilled everyone's glass. Jeffries took a sip and placed the glass on the mantlepiece. 'Excuse me a moment.' The others watched, perplexed, as Jeffries walked out to the hall, returning with a small wooden box in his hand. 'I have something for you, Frank.' He handed the box to his colleague. Smith frowned as he examined the box. 'What on earth is it?' He put his glass to one side and carefully flicked the brass catch open and lifted the hinged lid, smiling as he saw what was inside. The two wives exchanged a glance. Edith shrugged. Smith reached in and lifted out a small brass magnifying glass. The handle appeared to be ivory, smooth with use. Smith turned it over in his hand, inspecting his fingers through the glass.

105

'You're a proper detective now!' Said Jeffries. 'It belonged to my father. Look after it, my friend. And make good use of it!'

'I will indeed. Thank you so much. That's very thoughtful of you.'

Jeffries retrieved his drink and raised it as a toast. 'Ladies, we need a different set of eyes on our case. We're somewhat stuck and it's going nowhere. We need a woman's intuition.'

Jeffries would often discuss his more challenging cases with his wife, as he found that he was so close to a case he couldn't see the wood for the trees. He would never admit this to his colleagues, of course. The other officers would never let him forget it. Even if they probably did the same thing themselves.

Edith said, 'So from what you've told me so far, you've got no suspects, no motives, and no reasons why the trams might have been tampered with or why the photographer was murdered. It seems to me the crashes could simply be unfortunate accidents. The first tram had a fault, the driver tried to stop it from crashing, but failed, despite his heroic efforts. The second crash was caused by a wagon careering out of control. It's as simple as that. It does seem suspicious that a man, supposedly the driver of the wagon, was seen running off. Perhaps he was drunk and wanted to avoid arrest.'

Jeffries sighed. 'Perhaps. I'm not so sure. It's odd that two trams crashed in the same week, don't you think? Do you think the photographer had anything to do with the crash on the bridge? He was there taking photographs and seemed to have more money in his shop than I'd expect. And then he ends up dead. Murdered no less.'

Smith swirled his brandy around his glass, watching the golden liquid with concentration. 'Was our unfortunate photographer really standing in the street with his camera just at the exact time the tram crashed, then offering the photographs for sale to morbid customers?'

Ann smiled. 'Why not? It could all be a coincidence. He was taking photographs as was his business. The tram crashed, and he saw an opportunity to earn some extra money by selling photographs of the accident.'

Smith said, 'Yes, but it seems odd that he should turn up dead shortly afterwards. I don't like it. Something's wrong.'

Jeffries sighed. 'You're right. I have this feeling we're onto something.'

'Ah, my husband's feeling. It's never failed you before, has it, dear?'

'Well, when you've been in the police force for as long as I have, you get a feeling when something's not quite right. I can't explain it. Someone must have had a reason to damage the trams. Then the photographer, taking photographs and selling them to a ghoulish public, is murdered a couple of days later. And then there was the second crash that on the surface looks like a simple accident, but why did the driver of the paint wagon run off?'

Edith scoffed. 'Another coincidence. Those trams are death-traps. They're old, and perhaps it's time they were taken out of service.'

Ann agreed. 'You're right. There was an accident with one last year where a woman fell from a tram and was almost crushed beneath the wheels.'

Jeffries shook his head. 'Death-trap isn't accurate, I'm afraid, Edith. Until today there have been no injuries or deaths involving these trams. We've checked. The woman you refer to who fell was apparently drunk, and there was no fault with the tram. In fact, the driver stopped and helped the woman on her way. The trams may be old and a little worse for wear, but they do a good job. The fact that we've had two crashes in the same week suggests something suspicious, in my opinion. We just need to find out why. Who benefits from the crashes?'

Smith took a sip of his drink, leaning back in his chair. 'Jeffries is right. Something is afoot. The first crash seems to be a damaged brake lever, perhaps tampered with. But John, the engineer, didn't find anything to show us, despite his belief that something had blocked the mechanism. The second crash was supposedly caused by accident, but the wagon driver ran away after the crash. Did he deliberately run the tram off the rails, or was there another reason he didn't want to be questioned about the accident?' He turned to Edith. 'As you say, perhaps he was drunk.'

Edith looked at the two men in turn, deep in thought. Jeffries knew that look. 'Go on, dear. What's on your mind?'

Edith took a sip of her drink, placed it on the little table in front of her and clasped her hands in her lap. 'Well, you said you need to find out who benefits from the crashes, correct?'

Jeffries smiled, a familiar tingle on the back of his neck whenever Edith had one of her theories. She was good at that. Theories and ideas.

His wife continued. 'I received a letter from my aunt yesterday. She has just returned from travelling in America, and she visited San Francisco, among other cities. She mentioned that the trams there are being replaced with new ones. Streetcars, they call them. Anyway, she said they don't use horses to pull them anymore; they use a cable that runs under the road. Before they modernised the system, a horse-drawn carriage slid back, crashed into a building and killed the horses.' Edith let this sink in. 'Thankfully, none of the passengers was hurt, and the driver escaped with a cracked rib. But having experienced similar incidents recently, the town decided to modernise the tramways and use the new cable system.'

'A cable? How on earth do they do that? Surely a cable needs to be connected to the tram.' Smith looked at Jeffries and laughed. 'They wouldn't be able to travel far before the cable runs out!'

Edith shook her head. 'The cable runs under the road in a loop. It's constantly moving, sliding under the road. The streetcar has a grab contraption that grips the cable through the gap in the street when it wants to move and releases the cable when it wants to stop. The driver applies a brake to hold the car in place. They are very quiet and quite quick, apparently, and leave no messy roads covered in horse manure. The cable is turned on by a huge drum at each end. Driven by steam, I should think.'

Ann smiled. 'Sounds like you need to consider the cable alternative. Perhaps a company in the town wants to replace the old trams with new, cable-driven ones. A steam company, for example?'

Jeffries coughed and spluttered; the drink he'd been sipping suddenly gone down the wrong way. Smith slapped his colleague on the back. 'Are you all right, sir?'

Jeffries nodded, putting his glass on the table while wiping his mouth with his handkerchief. 'My God, Edith. That's it.' He turned to Smith. 'We haven't checked the local businesses. We've been focussing on people, not companies. We need to look at any business that might benefit from the demise of the old trams. There must be a company making cables or alternative ways to run the trams. Something that replaces the horses. Remind me tomorrow, we must check local companies and see if any fit the bill.'

Edith looked up at the clock on the mantlepiece. 'Good grief, is that the time? We must be off. Come on, Robert. We've solved your case, and it's time we bid goodnight to these fine people.'

The rain now thankfully stopped, Jeffries and his wife walked the short way home, her arm linked with her husband's, content in companionable silence. Jeffries smiled in the darkness. 'I'm rather excited about tomorrow. Hopefully, this case will take a new turn, and we can solve the damn thing this week.'

'Sometimes, you just need a fresh view of things. Frank seems nice. You're lucky to have such an interesting colleague. And I think I may have found a new friend in Ann.'

16

A flirtatious friend and a confession

I really don't have time this morning, but I must speak to John and find out what he was doing in the shop the day the photographer was murdered. I'm sure he couldn't have been responsible, but he must have seen something, surely. I'm tired; my night was interrupted with vivid dreams of the poor photographer lying on my kitchen floor, his eyes open; a deep, narrow line encircling his neck. He kept looking at me with black, empty eyes. While I looked at him, his face changed to John's, waking me with a start, the room swimming into focus in the dim light of the early morning.

Now, having persuaded William to join me, we walk quickly down the hill to the quayside, side-stepping people crowding the pavement. William's father is not due in the office until later this morning, so we won't be missed if we're quick. The day is bright and sunny, making our journey more pleasant. Five minutes later, we reach the quay area. We hopefully have enough time to speak to John and rush back to the office by nine.

We walk along the edge of the quayside, dodging crates and sacks haphazardly placed along the cobbled walkways, ready for loading onto the huge sailing ships moored up. Men aboard ships call out to the men working the cranes. Shouting orders. The air holds a pungent smell of fish and oil. As we hurry along, I update William with the devastating news about the dead photographer, and of John, coming out of the shop, seemingly agitated. William listens open-mouthed.

Hands in his pockets, William says, 'Why do you think that John was in the shop? There must be a decent reason. Perhaps it was completely innocent.' He shakes his head. 'I can't imagine John having anything to do with the photographer's demise.'

'I just don't know. I suppose I'm naturally suspicious. He came out of the shop, clearly angry at something. The photographer's wife was sadly unaware of her husband lying dead in the darkroom when I walked in. And she was obviously flustered. I noticed her button was undone. I think John was flirting with her, at the very least. We need to ask him what he was up to.'

We head for John's workshop, passing the little fishing boats moored up at the quayside, unloading their catch for the fish women in their dirty aprons to gut and scale for the market. Seagulls screech above in tense circles as they await their chance of a thrown-away scrap.

As I walk the last few yards to the workshop, William close behind, I notice the big timber doors are already open. John is leaning against the wall outside, speaking to a young woman who looks dressed for an evening. Her dress is bright, and she has lots of makeup on her small face. She must be younger than me, yet there's maturity to the set of her shoulders.

They both stop talking and look in our direction as they notice us approaching. John has a wide smile when he sees us. The girl pouts, tosses her head, and struts away toward the passageway to the side of the workshop. She briefly turns her head in our direction before disappearing around the corner, lost to the shadows of the alleyway.

'Good morning, you two,' John says, still beaming. 'What are you doing here at this hour? Shouldn't you both be at your office?'

'Yes, well, we need to talk to you first,' says William, standing a little too close to John. I stand to one side as William and John look at each other, John frowning in confusion.

'Go on,' he says.

'Carrie was on an errand yesterday. She had to get a document signed at a gentleman's home in Fore Street, opposite the photographer's shop. You do remember Carrie mentioning the photographer at the crash the other day, don't you?'

A subtle red flush creeps up John's neck. 'Yes, I remember Carrie mentioning the photographer. I'm not sure what you're getting at.'

The morning turns colder. Slipping my hands deeper into my pockets, I say to John, 'Let me help you some more, John. I saw you coming out of that same photographer's shop. You looked pretty angry.'

John looks at me, eyebrow raised. 'Yes, I was there yesterday. Why does that matter?'

'I went into the shop after you'd stormed off. I met Mrs Westlake, and while she was upstairs looking for a price list for me, I went into the darkroom. I knew my curiosity would get me in trouble one day.' I pause. 'Do you know what I found lying on the darkroom floor?'

'I have no idea, Carrie. You're confusing me. I went to see Mrs Westlake, we had a chat, and I left. That's it. It's not really any of your business.' He turned to walk back to the workshop.

'Really? So, you don't know anything about her husband lying dead on the floor of his darkroom?'

Turning back to us, his eyes wide, John says, 'Dead? What do you mean?'

Standing with my hands on my hips, I say to John, 'Yes, dead, John. He'd been murdered.'

'Murdered? Are you sure?'

'Well, he didn't die of old age,' says William, his arms crossed.

I step closer to John. 'It gets worse. While I checked that he was definitely dead, the police were not far behind. They smashed the door down, and I had to make a run for it. They probably think I did it.'

John looks around, lowers his voice. 'You think I had something to do with this? I didn't even see the photographer or, God forbid, kill him!'

113

John rakes his hand through his hair and looks from side to side before meeting my gaze again. 'What happened to him, Carrie? I swear I had nothing to do with it!'

I gather my thoughts. Is John telling the truth? I'm not sure I can trust him, but he looked extremely shocked when I told him the photographer was dead. 'I think he'd been strangled. There was a lot of blood, so he might have been beaten, too. Mrs Westlake obviously had no clue he was even in the darkroom. She told me he was at the studio somewhere here on the quay.' I glance around, wondering where the studio is before looking back at John. 'I almost tripped over Mr Westlake's body. Then the police officers arrived, and I ran out the back door.'

'Did the police see you?'

'I don't think so, but there's a problem. I left my umbrella behind, and I'm afraid they may have found it.'

'They might not have found it. Just deny you were anywhere near the shop. It could be anyone's umbrella.'

'It has my initials on it. And you still haven't answered my question. Why were you there in the first place, John?'

'I was enquiring about a family portrait I wanted to arrange for my father as a birthday present. The woman in the shop gave me some leaflets to look at. That's it, I swear.'

'I don't know why, but I don't believe you. Is that what you'll tell the police when they find out you were there? I won't tell them, but they're sure to find out.'

John thinks for a moment, watching a young woman as she walks past before looking back at me. 'Well, of course, you can't tell them I was there, or they will know you were there. Looks like we both have to keep quiet.'

I blink with clarity upon following his gaze. 'You really are the ladies' man, aren't you, John?'

'What do you mean?'

'You're always looking at young women. The waitress in the coffee shop; you know her as more than someone who serves you coffee, don't you? And you were very

114

comfortable with that other girl just now.' It suddenly hits me as I recall a flustered and red-faced Mrs Westlake, the third button on her blouse undone. 'You are having a dalliance with Mrs Westlake, aren't you? I knew you were a bit of a rogue, but she's married, John. Or she was. Probably makes things easier for you now that poor Mr Westlake is out of the way.'

William turned to John. 'Even I knew you were one for the girls, John, but if the police find out you were in the photographer's shop the same day he was killed, they might very well think you had something to do with it. They'll think you killed him to get him out of your way, so you can carry on seeing Mrs Westlake.'

'That's not what happened. I told you; I didn't even see her husband. Do you think I would have gone to see her while her husband was in the shop?'

I step forward and put my hand on John's arm. 'So, I was right. You were upstairs with Mrs Westlake. But why did you come out of the shop looking so angry?'

John lowers his gaze and shakes his head. 'She said she didn't want to see me anymore. Said she loves her husband too much and couldn't continue the relationship in case her husband found out.'

Perhaps he's telling the truth after all. 'You like her a lot, I can see that. You're sure you didn't see anything suspicious or hear anything while you were with her?'

John thought deeply. 'I certainly didn't see anything odd and I don't recall hearing anything. We were upstairs, and we'd just, you know, got dressed after…'

'We don't need all the intimate details, John.' I interrupt.

'Well, I was just putting on my shoes, and she says to me, "I can't do this anymore. This has to be the last time." I tried to change her mind, but she wouldn't budge. Whatever she felt about me, it wasn't enough to leave her husband. I didn't mean anything to her; I realise that now. That's why I was so angry. I felt rejected, I suppose. But I swear, I didn't see her husband or hear anything while I was with his wife. In fact, she said he was out. At a meeting or something. Anyway, I realised the time was getting on, and so I rushed down the stairs and out the front door and came straight to work.'

'Well, you've certainly got over her quickly. You seemed quite friendly with that girl we saw you talking to just now.'

'Her?' John smiles and shakes his head. 'She works upstairs in the studio. We chat now and again. She's nice, but we're just friends. I helped her with some problems she had with her brother a while ago. Gave him a job in the workshop, actually.'

I look up at the windows above the workshop. 'So that's the photography studio? Above the workshop?'

'Yes, the photographer rents the space from us. Or he did. Not sure what will happen with it now.'

I gaze at the studio above the workshop. Is it coincidence the two enterprises are in the same building? I shudder as a tingle runs down my neck. Something isn't right but I can't put the pieces together.

17

Thoughts, ideas, and a man at the window

Jeffries shook his umbrella as he entered the station, finding Smith already at his desk, surrounded by piles of paperwork. Jeffries slung his drenched coat and brolly onto the coat stand, pulled out his chair, and dropped into it with a sigh. 'Bloody weather.'

Smith leaned back, put his hands behind his head, looking up at the ceiling as if searching for inspiration. 'Well, I have had a wasted morning. I'm getting nowhere.'

Jeffries raised his eyebrows. 'What are you working on, Smith?'

Smith reached down and picked up a thick book from the floor and slung it down on the desk with a thump, dust blowing up around the clutter. 'If you remember, we had this idea that we should be concentrating on companies that might benefit from the demise of the trams.' He pointed to the heavy book. 'This is a directory of local businesses. I've made a note of each company that offers services that might be relevant, and I've sent a couple of constables out with a list of questions. They've just returned, and I've sent them to the canteen to have a cup of tea to prepare them for another session once I've finished this second list. So far, they've visited twenty-one businesses out of thirty possibilities, and none came back as a likely candidate. Three are no longer in business, and one that might be promising has diversified into electrical products. Quite interesting, if you like that kind of thing. Turns out this electrical company is trying to bring power into every home and business in the town.' Smith leaned forward and peered at his notebook. 'The Shute Lighting Company. Rings a bell, can't think where I've seen the name. Might be one to invest in if you have some spare cash, sir?'

'Spare cash, Smith? I'm a policeman, not a businessman. Shute Lighting, you say?' Jeffries pats his pockets. 'Where is that damn card Carrie gave me?'

'Ah, of course.' Smith slapped his hand on his forehead. 'I had completely forgotten about that. Didn't you make a note, sir?' Jeffries withdrew his notebook and flicked through the pages.

'Here we are. You're right, Smith. I made a note of the details on the card. *Mr Shute, Estuary View, Church Hill - £100. Monday Night. Tram 19.* Coincidence, Smith?'

'Let's see what the constables come back with after they've spoken to the other businesses I found.'

'Good idea. We need to compare notes and work out a plan. Let's go have some coffee. I think we both need it,' suggested Jeffries.

Smith smiled. 'Something stronger might be better, but a cup of coffee will do the trick.'

***

Later, at Deller's Café, a table by the window commandeered and their orders placed, they both had their notebooks open in front of them, a cup of steaming coffee in front of each man. Black coffee for Jeffries and Smith's favourite, the froth almost overflowing the cup. Jeffries told Smith what he'd learned from his conversation with the photographer's wife. Smith listened to his superior's account, looking smug as he turned the pages of his own notebook. 'It certainly sounds as if she wasn't cleaning that morning.'

'You're looking pleased with yourself, Smith. What did you discover from your examination of the darkroom?'

'Before that, I have some important details from her sister's husband.'

Jeffries put his cup down and shifted closer, a familiar tingling sensation at the back of his neck.

Smith continued. 'As you know, I called in on Mrs Westlake's sister to ask her to come over to the shop.' Smith consulted a page in his notebook. 'While she was upstairs getting her coat, I noticed her husband sitting by the front window, watching the world go by. I decided to talk to him while I waited. He told me now that he is retired, he sits in his favourite chair most days, looking out of the window. Watching the world go by, he said.'

'I hope my retirement is more interesting than that when the time comes. What was his occupation before he retired?'

'I'm not sure; I forgot to ask. But that's not important. What is important are the several visitors he saw calling on the photographer and his wife yesterday morning.'

Jeffries knew he was right to trust that tingle on his neck. 'Go on,' he said.

Smith continued, ticking off a list in his notebook as he spoke. 'By the way, he doesn't get on with the Westlakes; they owe him three months' rent, apparently. Anyway, according to Mr Goodchild, Harry let in two men at half past eight who were loitering outside a good fifteen minutes before Harry opened up. About half an hour later, the two men both left in a hurry. They split up, one headed for the town, and the other walked in the direction of the river.'

'Was he able to describe these two men?' asked Jeffries as he took a sip of his coffee. 'Height, clothes, anything like that. Or even better, did he recognise them?'

Smith shook his head. 'He didn't recognise them. Apparently, his eyesight isn't as good as it used to be. He said the two men were wearing overcoats and cloth caps, which could be anyone in the town, of course. He did say that one of the men walked with a limp, which might be useful.'

Jeffries made a note in his book. 'Who else did he see? You said there were several visitors.'

Smith turned a page. 'A few minutes later, a young man in overalls called. Mrs Westlake opened the door this time, not her husband. According to Mr Goodchild, she checked up and down the road before she let him in.'

119

'Interesting. Do you think that was the man you saw in the darkroom doorway before he scarpered?'

Smith put the details in order in his mind. 'It can't be. Mr Goodchild saw the same young man leave the shop through the front door about half an hour later. He said he looked angry - said he slammed the door - and walked down the hill in a hurry. The person I probably saw was the next visitor, who arrived a second later. This is where things get really interesting. The next visitor was not a man, but a young woman. Mr Goodchild was absolutely sure of this because soon before she had been with him in his dining room, witnessing him signing a legal document. When she left, he went back to his vantage point by the window and watched her as she walked across the street to the photography shop. No doubt about it. And now I think back, the person I saw could have been a woman. I just didn't expect to see a woman fleeing a crime scene at the time.'

'You'll discover that women are just as ruthless as men sometimes. Well, Smith, you said Mr Goodchild recognised her. I have a feeling I know who it was. Did Mr Goodchild see her leave, by any chance?'

Smith frowned. 'No, he'd left his post by then. Went to make some tea, I think. He said she was a young secretary from his solicitor's office and that's Carrie Grey of course. Which is most awkward as I know her father,' he said, reaching down to the side of his chair. 'This is her umbrella. I found it discarded in the darkroom. See the initials CG on the handle?'

'Well done, Smith! This case is getting more intriguing at every turn.' Jeffries thought momentarily. 'However, Miss Grey couldn't have killed Mr Westlake. She's too small and certainly not strong enough to strangle anyone, let alone a big man like Mr Westlake. It would take considerable strength to cause that injury. No, I think Carrie, unfortunately, found the body, but she didn't kill him. But why was she there in the first place? Mrs

Westlake said a young woman called in to ask about photography prices. It sounds as if Carrie was simply in the wrong place at the wrong time.'

Smith said, 'But why did she go into the darkroom? She had no motivation if she was just asking for prices, which is what Mrs Westlake said she was in the shop for.'

'That concerned me too. The way I see it, the two men, whom Mr Westlake let in earlier, are most likely to have killed him. Mr Westlake didn't stand a chance outnumbered. Perhaps they had an argument? It's usually about money.'

Smith suddenly had a thought. 'And that reminds me, sir. The papers Mr Goodchild was signing concerned the rent owed by Mr Westlake. It appears he rents the shop to the Westlakes, and they are months behind in arrears and are being threatened with court action if it's not settled soon.'

'But I met Mrs Goodchild,' said Jeffries. 'She's Mrs Westlake's sister. Seems odd that they are threatening to take the Westlakes to court over the rent.'

'Yes, I thought that too. But it was apparent that Mrs Goodchild knew nothing about this. It seems her husband doesn't get on with the Westlakes. Perhaps that's why he's getting heavy with the rent arrears.'

Jeffries drank the rest of his coffee, wincing as he watched Smith use a spoon to scoop out the froth left in his own cup. 'Interesting. Then we have the young man in overalls. Why did Mrs Westlake appear nervous about letting him in, and who was he? The only person I've met recently who wears overalls is that John fellow. You don't think it was him, do you?'

Smith grimaced. 'It could be anyone. There are hundreds of young men who wear overalls around here.' He shook his head. 'During all that time, the photographer was lying in his own blood on the floor and his wife had no idea. Or did she? She certainly seemed shocked to see his body, unless she's a good actress.'

121

Jeffries recalled his conversation with Mrs Westlake. 'As you say, she did seem genuinely shocked. I don't think she had a clue her husband had been murdered before we found the body. She didn't even know he was still in the shop. She was sure he'd left for the studio. Let's go over the facts again. A tram crash kills a woman when she is flung from the tram and dies from her injuries. A photographer takes photographs of the incident and is murdered soon after. An engineer has a theory as to why it crashed, but the evidence didn't make an appearance as promised. He seemed very sure that the brake held a clue as to the crash. It could still have been a simple accident. And what of the second crash? Very different scenario that time. According to witnesses, the tram was forced off the rails by a stolen delivery wagon.'

'We need to find that wagon driver.'

'Yes. Was Mr Westlake coincidently taking photographs of the area as he says, or did he know there was to be a crash, and he was meant to be there to record the incident? Did someone tell him to record the crash? Was he then murdered because he knew too much?'

Smith frowned. 'I don't like it, sir. Perhaps he was simply there at the right time, took the photographs and saw an opportunity to make some money. Perhaps he was murdered for a completely different reason. Don't forget the cash I found in the shop.'

Jeffries looked at his notes again. 'Let's go back to that later. It might be money paid to Harry for the photographs, but it seems a lot for a few pictures.'

Smith nodded. 'Miss Grey saw the photographer at the crash scene. Maybe she already knew him, and that's why she visited him. Then we have the two men visiting Harry around the time he was murdered. We also have the young man at the photography shop. Who is he, and did he kill Harry? My money's on the two men who visited earlier.'

'I don't think it was the young man on his own unless Mrs Westlake witnessed the whole thing. She let him in, remember. I agree, the two men must be the murderers; it's the only scenario that fits. Miss Grey is the curious one. She doesn't seem to fit into this at all. Why did she visit the photographer's shop? I don't believe it was for prices, otherwise she wouldn't have gone into the darkroom. And why did she scarper when we arrived?'

Smith pushed his cup to one side and stroked his chin. 'We still have to visit Mrs Brody and have a chat with her. Perhaps she can give us her account of what happened on the tram. She might have seen something untoward before the crash.'

Jeffries closed his notebook. 'True. The inspector will want us to visit her anyway, in case she has a reason to complain to the authorities. As far as I could tell, that seemed to be the inspector's main worry.' Jeffries looked about the café. 'I need another cup of coffee.' He raised his arm to attract the attention of the waitress. 'A bacon roll might be a good idea, too.'

18

A widow and a tea caddy

Saturday, and it's my day off. Having left it far too long, I'm on my way to see Rose's husband, who lives near the river. I hope he doesn't mind me calling in unannounced.

Clutching my bag, I hurry in the direction of Rose's house. William was able to find out where she lived through a friend at the council office.

The little side streets near Rose's home are quiet this morning. Most people use the main roads, as these back streets and pavements are not as well maintained. Muddy and rutted, they are best avoided.

Thankfully, the sun is out, and there's no sign of rain. I still haven't retrieved my umbrella from the photographer's shop. Hopefully, no one will realise it belongs to me. I can sneak in and collect it later. Leaving it behind was a reckless mistake.

I watch my step as I make my way along the pavement, arriving at Rose's house a few minutes later. William and I talked about this visit at length, and decided that the best way to approach this possibly unwelcome meeting would be to offer my condolences and explain to Sidney that I was with Rose when she died.

The house has no front garden, and the door is straight off the pavement. I reach up and knock with my fist, as there's no knocker. The screws that once held it in place are bent and rusted. The door's once glossy red paint is peeling off, and the wood is rotten at the bottom.

I wait for a twitching curtain or the sound of footsteps. I'm about to knock again when the door opens, and a man appears in the doorway. His hair is unwashed, messy without the sweep of a comb, his eyes are bloodshot, and he looks older than I expected. Grief can do that to a person, I think. His stubbled chin sprouts short grey hairs, the edges of his moustache also greying. His stoop reduces his height and bulk.

'Yes?' the man snaps. 'If it's money you're after, you can go to hell.'

This is beginning to feel like a bad idea.

'Are you Rose's husband? My name is Carrie. I didn't know your wife, but I was with her when she died.'

The man looks me up and down and then, to my relief, he opens the door wide and takes a step back, beckoning me in. 'I'm sorry. I didn't mean to snap at you. Yes, I'm Rose's husband, Sidney. Her widower,' he corrects himself. 'You'd better come in.'

He leads me down the dark hall, walking with his head down, dragging his feet.

The smell hits me straight away: spoiled food, spilt beer and whisky mixed with the aroma of a dirty house. Rose has only been dead for a few days, and her husband is already falling apart. The hallway is cluttered with an old bicycle, its wheel hanging off, leaning against the wall. A wooden cabinet, seemingly in mid-repair, sits abandoned at the foot of the stairs. I follow Sidney into the kitchen, squeezing past the abandoned pushbike, carefully avoiding the sticky beer stains on the floor.

The kitchen is no better and I fight the urge to hold my sleeve under my nose. Unwashed plates and greasy pans fill the sink, leftovers clutter the little table, and beer and whisky bottles jostle for space.

'I've been having a few bad days, as you can imagine,' Sidney says, filling the kettle from the tap. 'Tea?'

Despite the dirty cup he picks up, giving it a quick wipe with a grubby teacloth, I decide it would be rude to refuse. 'Yes, tea would be welcome, thank you. One spoonful of sugar, please.'

While the kettle boils, Sidney pulls out a chair, picks up a pile of dirty clothes from the table, and puts them on the countertop. He invites me to take a seat.

Sidney makes the tea as I sit and glance around the small kitchen. Pencils in a jar sit next to a muddle of official-looking documents on the table, weighed down by a tea caddy. I absent-mindedly move the documents aside to make room for my tea, revealing a pile of banknotes clipped together. I stare at the money. There must be nearly a hundred pounds here. I look up. Sidney is still fiddling with the cups, reaching across the counter for a sugar bowl. I wonder what he does for a living. Has to pay well, whatever it is he does. It looks like a lot of money at first glance. I wish I had time to count it but I dare not risk it.

I quickly cover the bank notes with the documents, and sit back in my chair as Sidney returns to the table with two cups of steaming tea, handing me a cracked cup. I turn it around to avoid a chip on the rim, holding it awkwardly before taking a tentative sip. The tea is actually quite good, not too sweet.

Sidney sits opposite me, holds his cup in both hands, and smiles weakly. He looks so sad, vulnerable even. His eyes are empty, forlorn. I could cry.

'So, you were with Rose when she died. The doctor said she didn't suffer, but I don't know if I believe him. She looked so peaceful when I went to visit her. To identify her.'

Warming my hands on my cup, I look Sidney in the eye. 'I held her hand while the doctor did what he could. She didn't look to be in any pain. I don't think she knew what was happening.'

Looking down at his own cup, absent-mindedly stirring the tea, he says, 'Rose should never have been on the tram that day. She doesn't normally go into town on a Tuesday. That's her day off.' Sidney looks up at the ceiling. He seems to have forgotten I'm here and mumbles, almost to himself, 'Why oh why did you ride the tram that day, Rose?'

He faces me again. 'Did you see Rose before the accident?'

'I wasn't actually on board. I was walking across the bridge on my way to work when the tram crashed. I ran over and tried to help her, but there was nothing I could do. There was nothing anyone could do.' I look at him, but he avoids returning my gaze. I ask, 'Have the police been to speak to you? They came to see me the other evening. They seem to think the driver was at fault, but I'm not so sure. What do you think happened?'

Sidney sits up straight, folding his arms. 'The police haven't talked to me, but a man from the tram company called in yesterday and said it was a terrible accident. They didn't seem to know what caused the crash.'

'What is it that you do for work, Sidney?' I ask, changing the subject. I'm curious to find out why he has all that cash.

'I'm a part-time maintenance man for the warehouses on the quay. Whatever's needed to keep them in good repair, really. Painting, clearing gutters, that sort of thing.' He looks at me, frowning.

Part-time maintenance work surely doesn't pay enough to leave a pile of cash, seemingly concealed. Sidney is hiding something, I'm sure of it. I wonder if Rose knew what he was up to?

I reach into my pocket for the card Rose gave me and slide it across the table. 'Rose gave me this card. Do you know a man called Mr Shute?'

Sidney holds my gaze for an instant, then glances down at the card. With a subtle shake of his head, he rubs the back of his neck and says, 'I do maintenance work for him sometimes. He pays well, but the work is fairly irregular, so I don't rely on it.'

'Why do you think Rose had his card?' I point to the card in front of Sidney. 'And what of the note on the back?'

Sidney turns the card over, and frowns. 'I have no idea. She hadn't met Mr Shute as far as I know. I might have mentioned him, I suppose. It's certainly her handwriting.'

'But when I spoke to her, she specifically said to talk to you. She said the crash was no accident. Why would she say that, Sidney?'

He slides the card back to me and abruptly stands, collecting the cups from the table, mine still with half a cup of tea yet to finish. 'I have no idea. As I said, I do maintenance work for Mr Shute occasionally. I have no idea why Rose had this card on her, and I don't know why she wrote that note on the back. Anyway, it's thoughtful of you to come and visit. I need to tidy up now. Rose would have hated to see our home like this. It's been such a terrible shock, and I have to go back to work tomorrow.' He turns to the sink and pours our unfinished tea down the drain.

I've obviously hit a nerve. There's something he's not telling me. 'I'm so sorry for your loss, Sidney. Rose seemed like a lovely woman. I'll leave you in peace now. Thank you for the tea.' I pick up the card and rise from my chair, turning to leave. Sidney follows me through the hallway to the front door. I turn and smile. He looks so sad. It must be awful to lose someone so close.

On the pavement outside, it's windy and starting to rain. I turn back to the front door to bid Sidney goodbye, but he's already gone back inside, the door closed.

I pull out my pocket watch. It's already 11 o'clock. The card Rose gave me is caught on the watch, and I nearly lose it in the breeze. I examine the card again. Shoving it back into my pocket, I make a decision. I need to visit Mr Shute to see what he'll divulge. I shove my hands in my pockets and put my head down against the stiffening breeze, walking quickly in the direction of the town. According to the card, Mr Shute lives a mile or so to the north, so I quicken my pace to beat the rain.

128

19

A big house and a horse groom

The gates to Mr Shute's house are at the top of a steep hill. My legs ache from the walk as I follow a gravel driveway, which leads through an avenue of trees towards the house and gardens. The house is imposing, built of red brick and with more chimneys than I've ever seen for one building. Through the back garden, I catch a glimpse of the views, stretching as far as the estuary. Dark clouds race across the vista, threatening rain. A shiny black carriage stands in the cobblestone courtyard in front of the house.

A groom tends to the horses, setting up harnesses. He's a young man in his twenties, finely dressed in a black jacket, matching trousers, and shiny boots. He notices me, and, smiling broadly, calls, 'Can I help you, Miss?'

I keep my distance. I'm wary of the horses as they scuff their hooves, impatient to get moving. 'I'm looking for Mr Shute. He's not expecting me, but I have his calling card.' I hold out the battered card Rose handed to me.

He takes the card from my outstretched hand, reads it and frowns. 'This card has had quite the journey, the state it's in. So, Miss, what brings you here, I wonder?'

I feel my face blush. 'Will you ask if he'll see me? I only need a few minutes of his time.'

'Wait here.' He heads to the house. Reaching the open back door, presumably the staff entrance, he calls through. A maid appears, carrying a bucket and mop, water dripping onto the floor. He says something to her, and they both look at me as I wait by the carriage. He hands the card to the maid, who glances at it briefly, shrugs, puts her mop and bucket on the step, and disappears back into the house. The groom looks across at me, still smiling. Is he flirting with me? He is quite dashing in his shiny boots. Come on, Carrie, focus.

A few minutes pass before the maid returns, beckoning me to approach the house. I cross the courtyard to a gravel path leading to the back door, the stones crunching under my feet. The groom passes me and touches his cap. 'Miss,' he says, still with that cheeky smile.

The maid purses her lips. 'Mr Shute will see you for five minutes; he's a busy man.' I follow her inside, quickly wiping my feet on the coarse mat.

The dark, narrow passageway has a scuffed wooden floor leading to a door that opens onto the main hallway. Paintings of stern-looking men and glamorous women adorn the walls. The black and white chequered pattern on the floor reminds me of a chessboard. Grand stairs sweep up to the floors above. There is a candlestick telephone on the wall. I'm fascinated, as I've only seen one of these contraptions once before. This one is an ornate affair, mahogany and brass. The numbered dial is ivory, the numbers black as coal. Most people don't like these new contraptions, preferring face-to-face conversations or cards carried by messenger boys. I quite like the idea of a telephone. The maid leads me across the polished floor and pushes open a door. 'Quickly now, Miss. Mr Shute is not one for having his time wasted.'

I squeeze past the maid and enter the room to find myself in a wood-panelled study, the décor dark, the walls a rich green. A painting of a steam-ship takes pride of place on one wall. Mr Shute signs papers at a huge mahogany desk next to French doors that overlook the garden. A little coal fire throws flickering light into the room. He looks up at me, smiling in a way that doesn't reach his eyes. With a nod, he beckons to the seat opposite him. 'Please sit, Miss.' He glances at Rose's card on the desk in front of him before sliding it to one side.

'Thank you for seeing me, Mr Shute.' My heart pounds in my ears. Come on, Carrie. Sherlock would be controlling this conversation, not the other way around. My chair feels much lower than this intimidating man. I have to look up to see his face properly. He looks even more menacing from this angle. I take an instant dislike to him.

'So, who are you, young lady, and what is this about?'

'Miss Grey, sir. Carrie Grey. I witnessed a tram crash on Tuesday morning and a young woman by the name of Rose tragically died as a consequence. She gave me that card with your name on it.' My confidence grows when I point to the card. 'I was curious about its meaning. I wondered how you came to be acquainted with Rose?'

Mr Shute picks up the card, turning it over. Frowning, he places it on the blotter on his desk, lining it up with a selection of exquisite, expensive-looking pens. He sizes me up, his elbows on his blotter, clasping his hands in front of him. 'I didn't know Rose, but she contacted me a few days ago. In fact, she was rather annoying and contacted me several times. Sent a number of messages. She even accosted me in the street on one occasion.'

'She obviously had a good reason to talk to you. What was so urgent?'

Mr Shute sighs, sitting back in his chair. 'She wanted to ask me about her husband. She said he was not the same man since he'd completed some work for me. I told her I didn't know what she was talking about.'

Mr Shute went on to describe how Rose had stopped him in the street one day, becoming quite distressed, telling him how her husband had become withdrawn lately and couldn't sleep at night. 'She made quite a scene. People walking by must have wondered what on earth was going on. Most embarrassing. I told her I have nothing to do with my workers. I have people who manage that side of things for me. She raised her voice. I was with a business colleague, and I can tell you, Miss Grey, it nearly cost me a new order. A big one at that.'

'And had her husband, Sidney, done some work for you, Mr Shute?'

'Well, yes, apparently so. I've no idea what her husband had done for me. I employ lots of men. Women too, as a

131

matter of fact. I can't possibly keep an eye on what they're all doing. As I say, I leave that to my staff.'

I consider my next question carefully. 'Is Sidney a practical man, a skilful worker, perhaps? Or just a manual worker?'

Mr Shute strokes his beard, looking down at the card. He looks up and gazes at me with a thin smile. His eyes are a bright blue, so cold I almost have to look away. 'I do recall Sidney, now you mention it. A pleasant chap and a good worker.' Mr Shute nods towards the door. 'He carried out some carpentry work in the hallway for me. Did a pretty decent job. So yes, I'd say he is a skilled worker.'

I can't think why Rose would be so anxious about her husband working in Mr Shute's house. It makes no sense. Unless Sidney had been working on something Rose wasn't happy about. Perhaps something dangerous. Carpentry work in a hallway doesn't sound dangerous.

'But why did Rose have your calling card? It seems odd, don't you think?' I persevere. 'And a curious note, wouldn't you say?'

Before he has a chance to reply, the door opens behind me, and the maid walks into the room. She is flustered and nervous, wringing her hands together. 'A gentleman wishes to speak with you on the telephone, sir. He says it's urgent.'

Mr Shute sighs. 'Damn telephones. They seem designed to interrupt every conversation. Please excuse me, Miss Grey.'

He rises from his chair, picks up a partly smoked cigar from an ashtray on the table and strides across the room. He closes the door behind him, but it fails to latch properly, leaving a small opening. Being increasingly curious, not for the first time and likely not the last, I quietly stand, tiptoe across the room, and listen at the door. *Listen carefully, Carrie.* Not now, Sherlock.

I hold my breath as I struggle to listen to Mr Shute's voice in the hallway. He sounds as arrogant as he was at his big mahogany desk. What a horrible man! I wouldn't want to work for him. His voice comes through the door, so it's not difficult to hear what he's saying.

'Well, I told you to arrange for some inconvenience, not to cause the damn thing to crash.' A pause. 'Yes, there's a young woman here now, asking questions.' Another pause. 'I trust you are still coming to supper this evening? We can discuss this properly here at the house.' A pause. 'Good, I'll expect you at seven. The others will be here as usual. Of course, good day to you.'

The receiver clatters back onto its holder and Mr Shute's footsteps march across the hall. My mind twirls. I need to be here at this evening's supper. I run to the French doors, turn the key and quickly return to the desk, dropping into the chair just as Mr Shute walks in. He returns to his chair, sits and pulls it closer to his desk, picking up his pen and dipping the nib into the inkwell.

'So why are you really here, Miss Grey? It seems to me that you've made an unnecessary journey for a simple card and your concerns about Rose and her unfortunate accident.' He pauses. 'It was an accident, Miss Grey. Awful, of course, but accidents do happen.'

'An accident perhaps, but I simply wondered what her connection was with you. As far as I can tell, she's a humble housewife and you're a rich businessman. I can't work out how your very different lives would cross. You've told me that her husband did some work for you, so that makes sense. But why did she give me your card while she lay dying in the street? She was trying to tell me something, I'm sure of it.'

Mr Shute smiles. 'Come now, dear. You're being quite dramatic. It's very simple. Her husband did some work for my company. And as I've already told you, as a result of his excellent work, he carried out some carpentry work here in the house. But I never spoke to him. Rose seemed to think the work upset her husband, and she was angry.

Other than that, I have no idea why she had my card with her, and I have no idea why she handed it to you.'

Mr Shute glances down at a document and signs it with a flourish. 'Now, if that is all, Miss Grey?'

I can't think of any more questions to ask, but before I stand, Mr Shute puts his pen down and twists around, reaching for a bell pull. 'Let me have Mr Jones show you out.' Pulling the cord twice, a bell rings faintly somewhere beyond the office. He turns back to his desk, draws on his cigar, and consults the papers before him. I have clearly been dismissed. A moment later, the door opens, I turn in my seat as a man appears in the doorway. He has a horrid scar on the left of his face. 'Sir?'

Mr Shute doesn't look up. 'Kindly show Miss Grey to the back door, would you, Jones? She's wasted enough of my time already today.'

I stand and walk across to the door. Then I suddenly remember the calling card, but as I turn to retrieve it, Mr Shute sweeps it up and tosses it into the fire. The hot coals ignite the card in a bright flame.

Mr Jones moves to allow me to pass. He closes the office door with a quiet click and beckons me to follow him the way the maid had led me earlier. I trail at a distance, peering around me as we pass through the hallway. Mr Jones wears grubby workman overalls and walks with a slight limp. He pulls open the back door with a flourish and gestures to the courtyard beyond. When I pass him, I cringe as he leans in close, his breath on my neck. 'Off you go, Miss. Best if you don't come back. Mr Shute doesn't like people wasting his time.' I turn to reply, but he's already walking back to the hallway. The door slams in my face.

The courtyard is empty, the horses and carriage having departed, the groom and the maid nowhere to be seen. The gardens look beautiful in the late morning sunshine. The lawns are freshly mown, having had the last cut of the season. The flower beds are still full, despite the lateness of the year. A gap in the hedge on my right leads to a path through the trees to the top of the drive. I walk up the path, under trees showing off their copper colours, the fallen leaves crunching under my feet. Reaching the top of the drive, I walk through the open gates, turn right, and trudge down the hill, smiling to myself as I recall my earlier dash to unlock the French doors. My heart races as I formulate my plan.

20

Picture shadows and missing ornaments

Mr and Mrs Brody's house was at the end of a terrace of grand townhouses in Southernhay West, overlooking a park, and a minute's walk from the police station. Jeffries didn't normally work on a Saturday, but after discussing things with Smith, they'd decided to make an exception to try and crack the case before another week went by.

Feeling confident, Jeffries walked up the short garden path, bordered on each side by neglected flower beds, standing out from the rest of the townhouses like a sore thumb. Smith followed, softly closing the gate behind him. The path was littered with fallen leaves, and a sheet from a discarded newspaper danced in the breeze, settling in the corner of the bottom step before being grabbed by the wind to begin its circular dance once more. The black door was complemented by a brass knocker and letterbox, dull through lack of care. That could do with a polish, thought Jeffries as he and Smith stood on the top step. Smith reached up, but before he could grab the knocker, the door opened, and a woman appeared, her hand flying to her chest.

'Oh, you gave me a fright! I was just on my way out. Can I help you?' Smartly dressed in a long dark coat and brown leather boots, the feather at the side of her wide-brimmed hat threatened to poke Jeffries' eye out if she stepped any closer.

Keeping his distance from the hazardous peacock feather, Jeffries held out his identification for her to see. 'I am Detective Sergeant Jeffries, and this is my colleague, Constable Smith, whom I believe you've already met. We'd like to have a word with you about the tram crash the other day. We won't take up too much of your time.'

Mrs Brody opened the door wider and beckoned them in, nodding to Smith. 'Hello again, Constable. Do come in.

I was only going shopping for tonight's supper; I'm in no hurry.'

Jeffries stepped over the threshold, pausing to wipe his shoes on the mat, smiling at Mrs Brody as he removed his hat. Smith followed close behind, removing his own hat and running his hand through his hair. Both men looked around the entrance hall while they waited for Mrs Brody to close the door and lead the way. The hallway was grand, certainly grander than Jeffries' house, with high ceilings and an ornate cornice. The ceiling rose had an intricate design but held a rather basic gas light fitting. Light poured through the large window over the front door, and more light shone through the open door to their left, revealing an empty room, save for a dusty table sitting alone in the middle. Jeffries had been to enough grand houses to realise something was amiss.

For a start, why didn't she have staff to go to the shops or see to visitors? Jeffries knew this area, one that was popular with professional people; doctors, lawyers. Most people couldn't hope to afford a house on this street, but those that did, had staff to attend to their every need. Jeffries couldn't see the point. He and Edith preferred to do their household chores themselves. He would feel uncomfortable, having people coming and going. Touching his possessions. Moving things around. Jeffries liked his things just so.

As the two men followed Mrs Brody, Jeffries spotted rectangular discolouration on the walls where paintings had once hung, and clean spaces on dusty surfaces where ornaments had presumably once sat. Smith noticed the only remaining item on the wall was a technical drawing of a great ship, displaying its internal workings. The two men shared a glance, both thinking the same thing; money problems.

Mrs Brody pulled out her hat pin and dropped her bag on the floor next to a small table by the foot of the stairs.

She paused to take off her hat and coat, hanging them on the back of a chair. Jeffries and Smith kept their coats on.

She led them to the rear of the house. The kitchen was through a door at the end of the hallway. The shelves were sparse, with just a handful of cups, a couple of saucepans and a block containing knives sitting on the worktop. The porcelain sink was empty, a dishcloth draped over the taps, limp and drab. Mrs Brody lowered herself into the chair at the pine table and beckoned for the two men to take a seat. 'I'm not sure how I can help with your investigation, but I will try all I can.'

Smith remained standing as Jeffries took a seat and leant forward, coming straight to the point. 'I appreciate you've already spoken to Constable Smith, but we were hoping that you can tell us more of what you remember from the day of the crash. Perhaps you could start from the beginning when you boarded the tram that morning.' Jeffries sat back in his seat. Smith watched Mrs Brody's face closely.

Mrs Brody sat back in her chair before telling the story of the day she caught the ill-fated tram. Her account didn't add anything to what the officers already knew, or from her first account to Smith on the day of the crash. How she survived and Rose perished was down to pure luck. Mrs Brody had sat on the left side of the tram while Rose had been on the right. Mrs Brody couldn't remember much about the actual crash.

Jeffries stroked his chin. 'How many other passengers were on board when you joined the tram?'

Mrs Brody thought for a moment, going through the scene in her head. 'There were two men sitting at the front. They were talking about work. Moaning about their boss, I seem to recall. An old woman sat at the back; she had her bags with her. Probably out shopping as was I.' Mrs Brody paused, her eyes flicking to the side as she tried to remember more. 'And that poor woman who died, she was on the other side of the tram. Such an awful thing to have happened. We didn't talk, just said good morning. I do recall she seemed to be preoccupied. I also remember she had on a bright blue dress. I forget what the others were wearing, but I certainly remember her blue dress.' Mrs Brody paused, gathering her thoughts, her eyes glistening.

'Preoccupied, you say? What do you mean by that?'

Mrs Brody thought back. 'Well, I don't know. She was quiet and just gazed out of the window, looking thoughtful, I suppose.'

Moving things along, Jeffries continued, 'Did the tram pick up anyone else along the route?'

'Yes. We stopped a short distance along the road before the hill. Three young men boarded and took the seats behind me, at the back of the tram. They were recounting their evening out the night before. They were a bit noisy, but they made the whole journey rather jolly. Their joking and laughing made me smile.' Mrs Brody smiled sadly at the memory.

'Go on, Mrs Brody. You're doing well. What happened then?'

'We moved off after picking up the new passengers. The tram reached the top of the hill at the junction. The driver started shouting. I looked to the front and saw him struggling with the controls. He seemed to be pulling and pushing a lever, yelling frantically. Then there was an almighty bang. The driver fell backwards, but managed to stand upright again, still hanging on to the lever and pulling and pushing.'

Mrs Brody looked up at the ceiling, her eyes shining with tears.

Jeffries leant forward and touched her arm. 'Can you remember any more, Mrs Brody?'

Mrs Brody looked back at Jeffries, and carefully wiped her eyes with a handkerchief pulled from her sleeve. She sat up straighter, nodded. 'I remember a tremendous cracking sound and a screech as the tram began running down the hill. The driver desperately pulled on the lever and shouted to everyone to hold on tight. The tram raced down the hill, rocking from side to side. We all held on for our lives. Time seemed to slow down as we rolled down the hill. Then the tram crashed onto its side. I think I was lucky because the tram fell on its right side and I was hanging from the seat, up in the air. The next thing I recall is being pulled from the wreckage onto the pavement. I sat in the street for a while, and I think someone helped me and talked to me. I recall someone checking me for injuries, wiping my face and helping me to stand. I remember seeing a doctor and a woman helping the girl in the blue dress. I didn't find out until later that the girl had died.' Mrs Brody looked towards the front door. 'A neighbour across the street told me.' She paused. 'I accompanied the poor driver to the hospital. I was quite unhurt but he seemed in a bad way and I wanted to help all I could.'

'Did you see anyone suspicious at the crash scene? Anything you remember at all on the bridge?'

Mrs Brody shook her head. 'Not really. There were lots of people. Some were helping, but most were just gawping.'

The two men sat in silence, hoping Mrs Brody would recall more details. Mrs Brody had other ideas. She stood and stepped across to the stove. 'I need a cup of tea. Would you two gentlemen care to join me?'

'That would be most welcome,' said Jeffries as he shrugged at Smith. If they learned nothing new, at least they'd get a welcome cup of tea.

Jeffries had been making notes in his notebook. He considered the scribbled words before him and closed his book. Mrs Brody placed cups and saucers on the table, poured the tea and offered the two men milk and sugar. Jeffries glanced at Mrs Brody. 'One thing that's bothering me, Mrs Brody.'

Mrs Brody took her seat and sipped her tea, wrapping her hands around the cup. 'What is that, officer?'

Jeffries held her gaze. Noticing his colleague's change of tact, Smith studied Mrs Brody's face. Jeffries said, 'I'm curious as to why you were on the tram, Mrs Brody. I would have thought a lady of your apparent wealth would have her own travelling arrangements without the need of public trams.'

Mrs Brody swept a loose strand of hair behind one ear, which did not go unnoticed by Smith or, indeed, by Jeffries as they both waited for her to answer. Nervous lady, thought Jeffries. Embarrassed lady, thought Smith.

Mrs Brody shrugged. 'You're quite right; I don't usually take the tram. We used to have a carriage with a driver who lived above the stable behind the house.' She looked out of the window towards the garden where the stable presumably sat empty, lacking both carriage and driver. She sighed. 'We've had to reduce some of our expenditures. My husband is a marine engineer. He designs ships. Or he used to before he lost his job.'

Jeffries shifted in his seat, feeling awkward that he'd touched a nerve. This information probably didn't have anything to do with their case. 'I see. There's no need to explain any further, Mrs Brody. I quite understand.'

Mrs Brody wrapped her hands around her cup. 'It's alright, officer. I knew that you'd seen the missing items, the gaps where paintings should hang, the lack of furniture and the cold rooms. We had to sell some paintings and furniture to raise money to pay the mortgage.'

As uncomfortable as he felt, Jeffries was compelled to ask further. It was an old habit. He had to delve deeper. 'Will your husband find another job, do you think?'

Mrs Brody smiled. 'He already has. It's not as well paid as the design work, but it will help until something more appropriate turns up. I'm sure we'll get back on our feet soon enough.'

Jeffries finished his tea and pushed the cup and saucer to one side. Smith took his cue and stood, pocketing his notebook. Jeffries was about to stand when he heard the front door open. A moment later, a man appeared at the open kitchen door. He wore a loose-fitting jacket and a grubby waistcoat. He looked at the two men sitting at his kitchen table, drinking his tea. 'Who are these gentlemen, dear?'

Mrs Brody busied herself with the tea cups, taking them to the sink before turning and wiping her hands on a cloth. 'They are police officers, just asking about the tram crash and if I remembered anything.'

Mr Brody took off his jacket and draped it over the back of the chair his wife had just vacated. He sat down and rolled down his shirt sleeves. His hands were grubby, with paint on the back of one hand and dirt under his fingernails.

'Terrible business. I hope you'll get to the bottom of this. It should never have crashed as it did. I'm an engineer, and although I design ships, it's obvious that these trams need a better design. They rely on a wooden handle to stop a vehicle that is pulled by horses, and those trams probably weigh more than a ton. Ridiculous.'

'We are asking everyone involved. Witnesses, the tram owners, the passengers. Everyone we can think of. I promise that we'll get to the bottom of this, sir.'

Mrs Brody stood next to her husband and put a hand on his shoulder. 'I'm sure the police officers are doing all they can to find out what happened. How did you get on today? Did Mr Shute pay you for last week?'

Jeffries' ears pricked up at the mention of Shute's name. Smith had a strange tingle at the back of his neck. He reached around to rub the area.

Jeffries looked at Mr Brody. 'You work for Mr Shute?'

Mr Brody had a broad smile on his face, his eyes crinkling at the corners. 'Well, it's not a full-time job, but Mr Shute is an old friend. He'd heard I was in some difficulty, having lost my job, so he offered to help by giving me work from time to time.'

'What sort of work?'

'Just ad-hoc jobs. I'm quite practical, and Mr Shute has a number of businesses under his belt, so there's always something to do. I've just finished a job for him, as a matter of fact. I was called out to fix a damaged lock on one of his buildings on the quay. Someone had tried to break into one of the workshops last night. The watchman sent a messenger to me to fix the damage as soon as possible. The thieves got away, but at least the building is now secure again.'

'I see. Well, we've taken up too much of your time. Thank you for clarifying a few things for us, Mrs Brody.'

'I'm not sure it was of any help, officers.'

'It all helps, Mrs Brody. Little details sometimes come together and complete a bigger picture for us.'

Mr Brody stood, pushed his chair back and joined the two officers at the kitchen doorway. Smith faced Mr and Mrs Brody. 'One more thing. Just to line things up, can you tell us where you both were on Monday evening, the night before the crash? From about 6 o'clock?' Smith watched their faces carefully as each answered.

Mrs Brody's expression was blank, her hands clasped together in front of her. 'I was home all evening, reading.' Mr Brody fiddled with his chin, his eyes flicking left and right. It was subtle, but Smith caught the movement easily enough. He'd make a useless poker player, Smith thought as he waited for a reply.

Mr Brody cleared his throat and looked to his wife. 'I was having dinner with old colleagues in The White Hart from about six-thirty. In South Street. The team I used to work with was celebrating a new contract.' He looked back to the officers. 'A contract that was won with my designs, as a matter of fact. Before I lost my job. Anyway, I booked the table myself. It was a combined celebration and an excuse to stay in touch with my old colleagues.'

Jeffries raised his hand. 'You still keep in touch with your colleagues, despite losing your job? That's unusual, isn't it, Mr Brody?'

143

Mr Brody fiddled with his moustache. 'Not really.' He shrugged. 'We are good friends. We've worked together for a long time.'

'I see. Go on.'

'As I was saying, we had dinner and a few drinks, and I came home about 11 o'clock.' He turned back to his wife. 'Isn't that right, dear?'

Mrs Brody scrunched her brow. 'Yes. I had been reading but had gone to bed at nine-thirty and was asleep by ten, but you woke me when you came home an hour later.'

Jeffries and Smith glanced at one another. 'Thank you both. We'll be on our way now. Oh, one more thing. You don't seem the type of man to enjoy manual labour. You seem overqualified for the job. Given your skills, I'd have thought a design position would be more suitable.'

'I'm sorry, I don't understand. Is there a question you wanted to ask me?'

'I'm curious. Why did you lose your job, Mr Brody?'

Mr Brody looked down, his face reddening. His wife had joined him at the doorway, and she reached out and took hold of his hand. He looked Jeffries in the eye. 'I had been gambling. On the horses. I'd lost a lot of money, and the owners of the design company were none too pleased.' He blushed a deeper red. 'I borrowed some money from the company without them knowing, and they sacked me. Quite understandable, of course, and with Mr Shute's help, I hope to pay all the money back within the year.'

Jeffries looked from Mr Brody to his wife. 'Thank you for recalling the accident, Mrs Brody.' Looking at Mr Brody, he said, 'I hope things work out well for both of you and you manage to kick the gambling habit, Mr Brody.'

***

On the walk back to the station, Jeffries was deep in thought. Without breaking stride, he said, 'This Mr Shute seems to crop up a lot. You mentioned the name when you listed the local companies that might benefit, and the name

144

was on that card Rose gave to Carrie. Now his name is mentioned by our Mr Brody. It could be nothing, but something's bothering me.'

'Got that feeling, sir?' Smith smiled.

'It might be worth visiting the factory that Shute owns. Have a casual look around, see if there's a connection. I've made an appointment for us to visit the mortuary on Monday so Shute will have to wait a couple of days. Don't let me forget, Smith.'

As the two policemen walked to the station, Smith asked Jeffries, 'What did you make of those two, sir?'

Pushing open the station door for his colleague, Jeffries replied, 'I don't know. Something doesn't add up. Mr Brody didn't seem the least bit bothered when I asked about his whereabouts on Monday evening. An innocent man would be annoyed at being questioned like that and yet, our Mr Brody didn't bat an eyelid. Indeed, he had an answer all lined up.'

'I'm sure we'll find that Mr Brody was with his chums for celebratory drinks at The White Hart. It's probably a dead end.'

'We'd better check, though. Perhaps you could go along to the public house this evening and ask around, Smith.'

21

Notes, thoughts and more coffee

The combination of steam from cups of tea and coffee has misted up the windows of Deller's. I order drinks from the waitress for William, John, and myself. Some patrons have ordered lunch already, and the aroma of stew and potatoes fills the air. I sit at our usual table, waiting for William and John to arrive, wondering what to tell them about my visit to Mr Shute's house, contemplating what Sherlock would do next.

Yesterday, while in the office, William and I talked at length about John and his indiscretion, deciding that John had simply let his heart lead him astray. He was obviously upset that Mrs Westlake had decided to end their relationship, but even he admitted it was a mistake, and now that her husband had been found dead, murdered, it seemed, ending their affair was probably for the best. We concluded that John was telling the truth; he didn't know anything about Mr Westlake's death.

Later, the three of us had met up briefly, outside the office, put our differences aside and decided to meet up properly now, go over what we had learned. That was before I spoke to Rose's husband and Mr Shute. I've already told William about my escapades. I wonder what John will make of what I've been up to and the plan I have in mind.

Now, food and drinks ordered, John crosses his arms and leans over the table, smiling at me. 'William tells me you went to see Mr Shute. He's a miserable bugger. It just shows that money doesn't buy you happiness.'

'I did, and yes, he's not the happiest of gentlemen, is he? While I was waiting here for you two, I scribbled down some thoughts to help us understand everything we know about Rose and the crash. Perhaps you two bright young men can fill in the gaps for me!'

William and John look at one another. Leaning back in his chair, William says, 'I've got some theories of my own. Tell us what you think so far, and let's put our heads together.'

I smooth out the napkin I've made notes on just as the waitress arrives with a tray of our drinks and pastries. 'Thank you,' we say in unison. We're a finely tuned team now, and I do enjoy being with these two.

With my pencil, I underline the first item on my list.

'Let's start with the calling card, where this all began. The card is a Shute Lighting Company card, and when I spoke to Mr Shute, he said he'd had one or two altercations with Rose. Shute wasn't clear why she was angry, and he said he didn't know why she had his card in her possession. I don't believe a word he says.' I underline item number two. 'Why was Rose so sure it wasn't an accident when she passed me this card?' Item number three. 'Then, we have the tram accident itself. Why did it crash?' I put a question mark next to the word 'evidence'. I push the list to one side. I know it off by heart anyway. 'The driver, Mr Hoskins, is an experienced man. He thought it odd that he had trouble with the brake, and we found that wooden wedge in the brake section.'

'Which mysteriously vanished,' says William.

'That still troubles me,' says John. 'Whoever gained access to the workshop and planted the wedge must have got in the same way to remove it later. They didn't break in, so they must have had a key, but I don't see how that's possible.'

William nods. 'If we can find out how they got in, that might point the finger at whoever this person is.'

I smile and pause for effect. My companions exchange looks, huddling even closer. 'The really interesting part is something I learned at Mr Shute's house. I haven't told you this yet.' I look at William and John in turn. William beckons me to continue. 'I overheard Mr Shute on his telephone. He said, "I told you to arrange for some

147

inconvenience, not to cause the damn thing to crash." I could only hear his side of the conversation of course.'

William puts his coffee cup down with a thud. John opens his mouth to speak, but I stop him with a raised hand. 'He definitely had something to do with the accident. He admitted it, and I heard everything. According to what I overheard, it seems the tram was never meant to crash, but why bother to interfere with it in the first place? I don't understand.'

'You need to tell the police about this, Carrie,' says William. 'It's proof Mr Shute had a hand in this. He may not have sabotaged the tram himself, but he must have instructed someone to do the dirty work for him.'

'But it's just my word. Mr Shute will deny it. Who do you think the police will believe? A young girl obsessed with Sherlock Holmes stories, already on their minds since the murder of the photographer? Or will they prefer the word of Mr Shute, the wealthy and supposedly respectable gentleman who employs most of the town's workers in his factories?'

I drain the rest of my coffee, now lukewarm. 'And another thing. Mr Shute's not a nice man, but his staff are no better. The maid was miserable and looked at me in disgust, and the servant who showed me out was rude, warning me to stay away.'

'What an odd bunch,' says William.

John says, 'What about the card that Rose gave you? Is that not proof? It might at least get those two police officers interested. They might feel more compelled to ask Mr Shute a few awkward questions.'

I sigh. 'I don't have the card anymore. Mr Shute destroyed it. Threw it into the fire when he'd closed down our conversation. Anyway, I've already shown those two detectives the card when they came to interview me at home. They didn't seem to take it seriously.'

'So what do we do now?' asks William, drinking the rest of his coffee and reaching for the last pastry.

'Let me get this straight,' interrupts John, absentmindedly twirling his teaspoon. 'The crash wasn't an accident. The tram was sabotaged; we have no doubt about that, despite losing the evidence. And don't forget the second crash just a day later. You think Mr Shute had a hand in tampering with the first tram but he wouldn't have dirtied his own hands.'

'Shute would have used his henchmen to do the deed. It's below him to do this. And it distances him from the crime, of course.' I say.

William wipes his mouth with a napkin. 'I've been thinking about the photographer. How does he fit into all this, and why was he murdered?'

I nod. 'He must have known too much. It always struck me as odd that he was on the bridge just at the right time. I think he was paid to take photographs. Perhaps he has contacts with the newspapers. He probably supplies photographs to the local paper when they need a bit more excitement to add to a story. People were already buying the picture cards from Mr Westlake's shop the next day. I noticed he had a display rack outside his shop full of photographs of the crash. Didn't seem shy to make a copper or two from a tragedy.'

'But was it really necessary to have him murdered? There must be more to this story for someone to crash two trams with dozens of people aboard. More might have been hurt.' I take a sip of my coffee. 'Or worse, the first tram could have crashed through the railings into the river, drowning everyone on board.'

'But what can we do, Carrie? It's out of our hands.' John says, reaching for his coat, draped across the back of his chair.

I stand and shrug on my own coat. 'I'm going to find out what Mr Shute's conversation was all about on the telephone earlier.'

William stands, checking his pocket watch. 'It's time we got back to the office. What's your plan, Carrie?'

149

I try not to smirk. 'I'm going to sneak into Mr Shute's supper club at his house later tonight and see what I can overhear.'

Their mouths drop open. William says, 'Are you mad? How will you get into the house?'

'Through the door I unlocked earlier, of course!' I give a wide grin and pull my scarf around my neck. Sherlock would be proud. 'Are you two going to join me to keep a lookout? That's if you haven't more important arrangements for this evening. What about you, John? Busy tonight?'

John looks at William and then says, 'No, I am available tonight.'

William looks at us both in turn. 'Count me in!'

I slide my chair under the table. 'I'm off home. I'll meet you on Church Hill. About two hundred yards up the hill is a postbox, set in a brick wall. You can't miss it. I'll meet you there at seven. Don't be late!'

I turn to John. 'And bring one of those fancy lights you use at the workshop. We might need it.

22

An oil lamp, a dark room and suspicious conversations

The heavy air loaded with rain presses against me as I stand by the postbox on Church Hill. William stamps his feet in a futile attempt to warm up. John is late. William squints as he checks the time on his pocket watch, the only light is from the almost-full moon. 'We'll wait for another five minutes. Ah, here he comes.'

John runs over to us. 'Sorry I'm late. Some of the other men were late leaving the workshop, and I had to wait before locking up.'

'Busy day today, John?' asks William, pushing his hands deeper into his coat pockets, his breath just visible in the dim light.

'Well, the tram crash didn't help. Put us back a fair bit, so we're working hard to catch up with the other work we have.' John smiles, rubbing his hands together. 'The extra money helps though, so I don't mind working longer hours.'

'Did you remember to bring the lamp?' I ask.

John reaches into his canvas bag and pulls out a shiny lamp. 'Of course. Would I let you down, Carrie?'

'Come on, the house is just up the hill and around the corner.'

Together we walk up the road that leads to the entrance to Mr Shute's house. The lane is dark, the moonlight struggling to penetrate the tree canopy above. The walk seemed shorter yesterday in the daylight but a few minutes later, we're all a little out of breath when we reach the entrance. We've warmed up from the trek, and the rain has stopped. We stand just inside the entrance, looking at the house at the bottom of the drive, illuminated with oil lamps placed strategically along the edge, showing the way. Light glows from most of the windows.

William turns to me. 'How are we going to reach the house without being seen, Carrie? We'll be discovered as soon as we start walking along the drive.'

I smile in the darkness. 'Don't worry, William. I noticed another way yesterday. There's a path that leads directly to the side of the house through the trees. Follow me.'

I lead them to a gap in the hedge and onto the narrow gravel path I discovered the last time I was here. 'We will be hidden from the house if we follow this path,' I whisper.

The moonlight shows the way through the avenue of trees, a pretty walk in the day, a little spooky at night. An owl hoots, and something small and furry scurries across the path in front of us, heading for safety in the undergrowth. A shudder runs up my spine.

We reach the end of the path, and I spot the French doors to Shute's study, the room beyond lost to darkness. I pray no one has noticed the unlatched door. Muffled noises reach us, the occasional chink of glass, raucous laughter and animated voices. This side of the house remains dark, so we should be hidden well enough.

There's a short gap between the end of the path and the house a few yards away. We wait behind a giant oak tree, watching. I point to the house and whisper to the others. 'Those are the French doors I told you about - our way in. Hopefully, no one's noticed they are unlocked.' I look at John, his eyes wide and bright in the moonlight. 'John, you come with me into the study as you have the lamp. Have a look around and see what you can find, I'm going to try and listen through the door, the guests will hopefully still be in the hall, before dinner is served. We'll give it about five minutes, then we must leave. Let's not push our luck.' I switch my attention to William. 'William, you wait outside and keep watch. Stay out of sight. If anyone appears, tap on the window and we'll drop whatever we're doing and make a run for it. Don't forget the way back through the trees, and we'll meet up by the entrance. Agreed?'

The others nod, and we peer around the tree, checking the front of the house again. It's all clear. I take a deep breath and step out into the open. The three of us sprint the short distance to the house, running along the grass and jumping over the narrow gravel path. We stop and huddle together in the dark recess of the flowerbed by the French doors. Gardening tools lean against the wall, discarded and forgotten. A rake and a fork rest against a rusty wheelbarrow. A pile of leaves swirls in the corner as a breeze picks up.

Satisfied we're ready for action, I reach for the handle and give it a tentative twist. The well-oiled handle turns quietly, and I gently pull the door.

It's stuck. 'Damn,' I mutter, but with a firmer pull, the door finally gives, opening with a slight squeak.

I hold my breath and listen, waiting for the voice of Mr Shute or a hand to emerge from the darkness and grasp my arm. My imagination is working overtime, making me jumpy. John gives me a nod, and we step over the threshold.

My partner in crime pulls out his small engineer's lamp, which he now lights. The lamp has a shield on one side so that the light is emitted only in the direction the glass lens faces.

The room is warm, embers in the fireplace dying down. The dark walls and cumbersome furniture look eerie at night, as though Mr Shute's desk may rise and attack at any second.

John flicks through the papers on the desk, the dim light produced by the little oil lamp throwing sinister shadows against the study walls. I quietly walk across to the interior door, slowly turn the handle, open the door an inch, and peer through the gap.

My skin prickles with goosebumps as I realise there are more people here than I expected. I count at least ten men standing with drinks in their hands. There are no women in the room, apart from the maid I saw earlier, circulating with a bottle, refilling glasses. I look across the room and see Mr Shute deep in conversation with another man who is obviously on the receiving end of some stern words. The man's face is red, and Mr Shute keeps interrupting him, holding out a hand to stop him from talking.

As I watch, Mr Shute leans in close to the man and points in my direction. I watch, rooted to the spot as the two men walk towards me.

There's no time. I softly close the door, rush across to John, grab his sleeve and whisper urgently in his ear, 'Quick, we need to go. They'll catch us if we don't go. Now!'

John quickly follows me to the open French doors. To my surprise, he grabs my arm before I can run outside. He closes the door with us inside, extinguishes his lamp with a twist of a brass knob, and pulls me close to him, drawing the curtains. He puts his finger to my mouth as we stand hidden behind the curtain. I can almost make out William through the glass, looking perplexed. I frantically gesture to him to hide, and he disappears into the shadows. My heart pounds in my chest. This is madness!

Through a tiny gap in the curtains, I peer back into the room. The door to the study opens, and the two men enter, Mr Shute leading the way, his cigar between stubby, stained fingers. In the light streaming into the room from the hallway, I watch as he reaches up and turns a knob on the wall by the door. A wall light flicks on. He has electric light in the house. Of course he does. Even though we're concealed, I worry they can see us through the curtains. John reaches down and, finding my hand, gently squeezes. I slow my breathing, but blood rushes in my ears. We're sure to be discovered.

The other man closes the door behind him as Mr Shute flicks a switch on a desk lamp. I quickly pinch the gap in the curtains closed as Mr Shute speaks. He feels frighteningly close. 'You were only supposed to disable the damn things, not cause them to crash. You were lucky the second one only crashed into a shop. No one was badly hurt, but the first accident caused the death of a young woman and several passengers were injured.'

The other man's voice rumbled low, laced with venom. 'You told me you wanted the trams disabled, Mr Shute. Your instructions were to cause a problem with the mechanics. That's what I arranged, exactly as you instructed.'

Mr Shute sighed. 'The police are sniffing around, naturally. Let's hope they don't make a connection with me. I can't afford to be anywhere near this. My company will be jeopardised if the police suspect I have any involvement. Investors will run a mile if they get a whiff of this.'

The other man speaks up, his voice low. 'What's done is done, sir. We can't change the past. All we can do now is keep to our agreement and deny all knowledge of this. Thanks to me, no one knows of our connection with the men who actually carried out the deed, and the trams are running almost empty now. People are walking instead; they are nervous about riding them, which was the point of the whole thing. I'd say it was a job well done, despite the poor woman getting killed.'

We hear a drawer sliding open. Mr Shute says, 'Well, let's hope so, for all our sakes. Here is your money, as agreed. I assume you've already paid your sidekicks. Make sure you all keep your heads down and your mouths shut.'

The other man mumbles something I can't hear, and the door to the hallway creaks open. I carefully peer through the gap in the curtains. The men are leaving the room. Just as I'm about to push John out of the French door, Mr Shute closes the study door after the other man leaves, turns, and sits at his desk with a sigh. He mutters something to himself and shuffles some papers around. Something makes him look up, and I swear he looks right at me. I can barely breathe. I tighten my grip on John's hand, silently urging him not to move.

I watch Mr Shute frown, sniff the air and wrinkle his nose. His cigar is now out. I hope he can't smell the oil from John's lamp. I can sense a sneeze building. I pinch the bridge of my nose, and the feeling dissipates.

Mr Shute looks around the room, frowning and stroking his chin. I follow his gaze as he looks down at his desk, considering the open drawer before him. He pushes the drawer closed and tidies the papers on the desk.

My sneeze sensation returns, and I pinch harder this time. It's too late! I emit a muffled sneeze that sounds more like a squeak.

Mr Shute jumps to his feet and takes two paces in our direction. 'Run!' I hiss to John, pushing open the door and shoving him out into the night. William appears from his hiding place, looking horrified, his eyes wide and his mouth open.

I turn and slam the door, grab the rake, and wedge it under the bottom of the door. It won't work for long, but it will buy us some time. Mr Shute appears at the window, shouting now, his face close to the glass. I step back into the gloom, next to the door, my back to the wall. I don't think he saw me. Mr Shute rattles the door, his angry face at the glass. Time to go. The others have already disappeared, swallowed up by the tree-lined path, and I run as fast as I can, across the grass.

William and John are waiting for me. The clouds have cleared, and I can just about make out the way back up the path, the silver light of the moon guiding us.

'What happened in there?' says William as we run, stumbling over the uneven path.

'Carrie sneezed. Shute discovered us behind the curtain,' says John, ahead of us now.

'Oh great. We're for it now,' says William.

'Come on, hurry to the entrance. He didn't recognise me. It's too dark.'

We run as fast as we can, dodging branches that crowd the path. I listen out for the footsteps of Shute's men in pursuit. Breathless, we reach the top of the drive as shouts erupt from the house. We might just get away with this.

A motor car engine fires into life in the distance. We turn and see a pair of bright lamps light up the drive as the vehicle races towards us. When it reaches the bend in the driveway, the engine sputters, and the lamps dim. The motor car stops in its tracks, emitting a hiss. A man jumps out, cursing.

John steps into the road and starts the long walk down the hill. 'Come on, you two. If he gets that engine going again, he'll be upon us in no time.'

We follow John as he strides down the hill. Then I hear a strange noise. I stop and turn to look, past the entrance to Shute's driveway, up the hill into the darkness beyond. I'm sure I can hear a steam engine from the top of the hill, the chuffing and hissing sound reminiscent of the trains that run behind my garden at home. A bright pair of lights head in our direction, illuminating the trees and hedgerow.

William stares at the lights, transfixed. 'The nearest railway is miles away. What on earth is a steam train doing way out here?'

John smiles broadly. 'That's not a train. It's a steam carriage!' He puts up his hand to wave the machine down.

'What are you doing, you fool? It might be one of Shute's men,' I shout to John, snatching his arm to stop him from grabbing the driver's attention.

John turns to me. 'I'd recognise this machine anywhere. It belongs to one of our customers. We maintain it for him. It's the only steam carriage in the town.' John turns back to the carriage, dangerously close, its lights almost upon us.

'Your customer it might be, but he'll mow us down!' I shout. William and I dive into the bank on the side of the road. John frantically waves his arms, jumping up and down.

With a hiss and a sigh, the brightly painted carriage screeches to a stop next to us. The driver, a smiling, jovial gentleman with a glowing cigar hanging from his mouth beneath an elaborate and highly-waxed moustache and wearing leather gloves and goggles, leans over the side. 'Well hello, John. What on earth are you doing out here in the dark, waving your arms like a lunatic?' He looks across as William and I, struggling to pull ourselves free from the brambles in the hedgerow.

John grasps my hand and tugs me to my feet. I pull twigs from my hair and step across to the curious carriage, William joining us. John shouts to the driver, his voice almost lost in the noise of the steam engine as it hisses. 'Mr Downe. Good to see you. No time to explain; can you take us to town?' He looks up the road. 'We're in a bit of a hurry.'

The driver's voice booms over the sound of the engine's patter. 'Of course, young man! Hop aboard. I'm heading into town anyway.' The back door swings open.

Behind us, on Shute's drive, we hear the motor car once again splutter into life, the engine roaring as the throttle is pressed. 'Come on, you two,' says John, pushing me in the direction of the rear door. 'Get in. William, come on, will you?'

The three of us jump aboard. William and I lean back into the plush leather seat behind the driver. John jumps into the front seat next to Mr Downe.

The driver looks at our frantic faces, peers back towards Shute's drive as the motor car appears, its lights illuminating the hedgerow, the driver looking left and right, before spotting the steam car.

'Ah, so you're not friends of old Shute's either. I take it you don't want to speak to those gentlemen in the motor car behind us? By the way, I'm Edward Downe. Everyone calls me Ed. Pleased to meet you. Right, John, watch the steam gauge and shout if it goes below the line; you know the drill.'

John looks down to monitor the steam gauge as instructed. I look behind us, spotting the motorcar racing out of the entrance, the wheels throwing up dirt in its wake.

John shouts to Ed, 'Steam's ok, sir. Let's get out of here. You keep telling me how fast this thing goes when you open her up. Now's the time for a demonstration!'

Ed laughs, pulls a lever to let out a huge plume of steam, and the car lurches forward. The only sound is the rumble of the rubber wheels on the roadway and the hiss of steam as the burners send more heat to the boiler.

Turning slightly, the side of his face visible in the moonlight, he shouts above the whooshing sound of the steam car. 'Any enemy of old Mr Shute is a friend of mine! Damn man is always trying to buy land from me at a ludicrous price. I don't trust him one jot.' Mr Downe faces the front again. 'Hold on tight!'

We grab anything we can as the steam car gathers speed, hurtling down the dark road. The steep hill helps us to accelerate, the hedgerows whizzing by at an alarming speed, my hair is blown all over the place and we all hang on for dear life.

Ed shouts back to us, 'This next turning is our chance to lose them. It's going to be sharp, so brace yourselves, gents. You too, miss!'

I look over the driver's shoulder. We're not going to make the turn, not at this speed. I tightly grip the seat in front of me and hold my breath. 'Hold on!' I shout to the others.

The steam car leans over as it turns hard into the dirt track leading to a farm, its name painted on a sign, blurred as we race by. I'm sure we're only on two wheels with the angle of the carriage. Thankfully, we somehow make the turn and skid to a halt next to a stable block. Ed frantically pulls levers and turns handles. The lights dim and then go out completely. The steam disappears, and the engine is silent. We wait, barely breathing, my heart pumping madly.

The chasing motor car races past the turning, its lamps illuminating the hedgerows as it disappears down the hill.

Ed twists around in his seat to face us, grinning widely, and slaps his hand on his thigh. 'Steam is the way ahead, not those infernally noisy, smelly petrol things. Let's go. No need to drive like a mad thing now. By the look of you three, I don't think you could stand any more racing!'

Still laughing, Ed flicks his spent cigar into the lane, pulls a brass lever, turns a handle, and the steam car slowly reverses out of the turning and back onto the road. He manoeuvres the vehicle to point in the direction of the town. The other car is nowhere to be seen. 'Well, that was fun! Where would you like me to take you?'

'Home please, Ed. I need a hot chocolate and an early night. I'm exhausted,' I say with a laugh. I turn to William, a broad smile plastered on his face. John is holding onto a handle in front of him, his other hand gripping a rolled-up sheet of paper. I hadn't noticed it before.

'What's that, John?' I ask.

John taps the end of the rolled-up paper on his forehead and winks. 'This, Carrie, is the answer to all your questions. Everything makes sense to me now.' He undoes the top two buttons on his coat, slides the roll inside, pulls his coat tight about him, and pulls his collar up.

I turn back to the driver. 'Ed, would you be kind enough to take us to Deller's Café by the Cathedral? Perhaps join us for a hot chocolate as a way of thanking you? Thanks to John, an early night will have to wait for another time.'

Ed releases a lever, and the car starts its descent down the hill. 'That sounds delightful, but I'm afraid I have a prior engagement. I'll drop you off right outside Deller's, though.'

And with that, the steam car gathers speed down the hill with gentle chuffing and the hiss of rubber on the roadway.

23

Hot chocolate and engineering plans

Later, having safely been deposited outside Deller's and watching Ed steam away in his contraption, we sit at a corner table, away from the rest of the coffee shop, though it's quiet tonight, with only two other customers and they are so engrossed in each other, they didn't even look up when we walked in.

We wait for our drinks, still wrapped in our coats, chilly from our open-top car ride. John reaches into his coat, pulls out the rolled-up sheets of paper he'd waved about earlier and lays the top sheet on the table, anchoring the corners with an assortment of pepper pots, salt cellars and cutlery. I peer at the drawings, a maze of lines and strange symbols. 'What on earth is this, John?'

'Looks like some kind of technical drawing.' William says.

John smiles. He doesn't say anything for a few minutes, his fingers tracing the lines from one end to the other. It means absolutely nothing to me. The only recognisable part is the Shute name and their business logo, stamped in one corner.

John leans back, crosses his arms. He puts his finger to his lips as the waitress arrives at the table with our drinks. She places a steaming mug of hot chocolate next to each of us, using the drawings as a placemat. As she walks off, John leans across the table, and in a low voice, says, 'These are electrical drawings. They show the electrification of the town.'

'I'm sorry.' I interrupt. 'The what? I'm lost already.'

'Patience, Carrie.' Says John. 'As I was saying, these show the proposed electric connections for the town. Basically, these show a plan to introduce electric power to every home and business.'

I lean across and I can see a pattern, now John has explained. I trace my finger along a thick line. 'This is the high street. And these are the tram lines. Ah, I see now. Shute's company will run their cables along the tram route, and split off into each building.' I point to a box shape. 'What are these? There are lots of them dotted along the route.'

John takes a sip of his drink. 'Those are a sort of repeating station. I have a limited knowledge of electrics, but I would think the power would have to connect here, with smaller cables running to homes and businesses.'

William leans back, folds his arms. 'What are you saying? Shute takes over the trams, builds new routes and installs power cables as he goes. That's astonishing. If he manages to connect up even half of the town, he stands to make a fortune!'

'Worth the risk involved with nobbling the old trams, then.' I say.

John moves the cutlery and condiments to one side and rolls up the drawings. 'We need to show the police these documents as evidence that Shute has a motive for shutting down the tram company. I shouldn't wonder he had a hand in the photographer's death, too.'

We sit in silence for a few minutes, enjoying our hot chocolate, each of us in our own thoughts. The other customers have gone and the waitress keeps looking at the clock, a cloth in her hand.

'Come on, it's time we went home.'

24

Dinner, alibis and fist-fights

Belly full from a hearty supper, Smith trudged down the hill leading to The White Hart public house. A welcome glow shone from the little crooked windows as he drew closer. The front door was open, and a man busied himself rolling beer barrels into a chute that led down to the cellar.

Smith arrived at the front of the public house just as the man rolled the last barrel into the cellar. He stood, arched his back and looked at Smith, a frown creasing his forehead before he broke into a wide smile. 'Well, I never. If it isn't Frank Smith.' He wiped his brow and hands with a dirty rag and shoved it into his pocket.

Smith smiled and held out his hand. The cellar man grasped it tight and shook it vigorously. 'Good to see you, Ernie,' said Smith. 'Working late, aren't you?'

'Late delivery. Flamin' nuisance. I should have got off ages ago. Haven't seen you since those last days at school, Frank. Last I heard, you was joining the police.'

Smith nodded. 'Yes, you heard right. I joined up just a few weeks ago.'

'Well, I never.' Ernie said again, standing back, his hands now on his hips.

Smith said, 'I'm on a case now, actually.'

'Oh? I thought you were off duty.' Smith raised a brow. Ernie pointed to his friend. 'No uniform.'

'Ah, yes. I'm in the new detective department. We don't wear uniforms. It helps us to blend in. And yes, I am on duty tonight.'

'Detectives? Sounds intriguing. I thought you police gentlemen walked around in uniform with fancy hats and capes, chasing criminals and dragging them to the courts.'

'It's a bit more than that, especially in the detective department. We have to solve crimes before we drag anyone off to the courts. There's a lot involved, a lot of head-scratching and thinking. I haven't actually chased any criminals yet.'

They stepped back as two men in oily overalls and heavy boots brushed past the two friends, eager to get inside to order their drinks. Piano music drifted through from inside, abruptly shutting off as the door closed.

Smith said, 'You might be able to help me, as a matter of fact. I'm looking for anyone who might know a Mr Henry Brody.' Smith held his arm up. 'Tall man with fair hair, carries himself well. He says he's a regular here, and I wanted to check his story that he had dinner here on Monday evening.'

'Henry Brody? Yes, I know him. Not very well, but I know who you mean. In trouble, is he?'

'He hasn't done anything wrong as far as we know. His wife witnessed an incident on Tuesday morning, and we just need to check everyone's whereabouts the evening before. It helps to give us a bigger picture.'

Ernie scratched his chin with a grubby hand. 'I was working on Monday, and I'm pretty sure he was here that night. It was busy, and I think he was with a big group. Celebrating something, now I think about it. They had a table for about ten men, I seem to remember.'

'That's what he says, so it sounds like he's telling the truth. Any idea what time he left?'

'I've no idea. I was busy all evening. Didn't even get a break that night.' He thrusted a thumb over his shoulder. 'The manager will probably know. He doesn't forget a face. Come in, and I'll introduce you.'

Ernie led Smith into a small porch with two doors leading off both sides. The left one was wedged open and led to the public bar where a man and a woman were in the middle of a song; the woman sang while the man played enthusiastically at an upright piano. The music sounded like the new ragtime style Smith enjoyed on rare evenings off. The other door led to the restaurant. Ernie opened this door, and the two men stepped into a short passageway with soft carpet. Gas lights lit the way, and oil paintings adorned the walls. They looked like portraits of local scenes to Smith, but he didn't pay them much attention. The passageway led to the restaurant at the very end, with two further doors along the right-hand side.

Ernie stopped at the first door, frosted glass in the top half, the word 'Manager' across the centre. Ernie knocked on the glass, and a voice called, 'Yes?'

Ernie turned to Smith. 'Wait here.' He turned the brass handle and stepped into the office, closing the door with a soft click behind him. Smith resisted the urge to lean in and listen to the muffled conversation through the glass. He could rely on Ernie. They'd been best pals at school but had lost touch through different paths since those innocent days.

A moment later, Ernie emerged from the office. 'Mr Hooper will give you a few minutes. He's busy, so don't take too long.' He leaned in close to whisper. 'He can be a funny bugger sometimes, but he seems to be in a good mood tonight, so you're lucky.' Ernie winked. 'I've got to get these barrels stored away, then I can get off home. We must get together sometime, catch up over a pint or two.'

Thanking his friend, Smith pushed open the door and stepped into the office. Illuminated by a single gas light on the wall and the fire flickering in the corner, the office smelt of tobacco smoke. The smoke from the offending cigarette wafted up from an ashtray on the desk. Smith let the door close with a click and glanced around.

The room was a miserable, dark space, every surface taken over with piles of paperwork and newspapers. A path between yet more piles of papers trailed through the office to a desk. Behind the desk sat a man in a leather chair, each looking as worn as the other. The dim light in the room didn't help Smith get a read on his age, but he estimated the man to be in his late fifties, possibly older. The man had a bald patch and wore glasses. The smouldering cigarette remained in a silver ashtray, the smoke spiralling to the ceiling. The manager looked up from writing on a document. 'I understand you are one of these new detectives I've read about. You have some questions about one of our patrons?'

Smith smiled to himself at the mention of the detective rank. 'Ernie's being over-generous with his description. I am Constable Smith from the Exeter Police. I am supporting the detective section on a case. I understand from Ernie that you are Mr Hooper, the manager?' Smith held out his ID card for the manager to inspect. The manager kept his eyes on Smith.

'Yes, I am the manager.' He pointed to the stained chair on Smith's side of the desk. Smith chose to remain standing.

The manager considered Smith with interest. He reached forward and picked up his cigarette. 'Who is it you're interested in? I'll see if I can help. I don't know all the customers, of course. I just run the place, pay the bills, hire and fire staff and so on.' Noticing the long drooping ash at its end, he deftly flicked the cigarette with a nail, sending the ash into the ashtray. Lifting it to his mouth, he drew smoke deep into his lungs and exhaled a circle of smoke into the air.

'We need to check the movements of a Henry Brody.' The manager's face flashed with recognition. Smith was sure of it. 'He says he was here on Monday evening having dinner with friends. I need to check if anyone can vouch for the times he arrived and left. He says he booked the table himself.'

'Old Henry, eh? The ladies' man.' The manager smiled. 'I know Henry well. Nice enough gentleman. Drinks here a fair bit. Plays cards occasionally.' Mr Hooper reached for a diary on his desk. A pile of invoices fell to the floor as he dragged the big book in front of him, but he didn't pick them up. He took another long drag on his cigarette and replaced it in the overflowing ashtray. Smith wondered how safe this building was, what with the glowing cigarette and the piles of paper everywhere. A disaster waiting to happen, he thought. He watched as Mr Hooper opened the book and leafed through the pages until he found what he was looking for. 'Monday evening, you say.' He ran his cigarette-stained finger down the page, then stopped near the bottom. 'Yes, here we are. Dinner for ten, booked in the name of Brody.'

'So he was here that evening?'

'Well, he booked a table, but I don't know if he was here, do I?' He closed the book with a thud and slid it to the edge of the desk. Dust motes flew and hung in the air. He smiled. 'I'm playing with you, constable. Yes, he was here. I remember it well because it was unusually early for Henry. He arrived first, then his pals joined him a bit later. They had drinks in the bar after dinner, but I don't know what time any of them left. You'll need to speak to the waiter or the barman.' He gestured to the door. 'You're welcome to ask around in the restaurant. The staff who were here on Monday will be working tonight.'

'Thank you. I'll do that. You've been most helpful.' Smith turned and walked to the door.

Emerging from the manager's office, he turned right and walked to the end of the passageway. He realised this detective business was all about asking questions time and time again, hopping from one person to another. Linking all the pieces. He didn't mind. Quite enjoyed the challenge.

Entering the restaurant, Smith noticed that the tables were laid with white tablecloths that had seen better days and silver cutlery that could do with a polish. An ashtray sat at the side of each place setting. Being early, there were no diners. The only activity was that of the staff, smart in their black and white uniforms, the women wearing newly pressed aprons, the men wearing black ties, putting the finishing touches to the table arrangements. At least the staff look presentable, thought Smith as he ran a hand over a creased tablecloth. Smith walked up to the bar at the far end of the restaurant. The barman, busy stocking his shelves with fresh bottles, spotted Smith in the mirror on the wall behind the bar. He turned to face him. 'What can I get you, sir?' Then, as an afterthought, 'Do I know you?'

Constable Smith leant on the shiny mahogany bar. He smiled at the barman. 'I've drunk in the public bar a few times. You might remember me from there.'

'That's probably it. Have you booked a table?'

'I'm not here for dinner.' Smith nodded in the direction of the manager's office. 'Your boss said I could ask you some questions about one of your customers, Henry Brody.' Constable Smith fished out his card and held it up to the barman, who squinted before pulling out a pair of smudged eyeglasses from his apron pocket. 'Can't see a damn thing without these.' Slipping his glasses on, he peered at the card. 'Constable Smith, eh?' He pushed the glasses onto his head and looked at Smith. 'Henry, yes, I know him. What do you want with him?'

'Do you remember seeing him at dinnertime on Monday night?'

The barman stroked his chin. 'Let me think. Monday was busy, and we had a fair few in that night. Almost a full house.'

'Monday. Henry Brody. Do you remember him being here that night?' Smith prompted, taking his notebook and pencil out, more for effect than anything else.

The barman noticed the notebook and, stroking his chin once more, said, 'Yes, Henry was here. There were ten of them. Mr Brody and his friends. They all had steak and plenty to drink.'

'Do you recall the time that Mr Brody left the restaurant?'

'It was a late one, I remember that.'

Smith nodded, gesturing to the man to get on with it. 'Go on.'

'I remember now. Mr Brody left at about eight, which is odd, come to think of it. The others carried on drinking and playing cards until we had to kick them out at midnight.

Old Brody normally likes to have a few drinks with his friends, but yes, he definitely left early. I remember wondering where he was off to.'

Smith scribbled these details into his notebook and put it back in his pocket. 'Thank you. Most helpful. Did you notice anything out of the ordinary, apart from him leaving earlier than the others? How did he seem to you? Was he his normal self?'

The barman reached below the bar and picked up a pint glass, pulled his cloth from his shoulder and started to wipe it clean. 'Well, he did seem like he was thinking.'

'Thinking?'

'That's right. Deep in thought he was. I remember asking him more than once for his drink order, but he seemed not to hear me. Hang on, here's Albert, one of Henry's drinking friends. He was here at dinner that night.'

The barman reached up and slid the glass onto a shelf above the bar. The glass clanged against the next in the row. He called over to a man who had just walked into the public bar, taking a seat at the end of the bar. Two other men were already seated nearby, drinks in hand, deep in conversation. 'Albert. You were with Henry on Monday night, weren't you?'

At the question, all three men looked over. The two strangers took in Smith, getting his measure. Smith stood straighter. Albert stood and sauntered across, standing next to him. 'Who wants to know?' He nodded to the barman, who held a glass under the beer tap and pulled the lever.

Smith considered the man before him while he waited for his drink to be poured. He wore a jacket, worn at the cuffs, a button missing from the right one. His collar was clean, his tie slightly askew.

'I'm Constable Smith, and I'm making enquiries about Henry Brody's whereabouts on Monday night. I understand you were here for dinner that evening.'

'That's right, a few of us were here.'

'Do you work with Henry?'

169

'We were colleagues at the engineering firm. Henry does the designs and we build them to his drawings. Until he left, that is.'

Smith frowned. 'Why did he leave? He was a bit vague when we asked him.' Smith knew, of course, but wanted to hear it from his colleague. From the corner of his eye, Smith noticed the two other men were looking away but clearly listening to the conversation.

'It was a misunderstanding. You'll have to ask Henry. It's none of my business. What's Henry been up to? Always seems like the perfect gentleman. A bit of a ladies' man, but I didn't have him down as a rogue.'

'He hasn't been up to anything.' Smith leant on the bar, trying to look relaxed. 'I just need to check his whereabouts on Monday evening. His wife witnessed the tram crash on Tuesday morning, and I'm just putting the pieces together.'

The fact that the two men at the end of the bar had stopped talking and were leaning in closer hadn't escaped Smith. The mention of the tram seemed to have piqued their interest even more.

'Well, I don't know Henry that well. We just work at the same place. Or used to. We play cards sometimes, have a few drinks, you know?'

'Monday night?' Smith prompted. It was like getting blood from a stone with some people.

'It was a celebratory dinner. A big project had just come in. All due to Henry's designs.' Albert paused as he thought back. 'Funny thing, though. He left early. We had barely finished dinner when Henry left. Didn't even say goodnight. Just slipped out. He thought no one noticed but we all saw him walk to the door and leave. Curious, but all that was forgotten once the cigars and cards came out.'

Smith took out his notebook again. 'What time did he leave?'

'Not sure. About eight or nine, I think. Is it important?'

170

Smith made some notes in his notebook and slid it into his pocket, along with his pencil. 'Maybe.'

The barman pushed a frothing pint of beer across to Albert. 'Can I get you a drink, constable? On the house, seeing as you're police and all.'

'Thank you, I'll have a half pint of your best, please.' He turned back to Albert, who was enjoying his beer, the froth lining his upper lip. 'Do you play cards for money with Mr Brody?'

Albert smiled and put his glass down. 'Of course. Ain't illegal, is it?'

'Not for small stakes, no. What sort of player is Henry? Does he win often?'

Albert threw his head back and laughed. 'Henry never wins, constable. He's hopeless. Hasn't got a poker face, you see. Gives himself away every time.' He shook his head. 'He did win once, but he lost the lot later on. He can't help himself. He either has so much money he doesn't care, or he's desperate to make up his losses.'

Smith considered this new information as he downed his beer. He thanked the two men for their help, and walked to the door. As he passed Albert's friends, he noticed them silently watching him. Smith pulled open the door and emerged into the cold night.

He walked along the dark street, heading home, deep in thought. He kept his hands in his pockets and his collar up against the evening chill. He was thinking about his conversation with Albert and the barman. Mr Brody had a gap in his movements that night, so where was he between eight and eleven when he claimed to be with his friends the whole time?

As Smith reached the junction at the top of the hill, he stopped to take in the view. The sight of the town, lit only by flickering gas lights, always made him pause. As he stepped into the street to cross to the other side, his home just a few minutes away, he became vaguely aware he was not alone. Footsteps followed behind him. Two sets. He

171

took his hands out of his pockets and quickened his pace. Turning the corner into the high street, he risked a quick look over his shoulder. Two men in dark coats and caps were about twenty yards behind him, closing fast. He decided it was no use out-running them. He'd have to face them and make the first move. He stopped dead, turned and faced the two men as they approached.

He recognised them instantly; the two men from The White Hart. Albert himself was nowhere to be seen. Smith considered the men before him. The man on his left was tall and skinny, had a slight limp. The other, short and fat, not fast on his feet, had a billy club in his right hand. The limping man appeared unarmed. The man with the club needs to be tackled first, Smith thought. The two men stopped in front of him.

Smith shifted his weight to the balls of his feet, taking a good stance with his fists clenched by his sides. His heart quickened, and he stood stock still. The two men sneered, appraising their quarry.

'There are two things that are going to happen right now,' Smith said.

The two men briefly glanced at each other. The limping man smiled as both men took a step forward. They were within range now.

Billy club man said, 'Yeah, and what's that?'

Smith held up one finger. 'First, you're going to turn around and crawl back under the rock you came from.'

The two men leaned forward, chuckling now.

'And secondly….' With that, Smith swung, catching the billy club man in the jaw with his elbow. There was a satisfying crunch as the man fell to the ground, moaning and clutching his jaw, the billy club bouncing out of reach. The limping man's chin dropped as he watched his pal fall to the ground. Smith regained his posture, held his arms wide, and brought his hands together with a slap to each of the limping man's ears. The stunned man fell to his knees, clutching his ears as he shook his head, grimacing. Smith looked down at the two men. 'Sorry, I couldn't remember what the second thing was. Oh yes! Always make the first move.' He crouched down next to the man now without his billy club. 'What do you want? Did someone send you to beat me up? Or did you just fancy your chances to rob me?'

Billy club man scrambled to his feet, limping man already hobbling away, still rubbing his ears and shaking his head. Billy club man scowled, pointed his finger at Smith. 'You just stop asking your questions. None of the gentlemen in The White Hart had anything to do with the tram crash. Especially not Henry. You're not welcome there, so take this as a warning. Next time, there'll be more of us, and we'll finish what we started.'

The two men ambled off, muttering under their breath.

Smith turned and walked briskly along the street, heading for home. That's enough for one night, he thought, rubbing his bruised elbow. Must be getting close. Ruffling some feathers. Wait till Jeffries hears about this, he thought with a smile.

MONDAY

25

A corpse and a clue

The morgue was busier than Constable Smith had expected, especially for a Monday morning. Probably been a chaotic weekend, with public house brawls ending in untimely deaths, and disagreements coming to nasty ends. It's more like a busy hospital ward, he thought, as doctors, mostly in white coats, some in suits, walked briskly along the corridors. They all carried something: a clipboard, a folder, a doctor's case. A distinct lack of stethoscopes or bedpans. Nothing for living patients, at any rate. Smith shuddered. Jeffries didn't seem bothered by any of it.

Constable Smith hadn't been in a morgue before. Mr Westlake was his first dead body, and he looked around the reception area, to distract himself from his thoughts – bodies opened up, skin and bones, knives.

Jeffries snapped his fingers next to the constable's ear. 'I said, Smith, how did you get on with your visit to the White Hart? Does Brody's alibi stand up? Are you even awake, Constable?'

Smith blinked. 'Sorry? Brody's alibi? Ah, yes. I went to The White Hart. The barman said Brody was definitely there last Monday, but he left around eight. So there's a gap of several hours as to his whereabouts because Mrs Brody said he wasn't home until 11 o'clock. We need to have a chat with him again.'

'Right, well done. Let's get this visit over with, then we'll decide what to do about our Mr Brody. And we must have a chat with Mr Shute. Each time I've sent a Constable to his house and factory, he's conveniently "out on business". His lackeys are very good at keeping Shute out of reach.' He looked at Smith, who had gone distinctly pale. 'First visit to a morgue, Smith? You might want to put some of this under your nose.' Jeffries smiled as he passed his ashen-faced colleague a little silver tin of white paste. 'It will disguise the smell.'

Smith dipped the end of a finger into the tin and wiped the residue as instructed. The smell was sweet, rather like marzipan. He hoped it would disguise the sour aroma he was afraid of. That distinct smell of death. He had once found the body of a cat in an alleyway. It had been dead for a few days, and hell, did it stink.

The officers patiently waited at the reception window while the sister in charge went to fetch the doctor. Do they call them doctors here? Smith wondered. Probably, he decided. What else would you call them? Morgue men, perhaps. Smith thought back to a crossword puzzle his wife had been working through the other evening. He couldn't recall the clue she struggled with but remembered the answer. Path something. Pathology, that was it. Pathologists, not morgue men and certainly not doctors. Those were for the living, not the dead.

Smith was brought to attention when a portly man in his mid-fifties approached and extended his hand. Jeffries shook it. 'Doctor Price, nice to see you again. Would be more pleasant in different circumstances, of course. This is my colleague, Constable Smith.'

Smith was grateful Doctor Price didn't offer him his hand to shake. He wasn't sure he could touch the same hand that had been handling cadavers. And even though they were indeed pathologists, they called themselves doctors. Very confusing, thought Smith.

'This way, gentlemen.' The doctor led them down a long corridor to a pair of doors marked Room 3. He pushed the doors open and walked into a brightly lit room with a high ceiling. The two officers followed, Smith reluctantly so. A semi-circle of raised wooden seats looked down onto a circular area. Upon a wooden table in the middle of the round floor lay a body shrouded in a white sheet.

'Welcome to our examination theatre, gentlemen. We often carry out post-mortems for medical students. They

176

have to learn somehow, and this is how I learned my craft. Many years ago now, but the basics are the same. Skin and bones haven't changed since my own student days.'

The room was empty of students now. Doctor Price led the two men to the table, and looked at Smith with a smile. 'No need to worry,' he said to Smith. 'He's dead. He can't hurt you.'

With a flourish and a fiendish grin, more to startle Smith than any practical reason, the doctor whipped the sheet off the body to reveal Mr Westlake lying on his back. Smith gasped, unable to look away.

Jeffries smiled. 'Don't take any notice, Smith. Doctor Price does this to everyone when it's their first time.'

Jeffries moved forward, followed by Smith a few paces behind, relieved that the ointment under his nose seemed to be working. Doctor Price reached up and pulled a cord hanging from the ceiling, moving a bright light closer to the body. To Smith's astonishment, the light was not gas but one of the new electric lights. The doctor saw him watching. 'We were one of the first places in the town to have electric light. It makes our job so much easier. Extraordinary, is it not?'

Jeffries had seen the electric light in the morgue before. 'What did you find when you worked on Mr Westlake's body, Doctor Price?'

'Ah, straight to business. Very well, Jeffries. I examined the poor fellow this morning and I quickly deduced strangulation as cause-of-death. The only other wound is a rather nasty cut on his head, but that wasn't fatal. He probably struck his head in the struggle, perhaps on a desk or bench nearby. There are no other wounds on the body, and he was otherwise a healthy man. His heart looked normal for a man of his age, and his lungs too. No sign of disease that I could see.'

The two officers peered at Mr Westlake's neck. Even Smith felt the urge to look closer.

The doctor checked his notes. 'The object used for strangulation was something quite thin and obviously strong. Not a rope, too thick. A length of string would be thin enough, but of course, that's too weak. See how the wound is deep, a quarter of an inch, in fact. I thought perhaps something more commercial, like wire, for example.'

Jeffries reached into his pocket and retrieved a magnifying glass with a polished wooden handle. 'Do you mind if I have a closer look?'

The doctor gestured for him to proceed, and Jeffries held his glass closer to Harry Westlake's neck, peering into the magnified image. 'Tweezers, please,' he said, holding out his free hand.

Doctor Price knew Jeffries liked to get involved and had anticipated this request. He promptly passed him a pair of tweezers.

Jeffries carefully picked at the neck wound with the instrument. Smiling, he extracted something almost invisible. 'Smith, I expect the doctor has some envelopes on his desk. Would you be so kind as to fetch one, please?'

Smith hadn't noticed a desk when he'd entered the room, but when he turned, he saw a small mahogany desk in the corner of the theatre. He strode over, found a small envelope, and returned to the examination table.

Jeffries held out the object from the dead man's neck for Smith to examine. Smith peered at it, squinting. 'Looks like thread, sir. From Westlake's shirt, perhaps?

'I'm not sure. It looks too stiff for that. Cotton thread is thinner than this. This is rather thicker than that. Seems very strong. And despite the bloodstain, note it's a cream colour. Westlake's shirt was white. Let's keep it for now. It might come in useful later.'

Smith opened the envelope, and Jeffries dropped the tiny length of thread inside. 'Seal that up, Smith. Write on the envelope the date and place it was found. As it's our first bit of evidence, you could also add 001.'

Constable Smith did as instructed and put the envelope in his inside pocket. He turned to the doctor. 'Did you carry out the post-mortem on the young woman who died in the tram crash, Doctor Price? A woman by the name of Rose James.'

The doctor covered Harry Westlake's body with the white cover, smoothed the sheet, and looked across at Smith. 'I didn't do it myself, but one of my colleagues did. The report said she died of blood loss due to a severed artery. She would have died within a few minutes of receiving the injury.'

'So no one would have been able to help her at the scene?' asked Smith.

The doctor shook his head. 'I'm afraid not. An injury like that causes death no matter what anyone does.'

Smith nodded. 'Thank you.'

Doctor Price clapped his hands and both men jumped. The sound echoed around the theatre. 'Well, if that is all, gentlemen? I have work to do. People don't stop being dead just because you're here.'

Jeffries shook the doctor's hand. 'Thank you, Doctor. Most useful.' Constable Smith reached over the table and shook the doctor's hand, his earlier feeling of discomfort now gone. 'Yes, thank you, Doctor.'

Once they were outside the morgue, Smith prompted Jeffries. 'What did you make of that piece of thread that you found in Mr Westlake's neck, sir?'

Jeffries smiled. 'Well, we suspected Mr Westlake was strangled, and Doctor Price has confirmed that. It was interesting that he was strangled by something so thin. And that thread. I wonder where it was from? In itself, too thin and breakable to have strangled him. Odd though, finding it in the wound on his neck. We shall have to see, Smith. The thread might mean something, or it might be a red herring.'

'I think we should have another look in Westlake's darkroom, see if there's anything connected to this thread of yours.'

'I think you're right, Smith. Why don't you do that? Pop in tomorrow and have a good look around. See what you can unearth.'

'Yes sir. Where are we going now?'

'Let's go and have a word with the tram driver. You can tell me all about your eventful evening.'

'Eventful?'

'Well, something must have happened. You've been rubbing that elbow of yours all day.'

26

The tram driver and a limping man

The day had turned windy, and a light drizzle soaked their coats as the two detectives left the morgue and made their way to the hospital. They had sent a message the day before to tell the ward doctor to expect them - Jeffries was keen to speak to the tram driver. As it was only a short distance from the morgue, Jeffries had decided they would walk. He regretted that decision now as they plodded through the miserable rain and wind, heads down and hands thrust deep in their pockets.

Jeffries kept up the pace. 'I don't like the way that our Miss Grey keeps cropping up. She follows us like a shadow. Do you think she has something to do with our case, or is it just coincidence, Smith?'

Smith walked quickly to keep up with his colleague. 'Well, she wasn't actually on the tram, and she was on her usual route to work, so she could just have been in the wrong place at the wrong time. Mrs Westlake described the young woman who visited her shop as having a bruise on her head, which we're sure was Miss Grey. And we have the discarded umbrella with her initials on the handle. She must have fled the darkroom when we burst in. The figure was the same height, same build. It's difficult to be absolutely sure, though. One thing's certain; she can't have been responsible for Westlake's death. She's just not strong enough.'

'I think you're right. She was probably in the wrong place at the wrong time. Again.' The rain eased as the sun tried to come out between the grey clouds. The two men reached the hospital and stepped inside the porch.

Smith took off his hat and shook off the rain. 'I think she was in the shop for completely innocent reasons, looked in the darkroom, saw the body and became hysterical. She dropped her umbrella and simply ran away when we

181

entered the room. She must have been worried sick we'd nail her for Harry's murder. Must have panicked.'

'Yes, I think you're right. Well, we've lost one of our tram crash witnesses now that Westlake's dead. He must have seen more than he told us, being there with his camera. Let's hope the driver can shed more light on what happened. We're running out of time, and I suspect the inspector will tell us to drop the tram cases and focus on the photographer's murder.' Jeffries reached for the door handle. 'Let's see what the driver has to say for himself. Hopefully, he's recovered sufficiently to talk to us.'

The detective sergeant opened the door for his colleague, the sharp smell of disinfectant hitting them as they both stepped into the gloomy entrance. Smith wrinkled his nose. 'It's not as bad as the morgue, I suppose.'

The two men approached the reception counter where a young, stern-looking nurse was working on some papers. She didn't respond at first, but then peered over her glasses at them.

Her hair was pinned up in a bun with a little hat perched on top at a slight angle. 'I'm sorry, gentlemen, but visiting hours are not for another three hours. No exceptions.'

She looked back down at the documents she was busy signing. The detective sergeant took out his police identification card and held it up for the nurse to read. 'Doctor Hughes is expecting us. We're here on police business which I think you'll agree is the exception to the visiting hours' rule.'

Reluctantly, the nurse put her pen down and looked up, holding her glasses slightly forward to read the detective sergeant's card. 'I see. You should have said you were the police. Wait here.' She left her seat and walked through a door behind her, leaving the two policemen to wait in the reception area.

Jeffries turned to Smith, pointing to his elbow. 'So what happened last night?'

'Ah, last night. Yes.'

When Smith had finished telling the story of the attack, Jeffries gave a low whistle. 'Some quick thinking saved you from getting more than a sore elbow there, Smith. And they warned you off, you say? We need to find these men and question them.'

Smith made a note in his notebook. 'Hopefully someone at The White Hart will know who they are. We could ask the barman, I suppose.'

The nurse returned to her post, pointed to the hallway. 'Go through that door and take the second corridor on the left. The ward is at the end, the last door on the left. Doctor Hughes is on the Hummingbird Ward.'

The two men nodded their thanks and walked across the reception area. Smith opened the door for his colleague, and they followed the nurse's directions. As they approached the ward, the door swung open with a crash, and a burly man in a dark suit and flat cap strode towards them. Dragging his leg slightly, the scowling man shoved past the officers and hurried to the main entrance. Jeffries and Smith watched the man hobble down the corridor.

Smith pointed to the man as he swung around the corner. 'That's one of the men who attacked me the other night, I'm sure of it.'

As the two men considered the implications, a doctor appeared at the same door, hair dishevelled and glasses askew. 'Damn him! Where has that scoundrel gone?'

Jeffries looked at the doctor's name badge. 'Doctor Hughes? Is there something wrong? We're the police; we have an appointment to speak with your patient, the tram driver. Who was that man we just saw?'

Doctor Hughes straightened his stethoscope around his neck. He had a tired look about him, and his creased white coat was stained with something that Jeffries didn't want to think about. The doctor pointed in the direction of the fleeing man. 'That man was pestering one of our patients. Your Mr Hoskins, as a matter of fact. He was upsetting the poor man, and I had to shove him out of the door. I don't know who he was, but he wasn't happy, as you undoubtedly noticed.'

Jeffries tilted his head to the doctor. 'Smith, go with the doctor and interview the driver. He knows you from the crash scene. I'm going to follow that rogue, see where he goes and find out why he wanted to talk to Mr Hoskins.'

'Be careful, sir. The man's a nasty piece of work.'

Jeffries hurried along the corridor, the man long gone, but there was only one way he could have fled. The doctor led Smith to the ward. 'This way, officer.'

Patients occupied all the beds, some asleep, some sat propped up reading books and newspapers, others staring into space. Nurses scurried about from bed to bed. Some carried clipboards, others pushed trolleys of medicines, and one or two carried discreetly-covered bedpans.

Smith followed Doctor Hughes to the end of the ward, where a bed was closed off by a curtain. The doctor pulled the fabric to one side and introduced Smith to Mr Hoskins, who was sitting up in the bed, his mouth cutting a deep frown. A discarded newspaper lay on the floor.

Smith walked to the side of the bed, retrieved the newspaper, and set it on the bedside cabinet. 'Hello, again, Mr Hoskins. Do you remember me from the crash? I was in uniform that day.'

'I'll leave you to talk, Constable.' Doctor Hughes hurried to his next patient.

Mr Hoskins watched the doctor leave and then nodded at Smith. 'Ah, yes, I remember you now. What happened to the uniform?'

'It's a long story,' said Smith as he took off his coat and sat in the only chair available. As he sat, crossing his legs, he realised the chair was too low to have a proper conversation, so he stood again and took out his notebook. Quickly flicking through the pages, he said, 'I just wanted to go over your story again to clarify things for our investigation.'

'Ah, I thought... never mind. Please go ahead and ask your questions.'

Mr Hoskins kept opening and closing his spectacles and tapping his finger on the lens. I'll have to keep a close eye on the patient as I ask my questions, Smith thought.

'From our conversation the other day, you said you'd been driving the trams for a number of years without incident.'

'Yes, ten years and proud of my time driving for the company. I started on the horse carriages and moved to the trams when they became more popular.' He smiled, having stopped fidgeting with his glasses.

'And you like the work?'

A quick tap on the lens. 'Yes, very much so.'

'On the day in question, you said the tram brakes were jammed somehow, as if there was a blockage. Do you remember more about that day?'

Smith watched him carefully. Mr Hoskins' eyes flicked to the right. Barely there, just a momentary flick, but Smith spotted it.

'The damn trams are old and unreliable. They are always breaking down, they almost jump off the rails most days. Bad maintenance by the engineering company is my best guess.' He had started fiddling with his glasses again, threatening to break them.

'I see, Mr Hoskins. We, that is, my colleague and I, heard the trams were well-maintained and had years of life left in them. Is it possible the braking mechanism had been tampered with? Perhaps preventing you from holding the tram on the hill?'

Mr Hoskins squeezed his spectacles so tightly that Smith was sure they would snap in two. 'Nonsense!' Mr Hoskins said, his voice faltering. 'I told you. The trams are old and badly maintained. Dangerous things. I am getting tired now, and I'd like to rest. Perhaps that's all the questions you have, officer?'

Smith frowned. Something was badly wrong here. Mr Hoskins was spooked.

He decided to leave things as they were for the time being. He wasn't going to get anything coherent with Mr Hoskins in this state. That chap from the corridor must've really riled him. Hopefully Jeffries will catch him. 'Of course, Mr Hoskins. I don't have any more questions for now. I'll leave you in peace.' Smith put his pencil and notebook in his pocket. He pulled on his coat, put his hat back on and made to leave, then stopped a moment. 'One more thing, Mr Hoskins. You had a visitor just before I arrived. A big man who walked with a limp and wore a scruffy suit and flat cap. Left in an awful hurry. He seemed angry. Anything you want to tell me about him? Was he troubling you?'

Mr Hoskins was already lying on his side, facing away from the constable. 'I don't know what you mean. I haven't had any visitors since I got here.'

Smith walked to the other side of the bed, reached into his pocket, and put his calling card on the man's pillow. 'If you think of anything else, please contact me at the station. We can have a quiet chat whenever you're ready. Good day to you, Mr Hoskins.'

With that, Smith left the driver to rest and made his way to the main entrance, wondering how Jeffries was getting on with his pursuit of the limping rogue who had obviously frightened Mr Hoskins out of his wits. Mr Hoskins had clearly changed his story. The way the man fiddled with his glasses was a sure giveaway that he wasn't telling the whole truth. And the flick of his eyes to the right. 'The eyes don't lie,' muttered Smith to himself as he walked past the nurse in reception. She frowned and shook her head as he passed by.

27

A chase and a plain envelope

Jeffries hurried along the hospital corridor, through the reception area, searching for the fleeing man. Porters pushed trolleys and stretchers, and doctors and nurses rushed in all directions. Jeffries couldn't spot the man anywhere. 'Damn, where the hell are you?' he muttered.

Through the white coats and blue nurse uniforms, he glimpsed a cloth cap. 'There you are, you scoundrel,' Jeffries said with glee, careful not to be noticed by his quarry. He wanted to see where the man went. Perhaps to a breakthrough in the case.

Jeffries followed the man out into the main street, keeping his distance for stealth.

After a hundred yards, the road split into two, Southernhay West to the left and Southernhay East to the right, with the gated gardens in between. The man took the western side and continued at a brisk pace, not slowed by his limp. The street was quiet, with only a few pedestrians meandering about. Jeffries tried to keep them between him and his man, aware he could lose him. Pulling his hat further down over his forehead, Jeffries strolled, as a gentleman out for an afternoon walk in the fresh air, the sun now edging out of the grey clouds as the rain eased.

The limping man slowed as he reached the junction with Cathedral Close and looked about him, getting his bearings. Jeffries quickly crouched down as if tying his shoe. He risked a quick glance and saw the man was moving towards the cathedral area. Jeffries stood and continued the chase.

They passed Deller's Café and headed for the row of shops on Cathedral Yard. The cream-coloured stone of the medieval buildings shone in the late afternoon sun. Jeffries was momentarily distracted and nearly missed the man ducking into the public house below the Royal Clarence Hotel.

Jeffries followed, pushing open the door to the bar and entering the dark interior. His eyes took a moment to adjust after the sunshine outside. The drinking house was busy for daytime on a Monday, and Jeffries easily melted into the crowd, scanning the room for his man.

The man slipped through the crowd with ease. This limp was something he had lived with for a long time, and had learned how to move swiftly despite his impairment.

Jeffries strolled up to the bar and raised his hand to grab the landlord's attention, who was chatting to the barmaid as she wiped a glass. The landlord nudged the woman in Jeffries' direction. She put the clean glass on the shelf, flipped the cloth over her shoulder, and approached the waiting detective sergeant. 'What would you like, sir? We have a new beer on tap today, strong and tasty.'

Jeffries looked at the beers on offer and pointed. 'Just half a pint of the Well Park beer, please.'

While the barmaid poured his drink, Jeffries surveyed the room, his eyes landing on his man seated at a small table in the corner of the room, deep in conversation with a gentleman dressed in a smart suit, a newspaper discarded to one side, his glass nearly empty. The two men leaned in close as they talked.

Jeffries paid for his beer and nodded a thank you to the barmaid, keeping a close eye on the two men across the room. As he watched, the limping man peered around, then said something to the smart man who reached down to a leather suitcase. With a practised turn of a key, he opened the case, reached in and took out an envelope. Taking another sip of his beer, Jeffries watched over the rim of his glass as the man passed the envelope to the limping man who, with another scan around the room, quickly opened it, took out a handful of pound notes, and fanned through them. He nodded, slipped the notes back and vanished the envelope into his coat pocket. The transaction had taken a few swift seconds.

Jeffries continued to watch from his position at the bar as the limping man stood, nodded to his companion, hobbled to the front door in his familiar way and stepped out into the street. Jeffries decided to stay with the well-dressed man, the financier. The man stood, picked up his newspaper and case, slung his coat over his arm and walked to the bar, raising his free arm to get the attention of the barmaid.

The barmaid smiled. 'What can I get you, Mr Shute, sir?'

Jeffries' ears pricked up. So this is the infamous Mr Shute, he thought.

'Hello, my dear. A whisky, please. The best you have. No ice or water, thank you.'

Shute certainly looked like the successful businessman that his reputation rumoured. There was something cavalier about the man, the way he tossed his newspaper onto the bar and straightened the lapels of his jacket. Jeffries considered what he knew about Shute. The card Rose handed to Carrie. The mysterious scribbled note and the mention of a hundred pounds. What Rose said to Carrie about the crash. The fact that Shute apparently helped Mr Brody with his financial troubles. Was it blackmail? Odd that Shute would help Brody out, especially as he'd foolishly lost the money playing cards. And Smith's discovery that Shute's company was diversifying into electrical services and products. Something nagged at Jeffries - that tingling feeling again. He rubbed the back of his neck.

Jeffries knew all about men like Shute, the kind that felt above the law because they had money and power. Sadly, some officers fell under the spell of men like Shute and let them get away with misdemeanours. Not Jeffries.

The barmaid reached up to the shelf for a glass and poured a generous amount of whisky. More than the

189

standard measure. The barmaid caught Jeffries' eye in the mirror behind the bar and winked. Jeffries looked away, his face growing hot. He turned to Mr Shute, who had pushed his newspaper to one side, both tram crashes dominating the front page. The bridge crash took up most of the page, with Harry Westlake's photographs taking pride of place. Jeffries cleared his throat and pointed to the headline. 'Terrible business, these tram crashes.'

Mr Shute sipped his drink, picked up his newspaper and turned to Jeffries. 'Yes, well, it was bound to happen sooner or later. Those old trams are death traps. The drivers struggle to manage the horses. The carriages are made of heavy timber. They are slow and, frankly, unreliable.'

Jeffries nodded. 'I never use them myself, but they do indeed seem to be slow and dangerous. It must be some weight for those horses to pull. What do you think caused the accident on the bridge? The second one seems like a simple collision. A delivery lorry lost control, apparently.'

Mr Shute slipped his newspaper under his arm and drained the rest of his drink. 'I should think it was either the fault of the driver or a mechanics failure. These trams are years old. What other explanation could there be?'

'Sabotage, perhaps? Maybe someone else wasn't keen on them and decided to do something drastic.'

'Bah! What nonsense. Mechanical failure, I'd wager. Pure and simple. Now I must be on my way. Good day to you, Mr...?' Mr Shute offered his hand.

Jeffries took Shute's hand and noted the strong grip. They considered each other for the briefest of moments. 'Detective Sergeant Jeffries. Good day to you, Mr Shute.' Jeffries drained his drink and left, the tingling still there on his neck.

28

A night in by the fire

After an uneventful Monday in the office (William was at court all day, so we couldn't even catch up after our adventure at Shute's house or discuss the ramifications of the documents John had taken from Shute's office), Father had suggested supper by the fire. He didn't need to ask twice. A storm was raging outside, the wind rattling the windows. A cosy night by the fire was just the ticket.

Over supper of a delicious meat pie and potatoes, we laughed and joked over my adventure in the steam car and the race through the lanes with my friends at the weekend. Father was alarmed at first, especially the part about me and John sneaking into Mr Shute's office, but when I told him the full story, I think he was a little jealous. He certainly smiled a lot, regaling his own stories of derring-do from his younger days.

Now, in the sitting room, our bellies full and with a glass of something in our hands, him with his favourite brandy, me with my sparkling wine, a rare treat indeed, we sit comfortably, listening to the storm, happy to read and talk a little. Father occupies his usual chair by the fire, now roaring away with fresh coal, and I've taken the sofa by the window.

Father looks up from his book. 'I received a letter today. Bad news, I'm afraid.'

I slip a bookmark into my book, close it and place it on my lap. 'Oh? What sort of bad news?'

Father retrieves an envelope from his pocket and holds it up as if presenting evidence. 'It's a letter from a solicitor. It concerns my brother.'

'Uncle James? Doesn't he own all those mills in the north? I seem to remember he made his fortune in the wool trade?'

191

'Yes. I think you only ever met him once, one Christmas. Anyway, according to his solicitor, he had a terrible accident in the mill. I'm not sure of the exact details, but he died from his injuries later in hospital.'

'Oh, I'm so sorry, Father. You must be devastated. Why didn't you say something earlier?'

Father takes a sip from his drink and slips the envelope back into his pocket. 'Well, we were having such a lovely evening. I didn't want to spoil things. He and I weren't close. I hadn't seen him in years. He took quite a shine to you, I seem to remember.'

I laugh, despite the sadness of the evening. 'Yes, I remember now. He was a fan of crime stories. I told him about Sherlock Holmes and introduced him to the weekly series in The Strand. I seem to recall he was later infatuated with the stories. I made a new fan of my friend Sherlock!'

'Indeed you did, Carrie.' He pauses. 'That reminds me. What do you plan to do next with your little adventure? Surely those two police officers have things in hand, and they don't need you getting in their way.'

I take a sip of my wine before replying. 'They are stuck in their ways, though Jeffries seems to have some bright ideas. I get the impression he's trying to prove himself to his superiors. His colleague, Constable Smith, the chap you know, he's a new recruit, so he's keen to shine as well. I like to think that William and John and I are helping in some small way. I was surprised the police didn't seem interested in Rose's card, so we decided to take matters into our own hands.'

My father settles his glass on the side table and raises one eyebrow, 'Perhaps you should lay things out for the two police officers. Tell them everything you know, as well as your theories. The people responsible for causing the crash and killing the photographer need to be caught and locked up. The sooner, the better. So, if you can help, you should tell them everything as soon as possible.'

'You're right, as usual. I'll go and see them as soon as I can.' I finish my drink and put the empty glass on the little table in front of me. 'I'll talk to William and John. Perhaps we can go to the police together. Hopefully, they will use the information to find the culprits before anyone else gets hurt.'

We sit in silence for a comfortable few minutes. My mother and father had known one another since school and were inseparable, marrying on my mother's twenty-first birthday. They had tried to have children from the start, but it took a couple of years until I came along. I often wonder how my father really feels, just the two of us. He doesn't show anything but love and support for me and has always encouraged me to be independent and happy in whatever I do.

It's this independent thinking that has turned me against the traditional path of finding a husband and having a family. Family life is the popular way to live, but I enjoy the freedom and will do so for a few years yet!

'Are you enjoying your new job in the office, Carrie?'

I set my book on the little table. 'Very much so. I'm grateful that you spoke to Mr Edwards. I don't think he would have considered me if you weren't friends with him.'

'Well, I merely gave him your name. You convinced him to employ you, so he must think highly of you.'

'He doesn't show it.'

'Mr Edwards is just nervous about employing a woman. You know how unusual it is for women to have a job like that. Give him time and he'll come around to the idea.' Father smiles. 'Mind you, you'll have to get some work done and spend less time chasing criminals. I take it he doesn't know about your involvement?'

'No, he doesn't.'

'Well, I suggest you speak with your friends and arrange to see the police soon. Then concentrate on your job at the solicitors. Perhaps you could become England's first female solicitor!'

'I'm not sure about that!' I glance up at the small clock on the mantlepiece. 'I think I will retire to bed now. It's late, and I have to be up early for work.' I stand, stretch and walk to the door.

Father stands, walks across to the oil lamp on the wall to extinguish it, the wall above dark from the fumes.

'Would you consider changing our lights to the new electric ones, Father?'

'Pah! Far too expensive. These work fine enough.'

'But what if the new electric system was made available to everyone, the cost might come down. Would you consider it then?' I smile, recalling the electric drawings John had taken.

'Whatever makes you think the electric will be made available to everyone, Carrie?'

'Well, you never know, Father.'

29

A late night and the Park Man

Smith gripped his walking cane tightly and, head down, shielded his face with the brim of his hat from The White Hart on the other side of the road. It was dark, but Smith wasn't taking any chances. He couldn't see anyone at the front door of the pub, but didn't want a repeat of his encounter the other night, and he needed to retrace Henry Brody's steps from The White Hart on the evening before the crash. Something wasn't adding up and Smith was keen to find out where Henry had got to during those missing hours. Once he was past the pub, he lifted his head and upped his pace.

He enjoyed a brisk walk, his cane swinging by his side, clicking on the path in time with his stride. He was aware mostly upper-class gentlemen walked with a cane these days, as was the fashion, and Smith had ambition. Promotion first, and then who knows? He wasn't planning on working on the streets for the rest of his career. He'd already noticed that some of the other officers, having spent years patrolling the grim and dangerous streets, had aged before their time. Wrinkles apparent from the pressure they had faced. The constant worry of what was around the next corner.

After many hints, his wife bought him the fine cane for his birthday, the handle a smooth ivory, the cane itself the best wood she could afford. The finest Ash no less. He didn't need it, but he was sure it improved his posture. Made him walk with purpose. A cane changed a man. Smith also knew that the heavy handle made a decent weapon should he be accosted in the street again. He wished he'd had it with him the other night. He might have avoided a sore elbow.

Brody's alibi was weak, with some hours unaccounted for, and so Smith set out to discover where he had got to that evening after he'd been at dinner with his friends. Smith headed east, taking the route Brody had most likely taken that night, assuming he'd headed home. Smith didn't know this for certain, but he had a feeling he'd made the right decision. It must be that police instinct Jeffries was always talking about.

This area of the town wasn't one that Smith liked to visit, especially at night. Glancing into dark and narrow alleys as he made his way, the streets quiet, Smith wondered what state Brody was in if he walked this same path that night. Probably a little worse for wear, Smith thought. Would Brody have been nervous, walking this dark road with menacing shadows and strange sounds? Smith couldn't help recalling the two men emerging from the shadows on his last evening walk.

As Smith reached a junction and stopped, trying to remember the route to Brody's house, a scuffle sounded from behind him. He spun around, his cane raised as he scanned the dark street. A woman appeared from one of the alleyways he'd passed earlier. A flickering gaslamp revealed she had a heavily made-up face and wore a flowing black skirt and a grey coat. The woman considered Smith with a cocked head and started walking towards him, her hips swaying as she tucked her hair behind one ear, smiling at Smith as he stood, transfixed. The woman halted before him.

'Looking for someone, sir? Perhaps some female company?'

Smith sighed, smiling despite his embarrassment at being accosted by a lady late at night. Indeed, a lady of the night. 'No, thank you, miss.' He pulled out his police identification and held it under the weak streetlight for her examination. 'Best be on your way, miss. Be careful, you never know who's walking these streets at night.'

The woman squinted at the card. She couldn't read the words but recognised the symbol from earlier visits to the police station when she'd been brought in by less friendly policemen. Coppers, they called them. Shame, this one looks cute, she thought. With a toss of her head, she turned on her heel and walked back to the alleyway, disappearing into the shadows.

Smith shoved the card back into his pocket and resumed his walk, deciding on the street to his right, thinking it likely Brody had taken a direct route. Perhaps he met the same woman. 'Damn,' he muttered under his breath. Jeffries would have something to say to him if he'd missed an important witness. It was too dangerous to go back and look for her. She might have someone looking after her who wouldn't appreciate Smith seeking her out. Asking questions.

Smith reached the bridge over the dark and swirling river, the quickest way to cross. The little ferries at the quay being the only nearby alternatives, but they didn't operate late at night. The bridge looked different in the dark, the lamps struggling to hold the darkness at bay. The trams didn't use the bridge at night, and indeed, none had crossed the river since the day of the crash. Smith recalled the scene where the tram had laid on its side on that fateful day.

To his right, in the doorway of the last house before the bridge, a man sat huddled under a thick coat that had seen better days, his face barely visible. A threadbare blanket lay in front of the man, held down by a few possessions. A battered tobacco tin containing a single coin and a button sat in one corner. An enamel cup and a small book, wrapped in string, held the other corners.

Smith reached into his pocket, took out a couple of coins, and dropped them into the man's tin with a clang. 'Thank you, sir,' the man gruffed. Smith nodded, more to himself than to the man. Smith's father once told him that everyone is just one or two steps from being homeless and destitute. 'Lose your job, fall ill, lose your home, and that's it, you're on the street. Simple as that.' It had stuck with

Smith over the years and he always gave something to those unfortunate enough to lose everything.

Smith turned in the direction of the bridge and walked a few footsteps before freezing. He realised he might have almost disregarded an important witness to Brody's movements that night. He walked back to the man in the doorway.

'Excuse me, sir,' Smith said, crouching in front of the man.

'What do you want? Want your money back, do you?'

'No, nothing like that. I hoped you might be able to help me, actually.' Smith dropped another coin into the tin.

'I'm looking for someone who may have passed by the other evening. Do you sit here most nights?' The man didn't look too likely to open up and talk. Smith needed a different approach. 'My name's Frank, by the way.'

The man nodded. 'My name's Brian, but most people call me the Park Man because I spend my days reading in the park. Books, newspapers. Anything to pass the time.'

'Nice to meet you, Brian. So, you were likely here on Sunday night?'

'Yes, I was here Sunday. I remember the church service, so yes, definitely here Sunday. I'm here most nights, but if it's too cold, I'll usually find somewhere warmer. Near the river can get chilly. Damp, too.' He pulled his coat tighter around his body, shrugging lower into the collar. He considered Smith, 'Get to the point, would you? I haven't all night.'

'Sorry, yes. Of course. I'm trying to find out if a gentleman walked by here late on Sunday night. Well-dressed, quite tall. He might have been drinking and wouldn't have put any money in your tin.'

'A lot of people ignore me and don't put money in my tin.' The man rubbed his chin. 'I assume you mean the posh bloke. Mr Brody, weren't it? Lost a lot of money lately. He the man you're looking for?'

'How on earth did you know his name and that he'd lost money?'

'He told me. When I dragged him off the ledge by the bridge.'

Seeing Smith's quizzical stare in the weak light, he continued. 'He walked right by me, and you're right, didn't drop a coin in the tin. Not at first anyway. As I said before, that's not unusual. What was unusual was although the gentleman was alone, he was talking to someone. Muttering away, he was. I realised he was talking to himself. Was having quite the conversation, actually.' The man snickered. 'I couldn't pick out any words, but he sounded desperate, angry even. I watched him walk onto the bridge.'

Brian went on to describe how he'd watched the man reach the bridge, where he stood motionless for several minutes, looking over the railings. Brian had nowhere else to go and certainly nothing better to do, so he'd watched the man to see what he did next.

Brian recalled that, to his surprise, the man looked about before climbing over the railings, stepping up onto the ledge on the other side. He had leaned forward, his grip on the railings the only thing preventing him from falling.

'I got close, sneaked up, like' Brian said. 'I reached out, grabbed the man's arm, and held on to him. He was strong, but I managed to hold him steady.'

'What happened next?'

'He went all slack. Like he'd changed his mind. I suppose I'd grabbed him at just the right moment. He sort of nodded to himself, clambered back over the railings, and stepped back onto the road.'

'You said he told you about the money he'd lost?'

'Well, we had a good old chat after that. I brought him back to my doorway here, gave him a shot of brandy and kept him warm while he let it all out. Told me everything. Told me his name was Henry. Henry Brody. He'd lost a lot of money through gambling. Daft man chased his losses. Lost the lot, he said.'

Brian went on to recall how Brody had revealed he'd lost his savings, and he and his wife were now having to sell everything to keep food on the table. He told Smith how Brody had eventually felt better after realising that ending it all was not the answer. After a couple of hours, Henry had looked better, having sobered up, despite the sips of brandy, and had decided he should be getting home. He said his wife would be worried about him.

Brian laughed at the memory. 'He even dropped a half-crown in my tin!' Bought some warm clothes with that, I did.'

Smith stood. 'One last thing, Brian. What time do you think he left you to go home?'

'It was twenty minutes past ten.'

Smith frowned. 'How can you be so sure of the time?'

Brian looked over Smith's shoulder and nodded at the church opposite. Smith looked across the street to the big clock on the steeple. There it was: Brody had an alibi.

'Thank you for telling me this. It's been really important. I'll be on my way now. Take care of yourself, Brian.' He dropped a couple more coins into the tin.

'You too, sir. You too.'

Smith strolled off in the direction of his own home, glancing back to the doorway where Brian huddled deeper into his warm coat, his hat pulled down over his ears.

30

A photography studio and a secret

Tuesday morning, there was still much to unravel and decipher. Jeffries and Smith were at their desks, trying to concentrate while workmen gave the station a fresh coat of paint. It was the inspector's idea to make the station a fresh and more productive workplace. The strong stench of paint and turps gave Jeffries a headache.

The two men spent an hour comparing notes. Jeffries summarised his pursuit of the limping man to the pub and the meeting with Mr Shute, and Smith recalled his meeting with the tram driver, whose nervousness and reluctance to talk to Smith had surprised both of them. Jeffries listened with interest as Smith told him about his conversation with Brian, the park man, and laughed out loud when Smith mentioned the reason Brian knew the time Brody passed by, despite not having a timepiece of his own.

'Well, that rather lets our Mr Brody off the hook, doesn't it Smith? Although I'm sorry Mr Brody contemplated jumping into the river. I do hope he sorts out his money problems. I didn't much like the man, but no one should feel the need to end their life.'

'Ah, I almost forgot,' Smith pulled out a rumpled envelope from his pocket. 'I had another look in Westlake's darkroom as you asked and found this under a cabinet. Lucky I saw it, just the end was poking out.' He reached in and gingerly pulled out what looked like a length of white string. He laid it on the desk and the two men leaned over to peer at it. Jeffries nudged it with his pencil, reaching into his pocket for his magnifying glass which he then held over the strange object.

'Well, I never. This is an interesting find, Smith.' He passed the glass to Smith who looked closely at the item in question.

'What do you see, Smith?'

'I can just make out a wire of some kind at one end. Two strands, twisted together. To make it stronger, perhaps?' He peered closer. 'It's covered with a cream thread that looks remarkably like the piece you found on Westlake's neck. It's a bit grubby. Could be dried blood. The wire is unusual, never seen anything like it before. What do you think it's used for, sir?'

'I have no idea. But it's covered in the same thread, as you say. Strong enough to choke a man? I do think it could be, Smith.'

Smith carefully picked up the wire and dropped it into the envelope. He removed the cap from his pen and wrote a number on the front. 'We need a secure place to keep any evidence we gather, sir.'

Jeffries opened his desk drawer. 'Drop it in here for now, Smith.' Smith walked around to Jeffries' side of the desk and placed the envelope in the drawer, alongside other envelopes and sheets of paper. He glanced at the framed photograph of the child on Jeffries' desk. 'Forgive me for asking, but I noticed the photograph earlier and I wondered who it was. You've not mentioned children so I assumed it was a nephew perhaps?'

Jeffries picked up the framed photograph, wiped the glass with the back of his hand and considered the image before him, his own face reflected in the glass. He placed it back on the desk, straightened it just so and looked up at Smith. 'It's my son, Smith. He died very young. Tuberculosis.'

'I'm so sorry, sir. I didn't realise. I've put my foot in it haven't I?'

'No, it's fine. It was a few years ago now. Still miss him, mind.' Jeffries smiled. 'He would have made a fine young man, that's for sure.'

Smith was about to suggest they leave the building in search of fresh air to talk about recent events, away from the stench of the paint, when the inspector bellowed from his room, 'Jeffries! Smith! In my office, please.'

Surprised that the inspector was in his office so early, the two men glanced at each other, both rolling their eyes at the same time. Smith pocketed his notebook and headed for the inspector's office. 'Come on, sir. Let's see what's up.'

Jeffries reluctantly shuffled his papers into a neat pile and dropped a paperweight on top. Picking up his notebook and pencil, he followed, an ominous ache in his stomach, suspecting he wasn't about to receive a pat on the back. The inspector will probably be wearing a smile as he points out the error of my ways, thought Jeffries as he followed Smith into the warm and stuffy office.

Once inside, the inspector said, 'Shut the door, Jeffries.'

The workmen's noise instantly reduced with the door closed. The two officers stood in front of the inspector's desk, waiting in silence. The inspector finished signing a document with a flourish and put his fountain pen to one side. Nice pen, thought Jeffries as he fiddled with his stub of a pencil, resisting the urge to prise out a particularly annoying lump of dirt from under his fingernail with the sharpened end.

The inspector drummed his fingers on the desk, considering his next words carefully. 'Well, gentlemen, I hope you two have made progress on these cases. Are you any closer to finding out what happened to the tram? Two crashes now, I hear. And what of our photographer friend? Do you have a suspect yet, gentlemen?'

The inspector had apparently forgotten the earlier deadline he had set to solve the case. Jeffries decided not to remind him of it. They certainly needed all the time they could muster. Jeffries leafed through his notebook, gathering his thoughts before looking up. 'We thought we had some evidence of foul play when we visited the tram workshop, but that turned out to be a false lead. We've spoken to a number of witnesses, including Mrs Brody as you suggested, and her husband of course.' Jeffries nodded to Smith. 'Constable Smith checked Mr Brody's alibi last night. His whereabouts for the night before the crash are accounted for.'

The inspector's head snapped up, his mouth open.

Before he could say anything, Jeffries interjected. 'Don't worry, sir. We were very discreet. Neither Mr nor Mrs Brody know that we were checking their stories.'

'Good. Go on, Jeffries.' said the inspector, relieved he wouldn't have to explain any of this to the chief inspector, him being friends of Mrs Brody.

Jeffries turned a page in his notebook, running a thumbnail along the top to straighten the paper. 'We spoke to the driver, as well as a woman who helped at the scene and we had a word with the photographer, Mr Westlake. We weren't happy with his account, and we wanted to speak to him again but, as you know, he was killed before we had a chance. You will remember that he was rather conveniently at the crash scene and ready with his camera. Someone must have instructed him to take the photographs as there's no other decent explanation for why he was there with a camera at the ready. When we spoke to him, he said he was taking photographs of the surrounding streets.' Jeffries turned to Smith. 'But we didn't believe him.'

Smith took his cue. 'We know it takes at least ten minutes to set up one of these camera contraptions. He must have had the camera set up on the bridge in readiness for the tram; he couldn't have simply moved it so quickly from where he says he was using it beforehand. His wife seemed nervous when we initially spoke to them both. She's hiding something, but we don't know what yet.'

Jeffries continued. 'Our focus is on the photographer and whoever gave him those instructions, especially as he turned up dead shortly after we interviewed him.'

The inspector picked up his pen and spun it in his hand, deep in thought. 'And a theory, Detective Sergeant. Do you have a theory? You seem to have no solid evidence.'

Jeffries considered revealing the length of wire Smith had found in the darkroom, and the matching piece of cotton thread he'd found on Westlake's neck, but decided against it. They still didn't know who the strangler was, and now would not be a good time to mention it. The inspector was clearly not in the mood for unsubstantiated ideas.

The inspector leaned forward in his chair; his arms stretched out as he tapped his fingers on his blotter. 'So, you have no evidence of the tram being tampered with. You have a dead witness, and no understanding of how that might be connected to the crash, if at all. He had taken photographs of the crash site, despite a camera taking some time to set up. Coincidence perhaps? Or was he told there would be a crash and later killed because he knew too much?'

Smith glanced at his notebook. 'We also found a wad of banknotes in Mr Westlake's shop, sir. More than a photographer would normally have in his possession. He was likely paid to be at the crash. Perhaps the idea was to send the photographs to the newspapers to be published thereby to establish how dangerous the trams are.'

The inspector shook his head. 'But why, Smith? Why take the trouble to damage these trams? It makes no sense.'

Jeffries cleared his throat. 'Motive, Means, Opportunity.'

'What on earth do you mean, Jeffries?'

Recalling his detective course, he replied, 'Sir, we need three things to find a suspect. They must have a motive—a reason to do the deed. They must have the means—the ability to do the deed. And finally, an opportunity—the suspect must have been in the area at the time the crime occurred.'

'And your point, Detective Sergeant?'

Jeffries counted off the items on his fingers. 'Mr Westlake had a motive—money. He was paid a substantial sum, hence the banknotes. He may have had the means as he was quite practical. Those camera contraptions and the darkroom take some skill to set up and use. And finally, opportunity. His studio is above the workshop where the trams are maintained and repaired. Trams are often left in the workshop overnight, and he would know that.'

Smith coughed, covering his mouth with his hand. 'If I may suggest something, sir?'

The inspector laced his fingers together. 'Go on, Smith.'

'I think we should take a look at Mr Westlake's studio. There must be a common thread there somewhere. The location is just too much of a coincidence. Plus, he was going to leave for his studio when he was murdered.'

The inspector lined up his pens and straightened his blotter. 'I agree. But make sure you take Mrs Westlake with you to open up. I don't want you breaking in.' He raised his eyebrows at Jeffries. 'We don't need a repeat of you kicking another door in. Let's hope that Mrs Westlake doesn't put in an expense claim for her husband's darkroom door, Jeffries.'

Jeffries reddened. 'Indeed, sir.'

***

Later at the photographer's shop, Smith was inspecting the portraits on the wall while Jeffries explained to Mrs Westlake that they needed her to accompany them to the studio. 'We're sorry about all this, but if I recall, Mrs Westlake, you told us Harry was planning to visit the studio the morning he was murdered, so there might be clues to be found.'

'Yes, he was due in the studio that morning, as I explained before, but I don't see what the studio has to do with Harry's death, Detective Sergeant. He was killed here in the shop, not at the studio.'

'We just need half an hour of your time, Mrs Westlake. It's just procedure. We need to check all possibilities to find out why your husband was killed.'

Mrs Westlake pulled on her coat and sighed, then ushered the two officers out onto the pavement, and turned to lock the door.

The three walked briskly down the hill, heading for the quayside. Jeffries removed his scarf. The day was warm, despite winter being around the corner.

The main quay area was busy as usual, with workers rushing here and there, carrying packages and pushing trolleys. Cranes lifted wooden crates onto waiting ships, and traders called out their wares to attract custom. As they approached the workshop, Smith looked up at the first-floor studio and noticed a large, arched window in the middle. A pair of smaller windows sat on either side. The studio must occupy the whole floor. Smith wondered how Harry had afforded the rent.

The studio was accessed by a narrow passageway next to the tram workshops. Jeffries glanced through the front doors as they walked past. Men were noisily cutting wood and shaping metal.

Jeffries had to shout above the din. 'Will you continue to rent the studio, Mrs Westlake?'

Mrs Westlake shook her head. 'I have no need of it now Harry's gone. He taught me how to take photographs, but I'm not very artistic and my heart's not in it anymore.'

They walked in single file. Mrs Westlake led the way until they reached the end of the passageway. Rotting vegetables, and other things Jeffries didn't want to consider, cluttered the gloomy walkway. Jeffries held his sleeve under his nose. The fruit and vegetable merchant clearly wasn't fussy about where he discarded produce past its best. A huge pile of wooden offcuts of all shapes and sizes leant against the wall, partly blocking their way. They halted at a metal stairway, the handrail rusty, the uprights broken and twisted. Mrs Westlake turned. 'Mind your footing; these steps can be slippery.'

At the top of the stairway was a window, its broken panes of glass replaced with wooden sheets. Next to this, a blue door, paint flaking, the hinges and padlock rusty with neglect. Mrs Westlake pulled an equally rusty key from her pocket and struggled with the padlock before it sprung open and dropped to the floor. Jeffries stooped to pick it up and passed it to Mrs Westlake, who placed it on the windowsill.

The two men followed Mrs Westlake into the studio. Light poured through the big windows, throwing a soft glow into the room. Both men could see how perfect this space was for photography. The high ceiling and white walls.

A door at the back of the studio led off to a kitchen. Jeffries peered inside and saw a basic sink, a small table, with two chairs, and a tiny range with a kettle on top. There was a cupboard on the wall, the door ajar, revealing cups and a tea caddy. A room with just enough room for two people to sit or make a tea or coffee.

They looked around while Mrs Westlake picked up letters from the doormat.

Jeffries held out his hand. 'Please don't touch anything, Mrs Westlake.'

Huffing, she strutted over to a desk in the corner of the room, pulled out a chair, the legs squeaking on the wooden floor. She sat, tossing the envelopes onto the desk.

The two men cast their eyes around the huge room. On the far wall, a large paper screen hung from a pulley system suspended from the roof beams. No doubt a photographer could quickly pull down different backdrops. A camera support was positioned in front of the scene, currently set to show a brown, mottled background. Jeffries assumed a number of different sheets could be displayed to suit the atmosphere the photographer was after. Flowers were set in vases on either side of the scene, their leaves drooping and petals strewn on the floor beneath.

The two men split up. Jeffries examined the camera equipment while Smith peered out of the front windows overlooking the quay below. There was something odd, but Smith couldn't put his finger on it. The largest of the windows reached from floor to ceiling, and the windows on either side, though smaller, let in as much light as the central one. The two windows on the right were partially covered with a blind that could be pulled up or down to control the light. The centre window was left fully exposed and had no blind that Smith could see. The single window on the left also had a blind, this one already pulled down. That's odd, thought Smith, as he walked across to the window on the left. 'The studio occupies the whole floor, doesn't it, Mrs Westlake?' he said over his shoulder.

Mrs Westlake didn't look up. 'Yes, we rent the whole floor.'

'Then why is there only one window on this side and two on the other?' Smith said, walking to the far wall and tapping it with his knuckles. The knocking sound echoed. 'This is a false wall. That's why there is a window missing. The other window must be behind this wall, in another room. Sir! Come and have a look at this.'

Jeffries strode across the floor, his footsteps carrying in the big room. Smith pointed to the front wall. 'See that there are two windows on the right side but only one window on this side? There's a missing window, and I believe it's behind this wall. Except there's no door.'

The two men walked along the false wall to a bookcase in the middle. They scrutinised the piece of furniture. Smith withdrew a book and slid it back into its place. Jeffries exclaimed. 'Look at that!' He pointed at a distinct groove in the floorboards, forming a perfect arc. 'This bookcase must swing out.' He grabbed the edge of the bookcase. It wouldn't budge. Smith was the taller of the two men, and he could easily reach the top of the wooden unit. He ran his hand along the top and stopped, fiddling with something that clicked. 'There's a lever of some kind. Try again, sir.'

Jeffries pulled again, and this time the bookcase easily slid in an arc, revealing an open doorway beyond, the door missing.

'Well, I never,' said Jeffries as he stepped through into the hidden room.

31

A hidden room, a bed and a notebook

Jeffries entered the hidden room followed by Smith, with Mrs Westlake close behind. Jeffries turned to look at the front wall. 'Ah, there is your missing window, Smith.'

His colleague smiled. 'I knew something looked out of place.' He turned to Mrs Westlake. 'Did you know about this room, Mrs Westlake?'

'Yes, I knew Harry had an extra space built.' She paused. 'It was for private photographic sessions.'

Although much narrower than the main studio, this room held similar paraphernalia: a plain white background sheet hung from the wall, and a camera mounted on a wooden tripod stood ready for the next session. Luxurious, deep crimson drapes hung over a four-poster bed with plump pillows and a matching bed cover. A small sofa sat in the corner of the room, facing the bed with velvet cushions at each end.

Jeffries touched the bed cover and scratched his chin. 'I don't understand the purpose of this. What are your thoughts, Smith?' He glanced at Smith. 'Why are you smiling like an idiot?'

Smith immediately stopped smiling. A hot flush spread up his neck as he cleared his throat. 'Well, sir. This is clearly for photography of a very private nature. Erotic, perhaps.'

Jeffries raised his eyebrows, his mouth slightly open. 'Ah, I see. Mrs Westlake, were you aware of the true purpose of this studio?'

Mrs Westlake stood at the foot of the bed, smoothing the cover as she considered the scene before her. She faced the officers, eyes flashing. 'As I mentioned, the studio is for private sessions. What is photographed in this room is none of my business.'

'Come, Mrs Westlake,' said Smith. 'You can't be so naïve that you didn't know what this room was used for.' Smith caught Jeffries' eye, who blushed, awkwardly clearing his throat.

'What Harry did with his time had nothing to do with me as long as the rent was paid,' snapped Mrs Westlake.

Smith walked over to a small writing desk and a thread-bare chair. The wheels squeaked on the wooden floor as he moved the chair away. He picked up a book of photographs, Harry Westlake's name written on the front cover in beautiful calligraphy. He slowly turned the pages. Each image was a street scene, depicting people going about their business outside homes and places of work.

'Anything of interest, Smith?' Jeffries joined him at the desk. Smith looked back at Mrs Westlake, who had sat on the end of the bed, her head held high, her back straight.

Smith handed the book to Jeffries. 'Look at these street scenes, sir. If these are Mr Westlake's photographs, then it looks like he was telling the truth. He was most likely taking pictures of the street on the day of the crash after all.'

Jeffries flicked through the pages. 'This is clearly a portfolio of photographs, ready to show prospective publishers, perhaps? Maybe he really was at the scene by chance, Smith.' He pointed to the little desk and handed the book back to Smith, 'Is there anything interesting in those drawers?'

Smith placed the book of photographs back on the desk and tried each of the three drawers, but found them to be locked. He turned his attention to the little shelves above the desk. From the middle shelf, he withdrew a small black book.

Opening the book, Smith randomly flicked through the pages. 'This seems to be a ledger of some kind. There is a column of names on one side that are either ticked or left blank, with a number against each name. I think they are prices, but I can't be sure.'

Smith continued to leaf through the pages. 'Some of the names are underlined, which could be significant. Ah, I see now. There is a total at the end of each page, so if I work backwards, I can see the prices are … ah.'

'What is it, Smith?'

'The numbers are pounds. For example, the name Mr Hallett and the sum of five pounds exactly. His name appears on each page, with the same cost each time. I can barely read the next name below, but the amount says three pounds. 'Is this the little black book you mentioned at the shop, Mrs Westlake? The one where your husband kept a list of his important clients?' Smith held it out for her to see.

Mrs Westlake stood, smoothed the front of her dress and approached them, running her hand through her hair. She took the book from Smith and flipped through the pages.

'Well, Mrs Westlake? We haven't all day.'

Mrs Westlake handed the book back, shrugging. 'It certainly looks like Harry's book.'

Smith and Jeffries glanced at each other. 'Where are the keys to these drawers?' Jeffries asked, pointing to the desk.

Mrs Westlake shrugged again. 'Harry didn't bother much with security. He probably hung them up on a nail under the desk for convenience.'

Smith bent and felt along the underneath of the desktop. Nothing. Then he felt along the back of the desk. 'Aha, here we are.' He held up a set of small keys on a brass ring, and tried a key in the first drawer, but it didn't fit. He moved to the next key on the ring, and this time the lock clicked and the drawer slid out easily. There was the usual collection of things one keeps in a drawer: a pad of paper, some paper clips, a rusty key, and half a dozen tiny nuts and bolts, which Smith assumed were for a camera.

The second drawer was empty, save for a dismantled timepiece, its parts strewn across the bottom.

Smith pushed the last key into the final drawer. The lock was stiff but with some persuasion, the key turned, and he

213

slid the drawer open. Inside were bundles of cards neatly stacked in rows. When Smith pulled one set out, he realised they weren't cards but photographs. He considered the identical piles in the drawer. Each batch of photographs was held together by a paper band and contained about twenty pictures. Smith ripped off the paper strip on one bundle and spread the photographs across the desk. Each picture was coloured and featured a barely-clothed woman. Some showed her lying on a bed, the same four-poster in the studio they stood in now. Some showed the woman standing in various poses against a different background. Some showed her completely naked apart from a well-placed scarf or shawl covering her modesty.

Mindful of Mrs Westlake standing next to them, Jeffries reached across, gathered the photographs, and placed them face down in a neat pile. He was too late. Her face had reddened and she began pacing the room, wringing her hands. Meanwhile, Smith turned his attention to the paper band. 'This one has a name on it. Mr Payne.' He reached for the black book and leafed through it. 'Here we are - Mr Payne, six pounds and five shillings. That fits my theory, sir.'

Jeffries sighed, motioned to Smith to continue. 'Please put me out of my misery, Smith. What the heck is going on?'

Mrs Westlake stopped pacing and sat on the sofa. Smith said, 'It's my theory that Mr Payne and other men have paid for sets of pictures of scantily-clad girls, and these were taken by Harry Westlake here in this hidden studio. Judging by the number of stacks in the drawer, I'd say he was on a nice little earner, and as producing colour photographs is such a new thing, I'd suggest that this is a lucrative business, hence the large sums in the black book and the wad of cash I saw in the shop.'

'We'll make a detective of you yet, Smith. Well done. But how does it help our case, and why was Harry killed? I thought we agreed his death was linked to the tram crash.'

214

'That was our original theory as we had nothing else to go on, but this changes everything. The question we should be asking is this - who has the most to lose if Mr Westlake's little secret comes out? It's not illegal, but it would be very embarrassing to a man buying these pictures. Potentially damaging to someone holding a responsible position if his secret were revealed to the press or his family, wouldn't you say?'

Jeffries thought about this. 'Perhaps Harry got greedy and decided to blackmail someone important, and they decided to pay him a visit to silence him.' He reached into a compartment on the desk, pulled out an envelope, picked up the pile of photographs and slipped them inside before sealing the end. He made a note on the front of the envelope before dropping it into his pocket.

Both men turned to Mrs Westlake. She looked up. 'I tried to tell Harry to concentrate on his portrait and street photography. I could see there was a market for a book of photographs taken around the town. Rich people like that kind of thing, and he could charge a premium, as his photographs are beautiful.' She shook her head. 'I told him to stop taking these ... these pictures. Of the girls.'

Jeffries walked across to the sofa and looked down at Mrs Westlake. 'Just tell us everything you know about Harry's activities, and perhaps we can work out why he was killed, Mrs Westlake. The truth this time, and leave nothing out. We're wasting time, and we need to find out what really happened.'

Mrs Westlake sighed, clasped her hands together and nodded at Jeffries. Smith had joined his colleague, Harry's black book in his hand.

'Harry loved photography. He was rather good at it and could see that photographs would soon become something everyone wanted. He had been learning how to produce pictures in colour, which is a new technique but very expensive and time-consuming. He knew that not all photographers are keen on colour, and he could see an opportunity if only he could afford the chemicals and the equipment. He built this little room for more discerning customers who are happy to pay for the service.'

Jeffries folded his arms. 'You must have realised he was being paid rather handsomely. Did you not wonder why that was?'

'I just thought he was selling more photography sessions. I didn't really get involved as long as we could pay the rent and put food on the table.'

Jeffries recalled Smith's conversation with Mr Goodchild. 'We understand from your brother-in-law that you were struggling to pay the rent, Mrs Westlake. Was business slow?'

Mrs Westlake looked down. 'It's true that we were having difficulty making the business work. Photography's a costly business. I don't know what I'm going to do now that Harry's gone.' She looked up, spread her arms wide. 'I shall have to get a job. Cleaning, perhaps.'

Smith coughed. 'Sir, if I may? I think we should focus on the names in the book. See if we can find these gentlemen and have a word with them. We should start with the names that are underlined.'

Jeffries smiled at Smith. 'Yes, you're right, Smith.' He turned back to Mrs Westlake. 'We will need to keep your husband's book and the photographs for the time being. The book will be returned to you in due course. The photographs will likely be kept as evidence for now. If you recall anything of importance, please come and see us at the station, Mrs Westlake.' □

The two men retraced their steps through the concealed door and across the main studio. Jeffries peered back at the row of windows. 'Counting windows! Whatever next, Smith?' He smiled as he opened the door to the outside stairs. Smith followed him down to the dreary passageway, stepping over the slimy vegetables once more.

32

The job and a proposition

I check the clock on the office wall. The hands haven't moved very far since I last glanced up. William is hidden behind an ever-growing stack of papers. The only evidence he is actually here is the occasional sigh or mumble. Mr Edwards is in his office, reading the daily papers with a keen eye on the death notices, ever hopeful that a client has passed away so that the firm can deal with the probate.

I've discovered that writing a will is not particularly lucrative, and local competition for clients is high. The biggest slice of the firm's income is derived from when Mr Edwards (or, increasingly, William) carries out the work needed on the deceased's estate. Checking investments, contacting the bank, speaking to the will's executor, and locating the will in the chaotic attic room where the files are kept. Our clients are clearly more valuable to us dead than alive. No other business relies on the demise of its clients. Apart from an undertaker, of course.

I've been thinking about the work William and his father do here since my first day in the office. I can't see why Mr Edwards doesn't diversify. William and I have revelled in our discovery at Shute's, and I have an idea. Taking a deep breath, I get to my feet, deciding to talk to Mr Edwards. My heart is pounding as I stand by the door, gently knocking on the frosted glass. I glance at William, so engrossed in his work that he's only just noticed I'm standing at Mr Edward's door. He raises his eyebrows in question. I smile as Mr Edwards calls out, 'Come in.'

I step into the office, warm as usual from the little coal fire glowing red in the corner of the room. Mr Edwards looks up, sets his pen down, and beckons me to the opposite chair. 'Miss Grey, take a seat. I was just thinking we should have a chat, since you've been employed here for a few weeks now.'

I sit in the plush chair at Mr Edwards' desk and clasp my hands together. I gather my thoughts, but before I can say anything, Mr Edwards says, 'How are you finding the work? Not too tedious, I hope?'

'I'm finding it very interesting, Mr Edwards.' Not true. 'I quite like being busy, sorting and filing the papers, dealing with the post and so on.' Partly true.

Leaning forward, his hands steepled in front of him, he raises one eyebrow, a thin smile forming on his face. 'Something's on your mind. What is it you wanted to see me about?'

Sherlock whispers in my ear. *'Come on, Carrie. It's now or never.'* Sitting up straighter, I explain to Mr Edwards that as a new arrival to the office, I have a unique viewpoint on the business. With a flush crawling up my neck, I tell him I've noticed the lack of new instructions and the ever-increasing bills in the post. He folds his arms as I continue. 'I think there's more business to be found with litigation cases, those that deal with ordinary people who have been dealt a bad hand. Perhaps they've been in an accident that is not their fault, and as a consequence, they find themselves destitute, unable to support their families.' Mr Edwards is silent for a moment, then smiles. 'Go on,' he says, with a wave of his hand. 'I'm interested in what you have to say.'

I describe how William and I have been looking into Rose's accident and explain that it might be worthwhile for the firm to act for Rose's husband to try and obtain some kind of compensation from the tram company. 'Or whoever was responsible,' I add quickly.

'And how would Rose's husband pay for this service, Miss Grey? I hear he is a manual worker and has little money available. How would our fees be paid?'

'Well,' I begin.

'Hadn't thought about that, had you? Litigation cases cost money, and if we can't prove who is responsible, who

218

will pay our fees? Or the rent for this place? Or your wages?'

My cheeks grow hot, but I push on. I explain how we would have an agreement in place that said that should the person involved, the victim as it were, be successful and win their case, our fees would come out of their compensation.

'And if they don't win?'

'Well, we'd have to be careful whom we help, I suppose.'

'I know you've been pursuing this case of the tram crash. Two tram crashes, in fact.' My face gets hotter. 'Not much gets past me, Miss Grey. Now look, I know you'd like a more adventurous job but I'm afraid this is as good as it gets. We deal with wills and probate. It's been the bread and butter for this firm from when my father ran things and his father before him. And on that note, I am requesting you stop pursuing this tram nonsense. Word is getting around, and the last thing we need is a scandal that affects my business. Perhaps you should start your own firm, Miss Grey, if that sort of work is of interest to you.' He smirks. 'Now, I have to get on, and I'm sure you have work to do. It was nice having this little chat.'

Mr Edwards notices my deep frown and shakes his head. 'Carrie, just leave the investigations to the fictional world of Sherlock Holmes. I gather he's a hero of yours? I've explained what your duties are. Now, if you don't mind, I have some probate documents to sign. It's how we make money here. To pay your wages, incidentally. Now, I don't want to hear more of your ideas, no matter how grand they seem. William tells me there are papers to file and several letters that need typing and posting.'

Mr Edwards picks up his pen and dips it carefully in the inkwell. He might see my ideas as lucrative eventually. I shall have to work harder to convince him. I stand and walk to the door. I'm just about to turn the handle when Mr

Edwards says, 'Of course, Carrie, what you do in your own time is up to you. Just don't mention the firm's name.'

'Of course, Mr Edwards.' An idea begins to form in my head.

33

A pleasant lunch and a meeting

It's Tuesday morning and William's father has sent us both on an errand, distributing leaflets around the local businesses to drum up new work for the firm. Unusually for Mr Edwards, he told us we could have the rest of the day off after we finish the deliveries. To make the most of this task, we rush from door to door, shoving leaflets into letterboxes as quickly as possible.

After delivering what seems like hundreds of leaflets, we call into Deller's for a coffee and something to eat before delivering the last few. It's an opportunity for me to learn more about William, who has been so nice to me since I started working at the office. I do rather like him and find his companionship enjoyable, especially during our recent adventures. I think he finds legal work to be rather boring, and would prefer to be chasing criminals, as would I.

We manage to get a table by the window, and we look out onto Cathedral Green while we wait for our food and drinks to arrive. I left it to William to choose from the menu, so we're both having fish pie, reputedly a treat at Deller's.

People wander past the window, most not in a hurry, enjoying the sunny October day. Mothers push their children in perambulators, and older children run and play on the path. Small groups on the grass talk and laugh, some of the men smoke pipes, and women sit on benches with friends, scarves wrapped tightly about their necks.

I turn away from the window and look at William. 'Tell me, William, how long have you worked for your father?'

'For as long as I can remember. I used to help during school holidays when I was younger, though I doubt I was actually much help. My father just needed to keep an eye on me.' William looks up as the waitress serves our food.

When she leaves, he continues. 'My mother died when I was really young, so it's just been my father and me at home since then.'

I dig my fork into my pie. 'I'm sorry, I didn't know. It's the same with me. My mother also died when I was young. I don't really remember her. I don't have any brothers or sisters, so it's just my father and me. He seems happy enough without a wife at his side. He has his hobbies, and he goes to regular meetings and dinners at his club.' I smile. 'We have our little squabbles, but we get on most of the time. He jokes about my infatuation with Sherlock Holmes, of course, but I don't mind. Actually, it's reading those stories that encouraged me to work in a lawyer's office.'

William tries hard to keep a straight face but fails. 'My father's not keen on women working in the office. He still thinks the office is a man's domain, but I think you've convinced him you're as good as a man. The last assistant left the position after a month. The two of them didn't get on at all.'

'I'll try and last longer than a month,' I say between mouthfuls of pie. 'I really enjoy the work, although our tram case and the photographer's murder have occupied my mind most of the time. It's difficult to concentrate on office tasks.'

William wipes his mouth with his napkin. 'Yes, me too. We'll have to get our heads down tomorrow. I know it's a bit of fun, this tram thing, but at the same time, we need to work hard at the office or my father will fire us both!'

I finish my pie and drain my coffee. 'How many more leaflets do we have?'

William peers in his bag. 'Not that many. I reckon we should head for the quay and deliver some there. There's a lot of money in shipping. Might be some decent clients that need help with their wills. It won't take long, then you can head home as you live in that direction anyway. No point in walking back to the office unless you need to.'

I get up and slip into my coat. 'Good. I can get home early for a change. Let's quickly deliver these last few leaflets before it rains.' Wiping the condensation from the glass and peering through the window, I spot ominous black clouds moving in from the west.

Later, having delivered the last of our leaflets, I rub my aching feet. The clouds have passed harmlessly by, and the sun is coming out again.

'Right, I'm off, William. I can't wait to slip out of my shoes.' That's when we notice John leaning against a pile of barrels by the quayside, chatting with a young girl who has her hand in his arm, taking in his every word. 'Typical. There's John with another one of his lady friends.' I keep my tone light. I don't want William to think I'm jealous or something absurd like that.

William laughs. 'Yes, he is one for the ladies, isn't he?'

As we walk over, John notices us and waves, saying something to the girl, who throws her head back and laughs before striding off. She glances at us as we walk down the slope towards John.

John smiles. 'Hello, you two. What have you been up to?'

'Delivering leaflets. Very boring. You finished for the day, then?' William asks, shaking his friend's hand.

John frowns as he looks over our shoulders. 'Hello, looks like we have company. Those men are the two coppers looking into the tram crash. I wonder what they're doing here?'

William and I turn to see Detective Sergeant Jeffries and Constable Smith walking over. 'This could be interesting,' I say. 'Looks like our afternoon off has just been cancelled.'

34

Joining forces

Jeffries and Smith emerged from the rank passageway, Smith leading the way. As they walked into the main quay area in front of the workshop, Smith looked up at the studio windows and thought he saw Mrs Westlake watching them from the end window. He shook his head. A trick of the light, he thought to himself. As they made their way along the cobbled road, heading for the station, Smith spotted three people standing in a close group next to a pile of barrels. He recognised Miss Grey and one of the men as the engineer from the tram workshop. John something or other. The other man was wearing a suit.

Smith nudged Jeffries and nodded towards the trio. Detective Sergeant Jeffries raised his eyebrows. 'I didn't realise our Miss Grey was an acquaintance of the engineer. I recognise the other man, the gentleman from Miss Grey's office. What are they up to, I wonder? I think we should have a word. Come on, Smith.' Watching out for barrow boys with their wares and men with trolleys, they crossed the street, carefully avoiding the horse dung dotted about the road.

Carrie spotted the two offices as they approached. She muttered something to the other two, and they watched Jeffries and Smith walk across to join them.

'Miss Grey, Mr Sparkes, good day to you,' said Jeffries. 'I didn't realise you knew our engineer friend, Miss Grey?'

Carrie blushed. 'John's really a friend of William's, whom I work with.' She looked at William. 'Will, this is Detective Sergeant Jeffries and Constable Smith. They are investigating the tram crashes. And the photographer's murder, I shouldn't wonder.'

William put out his hand and shook with the two officers. 'Yes, we met when you came to the office to see Carrie. Terrible thing, those crashes. And with the photographer getting himself killed, Exeter is becoming a dangerous place to live.'

Jeffries turned to John. 'Perhaps you have another of your theories, Mr Sparkes? It's a shame your idea about the tram brake didn't amount to anything. You had us quite excited in your workshop. Smith really thought he was going to pull something from that brake box. He was most disappointed, as was I.'

Carrie crossed her arms. John gave her a stern look and shook his head ever so slightly. 'Perhaps there was something,' said Carrie. 'Perhaps you just didn't reach deep enough.'

John gave Carrie a glare.

Jeffries tilted his head. 'Go on, Miss Grey. Do you have a theory too?'

Carrie sighed, ignoring the looks from John and William. 'The evidence was there the day before. It must have been removed before you checked. We saw it with our own eyes. The tram's braking mechanism had been sabotaged. There's no doubt in our minds, and we think we know why.'

Jeffries blinked like a fish out of water. 'I think you owe us an explanation, Miss Grey. Is there somewhere more private we could talk?'

John nodded towards the workshop. 'It's lunchtime, and the workshop will be quiet. We can talk in the office.'

'Lead the way, Mr Sparkes. This should be interesting.'

35

A theory, a drawing, and a door

I follow the others into the workshop, John leading the way. The other workmen lounge in the far corner, eating their packed lunches as we make our way to the office. They look over, heads close together, speaking in hushed tones. John reaches into his pocket for the office key and turns it in the lock. Standing aside, he holds the door open, and we file into the room.

The office is warm and stuffy, with the smell of oil filling the air. The only light is from a rear window, set high in the wall, cobwebs covering the glass. A large window provides a vantage point into the workshop.

There's nowhere comfortable for us all to sit, only a chair by the desk and a tatty, dark brown Chesterfield two-seater that has seen better days. A small table in the middle of the room is covered with unwashed, chipped coffee cups, an ashtray, and a pile of old newspapers. The policemen take the sofa, and John sits in the chair by the desk, crossing his legs. William and I remain standing.

The detective sergeant takes out a black pocketbook and pencil. 'Well, who is going to explain what's going on? Miss Grey, perhaps you can begin by describing the evidence you allegedly found?'

I take a deep breath, getting the details straight in my mind. 'John told us he'd found something in the tram's brake section that would have likely caused the tram to run down the hill and crash.'

'Go on,' Jeffries says.

'It's a long story.' I continue. 'But we all met here in the workshop the other night. John explained his theory, the same details he shared with you the following day. When we examined the brake box, lodged in the bottom was a doorstop - those things you see in posh people's houses, to keep a door ajar. Usually, they have the maker's name

226

carved into it, but this one was unmarked and made of plain, dark wood. Mahogany, perhaps, or Rosewood.'

Jeffries scribbles something in his book. 'So where is the wedge now?'

'Well, that's the problem. It was there when we looked, but it had disappeared when you inspected the tram the day after. The wedge was definitely there the night before. Someone must have forced their way into the workshop and removed it.'

Constable Smith glances up. 'And you're sure, John, that this would have prevented the brake from operating correctly?'

'It would certainly have made it very difficult for the driver to hold the tram on a steep incline. The tram would have operated quite normally until the holding lever was engaged to keep the brakes on.'

The detective sergeant looks at us all in turn. 'Let me get this straight. Let us assume the wedge or doorstop, or whatever this thing is, caused the crash. Who planted the wedge in the first place? Who had access to the tram while it was in your workshop?'

John continues. 'We had the tram here the day before the crash for a small, routine job. Two of us worked on it that day: me and my apprentice, and I was with him the whole time. So whoever tampered with it must have done so that night or I would have noticed something was amiss.'

'Who has keys to the workshop?'

'The only keys are held by the boss and me. We didn't find any signs of a break-in, so they must have got in with a key.'

'Was your boss in the workshop that night?'

'No, Mr Phillips was away that night. He took his wife to a party in Honiton, and they didn't return until the next day. He talked all day about his night away with his wife.'

Detective Sergeant Jeffries turns to Constable Smith. 'You'd better contact this Mr Phillips and check his story,

Smith. Speak to the wife as well, and see if their stories match up. Go on, Miss Grey. You said you know why the tram was tampered with.'

I nod to John, and he swivels around in the chair and unlocks a desk drawer before sliding it open. He reaches inside and pulls out a scroll of paper. It's the same one he took from Shute's office the night we sneaked in. I reach over to the little table, pick up the coffee cups and the ashtray and sweep the newspapers off the table. John unrolls the document and lays it on the table. I place a cup on each corner.

Detective Sergeant Jeffries and Constable Smith inspect the plans before them. 'What is this?' Smith asks, stroking his chin. 'It looks like an engineering drawing of some description.'

John smiles, clearly in his element. 'That is exactly right. These are the plans for the electrification of the high street. Produced by the Shute Lighting Company, these clearly show the proposed designs for a new electric-powered tramway system, and we believe the company is more than happy to see the demise of the horse-drawn trams. If they can convince the council to permit these plans, the lighting company will be able to introduce their new system throughout the town and beyond.'

Smith leans back on the sofa. 'Are you suggesting that Mr Shute has arranged to crash the trams just so he can introduce his own electric-powered versions?'

William answered, 'It's not as simple as that, I'm afraid. There's much more at stake here. Shute's lighting business stands to make hundreds of thousands of pounds from this venture. Show them, John.'

I slide the cups to one side and John lifts the top sheet away, revealing another below. This one seemed extraordinarily complex until John explained it to William and me yesterday.

The police officers once again lean over the drawings. The detective sergeant closes his pocketbook, the details too complex for him to put into words.

John pulls a screwdriver from his pocket and points to the lines with it, 'This drawing shows the complete electrification of the town. We think the Shute Lighting Company plan to introduce their electric trams to the planning department. The public will welcome any improvements with open arms, especially after the crashes with the old horse-drawn trams. But on top of that, Shute's company will have to lay electric cables to run the trams, so why not offer electricity to homes and businesses as well? They could easily run cables from the tramlines to every home and business along the route and beyond. The company stands to make a fortune.'

Detective Sergeant Jeffries frowns. 'I would like to know how you came about these papers. They are clearly not public documents, and the proposals are certainly not common knowledge, or we would surely have heard about them.' The detective sergeant looks at us all in turn, his eyes resting on mine as my cheeks heat up. Well, this is it. In for a penny, in for a pound, as my father says.

I cough, stupidly raising my hand as if in school. I quickly put my hand down again. Everyone looks at me. 'We found them in Mr Shute's study when we called at his home the other night.'

Detective Sergeant Jeffries gapes, 'You called in? No disrespect, Miss Grey, but I doubt that Mr Shute, the owner of the biggest company in the town, invited you to his house to discuss business plans. You'd better tell us everything.'

I glance out the front window into the workshop, hoping for inspiration. The engineers are back to work, the clanking of their tools coming through to the little office. 'I had already visited Mr Shute earlier that day because Rose, the woman who died in the crash, gave me a card with Mr Shute's name on it. Do you remember I showed it to you?'

Jeffries nodded, beckoned for me to continue.

'She was insistent that the crash wasn't an accident. Those were her last words.' The image of Rose dying in front of me steals my breath. 'I asked Mr Shute about Rose to try and find out how he knew her and why she had his business details, but he brushed me off and refused to talk about her. He was hiding something; I was sure of it.'

'What makes you so sure, Miss Grey?'

'We were interrupted by his housemaid. She told him that someone wanted to talk to him on one of those new-fangled telephones so he left the office for a few minutes. There's a telephone in the hallway.'

'Go on.'

'Well, I listened to the conversation. Through the door.'

Jeffries arched his eyebrows. 'And what did you hear, Miss Grey?'

'It was difficult to hear everything, but Mr Shute became angry and started shouting. Something about not doing anything to get anyone killed. He was definitely talking about the tram crash.'

'I see. Did he actually mention the tram?'

'I'm sure that's what he meant. He said "I told you to arrange for some inconvenience, not to cause the damn thing to crash." Or words to that effect.'

'What happened when Mr Shute finished his telephone conversation? Did he know you'd been eavesdropping?'

'I was sitting back at his desk when he came back into the office. He was still angry from the conversation he'd just had and he dismissed me. He didn't want to discuss the matter any further.'

Smith says, 'You say you called into Mr Shute's house later that day, during the night, I think you said? Did Mr Shute invite you?'

I smile. 'No, while he was distracted by the telephone call, I unlatched the back door, and we crept in later that night while Mr Shute was holding a party.'

'What? You all broke into Mr Shute's house?' the detective sergeant asks, raising his voice. 'This gets worse.'

'We didn't exactly break in.' I clarify. The two policemen frown. I detect a slight smile on Smith's face. Jeffries runs his hand through his hair, sitting up straighter as I continue. 'As I say, I had left the door open earlier. Anyway, that's not important.' I gesture to the drawings on the table. 'John found these drawings and realised their importance, so he, um, borrowed them.'

Shaking his head, Jeffries leans forward, elbows on his knees. 'Go on.'

'We overheard a conversation between Shute and one of his men that confirmed they had arranged for the trams to be tampered with. I don't think they intended for anyone to get hurt or die in the crash.' I omit the part about our escape and the race down the hill in Mr Downe's steam car.

Detective Sergeant Jeffries lets out a slow breath. 'This is all very good and extremely important information.'

'But?' I ask.

'But it can't be presented to my inspector, let alone a court. These documents were taken without permission. That's illegal. Any good defence lawyer will raise this with the judge, and we'll lose the case. We need solid evidence, lawfully obtained.'

Smith adds, 'At least we know where to look now. The photographer was a dead end - sorry.'

My head jerks up. 'How does the photographer fit into all this?'

Jeffries looks at me. 'We're not sure he is. It's most likely he was innocently photographing the houses and streets. We found a book of similar images in his studio. We believe there were other people, not connected to the crash, that wanted him out of the way.'

William asks, 'Why would anyone want a photographer killed?'

231

Jeffries says, 'I suppose you'll probably find out in the press soon enough, but this information is not official yet, so please don't repeat this to anyone. Our photographer friend was involved in some rather seedy goings-on in the studio above us.' He looks up at the ceiling. 'It looks like he was pushing the wrong people for more money, and they didn't like it.'

'Blackmail?' asks John.

'We think so, but we are in the early stages of that investigation, so please keep it to yourselves, or I might have to mention your little indiscretion to the inspector.' He glances meaningfully at each of us in turn, pausing a little longer on me. I wonder if they know it was me in the darkroom. I blush, and as if reading my mind, Jeffries says with a slight smile, 'I have your umbrella at the station if you'd like to collect it sometime, Miss Grey?'

I blush. Again. 'Thank you. I'll call in tomorrow.' *Careless,* says Sherlock's voice in my head. 'Yes, I know,' I say.

Jeffries frowns at me. 'Pardon, Miss Grey?'

Realising I've spoken aloud, I mutter, 'Nothing. Just thinking aloud.'

Smith takes out a black book from his pocket. 'Perhaps you could help us some more. We found this book in Mr Westlake's desk. Do you recognise any of the names, Carrie?'

He hands me the book, and I leaf through the tatty pages. The writing is poor and difficult to read. There are perhaps twenty names or more, but I don't recognise those that I can decipher from the scribbled writing. A number of the entries are initials rather than full names, and I am just about to hand the book back when I notice a calling card inserted inside the back sleeve. I take the card out and recognise it straight away. 'This is the same type of card Rose gave to me. It's a Shute Lighting Company business card with Mr Shute's name on the front.' I leaf back through the pages, pointing to one of the entries. 'There - GS. That must be Mr Shute.'

Smith takes the book back. Jeffries nods and says, 'His name seems to crop up an awful lot, and he's the same Mr Shute I witnessed meeting with our thug from the hospital. We should go and have a word with him. Perhaps a visit to his factory is in order. Well done, Miss Grey. You've all been most helpful.'

Jeffries walks to the door but stops as he reaches it, pointing to the corner of the office. 'May I use your washroom before we go?'

John frowns. 'Yes, but that's not the washroom. That's the door to the floor above.'

36

A locked door and a key trick

Jeffries narrowed his eyes at John. 'Why didn't you mention the door to upstairs before? That could be how someone got in to tamper with the tram!'

'That's not possible; it's always locked.' John reached up to a cupboard and opened the door, revealing three neat rows of keys hanging on hooks. He frowned. 'That's odd. The key is missing.'

Jeffries strode to the door, but Smith beat him to it. He turned the knob and pushed. 'Locked,' he said. 'Was that the only key?'

John joined them at the door. 'Yes, there's just the one. This door used to be for accessing the floor above before it was rented out as a studio. We've always kept it locked as the businesses are quite separate. We didn't give the tenant a key as it wasn't necessary.'

Jeffries had forgotten his need for the washroom. 'So where is the key now?'

John's face reddened. 'I think I know what happened.' He glanced at Carrie, who raised her eyebrows.

'Of course,' Carrie said. 'You idiot, John.'

Jeffries looked at John. 'Well? Let's hear it.'

John scraped his hand through his hair and sighed. 'I was having, erm, relations with Mrs Westlake. She has access to the studio above. It was her husband's studio really, but she used the space as well. I wondered why she suddenly told me she didn't want to see me anymore. What an idiot.' He started pacing back and forth before continuing. 'She was keener than I was. In fact, now I think back, she instigated the whole thing. I fell asleep on the sofa once after we spent the evening together here. We'd had a few drinks. She must have taken the key then. She was gone when I woke up, and I thought she had left by the main door, but it makes a hell of a racket when it's opened and closed. I thought it odd at the time that I hadn't heard anything. She must have sneaked out through this door instead and used the key to gain access the night the tram was here. Damn fool!'

Carrie touched John's arm. 'So that was why you went to see her that day and why she was in such a mood. You'd tried to rekindle your relationship, but she didn't need you anymore.'

Jeffries sighed and turned to the door in question. 'Smith, what on earth are you doing?'

Smith was on his knees, peering through the lock. 'I can see the key on the other side.' He pointed behind him. 'Hand me a sheet of newspaper and a pencil from the desk.'

Carrie swept up the requested items. 'Are you using the Sherlock method, Constable?'

'I am, indeed. Well noted!' He smoothed out the newspaper and carefully slid half of it under the door. It glided easily on the bare floorboards. Once in place, he gently pushed the pencil into the lock. 'Hopefully, I can do this the first time. It all depends on how the key was left.'

With a gentle tap, he nudged the pencil forward, and a second later, they all heard a clunk as the key fell to the floor on the other side. Ever so carefully, he pulled the newspaper towards him, and voila! The key lay on the paper, presented for all to see.

'Well, they didn't teach that on my detecting course. Well done, Smith. Open up the door and let's have a look.'

Smith unlocked the door and pushed it open to reveal a dark stairway rising to the floor above. He walked slowly up the stairs, feeling his way towards the faint glow from a partly glazed door at the top.

The others followed as he made his way up. When they reached the top, they could just about see each other in the faint light. Smith put his finger to his lips and pointed to the door. Voices came from the other side. Mrs Westlake's voice was raised, arguing with someone else, a man, his voice muffled by the closed door.

Jeffries urgently tapped Smith on the shoulder and, shaking his head, pointed back down the stairs. Smith frowned, the others unsure what was happening. 'Back downstairs,' whispered Jeffries as he led the way.

Back in the office, Jeffries quietly closed the door and turned to the others. 'We need a plan before we barge in on whoever is upstairs with Mrs Westlake. We need to use our suspicions to our advantage. I need to think.'

While Jeffries paced the room, muttering to himself, Smith stood by the door. John sat back in the chair by the desk, his foot nervously tapping the floor while Carrie and William took the sofa. Nobody spoke as Jeffries paced, hands clasped behind his back, his head down.

Suddenly, Jeffries stopped in his tracks. 'We need solid evidence. We really need to find that wedge planted in the brake section, as it proves the tram was tampered with. It's a long shot, as the perpetrator must surely have thrown it away by now. Any ideas?'

William looked at Carrie. 'You're the one who reads Sherlock Holmes. What would he do, Carrie?'

Carrie smiled. 'My thoughts exactly. Always trust Sherlock. Let's see.' She thought for a few seconds, slapped her thigh and stood. 'Sherlock would think like the culprit, so what would I do if I had the wedge? I would want to get rid of it as soon as possible. I could throw it in the river, but it's busy outside at most times of the day or night, and someone would surely see me. So, I would throw it away somewhere so normal that no one would think of it. After all, it's just a piece of wood, and the culprit doesn't know we'd previously found it, so a bit of wood wouldn't look out of place amongst other bits of wood.'

William spluttered. 'The woodpile in the alleyway!'

'Exactly, great minds think alike, William!'

Jeffries and Smith shared a look, perplexed. John explained, 'Workshops like this one get through a lot of wood of all shapes and sizes. We can't always use the offcuts, so the mechanics pile it up in the alleyway, and it's collected each week by the local coalmen. They then sell it at a cheap price to customers who can't afford coal.'

Jeffries was already striding to the office door. 'Well, what are we waiting for? Let's have a look at this woodpile.'

John's workmates paused their work to watch the group heading to the main door.

Jeffries stood in front of the mountain of wood, taller than he was and twice as wide. Smith scratched his chin. 'This might take a while.'

'Well, the sooner we start, the sooner we'll find it,' said Carrie, crouching down to begin the search.

'If it's here,' added John.

Jeffries took off his coat and jacket and hung them on a discarded shovel leaning against the wall. 'John, you keep a watch. Mrs Westlake and her visitors could come out of the studio at any time. Shout if you see anyone come out of that door.'

John positioned himself under the stairway, craning his neck to keep an eye on the studio door at the top.

Smith hung his coat and jacket on top of Jeffries' and pushed up his shirt sleeves.

The group made an unusual sight as they each picked up and discarded bits of wood. The timber was stored under a haphazard roof to keep rain off. The coalmen were only interested in dry wood to burn. Wet wood was no use to them.

Five minutes later, a number of smaller piles appeared around the tired group. Smith mopped his brow with his handkerchief, and Carrie wiped her hands on her skirt. Jeffries methodically picked up several pieces at a time and threw them on his own rapidly-growing pile while William took more breaks than any of them, his once-white shirt now grey with dirt.

Another five minutes passed, and Jeffries stood upright and checked his timepiece. 'Hell. A whole lot of searching and nothing.' He stretched his back and rubbed his shoulder. Smith threw a final handful of wood onto his pile, and the others stood upright and rubbed their sore muscles.

'Damn,' said William, kicking at the bottom of the remaining pile, now just a couple of feet high. His side of the pile tumbled to the ground, throwing up clouds of dust. Coughing, Carrie shouted, 'Wait! What's that?' She scrambled on her knees, no longer caring about the state of her skirt.

Jeffries stepped across and held Carrie back by her shoulder. 'Don't touch it!'

Carrie pointed to the base of the pile. 'Why ever not? It's what we've all been looking for. I can see it just there.'

Jeffries pulled out his handkerchief from his top pocket and handed it to Carrie. 'Pick it up carefully with this. I'll explain in a minute.'

Carrie took the handkerchief and pulled bits of wood out of her way. Gingerly, she grabbed the piece of wood with the white square of cotton and shuffled backwards until she could stand.

The others gathered around as she carefully opened the cloth to reveal the wedge of wood.

Jeffries held up a hand before anyone could speak, calling across to John, still in his observation spot by the stairs. 'John, is this the same piece of wood you retrieved from the tram the other day?'

John joined the others, examined the wedge in Carrie's hands. 'There's no doubt in my mind. This is the same wedge. Look, there's the mark the bolt made on the wood.'

They studied the hexagonal dent in the wood. Detective Sergeant Jeffries touched Carrie's shoulder. 'Well done, Carrie. This is solid evidence.'

'But why the handkerchief, sir?' asked Smith.

Carrie interrupted. 'Fingerprints! Of course!' Carrie beamed, looking at the confused faces of the others. Apart from Jeffries, who was smiling. 'Everyone has a different pattern of fingerprints - none are duplicated. Find prints on the wedge, and we'll possibly be able to find who's handled it.'

'Fingerprints? I've never heard of such a thing! Is what Carrie says true or just some fanciful idea from a Sherlock Holmes story?' asked William.

Jeffries smiled. 'She's absolutely right, William. I learned about this on my course. It's a new technique, but it is indeed possible to find prints on almost any surface. And as everyone's prints are unique, it's possible to match the pattern with the perpetrator's fingertips.'

Smith interrupted. 'The sergeant is absolutely right. I read something in the newspaper about it. From what I recall, it was the Harry Jackson case. In 1902 a burglary occurred in a house in London. The detective in charge of the case noticed a number of fingerprints on a newly-painted window sill where the criminal had entered the property. He arranged for photographs to be taken of the prints that were then compared to some prints from a known criminal. They matched exactly. Harry got put away for seven years.'

'Well, I never,' said William. 'There's just one problem with your theory. Who do we compare the prints with?'

Smith reached out and took the wrapped bundle from Carrie. 'First, we need to see if there are any prints on this wedge. We know John and Carrie have touched it already, and we'll need to eliminate them from the list, so we'll take a sample of their prints. Any other prints are likely to have been left by our culprit. Then, we need to take a sample from each of our suspects until we get a match.'

Carrie shook her head. 'No need to check our fingers, we both wore gloves when we held the wedge and John wiped it clean before he put it back.'

'So the only prints on this, if there are any, will belong to whoever removed it and threw it away.' Smith said.

'That's right. Should make it easier to find the culprit.' Carrie said.

Jeffries narrowed his eyes. 'But surely any criminal will refuse to give a sample. I know I would.'

John smiled. 'We have to trick our suspects into giving a sample. Perhaps by inspecting a glass or a cup after they've handled it.'

Carrie gazed up the steps to the door to the studio as it opened with a clang against the metal railings. A man appeared at the door, smoothed his hair and put on his cap as he descended the stairs, his hob-nailed boots clattering on the metal stairway. A second man trailed behind him, slamming the door shut behind him.

Carrie grabbed William and hissed to the others, 'Quick, we need to go!' She walked briskly to the end of the passageway and turned left, stepping behind a pile of crates. The others followed. As they huddled close to one another, Jeffries peered around the corner and watched as the two men marched off along the quay. One man had a limp.

'Did they see us?' asked John.

Jeffries said, 'They were so intent on rushing away, I don't think so. I recognised one of the men. The last time I saw him, I was watching him in the pub. He was the same man we saw at the hospital, Smith.'

'Ah, I thought I recognised him. The limping man. The same man who tried to give me a beating that night. I wonder why he was in the studio.'

'Smith, I need you to take the wedge to the station. Check for prints, and don't let anyone else touch it. If necessary, put it in the safe in the inspector's office.'

'Will do, sir. What are you going to do?'

'I'm going to have a word with Mrs Westlake and see if I can find out why our limping man was in the studio.' He turned to William, Carrie and John. 'Thank you for your help in all of this. We'll be in touch when we have more news, and please come to the station if you think of anything else. You've been most helpful.'

The three friends made their way to the river, Carrie bouncing like a cork in a stream. The others laughed at something she said as they rounded the corner. Smith turned to Jeffries, holding up the wedge, still carefully wrapped in the handkerchief. 'I'll be off then, sir. I'll put this in the safe back at the station and try and find out who might test it for us. We might have to wait a few days, though.'

Jeffries stroked his chin and nodded. 'Yes. Good.' He looked up at the studio. 'I'll have a word with Mrs Westlake and see what she has to say for herself. Good work, Smith.'

37

A confession and a safe place to hide

Smith made his way along the quay while Jeffries climbed the metal steps to the studio. As he reached the top, Mrs Westlake appeared at the door, a bunch of keys in one hand, her bag in the other. 'You again.' She said, closing the door and locking it quickly. She dropped the keys into her bag and faced Jeffries. He noticed her eyes were puffy and red, and there was a small cut on her neck. She slung her bag over her shoulder, put her hands on her hips. 'Have you found out who murdered my Harry yet?'

Jeffries touched his hat. 'Hello, Mrs Westlake. We have a number of leads to follow up, but I don't have any news for you yet, I'm afraid.' Jeffries nodded towards the closed door. 'I wanted to talk to you. Just a couple of questions, if I may.'

Mrs Westlake sighed, pulled the keys out of her bag and unlocked the door. She pulled it open and gestured that Jeffries should enter. With the door closed behind them, Mrs Westlake dropped her bag on a desk and tilted her chin. 'You have some questions?'

Jeffries removed his hat, placed it next to her bag and pulled out his notebook and pencil. He looked around the room, noticing the upturned camera support, documents strewn about the floor, a chair on its side. 'Who were the two men in here a few minutes ago, Mrs Westlake? They seemed to have made rather a mess.'

'They were customers of Harry's. I don't really know them.'

'Why were they here?'

'They were just picking up some photographs Harry had taken for them.'

Jeffries watched Mrs Westlake carefully. She was fiddling with her hair. He didn't believe a word she was saying. 'Come on, Mrs Westlake. You know that's not true. They didn't look like customers to me. The complete opposite, in fact. A pair of local thugs. I need the truth. I haven't got time to waste if you want me to find out who murdered your husband.'

Mrs Westlake pulled out a chair and sat, her head in her hands. She looked up, tears in her eyes. 'I'm sorry. They threatened Harry. Now they're threatening me. I can't tell you anything. They'll kill me if they find out I've spoken to you.'

Jeffries dragged a chair over and sat opposite Mrs Westlake. Leaning forward, he said, 'Mrs Westlake, we can protect you. Tell me everything about these men, and if they are threatening you as you say, we can arrest and charge them. They'll be locked away, and I'll personally ensure they are no longer a threat to you.'

Mrs Westlake sniffed, took out a handkerchief and wiped her nose. She sighed. 'I lied earlier. I knew what Harry was doing all along.'

'Go on.'

'The photography business has been failing for months. We were losing money, still are, and we're falling behind with the rent. We needed to find a way to earn more. The portrait business was struggling as people just couldn't afford the price we had to charge to make a decent profit. Harry needed a new venture. Something that didn't cost much but an idea for which he could charge a premium price.'

Jeffries nodded. 'He tried taking photographs of the town to make a book, but I suppose that's not it, is it? Whatever he came up with involved scantily-dressed ladies and a little black book, didn't it?'

More emboldened and eyes dry, Mrs Westlake said, 'That's right. He decided to use the studio to take photographs of women and sell them to discerning gentlemen. It would be a private club, very exclusive, and one that certain men, some of them famous or important in the town, would pay handsomely for.'

Jeffries sorted the details together in his mind. 'But it wasn't enough, was it? Harry got greedy and asked for more money, perhaps threatening to reveal what these men were buying. Is that correct?'

Mrs Westlake sighed. 'Yes. Harry knew these men would never want their secret revealed, so he asked for more money. Blackmail, I suppose you'd call it. But he picked the wrong men to threaten.'

'Who did Harry try to blackmail?'

'I don't know all the men he approached, but one was a Mr Shute. Those men who were here earlier work for him. They visited the shop a couple of times last week and told Harry they would ruin him if he kept demanding more money.'

'How did you know they worked for Mr Shute?'

'One of them let it slip. I heard the taller one mention the name. His pal told him to shut up.' She thought back. 'Both were nasty men, the sort you wouldn't want to cross.'

'I don't understand why they think you're a threat, though. With Harry dead, why come after you now?'

'Harry was a fool. After he was threatened, he agreed to destroy his records and promise not to reveal the names of the men on his books. He changed his mind, decided to keep the records, for security. It's the book those men were after. I tried to explain that I didn't have it but they didn't believe me. We were just beginning to earn enough money from the private club idea to pay our rent and save the business. We'd had a good few months with portraits and so on and a publisher had shown interest in Harry's idea of a photograph book of the town. I told him again and again not to demand more money from these men. Why wasn't he satisfied with the photography earnings? Why did he press for more money and risk everything?'

'Do you think the men who threatened Harry came back and killed him?'

'I think so. I don't know. I'm scared, Detective Sergeant. Scared for my life. What am I going to do?' She started to sob, her shoulders heaving.

Jeffries said, 'We can protect you, but you must tell me everything.'

She scrunched up her handkerchief, her knuckles turning white. 'They came to see me last week. They said that if I helped them with a job, they would leave me and Harry alone. They said that if I didn't do this one thing for them, they'd go to the newspapers to tell them about Harry's secret studio. They gave me their word and I stupidly believed them.''

'What did they insist you do for them?'

'They wanted access to the workshop below the studio. All I had to do was to leave the door that leads downstairs unlocked for them. I already knew an engineer from the workshop. I knew he had keys and was trusted to lock up, and so I befriended him. When I was in his office, I found the key to unlock the door.'

'This is John, the engineer downstairs?'

Mrs Westlake sniffed. 'Yes, that's him. We arranged to meet on Sunday evening. I flirted with him a little, plied him with drink, and he fell asleep. I unlocked the door and left the key in the lock on the studio side. Then on Monday night, I let Shute's men into the studio. They went down to the workshop and did whatever it was they wanted to do. They came back through the studio about half an hour later and walked out the door.'

'Were the men you let in that night the same ones here today?'

'Yes, they were the same ones but there was a third man on the Monday night. He wasn't here today. Now I think of it, he was different than the others. Not as nasty as the others. Not nasty at all. He seemed a nice sort, didn't really want to be involved, I could tell that much.'

Jeffries scribbled furiously in his book. 'So let's get this straight.' He looked up. 'Harry had a side-line going where he'd take photographs of scantily-clad women, which he'd then sell to his discerning clients. Harry saw a way to make his little venture even more lucrative, so he asked for more money from his clients to keep quiet. Blackmail, in other words. One of these clients was Mr Shute whose name, I can tell you, has cropped up more than once.'

Jeffries stood, paced back and forth, tapping his notebook against his leg, 'You don't know who else Harry was blackmailing, but we can assume their names are in his black book. Mr Shute's henchmen had intimidated Harry previously and told him to destroy his records and to stop threatening their boss. They might have returned to make sure Harry had got the message. These same men had threatened you and told you to get them access to the tram workshop, or they would reveal Harry's little scheme to the newspapers, thereby destroying your business. You opened the door for them last weekend, and they let themselves into the workshop through the door you'd left unlocked for them. Have I got that right, Mrs Westlake?'

Mrs Westlake blew her nose and wiped her eyes with a handkerchief. 'Yes, that's more or less what happened, officer.'

Jeffries sat back in the seat, scribbled some more, looked up from his notes and raised his eyebrows. 'But why were they here today?'

Mrs Westlake wrung her hands together. 'I now realise that I gave them access to the tram that crashed. I felt responsible, and I saw Mr Shute's thugs on the quay this morning. I told them I knew what they had done, that they had caused the crash. They just laughed in my face.'

Jeffries closed his book, dropped it in his pocket, and stared at Mrs Westlake. 'So they returned later while they knew you were alone and threatened you.'

'Yes, they pushed me against the wall, and held a knife to my throat. They threatened me. Told me to keep the secret studio quiet. Not to tell anyone. I tried reasoning with them, but they kept threatening me and told me to find a way to supply more pictures, even if it meant taking them myself. I told them that was impossible; only Harry knew how to make the pictures. Harry showed me how to use the cameras, but I don't know how to process the images. Then they smashed some camera equipment, overturned some furniture, and left.'

Jeffries stood and put his hat back on. 'Do you have anyone you can stay with for a few days? Just until this is over?'

Mrs Westlake thought for a moment. 'Well, there's my sister, but she lives opposite the shop. I assume you want me to hide somewhere further away?'

'Yes, across the road won't be safe enough. Is there anyone else?'

'I have an aunt in Sidmouth. I could stay with her, I suppose. How long will I need to stay away?'

'Just a few days. We're closing in on our culprits now, so it shouldn't be too long before we have these men in custody. Thank you for being honest with me, Mrs Westlake. Come on, I'll escort you to the station where we can keep you safe and warm while we arrange transport to your aunt's house.'

Jeffries walked Mrs Westlake across to the door, pushed it open, and stepped out into the sunshine, while she locked up. He led her down the stairs to the alleyway, keeping a lookout for her visitors. The streets were clear. Now we're getting somewhere, he thought. It's all coming together. 'I deserve a drink after that,' he muttered as he accompanied Mrs Westlake to the station.

38

A meeting room, a ribbon, and a noticeboard of links

It was Wednesday morning - over a week since the crash had brought the two men together. Jeffries and Smith sat at their desks, working through their notes, the crash scene photographs strewn across the desktops. Jeffries pushed the photographs to one side and held them in place with a tin crammed full with pens and pencils.

He told Smith about his interview with Mrs Westlake, Smith nodding as the pieces of the puzzle started, at last, to fit together. 'Did you manage to speak to John's boss? He and his wife were supposed to be at some party, weren't they?'

Smith said, 'Yes, I went to see Mr Phillips. I met his wife as well. Seemed like nice people. They mentioned the carriage driver who took them to Honiton and he confirmed that he picked them up and brought them home. So their alibi is sound.'

'There are so many aspects to this case. We have two crashed trams, both within days of each other. Then we have a photographer murdered in his own shop. Harry was threatening Shute, and we think it was his thugs that threatened and killed him. We know they are the men who tampered with the tram, but we can't prove anything yet.'

Smith released a sigh and stuck his pencil behind his ear. He leaned back in his chair. 'I work better with patterns. I need to see the case in front of me. This way of taking notes is just so confusing. There must be a better way.'

Jeffries rubbed his eyes with his knuckles. He'd tossed and turned all night and hadn't slept a wink.

'Well, the detecting course taught us how to approach suspects, observe, and take notes. They didn't teach us how to organise all the notes and evidence. Any ideas, Smith? I'm all ears.'

Smith stood, grabbed his notebook and a pile of papers. 'Bring all the paperwork, sir, and follow me. I have an idea.'

'Anything is better than managing this mess, Smith.' With a swipe of his arm, Jeffries brushed all the papers, notebooks and pencils from his desk into the wastebasket. He picked up the bin, and followed his colleague across the room to an office at the far end, side-stepping paint buckets and dust sheets along the way.

'When are they going to finish this infernal painting job?' muttered Jeffries, considering the office door before him, the screw holes showing evidence of a sign, long since removed. The door was locked, the key hanging on a hook at the top of the frame.

Smith reached up and unhooked the key, slotted it into the lock and turned. The lock clicked and Smith pushed the door open, gesturing for Jeffries to lead the way.

The room was dark and littered with broken office furniture. A noticeboard filled the wall at one end. Smith opened the blinds to let in some light. Dust motes danced in the stuffy air. 'I noticed this room earlier, any idea what it was used for, sir?'

Jeffries peered around and stood the wastebasket on one of the dusty desks, setting everything out onto its surface. 'It used to be a meeting room. Before that, it was the inspector's office, but it hasn't been used for months.'

'I can see that,' Smith said as he pushed a filing cabinet away from the noticeboard. He stood and gazed at the empty board, his hands on his hips. 'We need some pins, plenty of ribbon or string, and some blank sheets of paper. Oh, and a pair of scissors and pens or pencils. The thicker, the better.'

Jeffries was happy to be led for a change, so he left the room to collect the bizarre collection of items. Where on earth do I find ribbon? he thought.

A few minutes later, Jeffries shoved the door open with his shoulder and walked across to the noticeboard with a heavy box. He upturned the box, spilling the contents onto the desk. Smith raised his eyes when he saw the bright pink ribbon. Jeffries noticed his colleague's surprise that he had managed to find ribbon in a police station. 'I remembered a case from last year where a dressmaker was accused of murdering her husband. I raided the evidence room and found some of her spools of ribbon. I'm sure she won't mind. She's in prison for life.'

Smith smiled. 'I didn't doubt you'd find some ribbon, sir. Nothing in blue or green?'

'It was pink or nothing, Smith. Does it matter what colour we use?'

Smith shook his head, sat at the table, grabbed a pen, and pulled the sheets of paper towards him. Now intently focused, he wrote initials on some sheets, and on others he wrote place names. When he was satisfied, he pinned each sheet on the board. Then he fixed one of the photographs of the crashed tram in the middle of the board, followed by some of the provocative photographs they'd found in the hidden studio. He chose ones showing the girl wearing the most clothes, just in case anyone barged in unannounced.

Smith stood back to appraise his work and then reached for the ribbon and scissors. To Jeffries' amusement, Smith pinned a length of ribbon to each of the names and stretched each strand to other parts of the board. Jeffries nodded as Smith's idea took shape.

Gradually a pattern emerged of names linked to places. Jeffries immediately noticed the connection between GS (George Shute) and the crash, as well as a link to the studio through his thugs and Mrs Westlake. Shute's name was also linked to a sheet with the letters LM. 'Who's LM?' asked Jeffries, pointing to the board.

Smith tilted his head. 'That's our mystery man who seems to crop up everywhere. The one with the dodgy leg.' Smith pointed to the strands of ribbon leading from Shute's name. 'We can now see Shute's men include the limping man and his mate, plus the third man who only seems to have been involved with the first tram. The other two crop up everywhere.'

The two men considered the web of ribbon before them. Jeffries started to pace the room. 'Let's get this straight. We now know Mr Shute has a reason to nobble the tram system. His motive is that he benefits from the demise of the old trams because he gets his electric trams in service. And with that, his electricity company will eventually supply the whole town with power, making him thousands of pounds in the process. The tram system gives him an easy way in. So he has a motive. Let's look at his means and opportunity to carry out such a crime.'

Smith tapped his pen against his chin. 'He has the technical knowledge and his henchmen to do his dirty work for him, so he has the means. He has the opportunity, but not directly. He uses his thugs to do the deed. That way he keeps his distance from the evidence. Or so he hopes.'

'Go on,' said Jeffries.

'Shute paid our limping man to do the deed, which distances Shute from the crime. Unfortunately for him, you saw Mr Shute handing over a wad of cash to his man in the public house. The limping man found a way to enter the workshop from the studio. He must have had a connection with Mrs Westlake, possibly through Harry, to get her to steal the key from under the engineer's nose. Together with his accomplices, the limping man later tampers with the tram's brakes and sneaks back out again. Then, after the crash, he returns to the workshop and removes the wooden wedge to dispose of it.'

'But why three men to do the job, Smith?'

'That's easy; the limping man organises everything, one of his mates keeps a lookout, and the third man has the expertise to actually carry out the job.'

Jeffries stopped pacing. 'It all fits. We need to have a word with Mr Shute and his man. But why kill Harry and risk a hanging offence?'

Smith said, 'Perhaps Harry just knew too much and had to be silenced for good.'

He continued. 'I suppose we may never find out. And don't forget that piece of cotton buried in Harry's neck. That wire I found in the darkroom matched the thread you found on Harry's neck. We just need to link that wire to the limping man and the case is closed.'

Jeffries stroked his chin. 'The doctor said Harry had been strangled and that piece of cotton was quite deep in the wound on his neck. The wire you found in the darkroom is thin but very strong. And if twisted together, it could certainly be strong enough to throttle a man.'

Smith smiled at his colleague. 'If that small piece of thread turns out to be a vital clue, that was rather clever of you to spot it, sir.'

Jeffries spread his hands wide. 'Just good police observation, Smith. And don't forget, on the day Harry was murdered, we have a witness who saw a limping man leave the photographer's shop in a hurry. The same man was apparently threatening Mrs Westlake.'

'He's the one who, with his pal, tried to rough me up that night. They failed on that score, of course,' Smith added with a rueful smile, rubbing his elbow at the memory.

Jeffries scribbled notes into his notebook as his colleague spelt out his theories. 'It all sounds feasible, Smith. Well done.' He looked up. 'And the indecent photographs we found in the hidden studio? How do they fit in?'

Smith considered this. 'The photographs have nothing to do with the tram or the crash. Harry just happened to have found a lucrative side-line, and George Shute's name is in his little black book as a customer of the provocative photographs. That's how Shute knew Harry, and possibly how he found out about the door to the workshop below the studio. It's ideal. Sneak into the workshop from the studio, and no one would ever know. If it hadn't been for

252

your need for the washroom that day, we might have never realised there was a direct route between the two!'

'Yes, that was a stroke of luck, Smith. What about Mr Hoskins and the limping man? Why the visit to the hospital? Something was going on between those two.'

'Yes, what was that all about? Presumably, Shute sent him to warn the driver from revealing something. Mr Hoskins must have been scared out of his wits, so he clammed up.'

Smith peered at the board on the wall. Pinned up another piece of paper. 'We need to find out if we have a result from the fingerprints. The laboratory people are dragging their heels, though I think it does take some time to lift a clear print.'

Jeffries smiled. 'Yes, get onto them, Smith.' Jeffries walked over to the board to take a closer look. 'And what about our trio of curious sleuths, Carrie, John and William?'

'They are just that. Carrie happened to be at the scene when the tram crashed, William's friend works in the workshop, and they all got together to try and solve the crime themselves. They had some excellent ideas, and John was the one to find the link between Shute, the new trams and his plans to electrify the town.'

Jeffries stood. 'We need to have a chat with George Shute and put a name to the limping man. Come on, Smith. Let's pay Mr Shute a visit.'

39

A suspect in handcuffs and an egg sandwich

Smith threw a dust sheet over the noticeboard and followed his colleague out of the office, pausing to lock the door and hand the key to Jeffries.

The two men grabbed their coats and headed for the front entrance just as two uniformed officers crashed through the door, dragging a man in handcuffs. 'Let me go, you police bastards!' he spat. 'I paid for that whisky, fair and square, and I know your boss. He won't be happy you've pulled me in!'

Blood poured from the man's nose and purple circles surrounded both eyes. Jeffries recognised him immediately, 'Smith! That's the limping man, I'm sure of it. It looks like Harris and Cottem have collared our man for us.'

Jeffries strode up to the constables, keeping his distance as the handcuffed man twisted and kicked out, desperately trying to escape his captors as they dragged him to the main desk.

'Who's this gentleman, Harris?'

'This is Albert Jones. We caught him red-handed pinching a bottle of whisky in the high street. We've had him in before, sir, but he always finds a way to wriggle out of every misdemeanour.' Harris and Cottem struggled as the man thrashed about.

Jeffries realised that this could be the break they so desperately needed. He decided to use his rank to good effect. 'Perhaps it needs a new approach. Smith and I will interview Mr Jones. You two can join us in case the gentleman tries something stupid.'

The constables looked at each other and shrugged. 'We just need to book him in, sir. Shouldn't take more than a couple of minutes.'

Later, with Jones booked in, Jeffries and Smith sat at the desk in the interview room. Jones was escorted in, more subdued now, a smirk on his face. The constables shoved him into the chair opposite Jeffries and took a step back to the door, where they watched with interest.

Albert Jones grinned at the two detectives with a gleam in his eye. 'Well, this is a turn-up for the books, being interviewed by a couple of gentlemen not in uniform. Very interesting.'

Jeffries leaned forward. 'My name is Detective Sergeant Jeffries, and this is my colleague, Constable Smith. We have a few questions for you, Mr Jones.' Jeffries watched him for a reaction but the man's face remained passive. 'Now, I've spoken to my colleague here, and we both agree there's been some kind of misunderstanding. It would seem to me that perhaps you did indeed pay for the whisky, and the shop owner was confused. We're very sorry for the inconvenience.'

Jones looked behind him at the constables and then back to the two detectives. He roared with laughter. The constables were both red in the face, grimacing.

Constable Harris stepped forward. 'Beg your pardon, sir. Constable Cottem and me had this man bang to rights.'

Jeffries held up his hand. 'Not now, Constable Harris.'

The constable stepped back to the door, his neck and face still a rich crimson. His colleague simply shook his head.

Jones went to stand, still laughing. "I'll be off then, gentlemen. Care to remove these?' He held out his restrained hands.

It was Jeffries' turn to smile. 'Not so fast, Mr Jones. We still have some questions we need answers to.'

Jones sat heavily in his chair, leaning back and tilting his head to one side. 'Go on, ask your questions. This had better not take long.'

Jeffries consulted a page in his notebook, building suspense in the room. The constables leaned closer to get in better earshot.

Jones lifted his hands. 'How about we start by taking these off? I'm not going anywhere with four against one, am I?'

Jeffries smiled. 'I think we'll leave them on for now. So, Jones is it? Albert Jones?'

The man nodded and put his hands back on the table, the handcuffs clanking. 'That's right. That's me.'

Jeffries flipped over another page of his book. 'Who do you work for, Mr Jones?'

Jones blinked twice, mouth open. 'Eh? What's that got to do with anything?'

Smith leaned across the table. 'Just answer the question, Mr Jones.'

Jones rolled his eyes and shook his head. 'I work for Mr George Shute, a very important businessman in the town. I think he's friends with your boss, actually.' He smirked at the two detectives.

Jeffries continued. 'What do you do for Mr Shute?'

'Whatever he needs.' Jones shrugged. 'I look after his motor cars, carriages, the house, and I find men when he needs work doing in the grounds or in his factory. A jack-of-all-trades, me.'

Jeffries nodded. 'And how does he pay you for this work?'

'What does it matter? I'm paid just like the rest of the staff. Weekly and regular as clockwork.'

'So why was Mr Shute paying you with cash under the table in a pub instead of at the office? I followed you from the hospital the other day. You met with Mr Shute, who paid you with an envelope of cash in a very suspicious manner. What was the money for, Mr Jones?'

Smith put his elbows on the table. 'And while we're at it, why were you harassing a patient at the hospital the other day?'

Jones twisted in his seat. 'What's this got to do with the whisky I took from the shop?' he said to the two constables by the door.

They shrugged their shoulders. Constable Cottem said, 'It's out of our hands now. Detective Sergeant Jeffries evidently has his own way of doing things.'

Jones looked back to Jeffries and Smith. 'Look, how about you charge me with the whisky theft, and we can all get on with our day. Send me to the magistrate and have done with it. I'll take my chances in the court.'

Jeffries smiled. 'We would very much like to, but first, we need to know what you've been doing for Mr Shute recently.'

'Like I said, I do all manner of things for him. Depends what needs doing.'

'Including tampering with the town's trams?'

Jones laughed. 'What? I don't tamper with anything. You've got the wrong man. I don't know anything about any tram.'

'Come on, Mr Jones, we saw you with our own eyes accepting a suspicious payment from Mr Shute, and you were in the photography studio the other day, which is just above the tram workshop.'

'Doesn't prove a thing.'

'Not on its own, perhaps,' said Smith. 'But when all the pieces of the puzzle are assembled, you and Mr Shute seem to be in the picture at every turn.'

Jeffries pointed at Jones. 'We think Mr Shute asked you to tamper with the tram for him. We'll be talking to Mr Shute later today, and you can bet your life that he'll tell us everything to save his own neck.' Jeffries folded his arms. 'This is your chance to set the record straight. Just tell us what Mr Shute paid you to do, and we can nail him. We can put in a good word for you with the courts for cooperating. It's Shute we're after.'

Jones looked flustered, his face a bright crimson as a bead of sweat trickled down his left temple. He awkwardly wiped it away with his sleeve. 'Look, officers, I just do a bit of maintenance work for Mr Shute. He pays well, and I do what he asks of me. But I didn't tamper with no tram.'

Smith didn't need his poker skills to see that Jones was in the middle of a pack of lies, but decided to test his theory anyway. 'Mr Jones, my colleague here has got a little carried away.' Jeffries looked at Smith and was about to interrupt, but thought better of it. He knew Smith would have reasons for this new angle, and he trusted him, despite his lack of experience.

Smith continued. 'You've told us you work for Mr Shute. You carry out various maintenance tasks and so on, is that correct?'

Jones sat up straight in his seat. 'Yes, that's right. That's what I said.'

Smith noticed Jones' change in his demeanour. 'How did you get the key to the tram workshop?'

Jones wiped his brow, even though he had stopped sweating.

There it is, thought Smith. Everyone had a tell, and Jones' was wiping his brow. Smith would beat him in a poker game with no trouble at all.

Smith didn't wait for an answer. 'Did you pay Mrs Westlake, or did you have something on her husband? Something to do with the photographs he was making, perhaps?'

Jones wiped his brow again. 'I don't know what you're talking about. What is this nonsense? First, you're saying I tampered with a tram, now you're suggesting I had something to do with lewd photographs.'

Jeffries sat up straight. 'Who said anything about the photographs being lewd? We didn't mention what the pictures showed.'

Jones wiped his brow again and looked down. 'I'd like a drink of water. You can't keep me here without providing refreshment; it ain't fair.'

Smith looked at the constables. 'Get the man a cup of tea. He'll need it to keep his strength up. Make it good and strong with plenty of sugar.' He looked back at Jones, whose left leg seemed to have a life of its own as it bounced up and down. Another tell. This man was full of them.

The three men sat silently for a few minutes while one of the constables left the room to fetch the tea. Smith sat and observed Jones while Jeffries flipped through his notebook, tapping his pencil on the table. Jones continued to bounce his leg, the table vibrating in time with his knee.

Jeffries looked up as Harris returned with the tea. He also carried an envelope. Setting the cup down in front of Mr Jones, he handed the envelope to Jeffries, who glanced at it briefly, noticing the marking on the front. It was from the lab. As Jones sipped his tea, Jeffries carefully tore open the envelope and pulled out the result of the fingerprint test. He quietly read the report, his face giving nothing away.

Jeffries slid the sheet back into the envelope, placed it in his pocket and looked up. 'I think we should take a short break. Some new evidence has come to light, and perhaps Mr Jones would like to spend a few minutes gathering his thoughts.' Jones ignored him and drained his cup, setting it down on the desk with a bang. Jeffries reached across and used his pencil to slide the cup out of Jones' reach. Jones frowned as he watched the clumsy way Jeffries moved the cup. 'Afraid I've got germs, officer?'

Jeffries glanced at Smith and winked. 'Something like that.'

Smith smiled, realising what was in the envelope.

Jeffries stood and addressed the constables. 'Escort Mr Jones to the cells and get him a sandwich.' He looked at Jones. 'We'll continue this conversation later. If I were you, I'd spend your time in the cell getting your story straight.'

Jones stood and pointed at Jeffries. 'You'd better have a good reason for all this. Mr Shute will be unhappy I'm being held here. This is outrageous! I haven't done anything wrong.'

Constable Harris held open the door as his colleague led Jones by the elbow and guided him out of the interview room. With Harris on one side and Cottem on the other, they turned right, leading Jones along the corridor towards the cells, Jeffries and Smith following a few paces behind. Jeffries spoke quietly to Smith. 'We might have the breakthrough we need.' He tapped his pocket. 'This envelope contains the fingerprint results, but we need to check it properly and work out how to play this. This fingerprint testing is new and we don't want to play our ace card without being absolutely sure first.'

The two constables struggled with Jones as they manoeuvred past a decorator working from a stepladder, concentration on his face as he painted the intricate details in the moulding. Without warning, Jones twisted to one side and launched himself at the ladder, smashing into it with his shoulder. The painter wavered momentarily as the ladder tilted, then almost in slow motion, still holding his paintbrush, he tumbled to the ground, landing on his side.

The paint pot fell from the painter's grip and hit Harris, whose hands flew to his face as he desperately tried to wipe at his eyes. He released his hold on Jones and turned from side to side, blinded by the sticky white mess, hopelessly trying to clear his vision. Cottem struggled to hold Jones, twisting the wriggling prisoner's arm behind him to restrain him. Jones was the larger of the two, and stronger. With one fluid movement, he snapped his head forward, aiming for Cottem's nose. The constable saw the move just in time and stepped back, losing his grip on Jones' arm. Jones made his next move, launching himself towards the main office.

Jeffries rushed over to Harris, wiping the man's eyes with his handkerchief, shouting to Smith, 'Get after him, Smith. Don't let him get away!'

Constable Harris put his hand out to Jeffries for support. 'I'm fine, sir. At least, I think so.' He looked about him, blinking hard and squinting. 'Everything's a bit blurry.'

'Get yourself to the washroom and clean that paint from your face before it permanently damages your eyes.' Jeffries turned his attention to the fleeing suspect, now bolting across the main office, Smith and Cottem in pursuit.

Despite his limp, Jones moved faster than both the constable and Smith. Constable Cottem dodged a paint tin, kicked over by Jones in an attempt to slow his pursuers. 'Stop him!' Cottem shouted to no one in particular.

Jones kept running and, risking a quick look over his shoulder, saw the officers were a good twenty yards away. Turning back, he vaulted over a desk, landing awkwardly, and headed for the door on the far side of the big office, empty now for lunchtime, except for one officer, sitting at his cluttered desk, his handkerchief tucked into the front of his shirt.

Constable Macintosh was enjoying a cup of tea with his egg sandwich, freshly made by his wife that morning as she did every morning. He had looked up, mid-bite, when he'd heard the commotion of the step ladder crashing to the ground. A man was running in his direction, a scowl on his face.

Macintosh liked life behind the desk. He had never been keen on the roughhousing and pursuit that often came with making arrests. Today, he saw a chance to apprehend a criminal and impress his superiors. As the man loped past his desk, Macintosh extended his leg and winced as the escapee crashed into his shin and flew forward.

Jeffries had caught up with Smith, and together, they watched in horror as Jones, still bound by handcuffs, crashed head-first into a desk. He slid to the floor, unmoving, his head bent at an odd angle. Macintosh swallowed the mouthful of egg sandwich and took a slurp of tea before getting up to inspect the damage.

Jeffries and Smith ran over to the desk where their suspect had fallen. 'Damn,' said Jeffries.

'You can thank me later,' said Macintosh, returning to his lunch.

'Thank you? You blithering idiot! He's dead, you fool! He was our main suspect.'

Macintosh sat back in his chair, his sandwich now forgotten. His face had turned a sickly white. 'But I thought I would just stop the man from getting away. I didn't intend…'

Smith felt for a pulse. Nothing. Jones was definitely dead.

Jeffries beckoned to Constable Cottem. 'Get a message to the coroner; we have a dead body for him.'

The constable nodded towards the inspector's office. 'A messenger will take a while. I heard the coroner now has a telephone for emergencies, and the inspector has one in his office.'

'Really? I had no idea. Good man. Quick as you can, Cottem.'

Cottem strode to the inspector's office. Thank goodness the inspector is out of the station. There's still time to get a story together and clear up this mess, thought Jeffries.

Constable Harris appeared at the door to the washroom, wiping the remains of the paint from his face, his uniform a patchwork of white paint and dark blue fabric. 'What the hell happened?'

Smith stepped away from Jones. 'Jones is dead. Thanks to Constable Macintosh.' He addressed Jeffries. 'What now, sir?'

Jeffries considered his options and, coming to a decision, turned to Constable Harris, still gawping at the carnage. 'Harris, make sure that no one else enters this room without my permission.' He turned back to Smith, reached into his pocket and fished out the key to the meeting room. 'Smith, cover the body, then wait here for the coroner to arrive while I decide what we're going to do next.'

Constable Harris walked to the main door and stood with his back to it, surveying the scene. He watched Smith covering the body with a coat he found on the back of a chair. Constable Macintosh sat in silence, his tea cooling beside his abandoned egg sandwich.

The painters were told to go home for the day. Jeffries hurried to the meeting room he and Smith had commandeered earlier. He needed a minute to think. Once inside, he sat with his head in his hands as he considered the implications of Jones' death. 'Damn!' he exclaimed, slamming his hands against the desktop.

This case was going from bad to worse. He now had a dead suspect, killed by one of the constables in his haste to help, a near-blind constable, who thankfully seemed all right now he'd cleaned himself up, and a police station that looked like a war zone. Ladders and paint pots were strewn over the floor. The inspector will be furious, and they were still no closer to solving the cases on their hands: two crashes and a dead photographer.

He suddenly remembered the report from earlier. He pulled out the document from his pocket and considered the details, quickly skimming the text and considered the image of the fingerprint, the only one the laboratory could see with any confidence, according to the letter attached. He was astonished to learn that, as Smith and Carrie had said, the print could only be from one person. The problem was, who? Jeffries knew it would take hours to find and extract a print from Jones' cup, and no one in the station knew how to do it anyway. They couldn't ask the now very dead Mr Jones for his prints to compare them with. Or could they? Jeffries read on. Interestingly, the report told him that the print was especially distinctive because it showed a diagonal line across a thumb, probably an old scar.

Jeffries jumped up from his chair and rushed back to the office where the body lay, guarded by Harris and Smith. Both men looked at Jeffries as he rushed into the room, waving the report. 'Smith, uncover him for me. Let me have a look at his hands.'

Smith moved the coat to one side while Harris looked on from his position by the door, perplexed.

Jeffries knelt by the body and inspected each finger in turn. 'According to the fingerprint report, there should be a line on one thumb. An old scar.' Jeffries checked Jones's fingers one more time. 'Well, that's disappointing. None of his thumbs has a scar. I thought we had our man. It wasn't Jones who handled the wedge.'

Smith covered the body once more. 'I thought you had our limping man there, sir. We need to consider anyone else who might have touched the wedge. Jones we know about, and there's that fellow who was seen with Jones at the studio. The one who probably worked out how to disable the braking mechanism.' Smith held out his hand for the report, and Jeffries absentmindedly passed it to him, standing up and stretching. 'I'm getting too old for this, Smith. Ah, the coroner is here. That new telephone in the inspector's office is useful after all.' Jeffries stood aside as Doctor Price joined them next to the body. 'Another body, Detective Sergeant? You seem to be attracting them lately.'

Jeffries sighed. 'They do seem to be piling up, don't they? Smith and I witnessed this man's death, so it should be an easy one for you.' He looked across at Macintosh, who was still frozen at his desk in some sort of trance. Jeffries continued, 'We chased him through the office after he'd broken away, and he fell and hit his head on the desk.' He looked back at the body. 'Snapped his neck, I shouldn't wonder.'

The coroner crouched down and felt the man's neck. 'Certainly looks that way. I'll have a better look back at the mortuary.'

Jeffries looked across at Harris and Cottem. 'You two. Get this placed cleaned up before the inspector gets in. Use Macintosh here to help.'

Jeffries nudged Smith. 'Come on, I need a coffee. Let's go and get a sandwich somewhere. We need something to eat before we visit Mr Shute.' He glared at Macintosh, who avoided his gaze. 'Especially now we've lost our one and only suspect.'

40

An assembly line and a restricted room

Jeffries liked to visit people unannounced whenever possible. It tended to catch them by surprise. Especially his suspects. The less they were prepared, the more they disclosed. Hopefully, they'd catch Mr Shute in his factory today and learn something to help their case. A case that was looking more and more like it was full of dead ends. Their key suspect, Albert Jones, was dead, and they still needed to find a match for the fingerprint. Proving their case and putting away one of the town's most powerful businessmen was proving to be tough, even with the most solid evidence.

A tall brick wall surrounded the factory. The only way in was through a large, metal gate guarded by a stern man wearing an official-looking uniform and carrying a clipboard.

As Jeffries and Smith reached the gate, the guard looked up from his clipboard and approached them. He peered through the bars. 'Can I help you, gentlemen?' he asked, clearly not keen to help anyone who wasn't on his list of approved visitors.

Jeffries reached into his pocket and retrieved his police identification. Smith did the same. They both held up their ID cards for the guard to inspect. He squinted and moved closer. The man needs eyeglasses, Jeffries thought.

'Police, eh?' He peered at the sheet on his clipboard. 'I don't have you on my list. What business do you have with the company, sirs?'

'We don't need to be on your list,' said Jeffries as he returned the card to his pocket. 'Kindly inform Mr Shute that we are here on police business, and we wish to ask him some questions to help with our enquiries.'

The guard paused, pursing his lips. 'Wait here.' He turned and walked back to his little guard house.

Through the side window, the two policemen could see the guard talking into a telephone, saving the guard from having to walk to the main office when a query such as this presented itself at his gate.

'Useful things, these telephones,' said Jeffries. 'They seem to be appearing everywhere. I suppose they could catch on. It certainly got the coroner to the station in record time.'

'Give it a few years, and we'll all have one at home, I don't doubt. It's progress, sir,' said Smith with a smile, amused that his colleague was finally embracing the future, despite being significantly older than Smith.

'Mm, maybe,' muttered Jeffries, his eyes never leaving the guard, who was now returning.

The guard ticked off an item on his list before reaching for the gate lock. He lifted the metal bar, and with some effort, pulled the gate open just enough for Jeffries and Smith to squeeze through. Once in the courtyard, the guard swung the gate closed with a clang and slid the bar back into place. The fortress is secure again, thought Smith.

'Go up those steps to the front door and my colleague will escort you to Mr Shute's office,' said the guard as he pointed to the main building. With that, he returned to his post in the little hut, grabbed his newspaper, and settled in until the next visitor.

Jeffries and Smith walked to the front door as instructed. 'Charming fellow,' said Smith.

The front door opened, and another uniformed guard waited for the two men to reach the top of the steps.

Jeffries and Smith accompanied the guard along a dark corridor. The walls were painted a dull green, and the only light was from a long line of bare bulbs hanging from the ceiling. They buzzed and flickered. The guard said over his shoulder, 'We're having some issues with the generator today.'

Not a good sign that an electric lights manufacturer is having problems with their lighting, Jeffries thought.

At the end of the corridor was a grey door. The guard pushed it open and pointed to a sofa in what appeared to be a reception office. A woman in a white blouse and black skirt sat typing on a shiny new Remington, only pausing to slide the carriage with a crash for each new line. She didn't look up as the men entered. 'Please take a seat. Mr Shute will be with you in a few minutes,' she said.

Jeffries and Smith examined the paintings on the walls. Most featured scenes of the town. One painting showed the cathedral with Deller's Café in the background. Jeffries smiled, thinking of the times he'd enjoyed a coffee and a bacon roll or two in that same establishment.

Both men opted to stand while they waited for Mr Shute. Jeffries checked his pocket watch against the time on the big wall clock. Mr Shute made them wait more than twenty minutes before he appeared with another man at his shoulder. The man accompanying Mr Shute was tall and muscular. At least six feet tall. He stood to one side as if guarding the door, his hands clasped in front of him. He wore a scowl on his clean-shaven face. Probably a boxer, thought Jeffries, noting the crooked nose and mangled ears.

Mr Shute ignored the two officers and leaned in close to the receptionist. A little too close. Jeffries strained to hear what Mr Shute said. Something about Jones. Jeffries smiled. News is travelling swiftly, he thought.

Mr Shute looked across at the two officers, his eyes resting on Jeffries, a flicker of recognition passing his face. 'Gentlemen. So sorry to have kept you waiting.' Jeffries noticed Mr Shute glancing up at the clock before his gaze snapped back to Jeffries. Mr Shute clicked his fingers. 'Ah, yes. Detective Sergeant Jeffries. We've met before. Never forget a face. How can I help, Detective? My man at the gate said you have some questions.' Mr Shute held out his hand.

Jeffries nodded and shook Mr Shute's hand. 'Hello, Mr Shute.' He turned to Smith. 'This is my colleague,

268

Constable Smith. We'd like to ask you some questions about the recent tram crashes.'

Mr Shute nodded at Smith, smirking. He held Smith's gaze. Smith couldn't help looking away. Even though he'd dealt with many a lowlife, there was something about Mr Shute that made his stomach roil. 'I'm not sure how I can help.' Mr Shute glanced at the clock again. 'I'm very busy, so please make it quick, and I'll assist you if I can.'

The secretary had stopped typing and started straightening a pile of documents, trying hard not to look like she was listening. The man guarding the door hadn't moved a muscle.

Jeffries pulled out his pocketbook and pencil before asking, 'How long have you been in the electric light business, Mr Shute?'

Mr Shute blinked before answering. 'Twenty years this December. Although I was involved in many businesses beforehand. I fail to see the significance, Detective Sergeant. I'm sure that hasn't any bearing on your enquiries.' Regaining his composure, he continued, 'Look, just what is this all about? I am very busy and would rather like to get on with my day.'

I'll be the judge of what has a bearing on our case and what doesn't, thought Jeffries, itching to say it out loud. Jeffries gritted his teeth before continuing. 'As I mentioned, we are investigating the trams that crashed in the town, especially the one on the bridge. I recall you were reading about it in your newspaper when we met in the public house.'

'How on earth would I be able to answer any questions about the trams? I don't ride them myself. I have my own carriage.'

'Do you know a Mrs Rose James?'

Mr Shute's expression didn't change. He didn't seem to have any tells at all, thought Smith.

Shute shook his head. 'I don't know the name, sorry.'

'What about Mr Westlake? A photographer?'

Smith watched more closely. There! A twitch at the edge of Shute's left eye. Blink, and you'd miss it.

Mr Shute looked across at the secretary, who immediately started typing again. He looked back to Jeffries. 'Sorry, I don't know that name either. Anyone else you'd like to ask me about, officer?'

'You're sure you don't know those names, sir?'

Mr Shute shook his head and smiled.

Jeffries decided to try another angle of questioning. 'What do you make here, exactly, sir?'

Mr Shute fiddled with the top button on his jacket, then proceeded to list everything they manufactured, from light bulbs to signalling equipment to experimental motor systems – all electrical. Feeling on safer ground, Mr Shute held his arms wide as he described his products to the officers.

It seemed to Jeffries that if an object moved, gave out light or made a sound, there was a way to use electricity to replace whatever technology was used previously. Jeffries wasn't sure if he liked the new, electric future. He rather liked things as they were.

Smith, on the other hand, listened raptly, nodding at every product or idea that Mr Shute mentioned.

Jeffries scribbled all this down in his book, then looked up when he'd finished writing. 'You didn't mention vehicles or trams, Mr Shute. Is that something your company would make, perhaps? Surely an electric carriage or tram would be an improvement on the smelly petrol motor vehicles we see more of these days. Or the old horse-drawn trams?'

Mr Shute smoothed his beard. 'Ah. Back to trams again, are we?' He sighed. 'Vehicles are very expensive to work with. We focus on smaller, more profitable products.' He pulled out his timepiece. 'Now, if that is all? I have an important meeting in a few minutes.'

Jeffries paused, trying to think of another question to get to the bottom of this case. Shute seemed to have an answer for everything. They were getting nowhere fast. Smith jumped in. 'Can we have a look around, Mr Shute? It all sounds so interesting!'

'I can't see how that helps your enquiries, but it can be arranged.' He gestured to his man still standing by the door. Motionless. Jeffries realised the man hadn't even blinked. 'Harold here will show you around. Harold, show the officers around the main factory. I'm sure workshop number one will be of most interest.'

Smith noticed the look between Mr Shute and Harold lingered just a second longer than expected, his gaze a little harder at the mention of workshop one. Harold nodded.

'Well, if that's all, gentlemen, I'll leave you in Harold's capable hands.'

Mr Shute turned to leave when Jeffries said, 'One more thing, Mr Shute. Can you account for your whereabouts last Monday evening, the seventh of October?'

Mr Shute stood perfectly still, rubbing his chin. 'The seventh, you say?' He smiled. 'Ah, yes. I was at a rather fine dinner at the club. We raised quite a lot of money for a local children's home as I recall. Why do you ask?'

'It's just a routine question, Mr Shute. Nothing to worry about. Can anyone vouch for you, sir?'

Mr Shute raised a finger. 'As a matter of fact, I can do better than that.' He reached across the reception desk and from the top of a side-table, picked up a newspaper and leafed through the pages. He folded the paper back on itself and held up the page for the officers to see. Jeffries peered at the page. The photograph showed a group of men, smiling at the camera. 'What is it I'm supposed to be looking at?' He asked.

Mr Shute shook his head. 'Come along, Detective. Am I to do your job for you? The date printed under the photograph is the seventh of October - the night you are enquiring about - for reasons that are still unclear to me - and that's me, in the middle. Shaking hands with the mayor. Does that vouch for me that evening, Detective?'

Jeffries looked closer. The small printed words "October 7th" felt like a stab in the gut. They'd have to check, but it certainly looked as though Mr Shute was indeed accounted for on that Monday evening. With the mayor.

'Well, if that's all, I need to get back to work. This factory doesn't run itself.' Mr Shute said, tossing the newspaper back onto the table.

'Of course, Mr Shute. We'll be in touch if we have more questions for you.'

Mr Shute muttered something under his breath before heading back to his office, the door slamming shut behind him. Damn nosy police, Jeffries thought it sounded like. Good, he's getting nervous. He spoke quietly in Smith's ear. 'Get a constable to check his story, Smith. Find out what time he arrived and left this event of his.' Smith nodded.

Harold gestured to a door on the other side of the room. 'This way, gentlemen. Be sure to stay close. Factories can be dangerous places.'

The officers followed Harold along a corridor, descending metal stairs to a lower floor before coming to a set of double doors. Harold pushed open both doors and ushered the officers through, entering the factory. The doors closed behind them with a thud. Jeffries decided that the doors must be soundproofed as the noise on this side was deafening. Men were grinding, sawing, welding and hammering. Sparks flew about the huge workshop. The ceiling was at least twenty feet high, the steel rafters covered in dust and grime. The air was full of the acrid smell of scorched metal.

They walked along a designated pathway, distinguished by a thick rope hung between equally-spaced posts set into the floor, stretching the length of the building. The two officers could see a pattern in the chaos. Welders worked on steel sections on the left, while men worked on partly finished frameworks on the right, hammering and fixing

272

parts together. At the end of the workshop, completed parts were loaded onto racks. It all looked very organised.

'Where are those parts being sent next, Harold?' shouted Jeffries.

Harold leaned in close and shouted above the din, pointing to a huge set of doors at the end of the factory floor. 'To the paint shop over in another building. The paint shop has to be kept clean, so it's separate from this area.'

Harold pointed to an area to their left. 'These are electrical parts. They're for the new generators being built in the town to provide electricity to homes and businesses. It's the future.' He grinned. 'Be glad to get rid of the smelly gas lights, that's for sure.' Jeffries and Smith shared a look.

They continued past a huge machine that looked like a loom, the threads racing through the machine in a blur. The machine shuddered and whined as the threads ran through guides at such a speed that Jeffries and Smith could barely see what the machine was doing. Jeffries stopped and pointed to the machine, shouting above the noise it made. 'What's this machine making?'

'This is our new wiring machine. It's coating the bare wires in a cotton protector. The cotton acts as an insulator. Most insulated cables are insulated with gutta-percha, a natural latex material produced from tree sap, but it tends to degrade quickly.' He puffed out his chest, holding out a piece of the cotton for the officers to inspect. 'Sleeving the wire with cotton is a new method and will last much longer. The machine was shipped in from the US only last month. You're the first visitor to see wire insulated in this way.'

The two policemen inspected the sample in Jeffries' hand and glanced at one another, recalling the cotton thread retrieved from Harry's neck.

'May we keep this sample?' asked Jeffries.

Harold shrugged. 'Help yourself.' He turned and beckoned them to follow. 'This way, gentlemen.'

They passed a big set of closed metal doors so high that they almost touched the rafters. The number 2 was painted in the middle of one door, with Restricted Area - Authorised Personnel Only painted below in yellow.

Smith nudged Jeffries and tilted his head towards the door. Jeffries had already noticed it and shook his head. Smith frowned.

Harold stopped by a long conveyor belt full of electrical parts. He held his arm out, indicating the assembly area, and leaned closer so they could hear him above the racket. 'This is the lamp section of the factory. We make a new type of light powered by electricity. Light bulbs of all sizes and ratings and for all uses, from household lights to chandeliers that can illuminate halls and theatres. We borrowed the assembly line idea from a motor car factory in America. Have you heard of Henry Ford?'

Jeffries nodded. 'Henry Ford, yes. A customer can have a car painted any colour they want, so long as it's black. That's his sales pitch, I think.'

'Mr Shute met him last year, and he discovered that Ford was planning to create what they call an assembly line. We copied the idea here. As you can see, it works really well. The parts move down this belt, which is powered by electricity. The line runs at a constant speed, just slow enough for our workers to assemble the parts without having to move about the workshop. This process saves hundreds of hours. Before we set this up, the workers had to walk from one assembly area to another, pulling carts with the pieces behind them. Wasted hours, it did.'

The two officers watched, mesmerised, as the parts moved slowly past them. Workers picked up a part, fitted it to another in one swift movement, and placed it back on the line. They repeated this over and over.

Jeffries reached across and picked up a part. Harold grabbed it out of Jeffries' hand. 'You idiot, don't touch anything! This process is… oh hell! Look what you've done!'

They watched the domino effect as the other pieces bumped into each other, and the whole line of moving parts started to cascade off the side of the line. The assembly line workers jumped up, shouting and scrabbling to stop the parts from crashing to the floor. Harold reached across and thumped a big red button above the assembly line. An alarm sounded, and the line ground to a halt.

Jeffries nudged Smith and gestured towards the restricted area they had passed earlier. Smith nodded and took a step back behind a pile of wooden crates. He looked about him and walked quickly to the set of big doors, the one on the left had a smaller, man-size door set in the middle. Ensuring everyone was distracted by the chaos, Smith carefully pushed the small door open an inch or two. He peered through the gap.

He wasn't sure what he was seeing at first. The area was remarkably clean and virtually empty, except for a wooden tram-like vehicle in the centre. A man in overalls sat in a compartment at the front of the contraption. Facing forwards, he operated levers while looking straight ahead, brow furrowed. Another man, also in overalls, stood at the end of the room, a clipboard in one hand and a signal flag in the other.

The contraption was unlike any tram Smith had seen before. The body was shiny and had big windows along each side. There was another deck above, covered by a curved roof. Attached to the roof was a long metal pole that reached up to a pair of overhead steel lines, stretching from one side of the room to the other, held aloft by metal structures that almost reached the roof.

Conscious he needed to return before Harold noticed he'd wandered off, he watched as the tram moved forward almost silently, sparks showering from the end of the pole where it met the overhead lines.

The driver moved some levers in the cab, and the tram sped up a little as it moved along the short line. When it reached the end, the man with the clipboard raised his flag, waving it from side to side, and the tram came to a halt. The driver pulled back the lever, and the tram began its smooth run backwards, halting at its starting point.

'Time to go,' said Smith to himself as he closed the door and walked briskly back to where he'd left Jeffries and the chaotic assembly line.

The line was running again when Smith sidled up to Jeffries, standing with his arms crossed as if he'd watched the whole episode unfold. The supervisor turned from the line, scowled at Jeffries and wiped his brow with an oily rag. 'Now, please don't touch anything. The show's over, gentlemen.'

A look passed between the two officers as they followed Harold back to the reception area. Mr Shute was leaning against the reception desk, having emerged from his office, no doubt alerted to the commotion in the factory. The typist was enthralled with his every word, returning to her work as Jeffries and Smith entered the room.

Mr Shute pushed away from the wall, walked towards the three men. 'Everything all right, Harold? I heard the assembly line alarm a minute ago.'

Harold glanced at Jeffries. 'Just a jam on the line, sir. Nothing serious. I'll get back to work unless you need me for something else?'

'That's all, Harold. Thank you. These gentlemen were just leaving, isn't that right, officers?'

Jeffries had been scribbling something in his notebook. He slipped the pencil and book into his pocket. 'Yes, we need to be going. Thank you for seeing us, sir. The tour of the factory was most interesting.'

As the two policemen found themselves on the street outside the factory, Jeffries turned to Smith, holding up the sample of cotton thread between his fingers. 'This is the

276

same cotton we found on Westlake's neck, I'm sure of it,' said Jeffries. 'What do you make of it, Smith?'

'It certainly looks the same. And combined with the wire we saw in there, the two combined is strong enough to strangle someone. That's what I think.'

Jeffries smiled. 'Exactly. What did you see behind that restricted area?'

'I'll tell you everything over a sandwich and a coffee. After all that excitement, I'm starving.'

'You're beginning to sound like me, Smith. Come on then, but it's your turn to pay.'

41

A summary, a tram and an electric spark

Smith bought sandwiches and two steaming cups from the sandwich seller on the corner of South Street. Tea for Smith, while Jeffries had chosen coffee.

'These sandwich sellers are getting popular, Smith. Saves hanging around in the café, and we can eat outside on a dry day like this.'

Smith considered the grey clouds scudding across the sky. 'Let's hope the weather holds long enough for us to finish our food.'

Sitting on the wall surrounding the cathedral grounds with their food unwrapped, Jeffries took a bite of his sandwich, and wiped his mouth with his handkerchief. 'I do hope the station is all cleared up before the inspector gets back, Smith. We'll have some explaining to do.'

Smith spoke with his mouth full. 'What did you make of Shute's factory?'

'Ah, yes. The factory. Don't keep me in suspense. What did you see behind that door?'

Smith took a sip of his tepid tea, grimacing. He'd asked for sugar, but not two spoonful's.

He put his cup down on the wall. 'I couldn't quite make out what I was seeing at first. The area was enormous. The roof was double the height of the rest of the factory. A length of tram line was laid from one end of the area to the other. On it sat a tram, but it wasn't like the ones we see on the street. It looked sleeker. The windows were larger, and the sides were smoother. More curved.'

Jeffries downed the rest of his coffee. 'Go on.'

'The tram didn't have horse harnesses, although there was still space for a driver, just like a regular tram. On the roof was a long metal pole that reached up to a wire suspended between two metal structures at each end of the line. And this is the amazing part. Just as John described, the tram was being powered by electricity. As the tram moved, sparks shot from the top of the pole where it met the wire. It was like nothing I'd seen before.'

Jeffries finally understood. 'So, there are no horses and no noisy, smelly petrol engines. Just electricity?'

'Yes! It was so quiet and smooth except for the crackle of the sparks. No wonder Shute wanted it kept under wraps. This will revolutionise public transport.'

Jeffries screwed up his sandwich wrapping and threw it at a litter bin, scoring a bulls-eye. 'I'd wager a month's pay Mr Shute was behind the first crash, if not the second one. If he can speed up the demise of the horse-drawn trams, the way is clear for his revolutionary electric trams.' He shook his head. 'Did you notice how he pointedly told Harold to show us the main factory? He was obviously ensuring we were kept away from that big warehouse to keep that electric tram under wraps.'

Smith grinned. 'And don't forget what John said about electrifying the streets. Once the lines are installed for the trams, Shute can then offer his electricity to the whole town and beyond. It's a motive, sir. A bloody big motive at that.'

Jeffries sighed. 'All very good, having suspicions and making new discoveries, but none of it is actually hard evidence, is it, Smith?'

'Perhaps not, but it's a picture that is gradually coming together. Like a puzzle. We just need to put all the pieces into place and then present the details to the inspector.'

Jeffries thought for a moment. 'Come on, Smith. It's been a long day. I need to sleep on this. We need a plan.'

42

The attic room, cobwebs and a dusty desk

Thursday morning. Another day in the office when I'd rather be somewhere else. Mr Edwards' office door opens with a creak. I look up and see he's standing in the open doorway, smiling. 'Carrie, my dear. Could I have a word?' He disappears back into his office. I swear I heard him whistling a tune as he retreats.

Startled and jarred from my thoughts, I look across at William as he peeks around the stack of papers piled high on his desk. He smiles, rolls his eyes and nods in the direction of his father's office. 'Sounds like you've been summoned.'

'Why's he in such a buoyant mood today?'

William shrugs his shoulders. 'Who knows? Perhaps he's taken on a new client.'

I cap my fountain pen and lay it on my blotter, push my chair back and go to Mr Edwards' office. The door is still open. Out of habit, I tap on the frame and step across the threshold, the room warm with the little fire burning fiercely in the corner as usual. 'Mr Edwards?' I say, standing in front of his desk.

Mr Edwards signs a paper with a flourish, blots it and drops his pen into the holder on his desk. He leans back in his sumptuous leather chair, nodding to a pile of box folders on the chair beside me. 'Ah, Miss Grey, kindly take those files to the attic room and store them alphabetically on the shelves. Thank you.'

'Of course, Mr Edwards.'

Mr Edwards reaches across his desk for the post that I had set there this morning. 'Don't forget to wedge the door open, or it'll close and lock you in. There's no door knob on the inside. The last assistant forgot to wedge the door, and we didn't find him for over an hour.' He smiles. 'Not a pleasant experience, I believe, as the attic is the coldest room in this building.'

Having cautiously gathered all the files in my arms so as not to drop any, I take the back stairs to the attic.

Reaching the attic door, I put the files on a small mahogany table on the landing. The table leans against the wall to keep it upright, one of its legs shorter than its companions. It's seen better days: the top is stained with cup rings, and one drawer is missing.

The door to the attic room has a lock, the key in place, the handle once bright brass, now dull from neglect. The top half of the door is glazed with the type of glass that allows light through but is not completely transparent. Frosted, I think it's called.

The glass is dirty with years of dust.

The wedge hangs from a hook on the wall above the table. As I reach up for it, I recall the last wedge I held in my hand, from the wood pile in the alleyway, wrapped in a handkerchief. This wedge is wooden but different. It has a rougher finish, poorly fashioned into a wedge shape.

Pushing the door open, I reach down and shove the wedge underneath, ensuring it's firmly in place with a smart kick. Through the open doorway, a faint light from a grimy roof window does a reasonable job of lifting the gloom, revealing a small room with shelves on the wall to my right, a petite desk and a chair against the far wall, directly under the window. Cobwebs stretch between the wall and the dusty desk. An old pen stands to attention in a dry inkwell.

Satisfied the wedge is secure, I grab the files from the table on the landing and step into the cold attic room, a cobweb stroking the side of my face. A shudder runs down my neck.

I step across the little room and drop the files onto the desk with a thump, disturbing a cloud of dust. Stifling a sneeze with my sleeve, I look around me. The room has clearly not been used for years, apart from accepting old files.

The desk is small, with drawers on either side and a small gap in the middle, barely enough for a person's knees. I move the chair out from this cubby hole and push it to one side, its wobbly wheels squeaking in protest.

I draw my fingers along the top of the desk, leaving lines in the dust then turn my attention to the job in hand.

I only take a minute or two to organise the files, stacking them on the shelves along the wall in their correct order. Alphabetical, as instructed.

With a satisfied sigh, I step through to the landing and remove the wedge, reaching up and hanging it back on the hook.

The door swings closed with a click. I turn and step across the small landing. Inspiration strikes at the top of the stairs. Turning back, I look at the glass half of the door in front of me, take a step forward and reach up, touching the glass. With my finger, I write my name in capital letters, underlining each word. I like the way it looks.

'Have you completed that task, Carrie?' William appears on the landing below. I hadn't heard his footsteps. I quickly scrub out the words with my sleeve and take the stairs to join him. 'All done!' I say with a new enthusiasm. William shakes his head in despair. 'First my father is suddenly full of the joys of Spring, now you're suddenly happy. What is going on in this office today?'

I place a finger against my lips, hiding a smile. 'I have no idea, William.'

43

A plan and a hearty breakfast

While Jeffries enjoyed breakfast with his wife, they got onto the subject of his case. Edith didn't enjoy the sickening details of some of the crimes her husband worked on, but she was happy to discuss them and offer a fresh perspective. The excitement of her day was usually a game of bridge or a cup of tea with her close circle of friends, and so the crimes, horrible though they were, held a morbid sense of curiosity.

Jeffries had been frustrated with the progress of the cases of both tram crashes and Harry Westlake's death. They had leads and theories but no real proof that would nail Mr Shute or anybody else, for that matter. There was the cotton thread and some witnesses, but they needed something that would tie the whole thing together and make the cases watertight.

Edith listened intently then said, 'If only you could turn back the clock and catch this Mr Shute red-handed when he instructed his man to nobble the tram.'

Jeffries leapt up from the breakfast table so quickly that he almost knocked over his plate of kippers. His cup of tea clattered in its saucer. 'That's it!' he exclaimed, slinging his napkin onto the table. 'That's the answer. Why hadn't I thought of that before?'

Edith's hand flew to her chest. 'I didn't mean actually turn the clocks back. That's pure Jules Verne nonsense, darling.'

Jeffries waved his hands about. 'No. Of course. But we could perhaps encourage our Mr Shute to play his card again, but this time, we'll be ready to nab him when he makes his move.'

***

Later, in Deller's, Jeffries looked across at the door each time it opened, waiting for Smith to arrive.

Jeffries' coffee was hot and strong. With his drink, Jeffries had some scrambled eggs on toast. He hadn't quite finished his kippers at home before he'd rushed out, and the aroma at Deller's had triggered his appetite again. His intuition insisted today would be a good day.

He'd just finished his breakfast, wiping the plate clean with a crust of bread, when Constable Smith walked in and made his way to the table, signalling to the waitress. He sat opposite Jeffries as the waitress stood with her notebook and pencil at the ready. 'I'll have a coffee and one of your splendid bacon sandwiches, please,' Smith said to the young woman. She nodded, scribbled his order, then strode over to the kitchen.

Smith lined up the salt and pepper pots. 'By the way, Constable Harris checked Mr Shute's timings on that Monday evening. Apparently, he was at the club early as he had a meeting before the main event, and he didn't leave until midnight. A little worse for wear, as it happens. Harris tracked down the carriage driver and he confirmed he'd taken Mr Shute straight home, even saw him to his door as he was concerned that he might not make it, he was that drunk.'

Jeffries nodded. 'Well, we know he didn't carry out the sabotage on the tram himself. He definitely arranged it, I'm sure of it. Got his heavies to do the deed. I can't see Mr Shute getting his hands dirty.'

Jeffries considered the plate in front of him. Disappointed that it was already clean. 'Thank you for meeting me here a little earlier than our usual start time. I find we achieve more on a full stomach and the breakfast is much nicer here than the station canteen.'

'Happy to start with a decent breakfast, sir. I received your curious message just as I was leaving the house. Another minute and I'd have missed the messenger. What's on your mind, sir?'

Jeffries wiped his mouth and pushed his empty plate to one side. He drank the remains of his coffee and looked Smith in the eye, smiling. 'I have a plan, Smith.'

Smith sat back in his chair and glanced across at the waitress, hoping he'd have time to enjoy his breakfast. He could tell Jeffries was keen to get started with this plan of his, judging by his excited expression.

'Go on, I'm listening.'

'We need to catch our culprit in the act, and the only way we can do that is to engineer a situation Mr Shute will find irresistible. And when he makes his move, we'll be there to pounce on him.'

'I don't understand. How on earth do we make him do what we need him to do?'

Just then, John walked through the door with Carrie and William in tow. John was smiling from ear to ear. Carrie and William grinned behind him. They already know the plan, thought Smith.

Jeffries had sent messages requesting they all meet at the café. The three friends sat at the table. Smith appraised them. 'So, I'm the last one to hear this plan, I assume?'

Jeffries shook his head. 'Of course not, Smith. Our friends know there is a plan, but they don't know the details yet.' He pulled out his notebook, turned to the back and tore out a few pages, checking the name on the top of each sheet and passing them out like a card dealer at one of Smith's poker games. 'Each of you has a part to play in my plan, and timing is key. These are the details.' He turned to the new arrivals, signalling to the waitress. 'Now, what would you like for breakfast? It's my treat.'

44

A public garden and a line baited

The morning was almost gone, the time racing by at the office as William and I discuss ways to help Detective Jeffries with his daring plan. He left it to us to work out a way to get close to Mr Shute, to trick him into making a move. We rejected several of our own ideas, including William's daft plan of pretending to be lost in Shute's garden. I said we'd had our fair share of adventures in that garden, thank you very much. We sat looking at a newspaper cutting of Mr Shute and his wife, the photograph taken at a fund-raising event. Mrs Shute appeared several years younger than her husband, smiling for the camera, her hair held high in a fashionable bun. Mr Shute wasn't smiling. Perhaps he'd been asked to donate some of his precious money.

'We need to accidentally bump into them in a public place, when his guard will be down,' I say. 'Mr Shute must find time to relax, surely. Do you think he might accompany his wife somewhere, perhaps to show her off?' I take bites of sugary shortbread from William's biscuit tin.

'That's it, Carrie!' William exclaims, nearly knocking over the tin. 'I knew I'd seen him somewhere. He takes a walk after lunch every day with his wife.'

'Where?'

'There's a park near the courts called Northernhay Gardens. It's not close to Shute's house, so their driver takes them in the carriage and waits for them.' William smiles now. 'That's where we shall be when we bait our line. We don't have much time. It's gone noon already, but if we hurry, we might catch them. Father's meeting his bank manager, so he'll be ages. Come on, Carrie, grab your coat!'

Having shrugged on our coats and locked the office door, we dash through the streets to the park. As we get closer to the gates, we slow down. 'Best catch our breath before our leisurely stroll,' I pant. The stitch in my side fades as we enter the gardens with the warm sun on our backs. It's not too busy, so it will be easy to spot Mr Shute and his wife. We feign interest in the flowerbeds as we scour the area, walking slowly along the perimeter path.

As we start our second loop around the gardens, we both spot them at the same time, sitting on a bench. There are two other benches to the side of the one they occupy, set around a statue of the deerstalker, a foreboding man and his hunting dog, poised to catch their prey. I smile. How appropriate.

We walk casually up to the benches and sit at the one to the left of the Shute's, keeping our heads down. Mr Shute is deep in conversation with his wife when he spots us. He raises his eyebrows and smiles in recognition. 'Ah, Miss Grey. Enjoying the sunshine on this fine day?'

Mr Shute turns back to his wife. 'This is Miss Grey. I believe she works with Mr Edwards, the lawyer.' He's obviously looked into me, I think. I hadn't told him where I worked.

Mrs Shute nods. 'Yes, I've met Mr Edwards at some event or other.' She looks at William. 'I assume you are his son. You certainly look like him.'

William takes his cue. 'Yes, I'm his son William, and Miss Grey works with me at the firm.' He touches the brim of his hat. 'I'm pleased to meet you.'

Mr Shute crosses his arms and leans back, considering us. He turns to his wife. 'Miss Grey called on me some days ago to ask me some questions about the tram crashes.'

Mrs Shute shakes her head. 'Terrible business. I heard a young lady died in the bridge crash. So awful. Those trams are death-traps, so old and in need of repair. I'm not surprised they crashed.'

Mr Shute looks at William. 'What sort of law do you practice, Mr Edwards?'

William smiles, the conversation flowing as he anticipated. Come on William, I think. Keep him talking. Stick to the plan.

'My main interest is in corporate law. Fraud, embezzlement and so on. A lot depends on my father's wishes, though, as it's his practice.' I refrain from smiling, corporate law indeed. William is playing a perfect part.

I pull my coat collar tighter against the breeze. William glances at me, and I take this to be my cue. Looking at Mr Shute, I say, 'William is being bashful. He has a new client, don't you, William?' I look at William, then back to Mr Shute. 'His father has entrusted him with the company that runs the tram system. Apparently, due to the recent crashes, the tram company has found a new investor to help them modernise its fleet of trams and extend the service. William has been entrusted with drawing up the legal papers.'

Mr Shute subtly raises an eyebrow. 'How very interesting. Who is the investor, Mr Edwards? They must have deep pockets.'

William fiddles with his walking stick, drawing lines in the dirt at his feet. 'Carrie, you should know that some cases are confidential. I thought my father had taught you that on your first day.' To Mr Shute, he says, 'Miss Grey is new and forgets that some details are confidential to protect our clients. I'm afraid I can't disclose the investor's name, but I believe one of the trams is undergoing a new paint job as we speak. The engineers and painters are working day and night to ensure the tram is serviced and painted in her new colours for a grand procession at the weekend to announce the new venture.'

Mrs Shute says, 'I am surprised to hear that.' She turns to her husband. 'I thought you said the trams were so downright dangerous that they needed replacing.' Before Mr Shute could respond, she addresses William and Carrie, 'Of course, I don't take the tram as we have a carriage.'

Mr Shute looks red about the collar as he stands and reaches for his wife's hand. 'Well, dear. I think it's time we finished our walk. Jenkins will be waiting.'

Mr Shute touches his hat and bows slightly. 'Well, Miss Grey, Mr Edwards. Good day to you both.'

Mrs Shute stands, picks up her umbrella and adjusts her hat. 'It was nice to meet you both.'

With that, they walk briskly to the entrance of the gardens, deep in conversation. Mrs Shute peers back before they round the corner out of sight.

William stands and gives a stretch, grinning all the while. 'I think they bought our story. All we can do now is hope for the best. We've done all we can.'

45

A dark workshop, an electric light and a camera

Smith was already at the workshop with John, William and Carrie. Jeffries was nowhere to be seen. A newly painted tram sat in the middle of the workshop, resplendent in her fresh colours of cream and brown. The paint was barely dry. John's colleagues had done well, considering they were engineers, not coach workers. Certainly not painters.

Smith took out his pocket watch, tapped the glass and returned it to his pocket. 'Where the hell is Jeffries? We agreed to be in place at six o'clock after the workers left for home.' He turned to John and pointed to the bright light bulb above them. 'I see you managed to connect the electricity. The light is extraordinary.'

John smiled, holding up a thick cable, one end snaking into the rafters above them, the other connected to a small metal box in his hand. Two brass switches were screwed to the top, one larger than the other. 'Yes, we connected it up just before you arrived.'

Carrie frowned. 'How did you manage that? I thought there was a long waiting list to get connected. And it's expensive.'

John locked the main door and gave his usual mischievous smile. 'We are lucky that one of the foundries on the quay has the new power supply, and the boss is a good friend of mine. We managed to make a temporary connection to their factory. Hopefully, the cable we ran along the road is hidden well enough. We don't want someone to trip over it.'

Their conversation was cut short as the front door creaked open. Jeffries walked in carrying a large wooden box. 'Sorry I'm late. I had something to collect for our little event this evening. I've also arranged for two constables to conceal themselves outside. They're good men, Cottem and Harris. I've instructed them to stay hidden until we need them.'

Jeffries busied himself with the contents of his box while the others settled down for what promised to be a long night. Constable Smith watched Jeffries work, everything suddenly making sense. With a nod from the detective sergeant, Smith, Carrie and William hid in their respective spots. John stood next to the front door, waiting for the detective sergeant's instructions. The workshop now appeared empty. Jeffries took a deep breath. 'Right. We're all ready. John, the light, please.'

John crawled under the workbench, made himself as comfortable as possible in the confined space, next to William hiding in the same place. John flicked the switch on the metal box, and the workshop plunged into darkness. The bulb glowed for a moment before dying out completely.

The workshop fell silent, save for the occasional creaking ceiling rafter as it settled. The furnace dimmed as the coals began to cool. Muffled sounds came from the quay outside. Crates crashed and sailors shouted to quay workers as they worked late into the night, ready for the morning tide.

John and William were getting cramps, bent double under the workbench, John still clutching the metal box, the cable now hidden from view. Jeffries had found a hiding place behind the door that led to the welding area. His stomach rumbled. Smith stood with Carrie behind a tall cupboard, dusty and covered in cobwebs. Carrie shuddered, trying not to sneeze.

The workshop grew even quieter. The moonlight shone weakly through the skylight, though not enough to illuminate the scene as they waited.

Then, the squeak of a door opening. Steps across the floor above them. Muffled voices. More footsteps as the intruders made their way down the stairs to the workshop office. A pause, then the lock clicking and the door opening, the key having been left back in its place by John earlier.

Cramps and hunger quickly forgotten, John and William peered into the shadows from their hiding place. Jeffries held his breath, his heart beating fast in his chest. Carrie and Smith stood upright, backs to the cupboard.

Jeffries had the best view as two figures crept into the workshop. The one in front had a bag over his shoulder and held a dim lamp. The man with the lamp was large, but it was too dark to see his face. The other man, a few steps behind and looking about, was definitely Mr Shute. Jeffries had no doubt as he watched the familiar silhouette walk across the workshop floor.

The two men gingerly approached the tram, picking their way past toolboxes and piles of spare parts, their path barely illuminated by the little lamp carried by the first man. The two men walked past the workbench. John and William slunk back further into their hiding place. Carrie risked a glance around the cupboard but couldn't see much. Her hiding place was not in the best location.

Mr Shute turned to the man with the lamp. 'Well, get on with it, man. Don't bother with that wedge thing from the last time. We don't want another death on our hands. Two are enough for one month. All we need to do is make the tram fail. Cut the harness halfway through as we agreed. It will fall apart under strain, and the tram will stop. No nasty crashes, just another unreliable tram.'

The other man grunted something and set down his lamp to see the tram more clearly. He pulled a saw from his bag and leaned down to start cutting the harness frame.

As soon as the sound of the saw filled the quiet workshop, Jeffries shouted, 'Lights, John!' Within a split second, the workshop was filled with the most dazzling light they had ever seen. Jeffries leapt up and reached for the camera he had set up earlier. He paused a second before moving the lens in the direction of the two men and operating the shutter. A flash appeared from an arm above the lens, even brighter than the electric light illuminating the workshop. The flash emitted a loud crack as it burst for a second. Mr Shute, startled by this new light, covered his eyes, groaning.

The other man dropped his saw and ran for the door to the studio. 'Stop him!' shouted Jeffries. Smith was a few paces behind as the man toppled a pile of boxes. Smith stumbled as the crates cascaded across the floor, emptying the contents of machine parts as their lids broke free. 'Damn!' he yelled, struggling to keep his footing.

John and William pulled themselves from their hiding place. Carrie leapt from hers. 'William, help the detective sergeant with Shute. John, open the front door. We can head the other man off on the stairs outside. It's his only escape route!'

John fumbled in his pocket, withdrew the key as he sprinted to the door, Carrie following close behind. John slipped the key into the lock and swung the door open. He and Carrie ran to the passageway, to the metal stairs beyond.

Meanwhile, having jumped over the toppled boxes, Smith chased the henchman into the office. The man ran through the door, slamming it shut behind him. Smith reached the door as he heard the lock click. Grabbing the handle, he pushed repeatedly against the unyielding door. There was no time for keyhole trickery now. Remembering how Jeffries had forced open the darkroom door, he raised his right foot and kicked at the lock with the heel of his police-issue boots. The flimsy lock was no match for Smith's hobnailed footwear. The frame gave way, splintering with a crack as the door sprang open. Smith ran up the stairs in the dark, his quarry's footsteps echoing ahead of him.

Smith reached the studio above. Where the hell is he? Moonlight shone in through the big front windows. Smith was sure the man was still in the studio. He withdrew his truncheon from his belt, his shadow playing on the wall as he inched slowly across the studio floor. He was reminded of his fight with Jones and his chums in the street. On that occasion, he could see his attackers and had the upper hand, facing them as he did. This time, it was dark and Smith entered blindly into the studio's gloom, the moonlight now blanketed by dark clouds scudding across the sky.

There was barely a sound as the photography backdrop swung in the semi-darkness towards Smith, striking the side of his head. As he fell to the floor, he was vaguely aware of a figure running through the door to the night beyond. The man's footsteps clattered down the steel steps as Smith lay there, dazed, his head pounding. He reached up to his forehead and felt a sticky wetness. Blood. 'Damn!'

In the workshop, Jeffries had apprehended a very annoyed Mr Shute. 'You'll be hearing from my solicitor about this, Detective Sergeant. You have no right to handle me like a common criminal! You do know I am acquainted with your inspector?'

His legs planted wide, arms out, William stood in front of Mr Shute, preventing him from getting any ideas of escape. Jeffries tightened his grip on Shute's elbow as he handcuffed him. 'I don't care one jot about who your acquaintances are, Mr Shute. We know you caused the death of a young woman in a tram that you ordered to be sabotaged, you arranged for a second tram to crash, mercifully nobody was badly hurt, and we have evidence you were involved in Harry Westlake's murder. We have enough to convince a jury to send you down for a very long time.'

'Pah! Evidence? What evidence? You have nothing, Detective Sergeant. I admit I entered this workshop without permission, but nothing more.'

'I have all the evidence I need.' Jeffries turned Mr Shute to face the main door where the two constables were waiting, their faces grim, stamping their feet in the chilled air to keep warm. A police carriage stood waiting; the driver wrapped up against the bitter cold. The carriage's barred windows the only difference between a regular carriage and a prison one. 'Constables, get this man locked in the carriage. We'll question him later, and for God's sake, don't let him get away. Constable Smith will go with you to make sure nothing goes wrong.' Jeffries looked around. 'If I can find him.'

While Jeffries looked for Smith, Carrie and John appeared at the main door, faces red. Carrie shook her head, mouth set in a straight line. 'We were too late. He managed to climb the woodpile and leap over the wall. We lost him.' Jeffries nodded in the direction of the workshop. 'Never mind, we've got the main suspect. Mr Shute's none too happy about that, mind.' Jeffries looked around. 'Where the hell is Smith?'

As they all looked around the brightly lit workshop, Jeffries spotted Smith staggering from the office, clutching his head. 'What the hell happened to you, Smith?'

Smith reached the group and shook his head. 'He got away, sir. I'm sorry.'

Jeffries passed him his handkerchief. 'No matter, Smith. We've got Shute. Caught him red-handed. Here, clean yourself up. That looks like a nasty cut you've got there. Are you feeling alright?'

Smith took the cloth and gingerly dabbed his forehead, managing a weak smile. 'Yes, sir. It's not too bad. I think I need to sit down.' Smith pulled out a stool from the workbench and lowered himself onto it. 'Did you manage to take a photograph of the suspect, sir?'

Jeffries grinned and nodded to the wooden box. 'I did indeed, Smith.'

William laughed. 'I wondered what you were doing earlier. Fancy yourself as a photographer, Detective Sergeant?'

'Quite possibly. I'll need something to pass the time when I retire.' Jeffries called out to Harris and Cottem.

'Escort Mr Shute to the station and take Constable Smith with you. Make him a sweet tea. Get Mr Shute settled in a cosy cell for the night; let him stew for a while. No doubt he'll want to speak to his solicitor. He's going to need one.'

46

A treat for a job well done

The following evening, they had Deller's Café completely to themselves. John did indeed have a connection with one of the waitresses, and he'd managed to get the establishment opened just for them for a celebratory supper. Jeffries was paying. 'On expenses,' he'd said, but Smith suspected he was paying out of his own pocket.

They chatted while their food was served, a choice of a fine meat pie and mash, or pork chops with roasted potatoes. John poured the wine, and when everyone had a full measure, they clinked glasses to celebrate their success.

In between mouthfuls of food, Jeffries told them how the questioning with Shute had gone. Both he and Smith had spent the best part of an afternoon with Shute and his solicitor in the smallest, most depressing interview room they could find.

'He denied everything at first,' Jeffries said, shaking his head and smiling at the memory. 'Even his expensive solicitor looked dubious as Shute dug a deeper and deeper hole, contradicting himself at each turn.'

Smith tipped his head back and laughed. 'At first, Shute denied doing anything wrong in the workshop. Then we sprung the photograph of the exact moment Shute held the lamp as the other man sabotaged the tram. What a masterstroke.'

Jeffries reached into his pocket, withdrew a creased photograph and laid it on the table for all to see. Carrie picked it up. 'This clearly shows Shute being caught red-handed. It's a shame the other man's face is in shadow. Who was he?' She passed the photograph to William.

Jeffries frowned. 'We don't know. The ringleader was Jones, the limping man, of course. He died before we could get anything useful out of him. His sidekick was the other

297

one who followed Smith that night and is probably another of Shute's employees, I'm sure he'll make a mistake one day and we'll pick him up. The third man is a real mystery. The one that got away last night. He must have been the one who meddled with the first tram. He seems to be the clever one, the one with the technical know-how. After some prodding and questioning, Shute refused to say anything. Trying to keep his distance as usual, but this time it didn't do him any good. Especially when we produced the photograph.'

Smith took up the story. 'That's right. Jones we know about, there's no doubt he was the one in charge. The second man was his sidekick; I recognised both as being the ones who tried to attack me that night. The one I chased last night was taller and broader and is our mystery man in this saga. I suspect we'll never know his identity.'

Jeffries took a sip of his drink and turned to Carrie and William. 'Thanks to you two, Shute took the bait and arranged for the mystery man to get them access to the workshop. Shute evidently wanted to make sure the job was done properly this time, and that was his downfall. If he'd stayed away from the scene of the crime, he might have got away with it. As it was, he just couldn't trust anyone to do his dirty work without supervision again.'

'How did you know he'd taken the bait?' asked Carrie.

Jeffries smiled. 'We were watching you in the park, Carrie. We had followed you and William from the office. Then we followed Mr and Mrs Shute when they left. They met with their driver at the entrance, but only Mrs Shute climbed aboard. Meanwhile, Mr Shute walked down the hill towards the town. He led us to The White Hart. We had to be careful to remain discreet, so we watched from the Lounge Bar.'

Smith took up the story. 'We couldn't see the man he was speaking to, he had his back to us, but it was an animated conversation. Lots of arm waving and pointing by Mr Shute. He looked pretty angry. He passed an envelope to the other man, then got up and left. We moved into the public bar, but by then, the other man had disappeared. He must have slipped out the back door.'

'We didn't know what was going on for sure, but Shute had obviously arranged something, and so we hoped that our plan had worked. We were never certain until we heard them come into the workshop from the studio above. It was a long-shot, but it paid off in the end.'

Carrie leaned forward. 'I see. Shute originally paid Jones to sabotage the trams, but Jones was smart and didn't want to be directly involved, so he got someone else - the third man, the one that got away - to damage the first tram for him. The third man used the wedge to render the brake useless.'

William said, 'But Jones caused the second crash because he was seen at the scene. At least a limping man was seen running away. Perhaps he was getting desperate at that stage, so decided to do the job himself.'

Jeffries pushed his empty glass to one side. 'That's right. Then, when Jones died in the station, Shute had to go to the third man, Jones' accomplice, himself. Unfortunately, that man got away, so we'll never know who he was.'

Smith took a gulp of his wine. 'No point in getting down about it. We had a good result in the end. That was all down to you, sir.' He turned to the others and raised his glass. 'And to the three of you, of course. We couldn't have done this without you. Thank you!'

The group raised their glasses and clinked them together.

They sat in comfortable silence while the waitress cleared their plates. Carrie was the first to break the silence. 'What happens to Mr Shute now, and what of the trams? More importantly, the lighting company's big plans?'

Jeffries leaned forward, clasping his hands in front of him. 'The tram company looks like it'll go into liquidation, and the Shute Lighting Company, now managed by Mrs

Shute, will introduce their new electric trams. I suspect the plan for the new power stations will also go ahead.'

Smith said, 'So old Mr Shute's plan will come to fruition after all, albeit without him at the helm. Perhaps his prison cell will be lit with electric light.'

Jeffries laughed. 'Yes, that would be poetic justice, wouldn't it? Mr Shute will go down for a long time. He'll probably be found guilty of Rose's death. We have some more digging to charge him with the death of the photographer as well. We don't think Shute killed Harry Westlake himself, but we think he arranged for him to be roughed up. Obviously, it got out of hand.'

Smith added, 'In the end, Harry had nothing to do with the trams. He, unfortunately, met his fate after trying to blackmail Mr Shute with the threat that he'd expose him for buying lewd photographs.'

Jeffries cleared his throat. 'I was going to visit Rose's husband tomorrow to tell him we've solved the case and have Shute in custody.' He turned to Carrie. 'But I thought you'd like to give him the news, Carrie, as you'd been with Rose that day. If you'd be happy to, of course?'

Carrie held her glass out for a refill and said, 'Yes, that feels the right thing to do.' She turned to William. 'Would you tell your father I will be late tomorrow? I'll call on Sidney first thing in the morning.'

William topped up Carrie's wine glass. 'Ah, I forgot to tell you. My father wants to have a word with us both at 9 o'clock. Perhaps you can visit Sidney at lunchtime?'

'What does he want? Oh, don't tell me, another dressing down about my lack of interest in filing and administrative work.'

William shrugged. 'I have no idea, but probably best to get in early tomorrow, Carrie.'

The evening continued with everyone talking and drinking, the celebratory mood not abating until the waitress pointedly looked at the clock.

Later, outside the café, the night clear and cold, the group shook hands and slapped backs before going their separate ways. William accompanied Carrie, walking in relaxed silence.

They reached Carrie's house, the only light came from the hallway. Her father always left the light burning for Carrie if she was out after dark. William held the gate open for her. After a moment's awkward silence, William said, 'Don't forget to be in the office at 9am sharp, Carrie.'

Carrie stepped through the open gate. 'That's the second time you've mentioned that, William. What's going on? Am I about to be dismissed from my position?'

William smiled. 'You'll see. Just don't be late!'

47

A sign in a window

The following morning, feeling a little worse for wear after last night, I push open the door to the office. William is at his desk, early as usual, looking fresh and wide awake. Drink obviously doesn't have the same devastating effect on William that it does on me.

He looks up as I enter the office. 'Good morning, Carrie.' He glances at the clock. 'Nine o'clock on the dot. Good for you.'

I look across to his father's office. The light is off. There's no sign of Mr Edwards. I hang my coat up and drop into my chair. 'What was so important that I needed to be here early this morning? Where's Mr Edwards?'

William's lip twitches. He pushes his chair back. 'Come on, my father is in the attic room.'

I stand and wearily follow him through the door and up the stairs. There's a distinct smell of fresh paint. I wrinkle my nose. 'Had the painters and decorators in, William?'

William looks over his shoulder as he leads me up the stairs, a spring to his step. 'Father decided to spruce things up a bit. Smarten up the stairway and upstairs offices.' I frown. From the bills I see every morning and the lack of new clients, I wonder if it was a good use of limited funds.

As we reach the landing, something looks different. The little table is still there, but it's sitting upright now instead of leaning against the wall. There's a vase with fresh flowers on top and, hanging on the wall above, I notice a painting I don't remember from before. The door to the filing room is ajar, and I can hear voices inside.

William stands aside, beckoning me into the office, now bright and cheerful, the cobwebs swept away and the walls freshly painted. I gasp when I see the man with Mr Edwards.

'Father? What are you doing here?' My heart sinks. This is it, then. They must have arranged this. Mr Edwards is about to fire me, and Father is here to what? Tell me I told you so?

Something's not right, though. They are both smiling. In fact, Father positively beams.

'Take a seat, Carrie,' says Mr Edwards. 'I have a proposition for you.'

I pull out the little chair. It no longer squeaks. I sit at the desk which has been polished, a blotter in place in the middle, the inkwell holds a shiny new fountain pen. I look to William, leaning against the open doorway, his arms crossed.

My father is still smiling when he explains, 'Carrie, dear. You remember me telling you about my brother who died recently? Your Uncle James?'

I nod.

'Well, it turns out that he left a nice little sum to me in his will, and with little use for the money myself, I decided to put it to good use.'

I still have no idea where this is going. 'I'm not to be fired, then?'

My father laughs, William is grinning like an idiot. Mr Edwards Senior smiles, an unusual sight in itself. I allow myself a deep breath.

'On the contrary, Carrie.' He turns to William. 'William, if you would be so kind?'

William moves away from the door and points to the glazed part at the top.

There, written in gold lettering, in capitals, is Carrie Grey. Below my name, in smaller letters are the words Investigator.

I sit open-mouthed while my father explains that he will pay the rent for the office as well as all expenses for two years, "to get you established." Then, after that, it will be up to me to earn enough money to make the venture work. I still need to work for Mr Edwards, but part-time, just two days a week, to keep on top of the paperwork. The rest of the time, I can run the investigations, and William can offer legal help when needed.

I look at William. 'You knew about this?'

Arms crossed, leaning against the wall again, he nods.

'I saw you writing and scrubbing out your name in the dust, and an idea came to me. I knew you weren't happy, that your mind wasn't completely on the job and, with the way you helped the police to apprehend Mr Shute, it was obvious this would work.'

'But I couldn't have done it without you, William. And John.'

'Perhaps not, but you were the driving force behind it all. It was you who pushed things forward. You and Sherlock, of course,' he added.

I roll my eyes. 'Yes, Sherlock helped a bit, I suppose.'

William takes out his watch. 'Perhaps you should go and visit Sidney. We still have to finish setting up the office for you. The filing cabinets and sofa are due to be delivered shortly, and I have boring legal work to get on with.'

***

The gusts blow my hair into my face as I set off. I lean into the breeze, hands in my pockets as I walk along the road towards Rose's house. Dry autumn leaves swirl around my feet as I struggle to make headway against the wintry gale.

I soon reach Rose's house. At the front door, I reach up, surprised to see a new knocker has been screwed to the freshly-painted front door. Looks like Sidney has been busy.

I knock and stand back, and a short while later, Sidney opens the door. He takes a moment to recognise me, then smiles and steps back. 'Come in, Carrie. It's nice to see you again. Would you like some coffee? You're just in time; I'm making one for myself.'

The kitchen is tidier since my last visit. A pile of small wooden boxes sits in the corner of the room, next to the back door. There's a fresh bunch of flowers in a vase on the table. A pleasant aroma comes from the coffee brewing on the stove. Sidney beckons for me to take a seat at the table, and I shrug off my coat and sit down.

Sidney busies himself with the coffee and brings two cups to the table before sitting opposite me.

We sit in an awkward silence before I clear my throat and say, 'You may have heard that a man has been arrested in connection with the tram crash.'

Sidney puts his cup down, holding it with both hands, watching me with a straight face. 'Oh? I didn't know. I've been busy getting the house in order and trying to get on with my life.'

'That's good, Sidney. I know it must be difficult. Rose wouldn't have wanted you to live the way I found you on my last visit.'

'Yes, well. I'm still grieving, of course. I don't think I'll ever get over losing Rose. We had our moments like any other married couple, but we loved each other deeply, and I miss her terribly. I'm sorry, you said someone's been arrested. That is good news. Who is it they've arrested?'

I tell him about the case and how we all worked together to find the people responsible for the crash. Sidney listens with interest, nodding every now and again.

'I know Mr Shute. I did some work for him a while back.'

'You know him? I had no idea.'

'Well, not very well. Only as a boss.' Sidney picks up his cup, but changes his mind, puts it back on the table. 'He pays quite well but isn't a nice man to work for. Quite the bully, actually. I've seen his workers quivering when he lets loose with his words. If he starts with me, I give as good as I get.' Sidney considers the cup in front of him. 'No more work from him now he's in custody.'

I consider this revelation that Sidney knows Shute.

Sidney sweeps a hand through his hair. 'I'm pleased you did what you did, to find out who was responsible for

Rose's death. It won't bring her back of course, but I'm thankful to know a little more about what really happened.'

'You're welcome, Sidney. It's the least I could do, and I promised Rose I'd get to the truth. She must have been a lovely woman.'

Sidney's eyes shine as he drains the last of his drink. 'Yes, she was a fine woman.' He smiles. 'I think you two would have got on well, had you met in other circumstances.'

Sidney stands, walks to the sink and puts his cup on the draining board. He points to the pile of boxes by the back door. 'I need to finish tidying the kitchen. Would you help me carry these boxes out to the shed?'

I drain the rest of my coffee and nod. 'Of course. Anything I can do to help. I need to be back in the office soon, though, so I can't stay long.'

Sidney picks up a box and nods to another under the table. 'If you could bring that one for me?'

I reach down and slide the wooden box from under the table. Despite its small size, it's surprisingly heavy, and as I lift it onto the table, the lid falls off with a clatter. I can't help but glance inside. There are tight rows of small wooden blocks, neatly lined up, all shiny with varnish. The middle row is loose, one of its occupants missing.

I look at the blocks, confused. Then it hits me all at once. 'What are these things?' I ask Sidney.

'Oh, they are door wedges. I used to make them, but there's no money in selling them anymore. I make furniture now. It's more profitable and easier to find customers.' He puts his box on the table and reaches into my box and withdraws one of the wooden pieces, turns it over to show it to me. 'These made good money at first, but they seem to have fallen out of fashion now.' He drops it back into the box.

I gaze at Sidney, and a look passes over his face.

'It's you,' I say. 'You're the third man. You planted the wedge and caused the crash.' I scrape my hand through my hair. 'My God, Sidney. Your poor wife. How could you?'

Sidney flops down in a chair and puts his head in his hands. When he looks back up, tears run down his cheeks. He sniffs, wipes his nose on his sleeve. Leaning back, regaining his composure, he looks me in the eye. 'It was an accident, Carrie.'

'An accident? You made that tram crash. You, Sidney. It was no accident!'

Sidney shakes his head. 'It wasn't meant to crash - the wedge was meant to disable the tram, make people think they were unreliable. I was as shocked as everyone when I saw it crash.'

'Wait, you were there?'

Sidney loosens his collar. Holds out his palms. I notice a scar on his thumb. 'I was told to make sure the tram broke down. I knew the junction on the hill would be the first place the driver would need to use the lever. I waited at the junction.' Sidney pauses, thinking back, his face gone ashen. Recalling the horror. 'I saw right away what had happened. The brake had snapped. There was no way to hold the tram on the hill. I tried to run to the tram, board it and stop it somehow. But it was too late. The tram was too quick. And then ...'

I say it for him. 'You saw Rose on the tram, didn't you? You knew she was in danger.'

Sidney puts his fist over his mouth, afraid that if he says yes, it would definitely be true. It was no use. 'Yes.' He says, rubbing his forehead, his elbow on the table. 'I could see Rose through the window. She was looking straight at me. I don't think she saw me. She looked terrified. I watched as the tram ran backwards down the hill. I couldn't do anything to help.'

'Oh Sidney. You poor man.' I reach out and touch his arm. 'But why? Why did you get involved?' My mind was racing, trying to put the pieces together. It made no sense. 'Sidney?'

He wipes his eyes. 'It was Mr Shute. He had a hold over me. Rose and me, we were struggling financially. Rose worked but her wages were low and my work was sporadic. Maintenance work comes and goes. Sometimes we had no money at all.'

'What's that got to do with Mr Shute?' I prompt.

'I did some work for him occasionally. Then, one day, he happened to hear me talking to one of his workers. Heard me mention my money worries.'

'And what did he do? Did he offer you money?'

'Not directly. He said if I did a special job for him, he'd pay handsomely. I couldn't refuse. The job couldn't be done straight away. I had to wait a week or so before the opportunity arose. Then, one day, I received a message with a day and a code.'

'Ah, the infamous calling card. Monday night. Tram 19.'

'That's right. I already knew the place was the tram workshop. I was just waiting for a date. I was told the door would be unlocked. All I had to do was walk in and tamper with tram 19 to make it break down the next day. It was my idea to use the wedge. I had a basic idea of how the trams worked and how I could disable it.'

'But you must have known it was risky. That you might get caught.'

'Of course. I realised the risk I was taking. But I was desperate. I couldn't think of another way to get out of the mess we were in.'

He continues. 'The job was obviously illegal but the money was enticing. He offered me a hundred pounds. It was more than I would make in a year.'

Recalling the card Rose gave to me, I suddenly realise what had happened. 'Rose found out, didn't she?'

'Yes.' His eyes widened. 'How did you know that?'

'She told me. Not in so many words, but she said enough. And she gave me that card that led me to Mr Shute.'

Sidney nodded. 'She found the money. I didn't tell her what I had to do for it but she knew it couldn't be above board.' He sighs. 'She couldn't get it out of me, so she pestered Mr Shute. She didn't get anything from him either.'

'But why was she on the tram? You said she shouldn't have been on it.'

'I don't know. It's not somewhere she'd normally go at that time of day. I can only think that she was on her way to see Mr Shute again.'

'Well, she had Shute's card on her, so that's possible.'

I thought back to last night. The capture and arrest of Mr Shute. 'That was you again last night, wasn't it? You're the one that got away.'

'Yes, that was me. Shute threatened me. Said he'd get a message to the police, lay the blame on me. I had no choice but to help him last night. Then when the light came on and you all appeared, I just ran. Ran for my life. Are you going to tell the police?'

The thought had occurred to me. I was in a quandary. Has Sidney suffered enough already? Should I tell Jeffries? And William and John, they deserve to know the truth, don't they?

I smile. What would Sherlock do?

'I think you've suffered enough, Sidney. I'll keep this to myself on one condition.'

Sidney raises his eyebrows.

I point to him. 'Make Rose proud of you, Sidney.' I look around the little kitchen. 'I can see you've already started. Get yourself sorted out, find a decent job and make sure you don't accept any work from the likes of Mr Shute ever again.'

Sidney smiles for the first time since he confessed. 'Thank you, Carrie. I won't forget this.' He stands, lifts the box and heads to the back of the kitchen. 'Let's get these damn things out of the house.'

While Sidney struggles to open the back door with the box under one arm, I swiftly pull out my handkerchief and carefully pick up the wedge Sidney had taken from the box. I slip the protected piece of wood into my coat pocket. *Nice sleight of hand, Carrie. Your police friends will be impressed.* 'Not so fast, Sherlock. Sidney has suffered enough.' Deciding to keep the wedge safe for now, I follow Sidney into the garden to the shed at the end of the path.

AUTHOR NOTES

This story is fiction, of course, but it was inspired by a real event in my home town of Exeter, in the UK. On 7 March 1917, an electric tram, No 12, went out of control down the steep incline of Fore Street and crashed on Exe Bridge, killing one passenger, Mary Findlay.

The photographic studio of Henry Wykes overlooked the bridge at that time, so he was soon on the spot recording the accident with his camera. Within an hour he was selling postcards from his studio door of the disaster. Harry Westlake and his photography antics are pure fiction and are loosely based on Henry's actions.

If you would like to read more about the actual crash, the Exeter Memories website is a good place to start.
Ref:
https://www.exetermemories.co.uk/em/_events/tram_crash.
php

The contraptions featured in the book were in use at the time, although I've tweaked the dates a little.

The steam car featured in Carrie's race from Shute's house was inspired by a friend's car, the Stanley, still in use today. Steam, and even electric, cars were more popular than petrol until Henry Ford automated the production of his internal combustion cars.